Whistle for a Wind

How Wide the Heart

Elisabeth Ogilvie

Down East Books
Camden, Maine

Cover painting by Christopher Cart

Printed and bound at Versa Press, Inc., East Peoria, Illinois

3   2   1

Down East Books
Camden, Maine
Book Orders: 800-685-7962
www.downeastbooks.com
a division of Down East Enterprise,
publishers of *Down East* magazine
www.downeast.com

ISBN: 0-89272-625-3

Library of Congress Control Number: 2003109994

Contents

Whistle for a Wind   7

How Wide the Heart   149

Whistle for a Wind

There was an old superstition that one could raise the wind by whistling. At least to whistle for a wind might help to keep up one's courage or allay one's impatience, when actually there was nothing else one could do.

From *Sea Terms Come Ashore*

George Davis Chase
University of Maine

Foreword

Jamie Bennett lived at an exciting time in the history of our country; but so has everyone lived at an exciting time in history. Let's take a look at Jamie's particular period.

At the time of her transition from a district into a state, in 1820, Maine was busy and prosperous. No wonder Jamie Bennett felt constricted on his small island, with so many prospects open to a young, vigorous man. But his own industry, fishing, was the equivalent then of the Maine lobster industry today; it was one of the district's chief riches. It had been going on since long before Captain John Smith wrote about the abundance and size of the codfish on the Maine coast in 1616. The downeast salt fish dinner was fine enough for even the most elegant home; George Washington insisted on having such a dinner once a week.

Maine was a place of huge forests, if Jamie had wanted to strike inland and work at lumbering. But the sea was his element. Maine was active in the West India Trade, which had been flourishing then for well over a hundred years, except for the brief interruptions of wars and other international complications. With fortunes to be made in lumber and salt fish, no Maine man was going to be intimidated by the pirates who swarmed among these bright islands. The war of 1812, which had held up all American shipping for several years, had finished in 1815, and the exciting era of the brig was beginning.

The brig leads us to the shipyards. Wherever enough men could gather together by a cove or a salt creek, there was a shipyard. And because of the shipbuilders, Maine became also a state of beautiful homes built by ship carpenters, joiners, and carvers; and from those homes and those shipyards, men and vessels went out to cover the world. William King, who had fought long to make Maine a state and who became her first governor, was also one of her greatest shipbuilders.

Maine's struggle to become a state represented what Maine people have always considered the most important wealth of all—independence. To write their own constitution, to design their own seal, to choose their own governor, to consider themselves at last a free and sovereign state, equal to the others in the Union; this was what they wanted, and for it they kept up the long, quiet, but unremitting battle. They valued moral and physical freedom above all else, and so there was a bitter irony for them in the fact that Maine had to be tied to the slave state Missouri in the final contest before Congress. But they won their statehood.

In less than fifty years after that day in 1820, there were no more slave states. Those who were left to remember at first-hand the crusade for Maine's statehood were not surprised at the turn of events; they had always known, as we know today, that the freedom of body and spirit for which they stood is the prime wealth of a nation.

Chapter I

The spring bubbled up into a little pool in the midst of a leafy thicket of alders. As Jamie Bennett knelt to fill his buckets, he saw for an instant the trembling reflection of his tanned face, the big nose and the long jaw, the earnest deep-set eyes, and the brown lock falling over his forehead. Then he scooped a dipper into the water, and there were no more reflections.

He walked home with a wooden bucket in each hand; now and then a splash of icy spring water fell over his toes. It was good to be barefoot after the long day of wearing heavy boots, and balancing in the rolling boat to drag in one big codfish after another.

This was the hour of the day he loved best. The sea was quiet now after the day's wind, and the gulls were flying out to their ledges by twos and threes. The land birds were getting ready for the night; there were small twitterings all through the birch grove. When he left the grove, he faced the immensity of the ocean, spreading away from him for thousands of miles. Soon it would take to itself the rose and gold of sunset, but for the moment it was as blue as the larkspur in Pleasance Marriot's garden.

His home stood between him and the sea, just across the grassy ruts of the road, a low house with a huge square central chimney rising from the steep-pitched roof. The clapboards were dark gray with years of weathering; Jamie's grandfather had built the house, back in 1785. Beyond the grassy pasture on one side, and the garden and hayfields on the other, stood the family woodlots, rich stands of spruce and birch. But the trees had been cleared away between the house and the shore, and toward the road. In the mellow light the house and its small outbuildings seemed to be a part of nature, like the granite ledges that showed in the fields.

Smoke rose straight up from the chimney, which meant his mother was getting supper. Clover, the cow, stood at the pasture bars, staring toward the house. The gray cat appeared from the woods behind the barn and hurried across the yard, her tail upright and eager. She, too, was thinking of supper.

Jamie grinned. Clover was so big and Puss was so small, but they were just as hungry as he was. Clover could knock me down and gore me to death with those horns if she had a mind to, he thought, she's that much bigger than me. But the way I want my supper and my bed is just as big as the way she wants her hay and her tie-up. And Puss—I could put her in my pocket, almost, but that little body gets every bit as hungry and thirsty as mine does.

It was a strange thing, when you came to think of it. Look at a bird now, or the bees Mr. Whiting kept in his orchard. Just because a critter was as tiny as your fingernail, that didn't mean his feelings were tiny, too. If a bee took a dislike to you, didn't you run just as fast as if it were Ned Converse chasing you with his old cutlass?

He picked up his buckets again. As if this had been a signal, the hush was abruptly ended. The seven-year-old twins careened around the corner of the house, with young Sophia behind them; Clover lifted her head and let out an unhappy bellow.

"You git into this house!" Sophia shrilled at the twins. "You git inside and wash those hands and comb those rats'-nests out of your hair before I get old Ned to come and cut it off!"

The twins stood at a safe distance, their feet braced and their stomachs pushed out, and laughed at her. "Sophia, Sophia, go fall in the fire!" they chanted. They shouted it over and over, drowning her out. Clover bawled. Sophia went on scolding.

Jamie lengthened his step without spilling a drop of water, and was across the road and into the barnyard almost before they knew it.

"Margery, Albion!" he roared. The twins were bedraggled from an afternoon on the clam flats, their yellow hair snarled and sandy. They stared up at him with round fearful eyes as glistening blue as the sea. Suddenly he was no longer angry. They must have had a wonderful afternoon. But he didn't let his tenderness for them show. They must obey Sophia.

"You heard your sister," Jamie said sternly. "When she says 'Git,' you git. I want you all shipshape in ten minutes." He gave each a little push and they ran around the house without looking back. Clover bawled again from the pasture bars. Sophia pushed her thick black hair back from her hot face and said, "What makes them be such demons, Jamie? They'd rather be wicked than good." She was eleven, a slim, dark-eyed, anxious child.

"Maybe it's because they never knew Father," Jamie answered. "They can't remember when it was different. Here." He handed her a dipper of fresh water and she drank gratefully. She shouldn't, he thought, have to worry and scold at the children when she was still a child herself. She had been only four when their father was lost.

She looked up at him from the dipper and said proudly, "I remember him. And Mother was happy then. The twins don't know how Mother can be when she's happy. I remember . . . a little." She flushed. "Were we making an awful hullabaloo just now, Jamie?"

"I was thinking," he said dryly, "that they likely heard you as far as the harbor. They probably thought Clover'd gone mad and was trampling you all to death, from the blatting and the screaming."

She was appalled, and he grinned. "But it's more likely they said, 'That crew up at Bennett's Cove blows up enough wind in one squall to sail a ship to Montyveedio.' "

"I won't ever say another word to them," she promised fiercely, "not even if they pull the house down on our heads!"

"Words are fine," said Jamie, "if you've got an alder switch to back them up with. Where's yours?"

She glanced quickly back toward the house. "You know how Mother is about that," she whispered. "Yesterday she put it in the fire, and she cried and said, 'What would your poor father say if he knew his children had been whipped?' I tried to tell her I wouldn't really touch them with the switch, but she wouldn't believe me."

"I know," he said grimly. "But Father flicked me with an alder switch, and Lark too, and it didn't make us hate him. What would he say if he knew what little pirates some of his children are? I want him to think proud of us when he comes back."

"Do you really think he'll come back?" The hope in her eyes hurt Jamie. He put his big brown hand on her shoulder and gave her an affectionate shake.

"The whole British navy couldn't scuttle Charles Bennett," he said proudly, "let alone one of their press gangs."

"But Meg Erskine was telling me one day—" she was whispering again, casting furtive glances back at the house lest their mother should come upon them suddenly. "She was telling me how wicked cruel they was to the men, the keel-haulings and the cat o' nine tails and all; and suppose in some battle Father was took by the Barbary pirates!" Her lips trembled. "Look what they did to Ned Converse! They turned him into a madman! Oh, Jamie, I lie awake at night and think of it!"

As if I didn't, Jamie thought, shaken. As if I hadn't been lying awake thinking of it for all the seven years he's been gone. But he hugged the little girl to him, quick and hard. "They were cruel enough in the old days Meg's grandsir tells her about, that's certain. But this is modern times, Sophie. And we took care of the Barbary pirates once and for all when Mr.

Jefferson sent Commodore Preble over there. So you stop lying awake and fretting, you hear me? Wherever he is, Father's all right."

Of a sudden Clover bawled loud enough at him to split his eardrums. Sophia's arms were tight around his middle, her face was pushed hard against his chest. He set her away from him and said severely, "Where's Lark? He should've been home to milk before this."

Sophia, sniffling a little, sighed. "Well, you know Lark. We haven't seen hide nor hair of him since sun-up this morning." She gazed all around the yard, as if to discover their brother under the currant bush, or perched in the apple tree like a robin.

Then Jamie saw him at the edge of the spruce woods. He came, walking jauntily in his bare feet, his mouth puckered in a soundless whistle.

"You get into the house and help with supper," Jamie ordered Sophia. "Keep those twins inside. I don't want them flittering around me like a couple of pesky little midges. No, leave the buckets be. They're too heavy for you."

Sophia scurried into the house, holding up her long skirt to help her speed, and Jamie moved without hurry to the tall shadbush at the corner of the barn. He broke off a long, slim, supple switch. He was sympathetic with the way his mother felt about punishing the twins; they were her babies, born shortly after their father was stolen from his fishing boat by a British press gang. But Larkin was a different matter.

Jamie leaned against the weather-blackened wall of the tie-up, ignoring Clover's reproachful brown eyes, and watched his brother cross the field toward him. Lark was fourteen, a slight nimble boy with a way of walking as if he heard music, and a way of holding his curly dark head as if he were about to burst into song. It would be a gay tune, whether it was whistled or sung, because Lark liked merry things. He had been named Larkin for a cousin of their mother's, but it had been natural enough to shorten it to Lark. At two he could carry a tune and at five he knew all the hymns they sang at Meeting, as well as the old songs from England their father and mother sang to them. Lark at seven, tipping his head back like a bird, could melt your heart with "Greensleeves," or make you laugh and tap your foot when he sang, "Oh, the oak and the ash and the bonny ellum tree, they're all a-growin' green in my own countree . . ."

That had been when he was seven. Then Reuben Boyd sailed the boat alone into the harbor one night, and told how the British cutter had overhauled them just outside Matinicus Rock; the press gang had taken Charles Bennett and left him, Reuben, for dead in the bottom of the boat. After that, Lydia Bennett had not allowed Lark to sing any more. She could not endure to hear him. It reminded her too much of the lovely, happy days that had gone forever.

Lark had almost reached the barn now. He looked peaceful. Jamie wished he didn't have to discipline him, but something had to be done.

Suddenly Lark saw him, and the soundless whistle changed into a grin. "Welcome home, Cap'n!" he called. Jamie nodded.

"Same to you. We thought you'd set out for Dellygo Bay, or some such foreign part." Jamie spoke dryly, controlling his irritation.

Lark laughed, and shrugged his skinny shoulders in the homespun shirt. "No telling where I've been in my mind."

"I'd just as lief tell you where I've been," said Jamie slowly. "I've been standing all day in the wherry, hauling in codfish. I've caught 'em and split 'em and cleaned 'em, and sold 'em to Rich Gibson; then I had to wash down the wherry, and dig me a bucket of clams for tomorrow's bait. Then I walked home—a mile and a half from the harbor—and found not a drop of fresh water in the house."

Lark sucked in his cheeks and tapped one bare foot, staring at it. Clover mooed and he gave her a rueful grin. "Stow your gaff, old lady. Can't you see I'm about to be keel-hauled?"

"I don't object to the work," said Jamie, "because it's our living. But what does set my teeth on edge is a promise that's not kept. You got any good reasons for not going to the spring today, and for not getting my bait for me?" He sagged back against the barn. He was tired into the very middle of his bones. "And doubtless," he went on, "there's never a hoe been laid to the garden for a week."

Lark didn't answer. He gazed off toward the dark wall of the woods from whence he had come. Jamie wasn't surprised. Lark never had an answer.

"It's too much," Jamie said aloud. "Sophia and I have all we can fly to, and then we have to divide your chores up between us. No more, Lark." His eyes were heavy suddenly, and his waking at daybreak this morning seemed so many years ago that he wondered if he had the energy to thrash his brother. But he had to do it. "I have to do it," he repeated aloud.

Lark braced his shoulders as Jamie reached for him, but he didn't move away. His dark eyes stared into his brother's blue ones. His mouth grew pale and set, but it didn't quiver.

"Stop!" It was their mother's voice. "Don't you dare lift a hand to him, Jamie!" She came flying around the corner of the house, the twins and Sophia behind her. Under her cap her thin face was as pale as Lark's,

her dark eyes as wide; but they were frightened, where his were unafraid.
She ran fast in spite of her full long skirts, and seized the switch from
Jamie. "You can't do it," she panted. "You mustn't!"

Jamie said patiently, "I wasn't going to cripple him, Mother."

"I know, son, but I can't bear it." Her eyes filled with tears. Lark said
in a subdued voice, "I'll tend to Clover." He ran off toward the indignant
cow. Sophia grabbed a twin with each hand and hustled them back to the
house. Mrs. Bennett took a handkerchief from her apron pocket and
dried her eyes. Jamie had always been proud of his pretty mother, who
had laughed and sung with them so much in the happy days. But her
heart had been broken when Charles Bennett disappeared, and nowadays
they never saw the dimple in her cheek; she was much too thin, and besides, she hardly ever laughed. And it was the truth that the twins had
never heard their mother sing a lullaby.

"I'm sorry, Jamie," she said now. "It may be you're right about Lark.
And you do so much for us all, I shouldn't interfere. But it frightens me
to see you so violent with your brother. I'll have a serious talk with Lark
tomorrow," she promised him. "Now come in to your supper." She smiled
at him. "Beans tonight, and fresh johnnycake, and a bowl of blueberries
and cream afterward."

Suddenly he was so hungry his stomach hurt. He was also immensely
cheered. The Saturday night meal was always a good one, and tomorrow
was Sunday. There'd be no work. The very thought of it made him yawn.
He went with his mother toward the house.

Lark, leading Clover into the tie-up, was talking nonsense to her as if
the session with Jamie had been no more than a cloud passing overhead.
Well, perhaps the serious talk their mother promised would really work,
this time. Jamie hoped so, but not with all his heart. There had been
many "serious talks," and each time Lark looked sad, and promised to do
better. And the next day he was gone again.

Now Jamie was at the door, and the fragrances of supper came out to
him from the kitchen, the fire in the big fireplace snapped under a sim-
mering kettle. The combed and washed twins were soberly setting the
table made of pine planks scrubbed white. With a big scallop shell, Sophia
was skimming yesterday's thick yellow cream off the pan.

"I'll fetch you a piece of johnnycake to hold your stomach till we eat,"
his mother said, patting his arm. And as he sat in his father's chair by the
hearth, and stretched out his aching legs, he thought, I needn't plague
myself about Lark again till Monday.

Chapter 2

Early Monday morning, Jamie sat on his heels with his back against
Richard Gibson's salt shed, and looked sourly at the pinky *Minerva* lying
alongside the wharf. It wasn't the vessel that displeased him. She was a
handsome, able craft with her broad deep hull, and a stern as sharp as her
bow. And no matter what tremendous seas crashed into the harbor when
she lay at anchor, they could never throw the cable over her high
bowsprit. Oh, yes, the *Minerva* was a fine enough boat, like all pinkies,
whether twenty tons or eighty. Richard Gibson was always bragging that
she made less wake than a shad, and that when she carried him through
the heaviest seas he was as snug as in his own featherbed at home.

Well, there'd be no heavy seas today. The moderate summer winds
would fill her sails and send her gliding across fifteen miles of blue sea to
Stonehaven as smoothly as a seagull gliding across the sky. And the
thought of it caused a dry tightening in Jamie's throat.

He wanted to go. He had never been to the mainland in all his life.
Stonehaven wasn't mainland, but it was an island enough larger than
Brigport, and close enough to the mainland, so that a man could feel he
was touching great things at last. He'd heard how you could see the Camden hills green with summer, and how Limerock showed so clearly at
their feet, and that the dark wooded points below Limerock hid the shipyards of Thomaston and Waldoboro and Bremen and Bristol . . .

The names made him ache as he sat on his heels that warm clear July
day, with his back against a salt shed on the island of Brigport, twenty
miles out to sea. The names made a twisting in his stomach; for what they
did to him, they might have been as far away as San Domingo and Cuba
and Barbados.

Some of the men who were going to Stonehaven were already gathering, and he listened to their arguments about their errand.

"All a passel of foolishness," said Simon Pollinger, stumping along the
wharf as if it were the deck of his schooner. Simon was a big, heavy man
and his voice boomed out like the Voice of Judgment, and nobody would
think of differing with him. "Passel of foolishness," he repeated, glaring

at Captain Marriot. "All this folderol about being a state! We've always
been the District of Maine, and it's a fine-ringing set of words respected
everywhere our ships and our lumber and our salt fish goes. Why can't
we leave things be?"

The gold buttons on Captain Marriot's blue coat glittered like the July
sun itself. The seals on his watch chain shone. He smiled at Captain
Pollinger, and from the way he answered no one would ever guess that
before he retired from the sea he could raise his voice to be heard from
stem to stern of a barkentine.

"Now, Simon, we're all Maine men here, and you know as well as I
do that we've never hung to our mammy's skirts. We go to sea at ten and
we're sailing masters at twenty. Or—" and his keen gray eyes flickered toward Jamie —"we can haul in a giant cod with the best of 'em and earn
our living by a handline before we're fifteen. So why should the District
of Maine hang to Massachusetts' skirts forever? It's time we stood up like
men, Simon. And you know it."

Old Dougal Erskine, with the Scots burr still clinging to his tongue,
even though he'd been here since he'd come with the British in 1775,
cackled with laughter. "Aye, for three years now, ever since the
Brunswick convention when they tried to vote on Separation, and there
was foul play with the returns, Simon's been fair daft with thinking the
ayes might win at the next voting." He drew his long face down even
longer and waggled a bony finger at Captain Pollinger, but his deep-set
eyes were twinkling.

"It's those Federalist papers ye read, laddie. The *Portland Gazette* and
the *Kennebunk Visitor*. First they said 'twould be an end to free trade with
Boston, the Maine vessels would have to enter and clear with the Custom
House. Then the Congress put an end to that bogie by declaring all ports
free along the Atlantic seaboard." He took a breath. "And then—"

"And then," Simon roared, "they began trying to warn the people of
the District how much 'twould cost us to maintain a separate government.
And they're right, by the Great Horn Spoon! We'll be taxed within an
inch of our lives if the District votes for Separation today!"

A group of younger men had joined them at the edge of the wharf.
One wore a coat whose right sleeve was pinned up. Captain Marriot
pointed his gold-headed stick at him. "What do you say, Jonathan Gibson? You fought in Mr. Madison's War, back in 1812, and lost your arm."

"I say," said Jonathan Gibson mildly, "that if Massachusetts had given
us the proper kind of aid, the British could never have occupied the whole
of Maine east of the Penobscot."

"But the war finished in 1815," Simon protested. "And the District's been flourishing ever since! The war's over."

"Not for all of us," said Captain Marriot, and Jamie looked down at the wharf as all the men glanced over at him, remembering what had happened to Charles Bennett. There was a little silence on the wharf, and Jamie felt the sun hot on his brown head, and heard the gulls squabbling and screaming over fish entrails on the beach.

Then Simon Pollinger grumbled, "The talk's sailing far off-course, seems to me."

Captain Marriot clapped him on his burly shoulder. "Well, Simon, however the voting goes in the District today, we're all Brigport men first, last, and always." The rest agreed and a rumble of general conversations began.

But now the parson, Mr. Whiting, was walking down the wharf with Richard Gibson, and the time had come to cast off. The women, who had been talking in their own group at a little distance, joined the others to make their farewells to their menfolk. The gay voices rang in the quiet sheltered air of the harbor. Jamie tried to imagine his father among them, and his mother beside him, flushed and young and pretty again. His father would have been taller than any other man in the group, wearing his Sunday coat with as much of an air as Captain Marriot wore his.

His Uncle Nathan hailed him from the *Minerva*'s deck. "Come aboard, boy! You need a day's outing to keep you from turning into an old man before your time!"

Jamie shook his head. "I'd have gone with Hugh and Mark and the rest in Morgan Owen's sloop," he said stiffly, "if I'd wanted to go." Suddenly he was able to grin. "Be a pleasure to have the sea to myself today, with all the other boats on the mooring."

They laughed at this, and he felt better. If a man could carry off his longings with a joke, it was a good thing. He stood up, stretching his long legs, and went across the wharf to help with the casting-off. As the pink moved slowly on the floodtide toward the opening between high ledges of tawny rock, the women called last-minute messages.

"You keep away from them rum-shops, Alpheus!"

"Richard, don't forget my six yards of sprigged English muslin, if Mis' Gooding's got it in her shop!"

"We mustn't watch the *Minerva* out of sight," someone warned. "It'll be bad luck for her!" The women streamed up the wharf, their animated voices floating behind them, and Jamie was once more alone.

Yes, all the boys had gone, singing at the tops of their lungs about the

Maid of Amsterdam. And he'd have gone too, if there'd been some magic way of getting back before milking time. Lark couldn't be trusted to milk, and besides, more important, their mother wouldn't close her eyes all night with Jamie out of the house.

He turned his back on the pink before her sails had quite disappeared past the ledges, and walked slowly up the deserted wharf in the strong July sunshine. If he couldn't even go to Stonehaven, fifteen miles away, safe in the company of all the other men and boys of Brigport, how could he ever dare to dream of greater distances? Of the China trade; of the West Indies trade; of the shipyards? Time was racing, faster and faster; he was already too old to go to sea and catch up with his cousin Owen, who was First Mate of a vessel in the China Trade. But Owen's father hadn't been taken by the press gang; neither had Hugh Erskine's, nor Morgan Owen's. They could make their plans and carry them out in freedom because they had no responsibilities but themselves.

His feet had carried him away from the wharf, past Richard Gibson's store on his left, and up over a hill of yellow birches to where he could see Penobscot Bay spread out before him, and the *Minerva* striking out across that great blue floor toward the hazy purple waves of hills where Stonehaven blended into the mainland. A freshening breeze darkened the water; the *Minerva* caught it and suddenly she was winged out like a great beautiful bird.

Jamie swallowed hard. He turned and plunged back down the path the way he had come.

As he passed by the store, Amanda Gibson came hurrying out with a wooden bucket in her hand. "Wait, Jamie!" she called, and he waited reluctantly. She came up to him, innocently smiling, a short sturdy girl with a round face tanned rosy-brown, bright dark eyes, and curly black hair pinned up carelessly at the back of her head.

"Papa's left me to tend shop," she said, "and he's gone off without getting me a sup of fresh water. And I've been picking at a dry fish till I'm dryer than that cod is."

Jamie took the bucket and stalked off toward the well in the field opposite the store. She wasn't deceiving him; why, she could haul water, or row, or bring in a big cod on a handline as well as any boy. Almost as well. This was just an excuse to stop him. Girls were full of excuses. He had always thought Amanda was different, but now she was as silly as the rest.

Jamie brought up the bucket. A good dash of this icy water would bring her to her senses. Wouldn't she sputter! He decided against it and started back to the shop. She followed, humming airily. He set the bucket down on the doorstep. He wasn't going to carry it inside for her, she was perfectly able to do it for herself.

"I'm much obliged, Jamie," she said primly. "It was most kind of you. If you hadn't come along I'd have died of thirst, most likely." She seemed all ready to drop a curtsey, and he looked at her suspiciously. He couldn't think of anything to say, and he felt like slapping her.

"It's a pretty day for the voting, isn't it?" continued Amanda in her new tone. She looked up and down the road as if it were a wide thoroughfare bordered with great houses and fine shops, crowded with horses and people, instead of just a rough track with the woods on one side, and the rocky shore of the harbor on the other. "A real pretty day. It's a pity you couldn't have gone with all the others, Jamie. But then, what would I have done?"

"You could stop eating salt fish," suggested Jamie.

"Oh, thunder," said Amanda, sounding like herself when she lost a fish off her line. "Miss Prunes and Prisms! What's she want? My father doesn't carry any goods fine enough for her!"

Pleasance Marriot was coming down the road. Her silky little King Charles spaniel, brought by the Captain from England before he retired, ran ahead of her.

Amanda reached down and picked up her bucket. "If you're planning to get to the fishing ground before it airs up," she said, "you'd best be starting now."

So now she was telling him how to set about his work. "I'm in no haste," he said. "The tide's not right for me yet."

"Good morning!" Pleasance called out to them. The little dog frisked about their feet. Pleasance, in her flowered muslin and her bonnet, with the finespun shawl thrown lightly around her shoulders, could almost make you believe in the fine houses and the carriages. She smiled from one to the other of them, her eyes as blue as her gown and her fair skin only slightly flushed from the summer sun, while Amanda was not only tanned, but freckled.

"I've missed the sailing, haven't I?" she said breathlessly. "Papa warned me I should be late."

"I shouldn't think the sailing of my father's little vessel would be worth your notice," said Amanda, "after the big ships you've seen in Portland and Boston and New York."

Pleasance smiled at her. "Now, 'Manda dear, don't growl at me the way my Jupiter does when he steals a chicken bone." Her eyes flickered over the other girl. "Aren't your arms lovely and strong and brown? You make me feel so weak." And she lifted one of her arms in its full sheer sleeve, her slim hand drooping delicately from the wrist. Amanda, by now a dark red, struggled furiously to push down the rolled-up sleeves of her homespun. Jamie didn't know why she was so hot and miserable, but he felt sorry for her just the same.

"Amanda can do a lot of things other girls can't," he said. "You ought to see her load and fire a musket. Or split a big fish—"

Amanda didn't seem to appreciate it. She glared at him while she fought with her tight sleeves.

"You make me feel so useless," moaned Pleasance. "All I can do is play my poor little pianoforte . . . When are you coming up to see us, Jamie? You haven't been for a long time. Papa was just saying this morning—"

"Why don't you go and visit her now?" cried Amanda. "You don't have anything to do. Maybe she'll teach you how to play the pianoforte!" She rushed into the shop and slammed the heavy door behind her. The water rocked in the forgotten bucket, and they heard the big bolt driven across.

"Gracious," murmured Pleasance. "What a stormy girl she is! Jamie, walk up on Powderhorn Hill with me so we can see the *Minerva*."

"I've got to get to fishing," he said curtly. "You'll be safe enough on the hill alone. No bears on Brigport."

"Only one," Pleasance said to his back as he left her. "He's got brown hair that needs cutting, and a big nose and blue eyes, and such long legs you'd think he was wearing seven-league boots when he walks. He's named Jamie Bennett!"

Jamie was angry with both girls as he strode around the shore to his uncle's wharf, where his boat was made fast. A man had enough on his mind without these two pulling and hauling at him. For example, where was Lark now? He'd promised faithfully to be at the shore within an hour of the time when his older brother left the house; but the hour had passed, and the wharf was as empty as all the others whose owners had gone to Stonehaven.

Jamie stood quiet, listening for Lark's whistle somewhere back along the road through the woods. He heard robins, and the sweet plaintive voices of the yellow and black thistlebirds, but no whistling boy. All the grievances of the morning exploded in a great burst of anger. He looked longingly at a young poplar near the wharf. One of those boughs to sting the bare calves would teach young Lark his duty!

He set his bucket of clams aboard, his bundle of johnnycake and cheese, his stone water jug. He unloosed the line and pushed away from the wharf, setting the oars in the oarlocks. He gave one last look at the shore, and saw nothing but the tawny rocks and the sunlit wall of great spruce woods, and Pleasance in her blue gown walking from Gibson's store toward Powderhorn Hill. So much for Lark and their mother's "serious talk."

But by the time he had rowed among the pinkies and Chebacco boats, the square-sterned Dogbodies, the barrel-bottomed schooners and the yawlboats, and was heading out of the harbor into the little southerly breeze, his anger had melted. It was good to row, to swing his body into the smooth powerful rhythm that sent him swiftly forward over the sparkling water.

Jamie worked alone. Some of the men, like Simon Pollinger, were captains of their own boats, and the other Brigport boys and men, who went with them as crew, fished on shares. Rich Gibson owned a schooner that went to Labrador with a skipper and crew while he stayed at home, tending his store and buying fish. He took the mackerel by the barrel, but he dried the cod on racks, called flakes, in his big curing yard between the store and the water's edge.

Rich would buy Jamie's wherryload of fish just as quickly as he'd buy Simon Pollinger's schooner-load. He paid well, and besides, there was a government bounty on the cod. In turn, Rich made a fine profit for himself by selling to merchants in the West Indies and African trade. Some of the men grumbled about Rich's profits, and two of the older boys were even now building a sloop so they could get into the flourishing West Indies trade by themselves.

But the thought of Richard Gibson's profits didn't concern Jamie as he rowed out past the rocky islet called Tenpound. Now South Island lay ahead of him, and on the wind he could hear the bleating of Reuben Boyd's lambs. He rowed to the east of this island, passing close under the great towering mass of rock, Salvation Head. There was always a swell and a surge here, and a low thunder on the rocks. The wherry pitched and rolled, and Jamie had to work hard with the oars for a few minutes. Then he was out into quieter waters again.

When he was halfway between Matinicus Rock and the South Island, on an imaginary line that began on the highest point on the Rock and ended at the chimney of Reuben Boyd's house, he knew he was on the Chimney Shoal, his favorite fishing spot. He anchored, baited two strong codlines with clams, and dropped them overboard.

There was a little wait. He wasn't deceived by the strong tug of the tide on the line; he'd know the touch of a codfish when it came for the bait. He sat looking around him, completely at peace now, with the wherry rising and falling gently on the blue water, and the sunshine warm on his brown head and strong young shoulders. Seaward the horizon was as sharp as a line drawn by a schoolmaster's rule, broken only by the hump of Matinicus Rock. Once, when he'd gone fishing with his father and Reuben Boyd, they'd landed on the Rock and he had found it a strange kingdom rising out of the sea. It belonged not to people, but to the beautiful gray and white medricks with their swallow-tails and tiny red feet, and to the comical puffins who nested in burrows among the rocks.

Jamie had many things to think about as he waited for the fish to come. His unhappiness back on the wharf this morning, his annoyance with the girls, his anger with Lark, all faded into nothing. He was alone between sky and sea, surrounded by the tops of mountains whose age not even Mr. Whiting, the parson, could compute. It filled him with awe. He felt his heart beating hard. And at that moment something took his line.

After that there was no time for thinking. The cod were biting; he hauled first one heavy line over the side and then the other, re-baiting the hooks as fast as human fingers could move. To get each fish into the wherry was a battle, and some of them were nearly as long as he was tall. Before he could drag each one into the boat he must stun it into sluggishness with a stout oaken club. His calloused palms burned raw again with the cut of the codlines, his shoulders began to ache. Sweat ran into his eyes. But he was used to it. It was his work.

He had the wherry half-loaded before there was a lull. He sat down, flexing his legs cautiously. They had been braced for so long that they were trembling. He took a long drink from his water jug, and the still-cold spring water was sweet going down his throat. He took out a hunk of johnnycake.

It was halfway to his mouth when the fountain of water rose high in the air, not two hundred yards from him. It was beautiful, but it was terrifying, for Jamie knew what it was. His throat closed up, and the johnnycake fell from his hand. A whale had blown. He was no longer alone.

Chapter 3

Jamie sat without moving, staring until his sight blurred at the spot where the jet of water had arisen. He watched for the lazy rolling twist of the gigantic black body and the careless flick of a tail big enough to overturn a sloop, let alone a clamshell of a wherry. If he was lucky there'd be some sign to tell him whether the whale was coming toward him or going to the east'ard. That there might be more than one of them was a possibility he didn't dare to face.

As he waited, feeling far more helpless and tiny than the smallest seabird resting on the whole wide Atlantic, he remembered the stories about whales that he had heard all his life. Queer, he thought, swallowing to ease his throat, how you went fishing day after day on waters as familiar to you as the palm of your hand, and all the frightening yarns you'd heard were about things that had happened to other people. That time Uncle Nathan and Mark told how a whale had come up under their Chebacco boat, out by Matinicus Rock, and had nearly capsized them with a flourish of its tail . . . Oh, Jamie' d believed them, right enough, because the sweat had stood out on their foreheads when they told the story.

"There we set, hardly dassin' to let out a deep breath or shift a foot less'n it take too close notice of us! I was praying to my Maker the whole time, and weak as a babe once it'd passed by."

So there you sat, thought Jamie, and you waited . . .

Suddenly the huge, wet, black flukes of a tail broke water with a splash and disappeared. The whale was much closer to Jamie than the first sign had been.

He stared around him at the bright, empty sea. Not a sail anywhere. He was terribly frightened, but he knew he could not let his fear gain the upper hand; fear could turn a man weak as water and then how could he save himself—if there was any chance?

Better to jump than be dumped, he thought grimly. And thank Providence it was summer and not winter, though the water had a bone-aching cold even in summer. The tide should help him toward Gull Rock, if the whale didn't take a slap at him, after wrecking his boat.

Trying to move quietly he reached down to take off his wet, heavy leather boots. Quite suddenly the sense of nightmare fled before a real and invigorating rage. He'd worked hard for the catch that loaded his boat now and he didn't take kindly to the idea of losing it. And where would he ever get another wherry like this one, so some confounded, lazy, slow-witted whale could come along and crack it up with a flip of his tail?

His very helplessness infuriated him even more. He sat there among the pale bellies of his catch, and there was nothing in the world he could do but jump when the time came. And even if he reached Gull Rock safely, the Bennetts would be practically paupers, without a boat to their name. It wasn't fair!

He was so enraged by it all that when a strange shift of light and shadow in the nearby water caught his eye, he wasn't terrified. He should have been, he knew, while he stared over the side of the boat at the great black back spreading like a floor beneath him, just a little distance under the surface of the water. He could touch it that easy with an oar, he thought in wonder.

It seemed to take the creature an age to disappear, and all the time he was poised in readiness to jump. Then, all at once, there were only the sunshot green depths below him. In the manner of whales, it had let itself sink toward bottom and out of his ken. All the stiffening went out of him and he slumped on the seat. The sweat came out on his forehead; he put his hand up to touch it. The wetness was like a baptism and he realized with pride that he now belonged to that small but fortunate group who had whale stories to tell.

He even knew how he would begin it. "There I was with the wherry three-fourths loaded with some of the biggest, handsomest codfish you'd ever hope to find even out on New Found or Banquero—"

He laughed aloud and the sound was strong and good, startling a gull that was flying over him. Weaker than Puss he was, now that it was over, and his throat dry as the Sahara desert, and here he sat making up yarns to show himself a hero to all the loungers in Rich Gibson's store.

He pulled on his boots again, put the oars in the oarlocks, and began to row, standing up and pushing on the oars. He'd slake his thirst and fill his water jug at Reuben Boyd's spring on South Island, and rest awhile on dry land just to remind himself how sweet life could be.

South Island grew higher and higher above him. Reuben's chimney disappeared behind a grassy fold of land. The rocks gleamed yellow in the sun, and a fragrant land breeze blew warm against his sweating face. The swell sliding backward from the shore held him motionless each time, then the returning surge slid him forward. Rockweed floated golden-brown on the water, showing that there were ledges underneath.

With care he guided the wherry past barely submerged rocks to what passed for a beach. Reuben had a fine shingle beach in the cove that faced Brigport, but here on the ocean side there was only a long stretch of rock shelves and tumbled boulders. Jamie found a patch of small stones just wide enough for the wherry's bow to beach, and stepped ashore.

"Ahoy the wherry!" Reuben Boyd shouted, and Jamie turned to see him and his cosset lamb on the rise, silhouetted against the blue sky. He was a short, slim, nimble man who could pass for a boy at a distance, until you saw his thick graying hair and the way the years had weathered his face. He was smiling as Jamie came up to him.

"How's it happen you didn't row around to the cove if you planned to visit me?" he asked. "You run afoul of that sea serpent they been talking about for the last ten years?"

"No," said Jamie. The big pet lamb nuzzled his hand, and he scratched behind her velvety ears. "Good day, Poppet. I didn't mean to slight ye."

"No, it was a whale I saw," he went on, trying to be casual. "Come right up under me, near enough to touch."

"A whale, eh? 'There is that Leviathan, whom Thou has made to play therein,' as the Psalmist says. So if the Lord made the sea and put him in it, then you'll have to leave him be."

"And he can leave me be. Plenty of fish in the sea for both of us. He didn't drive me, either," Jamie added proudly. "I came for water."

"Well, fill up the jug, lad, and welcome to it." Jamie crossed the slope toward the path of alders where the spring was. When he came back, refreshed by a long cold drink and with his jug full, he dropped down beside Reuben on the warm dry turf.

"I reckon five minutes won't soften up my fish too much," he said.

"Any man who's just been amidships of a whale needs five minutes to thank his Maker in," Reuben agreed.

After a time Reuben asked, "Did they all get off to the polling at Stonehaven? I thought you'd go with 'em, to see the sights."

Jamie watched Poppet neatly clip off a Queen Anne's Lace blossom with her teeth. "Why didn't you go?" he countered. "You can vote. You're over twenty-one and you own property."

"It's nothing to me what happens," said Reuben. His brisk voice had become slow, suddenly. "State or District, what does it matter? I'll spend out my days here on South Island with my sheep, thinking . . ." His voice was slower still. "And remembering. I got a store of memories. My wife and baby son going with the smallpox, and then my best friend taken—"

Jamie rolled over on his stomach and put his chin in his hands. "Reuben," he said swiftly, "he was alive when you saw him last, wasn't he?"

"Alive and fighting!" The strength rushed back to Reuben's voice. It was the same every time Jamie asked the question, and he had asked it over and over again during the last seven years.

"Oh, he was a valiant man, your father! Two of them bold jack tars were measuring their length in the bottom of our boat, the last I knew, and he was going for a third! And the officer in all his braid and buttons looking on over the rail of the cutter, saying, 'We've got to have him, lads. He's an Englishman by the way he fights, no matter if he claims to be a rag-tag and bobtail American!' "

"So the press gang took him," mused Jamie, "with no more care for his home and family than if they were shooting a sea-duck."

"They'd have taken me," said Reuben, "if they hadn't thought I was dead from that slip on my skull with a marlin-spike. You see, I went for that pretty officer with his sly grin, and some bravo with a tarry pigtail cut me down. And there they left me to drift, with my face down in the gurry where we'd been cleaning mackerel . . ."

His voice went distant again, his pale bright eyes seemed to watch far horizons. Jamie said eagerly, "Then if they'd killed my father in the fight, they'd most likely have left him with you in the boat. They wouldn't have taken him."

"It was alive they wanted him. And there's proof that the British Navy had come to a pretty pass, when they had to go out and carry away honest American fishermen to fight their battles for them! And anyone who knows how long the press gangs ruled the seas, and still says Mr. Madison didn't have just cause for his war—I say to him, he lies in his teeth!"

"Tell me something, Reuben," Jamie said, and Reuben looked at him sadly. "I know what you figger to say, lad. You say it every time. You want to know if I think he could still be alive."

Jamie's blue eyes were steady on the man's faded ones. "Yes," he said.

Reuben laced his gnarled brown fingers together and stared at them. "And my answer is always the same. He might be. And then he might not. He could have died in India or Egypt. He might have died of scurvy, or of some sort of plague, or his ship might have been fell upon by pirates.

He might have tried to desert, or to get others like himself to mutiny, and in that case—" his words were very soft—"he'd have been hanged."

"And if none of those things happened," said Jamie harshly, "he could be on his way home now. Next week, next month, next year, he might come home."

"So he might," said Reuben, "but don't set your heart on it, lad."

Chapter 4

A few days after the men returned from the voting at Stonehaven, Captain Marriot rode into the yard one evening on Hector, the big roan. Pleasance was riding pillion behind him. The family spilled out into the yard, all but their mother, who hurried to put on a fresh fichu and cap. Jamie, as the man of the house, was obliged to help Pleasance down. She weighed hardly more than Sophia.

"Thank you, Jamie," she said, and he, meeting Lark's sparkling eyes, blushed angrily.

Captain Marriot handed the reins over to Lark and the reverent twins. Hector was the only horse on the island. Mr. Whiting often remarked dryly that if certain children showed as much admiration for him as they did for Hector, he could count himself a success at last.

The Captain swept off his hat in a courtly gesture as Mrs. Bennett appeared. Sophia was entranced. She thought that Captain Marriot was the handsomest man on Brigport; certainly the most elegant, in both clothes and manner.

"Good evening, James," said Mrs. Bennett.

"Good evening, Lydia." His gray eyes moved coldly over her face. "You're very thin and pale. How long has it been since you've spent an afternoon in the fields and on the shore with these children of yours?"

"I have no time for such actions."

He lifted one eyebrow. "Indeed. You had time once, when your children were smaller, and certainly more trouble than they are now."

Mrs. Bennett's face flushed, her lips parted and then shut again, firmly.

"Don't bully, Father," Pleasance said. "You're not walking the quarter-deck now, you know."

"Won't you come in?" Mrs. Bennett asked formally. She led the way, the captain close behind her, and Pleasance and Jamie following. Sophia slipped around them like a minnow, to walk near Captain Marriot and admire the fit of his seal-brown coat and the dignified way he carried himself.

"Father has come for a purpose, Jamie," Pleasance said in a low voice. "I only hope he succeeds."

"What is it?" asked Jamie. He glanced at her unwillingly. But she was not smiling at him, she was quite serious.

"I can't say. He must tell it. But if it works out as he wishes, this should be a very happy evening for you."

He couldn't imagine what it was, and he was uncomfortable. He liked to understand things, he hated to be surprised. He wished they hadn't come, anyway. They were too fine for his kitchen, and he felt like a hobbledehoy in his work clothes, not knowing where to put his hands or his feet, and so miserably hot he felt all afire. He stood stiffly by the tall dresser where his mother kept her blue willowware.

She felt easy enough, to have them here. She sat with her hands in her lap, exchanging comments about the weather. But why did Pleasance have to keep looking toward the dresser? Hadn't she ever seen blue willowware before? Why didn't the Captain get to his mysterious business?

Then, suddenly, it was out. "I met an old friend of mine at Stonehaven Monday," the Captain said. "He's associated with William King, building ships at Bath. You know what the shipbuilding business is in the District today. During the Blockade and the war, it all but died. But today it's never been more alive. It's the lifeblood of Maine—of the Union itself!" Suddenly he smiled at them. "And there's a berth for this boy in it. I've spoken for it. It means clear sailing for him from now on. Twenty years from now—perhaps only fifteen, or even less, if he applies himself—he may have a shipyard of his own."

He got up and came across to Jamie, put his hand on the boy's shoulder, and looked into his eyes. "Let your cousins go to sea, boy; you'll build the ships for them."

Jamie's heart gave a great lurch. In the space of an instant his life had been changed; now he truly stood on the brink of the great world. His jaw felt loose. He wanted to smile at the captain, but he felt as if his face might dissolve altogether. He turned toward his mother, and her name came out in a croak.

"Mother—"

"No," she said. She was so white, so still, that his joy turned to terror. They all looked at her.

Pleasance said with alarm, "Are you feeling ill, Mrs. Bennett?"

"Yes, I am," she answered. She didn't take her eyes from Jamie's face. "I'm very ill. You don't know what you're doing to us, James Marriot. I can't let Jamie go away."

Captain Marriot strode across the room and stood looking down at her. "See here, Lydia, I'm not suggesting that the boy go to sea! He'll be snug on land, and learning a good trade, and a word from me will make sure he won't run afoul of the grog ration."

"I need him here."

"You and Charles promised when you named the boy for me that you'd let me give a hand with him when the time came," the Captain said sternly. "Well, when he was ten and I wanted to start him off as a cabin boy along with his cousin Owen, you wouldn't let him go. Look at Owen today—First Mate in the China trade."

"That was seven years ago," said Jamie's mother. She held a handkerchief to her trembling mouth. "You know what happened seven years ago! His father had just—gone. How could I have let Jamie go?"

Jamie went and stood beside her chair. "It's all right, Mother, I'm not going away. I—" He had to swallow before he could tell the ridiculous lie. "I w-wouldn't want to go anyway, with the c-cod running so good and the m-mackerel coming any d-day now."

The Captain blazed at him. "Don't give me any of your slack, boy! If you lied like that to me aboard ship, I'd see you had a taste of the rope's end. You know you want to go. It's turning you green, you want to go so much. You want to sail to the West Indies with Hugh Erskine and Mark Bennett next winter. And it twists in you all the time, to think of what Owen Bennett's seeing halfway around the world from here! Bennetts are doing these things, and you're a Bennett, but you're here on this island, and you look me in the eye and say, 'I can't leave my cod and my mackerel!' "

"Father—" Pleasance was at his elbow. "You're upsetting everyone, and I told you not to bully. Let's go home, and leave Jamie and his mother to talk it over."

"There's nothing to talk over," Jamie's mother spoke with quiet finality. "I need Jamie here."

"For the few dollars a day he gets from Rich Gibson for his fish?" the Captain demanded. "Why, he'd be sending you home twice as much from

Bath! What's the matter with young Lark? Put him in the wherry for a change!"

"Father—"

"All right, all right, girl," he said furiously. "All this pulley-hauling is getting me nowhere. And don't tell me I've gone at things sternforemost again. And heaven help me," he thundered, "if I ever sing out to a woman again—even if the breakers are pounding off her port bow!"

He left the house abruptly. "Lark!" they heard him shouting. "Look alive there! Bring me my horse!"

Mrs. Bennett arose and went into her bedroom. Pleasance said in a low voice, "I'm sorry, Jamie."

"What for?" he said staring straight ahead. "I told the truth. I like to fish. That's all I want to do." When he did look around, she was gone, and Sophia had slipped away too.

He went out and down toward the shore at a long fast lope, trying to get out of sight before anyone could hail him. When at last he was down over the bank and on the pebbly beach, he felt safe. He walked slowly along the water's edge. It was early evening and the sun laid a golden light over the rocks and turned the grass to a peculiar, brilliant green. The air cooled his hot face.

What had just happened in the house was like a bad dream. Still, his mother had been right to say she needed him; young Lark was no help at all without someone to bring him up with a round turn. And there was another reason. Jamie remembered how it had been when his father was first lost, and he and his mother kept hoping against hope that the officers of the press gang might take pity and return him, or that by some miracle he would escape. And so in this one way Jamie was closer to his mother than the others, and he knew how afraid she was to let him out of her sight. "What if something should happen to you?" she'd said, when he'd wanted to make a trip to the Banks with Captain Pollinger last year. And through his disappointment he had understood her fear, and respected it.

He respected it now, but he couldn't pretend nothing had happened. Captain Marriot had actually said those words to him; there was a berth for him in the great William King yards at Bath. For him, Jamie Bennett! There was a sort of grim comfort in thinking that Jamie Bennett's berth would exist until Captain Marriot got word to his friend.

He had gone a long way while he was thinking, past his own woodlot and Thaddeus Boyd's pasture. He came out on a sharp, steep point of rock below Thad's grove of tall spar spruces, and stopped.

In a little cove just beyond, on the turf well above high watermark,

Hugh and Mark were building their schooner. They spent every possible hour there. They were there now. The sound of their hammers was clear in the still air as they planked the rounding sides. With only her hull yet built, the little schooner was already a gallant shape. Jamie watched for a few minutes from the point. He didn't want to go any nearer. It seemed to him that happiness showed in the swing of Mark's broad shoulders, in the cant of Hugh's fair head. He turned abruptly away from the shore, and made his way through Thad's spruces to the road.

Beyond the place where the road turned off for the harbor, a rough track led toward the southern point of the island, where the deepest woods were, and where no one lived but old Ned Converse. If he followed the track—giving old Ned's place a wide berth, of course—he could find real solitude for the hour or so of daylight left him.

But as he passed the harbor road, someone called his name. He stopped and looked around, and saw Amanda Gibson walking up between the stone walls. For once her hair was done neatly under a cap, and her sleeves rolled down. But her white kerchief made her look brown as a Gypsy.

"I was just coming to your house," she said happily. "Where are you bound? Down toward Southern Point?" She didn't give him a chance to answer. "Listen, Jamie, that's what I wanted to tell you about. I've been saving this for you—not another soul on earth knows about it." She became suddenly solemn, crossing her heart and rolling her eyes skyward.

"Well?" Jamie felt guilty for sounding so bored; he and 'Manda had always saved secrets for each other. But couldn't she see they were grown-up now? he thought crossly.

"Well," she began, "I rowed all the way down the south side this afternoon—all alone—and I landed on the sand beach and went up the path to the Beach field and I went almost as far as the old stone Frenchie house, and—" She stopped, excitement shining in her eyes and curving her mouth. "And what do you think I found? Guess!"

"A Frenchie," said Jamie.

She squealed. "Oooh, if I had, I'd have died from the fright!"

"And he'd have been about two hundred years old, most likely," said Jamie. "What did you find? Ned Converse sharpening his cutlass?"

"Blueberries!" she said ecstatically. "The ground was blue with them, and they weren't all ripe yet, either. And they were so big, Jamie! And so thick! I swear nobody's ever picked there. I'd have taken home a mess, but I was afraid somebody'd ask questions, and I wanted to save the patch for you and me."

"You better tell somebody else," he said roughly. "I'm past the age for wanting to pick blueberries. I've got too much work to do. And when I get by myself for a spell, I don't want any female trailing after me."

You'd never see 'Manda's lip quiver. She tucked it under her teeth. "Oh, I see," she said proudly. "And thank you kindly for speaking so plain. I prize honesty above all."

Her chin went up as high as the pennant at a masthead. She swung around and left him, squaring away for home like a full-rigged vessel before the wind, and he was bitterly ashamed of his cruelty.

But he forgot about her at once, absorbed in his thoughts. He saw himself in twenty years, a man as important to the District of Maine as William King or Peleg Talman; sending his cousin Owen to sea as master of a ship he, Jamie, built and owned. He saw himself in an office looking out over the busy yards; presiding at launchings; returning to Brigport like Captain Marriot, with fine clothes, glittering seals on his watch chain, a gold-headed cane. He would even have a horse, not a roan, but a great black stallion.

He looked around him and felt an unpleasant shock. He'd meant to cut off through the woods before he reached Ned Converse's place, and here he was in plain sight of it, and Ned himself was stumping across the yard. He had only to look up the cleared slope and he could see Jamie against the woods. Promptly Jamie sat down, hoping that a big boulder on one side and a clump of bay on the other would make him inconspicuous.

He wondered what the man was doing as he limped back and forth. His cow grazed quietly in the stone-walled paddock beside the house. His pigeons were picking their way over the turf like so many chickens. It was a peaceful enough scene. You'd never guess, Jamie thought, that Ned's name was used to frighten island children into good behavior.

He had been on the island for as long as Jamie could remember. Everyone knew why he was a madman. As a young man, he had been a sailor on an American ship that was taken in the Mediterranean by the Barbary pirates; and he had spent seven terrible years as a slave before he escaped. The islanders agreed it was enough to drive any man crazy, being chained to an oar in those heathen pirates' galleys for seven years, with rags for clothes and nothing on his head to keep off the burning Mediterranean sun. They stood around in Rich Gibson's store and talked it over and said Commodore Preble should have strung up every man-jack of those savages when he went over to Tripoli. And then they usually agreed that they were sorry enough for Ned, but it was too bad Captain

Marriot had discovered him in Liverpool. Jamie remembered such a conversation; he had been about eight, and had gone to the store with his father.

"What else was James Marriot to do?" his father had argued reasonably. "Here was an American seaman, lame, sick, half-blind, not a penny, wandering around the waterfront trying to find a way home. You'd have picked him up if you'd been there. It's only Christian charity."

"Aye, aye," said Thaddeus Boyd, "but couldn't he have dropped him in New York or Savannah? After all, it's not as if Ned was a Brigport man to begin with."

"The Captain ought to've sounded us out before he let Ned drop anchor here," someone else growled. "He'd no right to give him a holding, even if Southern Point does belong to him. It's a matter that concerns all of us."

"Charity concerns all of us, too," Jamie's father had answered in his slow deep voice. "Do you begrudge a man safe harbor after seven years of worse nightmares than we'll ever know?"

"But he's mad! He's a danger!"

"How is he a danger?" Charles Bennett demanded, and Jamie had been proud of him.

"Threatening our young'uns with his cutlass," Thaddeus Boyd cried. "Why, he like to took off my Israel's ear when the boy was only trying to get us a mess of seabirds last fall."

"Israel could have gone some other place for his seabirds besides Ned's cove," said Jamie's father. "Ned thinks Providence appointed him to protect the birds that come there. There's no call for anybody—child or man—to torment that poor soul." His strong hand tightened on Jamie's shoulder. "I've given this lad my promise; if I ever know of him plaguing Ned Converse, he'll be thrashed within an inch of his life."

Ned had built his house in a haphazard fashion from the ruins of one of the little rough field-stone houses built by the French fishermen long ago, long before the first English settler came. Captain Marriot had bought the cow for him, and Ned had put up a lean-to shelter for her. He kept a few hens, which he could never bring himself to eat. One year Jamie's father had given him a little pig, thinking it would guarantee Ned a good supply of bacon and salt pork, but Ned hadn't killed the pig, either. He had named her Clytie and let her sleep in the house until she was too big, and then he made her a little house of her own close to the door. Eventually she died of old age and overweight. But for a long time, whenever Ned came limping up to the harbor, the children he passed would run after him—at a safe distance, of course—yelling, "How's Clytie? Does she sleep in your bed?" They had a rhyme they shrieked at him. "Ned, Ned, puts the pig in his bed; he sleeps on the floor with his head out the door!"

Then Ned would round on them, waving his good arm, glaring hideously from his good eye—and the black patch over the blind eye seemed to glare just as terribly. The children would run back, screaming, and then start after him as soon as his back was turned. He reminded Jamie of the old ragged-winged raven who sometimes flew over from the South Island and was set upon by the crows.

As he watched Ned now, he realized at last what the man was doing. He was taking down the crude cow-shed, battered into final shapelessness by the spring storms. Board by board, log by log, laboriously he wrenched each part free and stumped across his yard to stack it in its proper pile. His leg seemed to drag more than usual, and sometimes he stopped to wipe his face; Jamie could almost tell when he took a long, heavy breath.

Jamie watched, uneasy and pitying. Whenever anybody else on the island began a barn or a house, everyone gathered to have a "raisin'," and it was a fine occasion for hard work and laughter and good food. But no one cared or knew what Ned was going to do. Jamie wondered how the man planned to drag heavy stones into place for the foundation of the new building, or, sole alone, to set the corner logs in place. He wished he dared to go down and lend his shoulders for the job, but what if Ned took him for one of the pirates, and went for him with his cutlass?

He felt so uncomfortable about it all that he grew angry, and could almost sympathize with the ones who said Ned shouldn't be here. If Ned were elsewhere, Jamie Bennett would not have to feel guilty along with all his other disagreeable sensations. He didn't have time to feel sorry for anybody; for Amanda for running after him like a puppy dog, for Ned for being gray and old and lame and crazy.

And then the sunset light caught on the sails of a tops'l schooner on the horizon, heading for Boston, or New York, or even farther. And the sight of those sun-gilded sails caused such a twist of longing in Jamie that it was like a pain. She was going somewhere; but Jamie Bennett wasn't. Jamie Bennett was rooted on Brigport for the rest of his life.

He rose quickly, not caring now whether or not Ned saw him, and hurried away until the woods shut off the horizon from him.

Chapter 5

The cod ran thick, and the weather held hot and fine. The women picked berries, tended the gardens, and dried fish for the family's consumption. Everyone has special tasks to complete during the good weather. Pleasance tended her garden and her herbs. For all her youth, she knew as much of herbs as any woman on Brigport, and more than most of them. Her mother had handed the knowledge down to her.

Amanda Gibson must have been very busy helping her father. At least she stayed away from Jamie's house, and even his mother noticed it. "I do think Rich Gibson works the girl too hard," she said.

It was at the table one night, and Lark looked down at his supper, and snickered. " 'Tisn't Rich that's hard on 'Manda," he said. He wouldn't say any more, but Jamie could have cuffed him just the same.

Jamie's friends also were busy, in the time they could spare from fishing. Mark and Hugh worked on their schooner. Old Dougal, Hugh's grandfather, was stitching a suit of sails for her. Morgan Owen and his father were building lobster traps; they intended to try their luck at lobstering when the summer was past and the critters had put on their new hard shells.

When it was haying time, the islanders had to let days of superb fishing weather go by while they mowed and raked their fields. But they were salt-water farmers, these island men, and they could take a genuine satisfaction in a rich spread of ripe hay, sweetly cured in fine, dry, hot weather and filling the dusky mows with a summery fragrance that lasted through the winter. It meant the very existence of their cattle throughout the bleak bad months, and so it was to be treasured like gold; it was as important as the provender for their own mouths.

Jamie was a good man with a scythe, and before he cut his own hay, he always put in a day helping to mow his uncle Nathan Bennett's fields, leaving the cut hay for the women and girls and small boys to rake into long rows. Then his uncle and his cousin Mark came with their scythes to help mow Jamie's fields. He found a great pleasure in the clean rhythmic strokes of the three scythes working in unison down the meadows, the ripe grass falling from the blades, the sun hot from a deep blue sky over a deep blue sea, and a dry wind blowing from the northwest.

Then there were the brief spells of rest on the stone wall at the edge of the woods. He drank cool switchel from the big earthen jug and wondered how anything anywhere else in the world could taste better than this drink composed of cold water, ginger, and molasses.

Uncle Nathan sang out, "Let's be at it again, lads!" And then went back out into the blazing, sweet-scented heat to the tune of Mark's whistling.

Uncle Nathan had a team of oxen, Damon and Pythias. When they had hauled all his hay to the barn, then Jamie could borrow them. But Uncle Nathan had three hayfields to Jamie's one, and while the boy worked for his uncle his pleasure was overshadowed by the fear that the good weather would break before he could get to his own hay. He studied his father's old barometer anxiously for signs of falling, but it stayed high; Sophia and the twins turned and raked the hay at home, while Lark went along with Jamie. Lark and a couple of cousins close to his own age rode the rick and tramped down the hay. It was great sport for them. They were being useful in a painless fashion.

"I wish haying went on for another month," Lark said one night when they were on their way home.

"You'll change your tune when we get to our own place," Jamie said. "Sophie and the twins'll be aloft in the rick, and you'll be pitching hay up to them."

Lark gave him a wicked grin. "Will I, now? And me still a growing boy, who gets aches and fever so easy?"

"We'll have Pleasance brew you up a tea for your aches and fevers," Jamie answered calmly. "I hear she makes some real vile-tasting concoctions. They get a man on his feet in spite of himself."

He reminded himself that he was the older brother and knew better than to flame out at Lark's foolishness; but at the first opportunity Lark would cry "Too much sun!" or "A stitch in my side!" He'd lie limply in the shade for a few minutes, until the rest had moved away down the field, and then he'd be up and gone.

It was true that he'd come back with his old straw hat full of raspberries for their supper, or he'd have spotted in a secret place a wild apple tree that later would give them a basket of fruit. And Jamie would enjoy the fruit as much as the others did.

But the fact would remain that Lark had escaped the long hard task of getting the hay in, just as he managed to escape most of the other long hard tasks. What sort of man would he be? Jamie sighed, and Lark laughed.

"Do you have the weight of the world on your shoulders?"

"Not entirely," said Jamie dryly. It wasn't that Lark was cruel, or really dishonest. But he was as hard to keep in one's grip as a lively herring. Pray little Albion wouldn't be another such lithe and slippery fish.

* * *

The day when Damon and Pythias came to haul Jamie's hay, the weather reached a rich blossoming of heat. There was no wind, and a hot dry breath rose from the ground to meet the heat of the sun.

The oxen stood patiently in the hayfield, twitching their dark hides to keep off the flies, chewing their cuds, gazing with their round soft eyes at the twins who ran back and forth under their noses. Margery and Albion had made wreaths of red clover and buttercups to decorate the beasts' horns, and the pair calmly accepted the children's attentions.

Betsey Gibson and Sophia tramped, while Jamie and Lark pitched the hay up to them in great loose fragrant forkfuls. The boys had taken off their shirts, and their brown shoulders glistened with sweat. Lark, who had started off gaily enough, was muttering before a half-hour had gone by.

"Flies. Light on me and stick like I was painted with molasses!"

Betsey and Sophia giggled appreciatively. "Go put your shirt on again," Jamie said.

"I'd sooner wrap me up in a fleece," Lark grumbled. "I've hayseed in my eye, too."

"You did have," Sophia corrected him from up above. "But I got it out for you."

"You keep out of this!" He glared at her, drove his fork into the ground, and leaned on it. "Listen, Jamie, we aren't from Africky or the West Indies! We aren't made to strive so hard in this heat! It can kill us!"

Jamie pitched up a forkful of hay to the girls, then pushed back his torn straw hat and considered his brother. He thought of a number of things to say and then decided against it and went back to work. Lark spread out his hands, shook his head over a blister, and with infinite caution took hold of his fork again. He flinched dramatically as he stabbed the fork into a pile of hay, and heaved the weightless, sweet-scented mass upwards as if it were a thirty-pound codfish at the very least; his slender body all but reeled backward with the effort.

Jamie watched him from the corner of his eye. How long would it be before Lark gave up? Lord, it was hot! The heat had a smothering breathlessness; you could almost see it around you like a thin gray mist overlaying the summer brilliance.

"Heave ahead, Sophia," he called up to her. She touched the oxen lightly with the long whip. They moved forward slowly, unconcerned, as if they were too rapt in their own reveries to be annoyed by the giggling, tumbling girls in the rick and the yellow-haired twins who brought them crumpled handfuls of green grass, shouting with laughter as they did so.

Suddenly Lark threw down his fork and clapped his hands over his ears. "They're killing me with their noise!" he gasped. "It's slashing through my head like an axe!"

"I can send the young'uns away if they're giving you that much pain," Jamie said mildly. Lark shook his head.

"It's too late," he moaned, closing his eyes. "I was trying to bear up, I wasn't going to show how I felt, but I can't take another step." He tottered away from them toward the nearby woods, his shoulders bent, his hands still to his ears. He looked so frail and ill that Sophia began to worry.

"He is a mite pale," she said.

"Pale as skim milk," said Betsey in awe. They watched Lark collapse by the wall like a mainsail coming down.

"Remember," asked Betsey almost reverently, "how Uncle Oliver Burton was took of a hot day in the hayfield? And he had such a prodigious pain in his head first, but he kept on toiling, and then all of a sudden he fell on his face and he was dead?"

"I remember about Uncle Oliver Burton," said Jamie grimly, "and doubtless Lark remembers too." He drove his fork into a heap of hay and flung it upward into the rick. Lark remembered the sudden death last year, and was trusting the rest of them to remember the heat, the pain in the head . . . Who then but someone bent on his destruction would dare to summon him back to work? And what's more, Lark would never again be expected to work in the fields.

So frail, poor lad. Not long for this world, I don't doubt. Jamie could just hear the voices. He set his jaws hard. If he had to do the work without Lark, so be it. "Get along there!" he shouted to the oxen. The heat pressed down on him as thick as fog. He glanced at the sky. Over there in the west the mainland was blurry, the sky was grayed lavender. And there was something else, just beginning to rear above that hot shadowy color; the rounded, faintly pink, mass of a thunderhead.

Thunder. He realized then that he had been afraid of thunder all along. The fine haying weather had worn itself out. The thunderstorms were coming, and he had barely begun on his task. Of course there was no great wind yet to hurry the storm along, but soon the pale blue sea would darken under the first scuds. Even as he looked, a dim flicker of lightning forked down through the gray-lavender light over the main-land.

He said nothing to the girls and worked stolidly. Such thunderstorms as followed long dry periods on the island were ferocious; cloudbursts and hail and then perhaps weeks of fog to ruin the gardens and spoil the hay. His beautiful hay, so free of poisonous weeds to hurt Clover or make her lose her calf.

If he lost it—and the certainty of loss had him by the throat—it was the end of Clover, for no one else on the island had any more feed than what they needed for their own stock.

He had led Clover home from his uncle's barn five years ago, when she was a silky calf with a white star on her forehead; he had taught her himself to drink from a bucket. It wasn't just the milk and the cream, the cheese and butter, that they'd lose with her, it was the patient lovingness of Clover herself.

He drove his fork violently into the ground and strode off toward the stone wall. Sophia called after him but he didn't look back.

Lark lay comfortably in the shade, his arms behind his head; staring with tranquil brown eyes into the branches of a maple. Whatever his thoughts, they must have been sweet, if one judged from the dreamy smile. When Jamie stood over him, Lark took his gaze from the maple bough and said drowsily, "Hail, fellow, well met! That's an ancient Roman greeting."

"You don't look pale to me," said Jamie. "You look just about as stalwart as anybody on this island." He leaned down abruptly, grabbed Lark by his bare shoulder, and hauled him, struggling and squirming, to his feet.

"My head!" Lark gasped, and Jamie shook him.

"I'll rattle your wits into place for ye!"

Red flashed into Lark's face. "You leave me be!" He spat the words out venomously. "Might be you're bigger'n me, but that gives you no right to lug me around by the scruff of the neck!" He twisted and lunged at the same time, taking Jamie by surprise, and wrenched himself free. He bounded to the top of the wall and stood there panting.

"Now try and rattle my wits into place, bully boy!" he shouted. As

Jamie took a step toward him, he swung one foot out in a savage kick. Jamie was more conscious of astonishment than of anything else. Why, Lark was a real little gamecock!

"Aye," he admitted quietly, "I'll grant that you're all set to repel boarders. But take a look to the west'ard and then tell me; which of us is to slaughter Clover when there's no feed left for her? Are you brave enough for that?"

"What's Clover got to do with us?" Lark demanded. But as Jamie, without answering, looked out across the hot field to the western sky, Lark's gaze followed. The thunderhead towered high now, a magnificent sculpture of cloud; beneath it the mainland was hidden in rain and even here on the island, twenty miles away, the sunlight was beginning to dim.

"Gemini!" Lark breathed.

"Good weather's lasted too long to be true," said Jamie softly. "S'pose this didn't turn out too bad . . . mebbe we could dry out our hay. But the moon's about to change and we may have naught but fog and easterly wind for weeks." He didn't look at the slim boy on the wall, but started back to the hayrick and the oxen. He'd get in every wisp he could, anyway.

"Heave to, man!" That was Lark calling, and the sound of Lark's feet running. "I'm coming aboard!"

Chapter 6

Jamie didn't show his happiness. But suddenly the menace of thunder had become a challenge and he felt his whole mind and body rising to meet it with something like delight. As he and Lark picked up their forks he sent the oxen ahead and called to the twins.

"Put for the house, now, and fetch the switchel jug to the end of this row—we'll have a quick drink, and then you can go down the field and wait at the end of the next row." He tossed hay into the rick and squinted at the girls. "You two getting light-headed with the heat? If you are, get down now. We'll have no time to lug you off the field."

The boys worked in grim silence. The pale blue of the sea was graying, glinting with silver from a veiled sun. There was no relief in the wind from the stifling heat. Jamie's eyes burned as the sweat ran into them, sweat itched maddeningly down his spine, his trousers felt incredibly thick and seemed to impede his every motion. The tenseness of his muscles grew with the approach of the storm, and made his shoulders ache; he realized this, and tried to relax, to work as he had always worked, with an easy rhythm, but whenever he glanced from the sky to the long rows stretching away from him, the tightening began in the nape of his neck and ran like fire into his back and shoulders.

If he felt like this, what about Lark? They weren't wasting their breath on words now, but he glanced at his brother and saw that Lark's face was set and still; he looked older than fourteen, older than the gay impertinent boy who had defied him exultantly from the stone wall an hour ago. It was as if he had suddenly begun to grow up.

Clover mooed from the pasture wall beyond the barn.

"She always hated thunder," Lark said.

Jamie shouted at the twins, who had been told long since to stay out of the team's way. "Take Clover to the barn!"

Betsey exclaimed fearfully, "Them clouds is as full of lightning as plums in a pudding! I'd best start for home!"

"Go then!" Sophia was scornful. "We don't need you."

"I'll go when I'm ready, Sophie Bennett!" Betsey stuck out her chin in a way that Amanda had, and Jamie had to grin in spite of his anxiety. If Amanda were only here, now, wouldn't they be a crew? Come to think of it, this was the first haying Amanda had missed.

A strange light lay over land and sea. The water was the color of slate, the white caps that appeared under the freshening wind shone unearthly white. Mrs. Bennett appeared at the house door to watch them and her cap and kerchief had the same glittering whiteness against the darkness of the house and the brilliant unnatural green of the trees beyond it.

"The way the thunder growls," Lark said tightly, "puts me in mind of a lion waking up."

"It'll be a real handsome storm," said Jamie. Their eyes met for a moment and for the first time they were not two brothers but two men standing side by side to meet a common enemy. They worked with renewed vitality.

At last they had finished, with the thunder sending the first long rolling salvoes over their heads and the rain not yet falling, though the black clouds were heavy with it. The birches and maples bent before the strong winds and the tops of the spruces swayed; the sound of the wind through the woods was like boiling surf in a storm. Mrs. Bennett waited at the gate, glancing anxiously from her children to the sky. The twins ran ahead of the team as they pulled for the barn. Lark and Jamie walked on either side of the oxen, the girls still rode the rick, weary and quiet, but proud.

Then the rain came with a hiss and a crash. The lightning flashed white across the island. The storm was upon them at once. Mrs. Bennett collected the twins and ran to the house. "Go in," Jamie called to the girls. "We'll do the rest!"

He and Lark were alone in the barn—alone except for the chickens underfoot, Clover, Damon, and Pythias, and the barn swallows feeding their young in the mud nests along the beams. The rain on the roof nearly drowned out the thunder itself. The boys sat on their heels with their backs against the wall, resting, not speaking. The scent of the hay filled the darkened barn.

Then came the hailstones, bouncing and clattering. At last Jamie looked over at Lark and grinned. "Told you it'd be a real handsome storm."

"And there's another one behind it," said Lark. He climbed into the rick, stretched, and picked up his hayfork. "Well, let's stow it away."

Jamie nodded, but he was troubled. There was something that had to be said, if only he could think of the right way to say it. But it was his way to be blunt, so he plunged in all at once.

"If you'd run off today when you had the chance," he said, "I couldn't have got the hay in alone. I'm much obliged, Lark."

"What for?" Lark shrugged. "It's my hay too, isn't it? She's my cow as much as anybody's."

"I'm glad you feel that way. Everything here belongs to you as much as it does to Mother, or the young ones, or me. Only—"

"Only I don't very often act like it, is that it?"

"That's it," said Jamie.

There was a new uneasiness in Lark, who had never in his life showed doubt about anything. He gave Jamie an almost shy glance and went on pitching hay into the mow. Out in the field, racing against time, he had looked grim and mature. Now his troubled expression made him seem very young.

"If you've anything fretting you," Jamie said hesitantly, finding it hard to lift his voice above the roar and splash of rain, "you'd ought to rid your mind of it before it gets you ailing."

Lark turned to him with a smile; for a long time afterward Jamie remembered that smile in the dusky gloom. And then the smile died. "I don't reckon there's anything I can tell you," he said, and turned back to his work.

There was something, Jamie was certain-sure. He wished he could reach out to his younger brother, but he didn't know how. All he could do was to be grateful for what this day had shown him of Lark, to remember always that the hay smelled sweeter than it had ever smelt because he and his brother had worked side by side to save it, and to hope that, whatever Lark's secret, it was nothing shameful.

Chapter 7

Jamie had guessed right about the weather. The day of thunder was followed by a week of damp easterly winds that would have mildewed and rotted the hay.

After a week the wind changed again, going out around southwest. The first mackerel of the season appeared, and when Jamie was fishing he could have counted fifty sails at least, around and beyond the Rock. Men came from Stonehaven to fish for mackerel in these rich grounds.

One day when he was rowing toward the Rock, Jamie ran into a school of the lively blue and silver-striped fish, and was glad he had small lines with him as well as the heavy codlines. While he was catching mackerel as fast as he could throw his line over, Rich Gibson's schooner *Eugenia* sailed past South Island, going toward Monhegan, a small blue hump on the horizon. If luck was with her, the *Eugenia* would come back in a few days with all her empty kegs loaded with salt mackerel, and her crew would share richly.

While he was busy with the hay, Jamie had had no time to think of anything else. But the sight of the *Eugenia* roused all the old ache within him. He stood balanced in the lightly bobbing wherry and watched the schooner pass beyond the Rock; she might have been a clumsy, barrel-bottomed thing, but she was beautiful to him, for she was going somewhere. She wouldn't touch any foreign ports, and salt water was salt water, true enough. But it would be an adventure for Jamie simply to be on another part of the same ocean.

That night he sat on the front doorstep and watched the stars twinkling over the sea. Behind him the door was open; his mother sat at her spinning by candlelight, and Lark hunched at the table reading a book. The younger children were in bed.

How would it be aboard the *Eugenia* tonight? Jamie wondered. How would the sky look to a man lying on her deck in the dark, while she rocked at anchor like an enormous cradle? Out there you could see the whole sky, from horizon to horizon. There'd be the murmur of the water against her round sides, the creak of the masts, a snatch of song or rumble of laughter from below . . .

The night was warm but gusts of wind came, and the candle flame danced wildly. "You'll ruin your eyes, Lark," Mrs. Bennett said, "reading in that light. Larkin!"

Lark said thickly, as if from a great distance, "What is it?"

"Your eyes! Do you want to be blind before you're twenty? What are you reading?"

"It's a new book called *Ivanhoe*, by a man named Walter Scott," said Lark impatiently. "Let me be, Mammy dear. It's full of knights and jousting and wicked Normans."

"If you must be spoiling your sight, you'd be better off to be reading your Bible."

"But Mr. Whiting lent it to me, Mother," Lark became sweetly persuasive. "And he's the parson."

Mrs. Bennett sighed. "I don't know what the clergy is coming to," she murmured. "Our dear Dr. Hall, at home, would never have given his own children such a worldly book, let alone his flock."

"But Mr. Whiting is very worldly," said Lark mischievously. "Look how he plays his flute at all the sociables."

Mrs. Bennett sighed more deeply. The pleasant whirr of the flax wheel was drowned by the sound of the rising wind in the chimney and in the tops of the spruces. Fireflies danced in the darkness. Jamie stared at the sparkling Big Dipper, and from custom he followed the pointers to the Pole Star. If, at this moment, he were on a ship, somewhere in the warm South, he might be at the helm now, steering by far different stars from these.

The candle almost blew out, and Lark and his mother both exclaimed. Jamie got up to go inside and shut the door; and at that moment the harsh clang of the school-bell was borne to him on the wind. He stood still in the open doorway, listening, listening with his whole body.

"What is it?" cried his mother, seeing him stiffen. Lark looked up dreamily from his book and then became alert. His stool clattered as he pushed it back. He ran to the doorway and listened too. All the mischief in him was gone as the bell kept ringing, its wild alarms tossed and broken by the wind.

"A fire?" he said huskily.

"Let's pray not," said Jamie. They pulled on their boots and set off. Their mother watched them from the doorway, her fingers against her lips. She knew this was one time when her boys must join the men and take the danger as it came, whatever it might be. Fire. What if it should be fire, which islanders dreaded above all storms and sickness? As yet no shaking red glowed above the black wall of woods around the house, but in the next five minutes the first faint, terrible radiance could appear. Fire could start at one of the furthermost points and race over the entire island, swallowing up tinder-dry woodland, fields baked by a hot July, home and barns, people and animals . . . How could a little handful of men and boys hold it back when this wind was driving it; and there had been no soaking rain for weeks?

Lydia Bennett went back into the house and shut the door. She began to gather the family's few valuables together. If the boys found out it was a fire when they reached the schoolhouse, Lark would be back to help her get the children and Clover down to the shore. The twins would take turns carrying their gray cat . . . She went to the door and looked out again. No red light yet dimmed the stars. She returned calmly to her work. It was only the ever-present prospect of losing one of her sons at sea that could make Mrs. Bennett too weak and frightened to carry on.

When Lark and Jamie reached the schoolhouse at the high center of the island, their lungs aching from the long steady run, they found young Johnny Owen in the entry, pulling on the bell-rope for all he was worth. In the smoky light from his lantern, his small face was wild with excitement.

"It's a ship ashore!" he shouted at them importantly. "Down off the Thrasher! You better heave ahead and get along down there!"

As they left the schoolhouse, they found several more men and boys converging on the building from different directions. They shouted the news at these, and set off at a run. The Thrasher was a treacherous ledge just off the southern end of the island.

The boys kept at a steady trot through the woods and by Ned Converse's place, on and on until the forest thinned and they came out on wide fields high above the sea. The few trees here were stunted and wind-twisted black shapes against the stars.

Here, close by the edge of the woods, stood the ruin of the little stone house where Amanda had found the special blueberry patch. Jamie remembered it for an instant, the way one remembers slight, safe things in frightening moments. Then he forgot it as he saw the lanterns moving like big fireflies far ahead of him; he knew they were clustered at the edge of the field high above the Thrasher.

In the woods he and Lark had not been so conscious of the wind, but now as they trotted across the fields, it rushed at them in great gusts, and the crashing of the surf seemed to surround them like a ring of thunder.

They heard fragments of voices, as small and inhuman as seagulls' cries. Suddenly Lark grabbed Jamie's arm. All his brashness was gone. "I don't want to go!" he shouted above the long, rushing roar. "I don't want to see it!"

Jamie knew what he meant. He didn't want to see the ship break up, and the men struggle in the deadly stretch of surf between the Thrasher and the shore.

Lark had let go of his arm and was backing away toward the safe shadows of the woods. Jamie caught his wrist and held him fast. "I don't want to see it either!" he shouted at his brother. "But we've got to go and help all we can!"

"Not me!" Lark's voice broke, and he fought against Jamie's steely fingers.

"Cut for home then," said Jamie. "If you figger you aren't man enough to do a man's work here."

That did it. Lark came along with him, catching his breath now and then as he stumbled. At last they reached the edge of the land. Every able man on the island had turned out, and all the boys who were big enough to bear a hand. Below the fields, the combers rushed in from open sea, long smears of luminous white, to bury the breaking ship again and again in foaming tumbles of surf. There was a continual splintering and creaking, a gleam of ripped and drenched sails, and such a confusion of voices all around there was no telling whether the hoarse cries came from the seamen or the islanders.

The boat had smashed down hard across the rigid spine of the Thrasher. There was no possibility of reaching her with small boats, not from any angle; and the tide was ebbing too. But the islanders had gotten several lines out to her, and the crew was trying to make their way ashore, using sheer wrist and shoulder power to hang to the lines and drag themselves through the surging white water.

Halfway up the steep bank between beach and field, a crew of island men manned the lines, keeping them taut. At the foot of the slope others waded out again and again into the surf to lay hold of the exhausted sailors, and help them to dry land.

Jamie looked for the place where he would be most useful. Someone grabbed Lark by the shoulder and bawled at him, "Git down to the harbor and tell my missus to blow up the fire and git some beds ready—spread the news—" Lark was gone.

So he was spared, but at the same time he was being useful. Jamie ran down the steep path to the beach. He had to go a little way along the hard wet sand; he came upon several active figures and thought they were rescuing men who had been washed away from the lines. But as they came splashing ashore, hauling something between them, it was no human shape he saw in the clear starlight, but something large and bulky. There were others like it piled above the tide mark. Bales or chests of some sort. But he had no time to investigate.

"What's the cargo?" he shouted at the salvagers as he passed them, and Israel Boyd's voice answered.

"Bales of raw linen! Bobbing ashore like net corks!" Israel's brother, Tim's deep tones chimed in jubilantly.

"Wade out and get a holt of one, boy, and make your mother happy!"

"I'd rather git a holt on a man!" Jamie yelled over his shoulder.

"There's so many now they're falling all over each other," Israel called after him. Jamie went on. Trust those two to discover the cargo and make hogs of themselves salvaging it while the rest saved lives. It was said on Brigport that Thaddeus's boys would steal South Island if they found it adrift.

Here were the workers finally, splashing out hip-deep into the swirling water, slipping on rocks covered with seaweed, clutching at the shipwrecked men and dragging or carrying them ashore.

"Give a hand, here!" someone shouted from the noisy dark. "Man with a broken leg—I can't get him in all by myself!" It was Jamie's cousin, Mark Bennett.

Jamie yelled, "I'm coming," and ran out. His foot slid sidewise on a slimy rock, but he kept his balance and reached his cousin's side. Bracing their feet wide apart against the force of the water rushing in and then drawing out, they made a seat of their hands and wrists, and carried the man in. They put him down carefully on the dry soft sand. "Thank 'ee kindly, mates," he panted. "Thank 'ee kindly." He lifted himself on his elbow, gasping, and stared out through the starlight past the confusion of black figures and surging phosphorescent water. The ship now lay far over on her side; from this distance one could hardly tell that the strange black shape was a ship at all.

"So that's the death of the *Cynthia*," his voice croaked hoarsely. "We cleared New Bedford three days ago and set out all a-taunto for Halifax. And now look at her!—with the sea a-pourin' over her and through her, and breakin' her up with no respect for the lady that she's been." He dropped back wearily and put his arm across his eyes. "I'd take my oath on it, so would every man-jack of us that was on deck—we saw the light and took it for Saddleback—"

"Saddleback!" exclaimed Jamie. "Why, man, Saddleback's fifteen miles to the north of us."

"But there was the light," the man protested angrily. "And by the time we'd got our senses and the skipper cal'lated we was off our course, we was well in past the top o' that island to the south'ard, and sails set, and we come down on them rocks fit to split her wide open. And it did. And the light was gone."

"What light?" Tim Boyd's deep voice boomed behind Jamie. "What's the man raving about? There's no light on this shore—there's not a house where a light could show." He stooped over the man. "You sure your helmsman hadn't been tippling the skipper's brandy?"

"There was a light," the man repeated through chattering teeth. "We all saw it. If you can't take Bob Crockett's word for it, listen to the skipper. He's a fine young gentleman, is Cap'n Jeremy Thorne." He stared toward the knot of figures at the edge of the frothing tide. "They salvaged him yet? He was just hanging on by his eyelids when I went over the side."

Mark was returning. Jamie could see him plain in the starlight; he walked slowly, and well he might, with his clothes sodden with sea water and his legs and ankles lame from all the tumbles he'd taken on the rocks.

"Where's the skipper?" the man shouted at him. "They'll believe him when he says there was a light!"

"They won't believe anything he says any more," said Mark. He was usually a loud, cheerful boy, but now his voice was flat and tired. "He lost his handholt on the line."

"He can swim!" Bob Crockett said defiantly.

"Nobody can swim in that white water," said Jamie. Suddenly he wanted to sit down; a sickness at his stomach had spread in some queer way to his legs.

"Morgan Owen brought him in," Mark went on. But Bob Crockett seemed not to have heard him. He lay on the sand shivering in his wet clothes, his broad face turned upwards. He stared fixedly at the stars and said never a word.

Chapter 8

Bob Crockett was the only one of the rescued men who was unable to walk. The others were taken to the village by foot through the woods, but Bob was wrapped in blankets and carried on a litter.

The next afternoon a service was held for Captain Jeremy Thorne. Almost everyone attended. The *Cynthia*'s crew, bandaged where it was necessary and clad in borrowed clothing, made a tight little group among themselves.

In the churchyard, tall spruces brushed a bright blue summer sky, and the big, billowing, fair-weather clouds from the northwest sailed slowly overhead. Beyond Mr. Whiting's pleasant dry voice, there was the peaceful drone of the wild honeybees that climbed over the early goldenrod and asters. Far in the sky the black-headed laughing gulls soared and dived in some mysterious pursuit. It was the kind of weather Jamie loved, but as he stood beside his mother and Lark, he knew he would never again awake to such a day without remembering Captain Jeremy Thorne.

When they were leaving the churchyard, Captain Marriot stood in the road in his fine black broadcloth coat, his tall hat still on his arm, and spoke to every man who passed him.

"Come to my house this evening before sundown," he said quietly. "There's a matter which concerns us all." His usually ruddy face was pale, and his lips were pressed into a straight hard line.

"What can be the trouble?" Mrs. Bennett asked, as she and her sons moved out of earshot.

"It was a strange light lured 'em onto the rocks," Lark said excitedly. "Dougal Erskine claims it was a will-o'-the-wisp! Only in Scotland it lures people into bogs, but he says it must have changed its ways here."

"Don't talk such foolery," Jamie said, but he was uncomfortable.

On the way to the Marriot house that evening he fell in with Morgan Owen and Hughie Erskine. Hugh's grandfather had grown up in the Hebridean islands of Scotland, and Morgan's father had come from Wales, so both boys had vivid stories to tell of fairy lights and other suchlike things.

They laughed as they told of them, but their laughter was uneasy.

The square handsome parlor of the Marriot house soon filled with men. The crew of the *Cynthia*, all but Bob Crockett who was bedded down at Simon Pollinger's house, kept to themselves near the fireplace. Jamie slid in behind Pleasance's pianoforte, perching on a wide windowsill where he could glance out now and then at the harbor in the sunset light.

Captain Marriot, still cold-eyed and severe, presided, calling upon the crew members to give their stories. As the rough, halting voices went on, Jamie looked out and saw Amanda Gibson on the end of her father's wharf, fishing for flounders.

Simon Pollinger was reading aloud Bob Crockett's statement. That finished the testimony about the light, and there was much clearing of throats and shifting of feet. Captain Marriot tapped for order on the table before him.

"Who gave the first warning of the disaster, so that the schoolbell could be rung?" he asked.

Tim Boyd was on his feet. " 'Twas me, Cap'n," he said eagerly. He was a big, rangy young man with rough sandy hair, and Lark had said once that he had a face like a turnip.

"I was on my way home from gunning seabirds, following the shore, and I come out on the Point opposite Tenpound and I looked down across the channel between us and South Island and there she was." He stared dramatically into space. "I seed her lights, and her full spread of canvas sort of shining in the dark, and I thought to myself first 'twas a ghost ship, the *Flying Dutchman* mebbe, and I like to fell off the rocks with being so scairt—and then—" He laughed in a manly fashion. "Then I come to my senses like, and says, 'Now, Timothy, ain't Parson Whiting told you over and over they's no such thing as ghosts or ghost ships? That vessel's good oak and canvas, and she's riding for the Thrasher!' "

He paused and looked all around. Thaddeus, his father, nodded his grizzled head approvingly. Tim might have been a poor scholar, but he could certainly get things said. Israel, his brother, stared at the floor.

"No wonder she struck," Jonathan Gibson said, "if you took all that time to talk to yourself about her before you sung out."

Thad glared at him, and Tim flushed angrily. A red turnip, Jamie thought. "It all happened in a minute, like!" Tim roared. "I reckon I got back to the harbor faster'n you ever traveled in your whole life, Jonathan Gibson!"

There was a murmur of displeasure in the room, and Captain Marriot tapped for order. "Continue, Tim."

But Tim's moment of glory had been shattered. "I come to David Owen's place first," he said sulkily, "and I roused 'em out, and they sent one of the young'uns hypering off to the schoolhouse. And I got m' brother and m' father and we went down to Southern Point. And that's all."

That's all, Jamie thought, except that you and your brother spent your time saving the cargo instead of the men.

Then the first mate of the *Cynthia*, a slight dark young man, stood up. "There's something the men have asked me to say, Captain Marriot. I don't like to say it, but it'll be brought up sooner or later. Better to have it over with."

"I think we all know what it is, Mr. Hathaway," said the Captain.

"You suspect there's been wreckers at work, do ye?" Simon Pollinger rumbled, and there was a stir of wrath in the room, as if someone had poked at a hornet's nest. A cold prickle moved along Jamie's spine. David Owen called out in his lilting Welsh accent, "We do be all Christian folk here, Mr. Hathaway, not murderers!"

The mate looked around at them steadily. "I said I didn't like to mention it, but the men have asked me to bring it up."

Behind him the crew made a tight hostile group. The room was full of confusion. Some of the island men rose to their feet, muttering angrily. Captain Marriot rapped for order. "This is no way to carry out an inquiry!" he shouted above the uproar. "Either we examine this in an orderly fashion and prove to these men that we have no wreckers on this island, or we let the name of Brigport be forever muddied!"

"That's right, Cap'n!" It was Thad Boyd's voice resounding over the rest. A stout, square-built man, he moved with astonishing speed and set himself in the exact middle of the French carpet. "I got something to say here!"

The others, both sailors and islanders, fell quiet, and Captain Marriot nodded curtly. "Speak out, Thad. This is no time to hold anything back."

"Well, it's not a thing a man wants to be saying," said Thad, "and when my boys told me about it they begged me not to make use of it unless'n I had to. But I reckon I have to use it now, and pour oil on troubled waters, you might say."

There was a nervous clearing of throats and shifting of feet. Thad Boyd was always long-winded. Captain Marriot watched him from under his eyebrows, and Thad hurried on.

"The boys got to the Point before me, on account of me stopping to rouse up everybody on the way, and who'd they run into up there on the bluff above the sandbeach but Ned Converse!" As the ripple of surprise flowed around the room he said triumphantly, "You all know how he wanders around half the night when folks in their right minds are sound asleep. He wouldn't have no talk with my boys—just up jib and away for home like he thought the pirates was after him again. But—" Thad dropped his voice dramatically, "He had a lantern with him . . . We talked it over afterwards, when the men kept swearing they'd seen a light, and we figgered old Ned was out there prowling around—all innocent-like, I'm sure of it—most likely he didn't even know where he was, he's that addled in his head—and caused that poor vessel to run ashore."

"Seems as if it could've happened that way," somebody said. There were murmurs of agreement, and Jamie felt the general relief in the room. The word "wreckers" had caught them all by the throats a little while ago. Mr. Hathaway, the first mate, conferred with his men and then rose.

"The men are satisfied, Captain Marriot. It seems to be a logical explanation. But a hundred explanations won't bring Captain Thorne back to life, or restore the *Cynthia*. Do you intend to let this madman wander free and cause more disasters?"

Captain Marriot pulled at his lower lip and stared at the notes on the table before him. "I always swore Ned should be locked up," Thad was saying.

"Well, I dunno but what I believe it now," someone else muttered. "It's the shame of Brigport!" one man exclaimed. "Git him off'n here to-morrow!"

Captain Marriot looked up. His gray eyes were icy. They ignored all else in the parlor and picked out Mr. Whiting. The minister, a lean, white-haired man in black, had been sitting quietly through the meeting in a corner of the room. As Captain Marriot called his name, they all turned toward him eagerly.

He stood up then, tired and grave. "This is a tragic business," he said slowly. "But it seems to me that it would only add to the tragedy of it if we cast our poor Ned adrift. I would suggest that we try to show Ned what terrible harm he has done, and impress it upon him that he must stay indoors at night—or at least not take a lantern with him on his wanderings."

"Splendid, splendid!" Captain Marriot looked happy in his relief. "Do I hear any objections to Mr. Whiting's plan?"

Simon Pollinger heaved himself to his feet. "I got one, Cap'n. Who's going to get the facts through Ned's thick skull?" He squinted at Mr. Whiting and pulled at his massive chin. "Not meaning impertinence or disrespect, Parson, but do you reckon you can convince him?"

Mr. Whiting smiled sadly. "I wish I could. But you all know Ned has little use for the clergy."

"Cap'n Marriot!" called out Jamie's Uncle Nathan. "He'd ought to listen to you!"

Captain Marriot shook his head. "Ned washed his hands of me when I retired from the sea."

"It all comes to this," Simon grunted. "Who's goin' to bell the cat?"

"Why not you, Simon?" someone spoke up, and there was an immediate enthusiastic response in the room.

Simon glared around him, rubbed his hand over his gray head, and then said abruptly, "Well, if anybody can lay into Ned Converse and make him look alive, it's me. All right. I'll give him a hail now." He stamped out of the room and everyone made way for him. Captain Marriot stood up; the meeting was over.

Jamie slid out around groups of talkers and into the big square hall. Pleasance called to him softly from the head of the stairs; he gave her a hasty wave and hurried out-of-doors just ahead of the men from the *Cynthia*. Tim and Israel Boyd were with them, Tim saying earnestly to the mate, "Talk to him! I swear they'd ought to hang old Ned. Tomorrow!"

Captain Pollinger was halfway down the flower-bordered walk to the road and Jamie had to run to catch up with him.

"Cap'n Pollinger—"

The big gray man scowled at him. "What is it, boy?"

Jamie had hardly known how he was going to say what was on his mind, but it burst out all at once. "Can I go with you to see Ned?"

"You think it's like going to gape at a dancin' bear? He was a good seaman before he lost his wits."

"I don't want to gape at him or plague him! I just want to go with you, that's all."

Simon shrugged. "Come along, then. But if Ned don't like the cut of your jib, out you go. I can't get an idea through his head if he's all fretted up with something else."

* * *

As they went down the slope to Ned's house, the pigeons flew up in a cloud, their wings making a rushing sound. Simon tramped on toward the small huddled house without looking left or right, but Jamie stared

around him, trying to see everything at once. He was tense with ex-
pectancy, as if any moment Ned might burst from the alder swamp or
come storming out the door, swinging his cutlass and shouting curses.

But nothing broke the usual sunset hush save the soft sounds of pigeons as they settled to earth again, and the voices of the small birds in the
woods. The cow, at the far side of the paddock, gazed at them indiffer-
ently. Simon reached the crude door set into an opening of the original
stone house, and knocked. Jamie saw where the old man had managed to
roll some big logs into position on the rock foundation of his new barn;
but how had he ever managed alone, to pry out the big rocks and drag
them home and get them into position to receive the logs?

Simon pounded again, and shouted, "Ahoy the house! Heave to,
Ned!"

Then suddenly Ned was in the doorway and before Jamie had time to
swallow his nervous astonishment, the man was saying, just like any other
man, "Simon Pollinger. I ain't seen ye since Adam was an oakum-boy.
How are ye, old Shiver-the-mizzen?" He was even grinning. He had only
a few teeth left, and his face with its broken nose and scarred forehead
had been burned permanently by the long years in the Berber galleys; the
black patch added to his ferocious appearance. He cropped his white hair
as best he could, hacking at it with a knife. So his grin was almost as
frightening as his scowl would have been, but there was no mistaking the
heartiness in his voice. Simon was just as hearty in his directness.

"I'm fair, Ned, fair. I'm winterin', but who isn't? I'm aboard to have a
word with ye, Ned."

"But not in the cabin," said Ned firmly, coming out and shutting the
door behind him. "It's like Barney's brig in there—both main tacks over
the foreyard." He squinted his good eye past Simon's big shoulder.
"Who's that stowaway a-lurkin' there?"

The gleaming eye surveyed Jamie from head to foot. He tried to smile
and nod, but his face felt stiff. Simon saved him.

"That's no stowaway. That's Charles Bennett's boy. And that brings
me to my business, Ned. Speakin' of sailors and salt water . . . Where was
you when that vessel struck on the Thrasher t'other night?"

"Down on my shore," said Ned promptly. "I was haulin' up my yawlboat—she was a-poundin' around down there in that wind and tide like
she was bound to scuttle herself. I'd just got her above high watermark
when I heard that vessel strike, and the voices a-cryin' out." His face went
bleak. "It was a sound to bring the dead up all standing from their
graves."

Simon nodded. "What'd you do then, Ned?"

"Set a straight course for the house and took my lantern aboard. Put for the Southern Point a-flukin'—"

"You wasn't out there with your lantern before she struck? You wasn't tackin' back and forth along the bank kind of absent-minded, like?"

"I was not," said Ned sharply. There was a deadly intelligence in the good eye, as if he guessed at the direction of Simon's questions.

"Did you see anybody up there?"

"Them slack-jawed sculpins of Thad Boyd's crossed my bow! Asked me what I was up to. I asked them if they'd roused out the village, and they said aye, so I put for home. How much of the cargo did they git for themselves?"

Simon, staring at the ground and thoughtfully pulling at his chin, didn't answer.

"They got most of it," Jamie heard his own voice with surprise.

Ned nodded. "So they would. Chaw-mouth scavengers!"

"Well, Ned," Simon said, "I've transacted my business. I reckon I know the truth when I see it. But like Mr. Whiting says—a word to the wise; you stay home with your lantern next time a vessel goes on the Thrasher. Then nobody can name you as a menace to navigation!"

"You think it's likely to happen again?" Ned asked shrewdly, and Simon shook his head. His heavy gray eyebrows were drawn forbiddingly toward his big nose. "I ain't thinkin' anything of the sort. Good night to ye, Ned." He strode across the yard. As he passed Jamie, the boy fell in behind him; but an irresistible impulse drew his head around and he looked back at Ned. He stood against the wall of his little house, his seamed brown face melancholy as he watched Simon's departure. The black patch, the withered arm, the dragging leg; they were all pathetic enough. But what struck Jamie to the heart was the man's loneliness.

His pace slowed even before he knew what he was going to do; it was as if he were controlled from without. He kept staring back at Ned. What if Father came home, looking like this? What if he'd known such terrible things that he couldn't forget them, and folk called him mad because of it?

No. It would be better for Father to be dead than like this! His father had been tall as a spar pine, with a high head and a proud walk, his keen eyes full of humor and kindness. He could never, never, be a half-mad derelict like Ned Converse!

Or could he? . . . Simon was halfway up the slope now, but Jamie had turned back, walking slowly, but always toward Ned Converse. Suddenly the fierce, sad eye lit on him.

"Who are ye?" the hoarse voice demanded. "Git, before I cut ye down!"

"You know me," said Jamie. "I'm Charles Bennett's boy."

"What do you want of me? I'll not let ye kill the seabirds in my pond!" He fumbled with the latch of the door. "I know how to repel invaders! I cut down five of them cursed pirates before they split my skull." He touched the cruel scar across his forehead.

"I'm not an invader," Jamie said. "I—I want to help you build your barn."

The man screwed his good eye almost out of sight. Then he said in a harsh whisper, "Build my barn!"

"Yes sir," said Jamie, and the miracle was that he was no longer afraid.

"Well, I'll be jiggered," whispered Ned Converse. "I'll be jiggered."

Chapter 9

Jamie told no one what he was doing, but since he had a habit of going alone for long walks, no one questioned it when he disappeared after supper each night. No matter how tired he was from a long day of fishing, he went to work on the barn without fail. He and Ned accomplished more in the last few hours of daylight than the man could have done alone all day.

Then one night at supper Lark took it into his head to plague Jamie about his mysterious errands. "Are you courting Pleasance, or 'Manda, or a mermaid?" he demanded. The twins giggled, and even their mother smiled faintly. Only Sophia was indignant.

"Nobody asks you what you do all the time!" she flared at Lark. "And maybe it's a good thing, too! Maybe you're ashamed to tell what you're up to!"

"Sophia, Sophia, go fall in the fire!" Lark chanted at her, which sent the twins into fits of pure mirth, and Jamie arose and led Lark away from the table by his ear. He set Lark outside and shut the door on him. "You can't come in until Sophie says so!" he shouted through the door.

"But why do you go out every night, Jamie?" Margery asked earnestly.

"He doesn't have to tell you, either!" said Sophia, and then Jamie understood. He hadn't told Sophia his secret, and though she jealously guarded his right to privacy, she would be desperately hurt if he should tell the others before he told her alone.

He reached over and pulled one of Margery's yellow locks. "To make little girls ask questions," he said.

"That's no answer," Albion stated belligerently. Jamie grinned, and looked around to meet once more his mother's gaze. This time she was concerned with him, not with Lark. Her dark eyes were steady and thoughtful under the white frill of her cap. And he knew, as if she had already asked the question, that in the next instant she too would ask him where his walks took him night after night. Doubtless she'd taken them for granted until all this pulley-hauling began. And he couldn't tell her. Such a frightened thing she'd become since the loss of her husband; she'd see only disaster and terror in his friendship with Ned. And Sophia and the twins, if they knew, would be having nightmares about it.

But she was going to ask him. He knew it and the young'uns knew it; they were waiting. He was saved by a furious pounding on the bolted door.

"Look alive in there!" It was Lark. "Show a leg! There's herring puddling in the cove!"

The twins and Sophia were away from the table as swift as herring themselves, and Jamie was almost as fast. Mrs. Bennett glanced with a rueful smile at the half-emptied bowls and then rose to follow her children to the shore.

The twins and Sophia launched Grandfather Bennett's old wherry, over whose rounded sides they fished on calm days for the lazy flounders and the fast-striking little pollock. Jamie went into the fish house to gather up the intricately knotted mass of twine that was the gill net he'd knit last winter, and then he and Lark rowed out to the mouth of the cove to set the net. It hung like a lacy curtain in the clear water, wavering slightly in the tide but for the most part held taut and straight between the weights along the bottom and the floats along the top.

"Now we'll fetch 'em in!" Lark exulted. "We'll have salt herring laid away for winter that we caught ourselves, in our own cove—none of Uncle Nathan's charity!"

"None of that slack, now," Jamie rebuked him. "We might be glad of his charity, as you call it, before the frost is out of the ground . . . Might be this net won't fish, after all."

"Why shouldn't it fish?" demanded Lark. He leaned far over the side, gazing at the net until the deepening water hid it from his sight.

In the cove each blue ripple was edged with gilt; Jamie's oars stirred whirlpools of gold. The mark of the herring was as plain across the water as the scud of a catspaw breeze. They made a small but continuous splashing. What a fine evening it was! And if his net should catch something—he stiffened his face lest his grin of delight should break through. He'd never made a gill net before. There could be any number of things the matter with it.

"Might be they won't like the smell of it," he said aloud. "Or the color—"

"Of what?" asked Lark, sitting up.

"Let's go in." Jamie pulled for the shore.

After that there were the clean-scoured kegs to be fetched, and the salt, just in case the net did fish. And there was supper to be finished, with the young'uns prattling so fast and furious about the prodigious catch that no one remembered what they'd been talking about before Lark had sung out. After the tide had turned, he and Lark went out to the net again. They saw it before they came to it; it shone through the dark water with a cold white fire. When they were close upon it, staring down into the water, it was even more wonderful in its brilliance. What had been a lacy curtain of twine was now a radiant screen of some strange, unearthly substance.

"There must be one in every mesh," Lark whispered reverently. "She fished, Jem. She fished!"

"Aye," Jamie answered, his face gone stiff again. "She fished. Ship your oars, and turn to. We'll take her in."

They began to pull the net into the boat, and the weird fire of phosphorus rubbed off on them with each fish they plucked from the net. Their hands were spattered with blood and luminous scales, their clothing was dappled with more scales. The clean acrid scent of fresh herring was good in their nostrils. They worked steadily, hardly speaking.

In a curious way Jamie was reminded of the afternoon when he and Lark had taken the hay in. Lark must be tired now from standing braced in the boat, his hands must be aching and raw, but there was never a word from him. Except for his slightness, he might have been a man working there opposite Jamie, or at least as old as Jamie.

It was a troubling circumstance. It made him wonder about Lark, but it didn't make him rejoice. Instead it set him to puzzling if he himself were at fault somehow because Lark was so wayward.

Might be he, Jamie, was doing something wrong, to drive the lad away. There was energy enough in him, and purpose; he showed it in flashes as dazzling as lightning through night clouds. But what if Jamie was too stern, too unfriendly? Arrogant. The word came so clear that Jamie's head jerked up and he stared at Lark across the chilly glow of the scaly net between them. But nobody had said it; the only sounds were the chuckle of the tide bubbling past the boat, the wash on the shore, the rise of the wind through the trees.

Am I arrogant? he asked himself. Do I think too proud of myself? It was in his mind to ask Lark, at this moment, but his tongue became suddenly thick and shy. In the next moment Sophia yelled from the shore.

"Are you still alive out there?"

"Alive, alive-o!" Lark called back. They had most of the net into the wherry by then, in folds around their feet. There was no opportunity to ask Lark the question, and Jamie was relieved.

By the time they had finished cleaning the fish, by the light of half a dozen guttering candles in the fish house, they had enough and plenty for their winter's use; tired, aching in legs and shoulders and wrists, they were yet giddy with self-satisfaction as they arranged a layer of fish, a layer of salt, then fish and salt again until the contents reached the top of the keg. Then the boys stumbled up the path in the dark, to scrub up on the wide doorstep with the candlelight shining out through the open door, and the twins half-mad with the jubilation of the catch and of being allowed to stay up so long after dark.

Inside there was a roused and crackling fire, and scalding tea brewed for them by their mother. As he sat at the table opposite Lark, sipping the hot drink and eating gingerbread, Jamie suddenly remembered the nights he had laid awake upstairs listening to the kitchen sounds. His mother had made tea for his father, when Charles Bennett had come home after dark from some such occupation. But this was the first time she had blown up the fire again to make tea for her sons.

She had known that it was men's work they were doing. Did he dare to hope, he wondered cautiously, that she knew he was a man at last?

No one ever thought again to ask him what he did on his long solitary walks.

Chapter 10

To be with Ned was to enter another world. Sometimes they worked silently at their building, and Ned's face was as hard and blank as a face carved from rock. Then Jamie's thoughts ran free, and while he hammered he wondered how he would feel if he were helping build the schooner with Mark and Hughie. It was not a pleasant comparison, and yet he was glad enough to be helping Ned. The hard work eased his secret unhappiness.

And then there were the times when Ned talked. He might talk as any old sailor would talk to a boy, in bits and pieces of his past life; he might tell of the Algerian Corsairs overhauling the ship, in such vivid terms that Jamie dreamed of it afterwards, and awoke sweating.

At other times Ned's memories overwhelmed him and then he spoke as if to a crowd of companions and enemies unseen by Jamie; but as he listened to Ned's threats, defiances, and reassurances, the others were almost as real to him as they were to Ned.

"Turn Mohammedan?" Ned roared. "Never! Make me a slave! The mines or the galleys, it's all one to me—I'm still Ned Converse of Connecticut, and you can't change me!"

Then he comforted a frightened comrade. "Put the iron in your knees, lad. Don't let that gimbal-jawed pagan see a Yankee strike his colors."

And then, his eyes running over with tears, he hailed the arrival of the French frigate that had saved him. And as he talked, Jamie knew the tears were not all for joy.

"Those dirty devils!" he cried, his voice breaking. "They know they're beaten, they'll butcher us where we sit in chains! They're coming at us now! Are we to be cut in pieces before the French come aboard?"

He had been one of the few who had survived the butchering. "But the captain and the mate," he said sadly, "they'd sent them to the mines instead of to the galleys—there was no French frigate with forty-eight guns could get them."

"Maybe when Commodore Preble went over there, the captain and the mate were set free," Jamie suggested. Ned shook his shaggy white head.

"No, no," he said. "They'd never have lived that long."

* * *

One day when it was too foggy and windy to fish, the wet weather
got into Ned's bad leg so he couldn't work, and Jamie found himself with
an empty afternoon. It was rather a wonder; he couldn't remember such
an afternoon in years. The haying was done, the garden needed only to let
the potatoes and turnips and cabbages grow in peace; his mother had
taken the twins and gone to call on his Uncle Nathan's wife for a few
hours. Only Sophia was at home, watching him with wide shining eyes as
if at any moment he might suggest something wonderful to do.

"Let's go for a walk," he suggested, and she was as eager as a puppy.

"I love to walk in the fog!" she said excitedly. "Nobody can see you,
and you can't see anybody, and it feels so wet and soft against your
face . . . It's like being inside of a big cloud."

They had not gone far along the road, always encircled by a thin
white wall, when two figures appeared hazily out of the mist. The bigger
one hung back, and Jamie recognized Amanda. When she saw him she
leaned down and made quite a business of tying her shoe. Betsey ran forward eagerly to take Sophia's hand.

"We were just coming to get you, Sophie!" she cried excitedly. "
'Manda knows where there's some beautiful blueberries. We wanted you
to go with us. Unless—" She looked disapprovingly at Jamie—"you have
to go some place with him."

Jamie grinned. "I suppose," he remarked to Amanda's bent head as
she went on fiddling with her shoe, "if you caught me anywhere near
your blueberries you'd wring my neck and hang me up for a scarecrow to
keep the gulls off."

"I never said you couldn't go up there," she said in a muffled voice.
"You didn't want to, that's all. You got bigger things to do than pick blueberries."

She straightened up and regarded him with her honest dark eyes, as if
daring him to be cruel again, and he wanted suddenly to tell her about
Ned. The words were already in his throat, but he swallowed them back;
he had promised himself he would tell no one.

Instead he answered simply, "I was ugly that day, 'Manda. But I'm
not like that now. Let's go find your blueberries."

"I reckon the gulls have got 'em all by now," she grumbled, and then
grinned at him.

They took the path toward Southern Point, but when they reached
the edge of the woods, they didn't go out across the open fields above the

sand beach, but turned left toward the stone shell of the French fisherman's house. It was half-hidden by big clumps of shiny-leaved, fragrant
bay. They swung wide around it, tramping through early goldenrod and
blackberry tangles. The blueberry patch was on the slope between the
house and the shore, and Amanda had been lucky; the gulls hadn't bothered. This little spot remained rich and blue.

Wrapped in the fog Jamie and Amanda picked with expert speed, not
bothering to talk. The little girls chattered like sparrows, moving from
clump to clump.

"If you aren't going to settle down to this," Amanda warned them,
"you pick around the edge of the patch. I'm not going to have you staving
through here like a couple of heifers got into the garden."

Sophia and Betsey giggled, and did settle down, for all of five minutes. Then they were on the move again, roaming always up the slope
rather than down to where the heavy swell boomed unseen on the rocks.
The fog thinned, then thickened, swirling around Jamie and Amanda
like wet white smoke. Suddenly it blotted out the children and the sound
of their voices as completely as if they had dropped off the earth.

"There," said Amanda comfortably. "I always say that taking young
ones berrying is like taking along a couple of puppy dogs. They can run
around in the field and tire themselves out." Then, shyly, she added, "I
heard about the shipyard. I'm sorry, Jamie."

"It's all right," He went on picking berries. "I don't know how I'd
make out, living ashore. 'Twould be like putting a gull in a cage."

Apparently Amanda thought it was time to change the subject. "Was-
n't that a terrible wreck?" she exclaimed. "Do you think Ned will make it
happen again?"

"I don't know if he made it happen the first time," Jamie said shortly.

Amanda sat back among the blueberries and gave him a long steady
look. "Then who did?"

Jamie shrugged. "I dunno. Mebbe it's what Dougal Erskine says—a
will-o'-the-wisp." He picked rapidly, enjoying her startled silence. Then
the words rushed at him.

"Cap'n Simon wouldn't make any answer, either! You're as bad as he
is!" Anger turned to pleading. "Please, Jamie, tell me what you think. I
won't tell anybody, cross my heart!"

"Listen," said Jamie. "If it wasn't Ned out here with a lantern—and I
don't believe it was—it was somebody else who'd no thought of causing a
disaster, and after it happened—well, they were scared to tell of it. Same
as I'd be, for fear somebody'd accuse me of being a wrecker."

"Well—" She bit thoughtfully on her lower lip. "I'd hate to be the one. He must have some mighty fearsome dreams."

She looked around at the wreathing fog with awed eyes, and it was at the same moment that the screams came from the slope above. Jamie was on his feet and across the juniper as if nothing stood in his way. Amanda was close behind him. He thought he would never find anything in the fog—he felt as if he were lost in a wet, white world full of children's screams—and then Sophia and Betsey plunged blindly out of the mist, holding hands; they rushed at Jamie and clutched with all the strength of their fingers. They pushed their frightened faces against his ribs and he hugged them hard.

Amanda kept pulling at Betsey trying to make the child face her. "What is it?" she cried. "What is it? Answer me, you silly goose!"

"Leave them alone!" Jamie shouted at her. Sophia sobbed against his shirt. "Let's go home right now, Jamie. Let's go home, please!"

"Yes, let's go home!" came Betsey's wailing echo.

"Not till you tell us what ails you," Amanda argued, but Jamie scowled at her.

"Get the berries and we'll go home."

She tightened her mouth, but she obeyed him. Then they started up the hill, but the little girls balked like two terrified calves. "Not near the stone house," moaned Sophia. "Not near the stone house!"

Jamie couldn't imagine what they had seen or heard to put them in such a state. Amanda was white around the mouth and her dark eyes shifted uneasily from side to side, as if straining to see demons through the swirling fog. They made a wide circle around the stone house, and at last reached the path that led through the woods and home.

Once they were inside the shelter of the trees, where the sound of surf was muted, the children became quieter.

"Now," Jamie said in as masterful a tone as he could manage. "Tell us what happened. What did you see?"

Betsey promptly ducked her head against her sister's shoulder, but Sophia fixed her eyes on Jamie's face. "We didn't see anything," she said bravely. "We found a real handsome lot of berries amongst those blue spruces—you know the ones close to the—the stone house?"

Jamie nodded.

"Well, we were picking away and telling how we thought to surprise you and 'Manda with 'em . . . and then we heard it."

Betsey's hands went over her ears, and Jamie was proud of Sophia for the way she kept on. "It was a—horrid kind of noise, Jamie! Like some-

one was choking and choking, and they couldn't get their breath, and—
and—" Her hands came out for him again. "And I don't know if they
ever got their breath, because we ran away!"

"What do you suppose—" Amanda began uncertainly.

Jamie looked back along the path. "I don't know," he muttered.
"Seems like I ought to go back and see—"

Sophia's fingers had a wiry strength. "No, don't go back—don't leave
us here. Old Ned—"

"Old Ned won't hurt you," said Jamie.

Amanda said sharply, "Maybe 'twas him making the noises, to scare
us off. Come on, Jamie, let's get these young ones away from here."

"You take them—I'll go back."

"And walk by Old Ned's place, or maybe meet him face to face?" she
demanded. Betsey burst into fresh wails. Sophia said nothing, but
watched Jamie with a silent pleading until he gave in at last.

* * *

Amanda and Betsey turned off at the road to the harbor. Jamie hurried Sophia home. She was much calmer now and told him the story
again. It was just as dreadful as it had been the first time; it tightened
Jamie's scalp uncomfortably even while he strove to find a reasonable explanation of it.

"It's likely somebody was having a game with you and Betsey," he
said. "Maybe Stephen or Robby Owen—they're great ones for plaguing
the girls."

"But they aren't any bigger than Betsey and me," Sophia objected. "I
don't see how they could make such big noises."

Jamie laughed. "When I was twelve I could bellow like Uncle
Nathan's bull if I was so minded."

"Well—" She gave him a doubtful glance. They had reached their
own gate, and through a thinning in the fog they saw the twins playing
with the cat in the yard, and Lark leading Clover across to the barn.
Jamie patted his little sister's shoulders.

"Go on home, young one. They're all there—you won't be alone."

He gave her no chance to protest, but walked quickly back to the
road and didn't look around when she called.

He didn't enjoy his errand. The fog was thickening and the night was
drawing on; the woods had never looked so dark or felt so haunted as
they did now. All the birds that usually made soft talk and flutterings in

the branches were in some other part of the forest.

When he reached Ned's clearing, he hesitated, and looked fondly at the small half-finished barn. What if Ned did have rheumatism in his bad leg? Jamie could work alone. He could go down now and do a little work before supper. Wasn't that a much more worthwhile chore than to go prowling around the old stone house in the fog? Most likely he wouldn't see or hear anything to tell him what had frightened the girls. The more he thought about it, the more he was convinced it was some young rapscallion having a game with them.

It was all very logical, but it didn't deceive him in the least, and so he went on past Ned's place. The path made a sharp turn, and his indrawn breath whistled as he came face to face with a looming figure. It was Timothy Boyd.

"Evening, Tim!" he sang out, and Tim stopped, running his hands through his thick sandy mane.

"Oh, it's you. What you doing down here? Ain't you scairt the witches'll git ye?"

"I might ask you the same thing," said Jamie.

Tim shrugged his heavy shoulders. "I don't fear anything. I got charms against 'em all."

"Then you're just the man I want," said Jamie. "Cruise back to the Point with me for a bit."

"I just been there." Tim was suspicious. "I been walking around the shore, piling up driftwood above high watermark, and nobody else is to lay a finger to it. Understand? What I've lugged up out of the tideway is mine."

"I don't want any of your cultch," said Jamie patiently. "I just want you to go back and look around the old Frenchie house with me. Sophia and Betsey Gibson were picking blueberries around there this afternoon and they heard noises that like to struck 'em dead of fright."

Tim's face changed from suspicion to astonishment and awe. He caught Jamie's arm in a painful grip. "I got no charm against that, boy! You'd have to kill me to drag me anywheres near that place!"

"Why?" Jamie demanded skeptically.

"Don't you know the story about it? You, born and bred on Brigport?"

Jamie shook his head. Tim threw a fearful glance over his shoulder, then pushed Jamie along ahead of him, away from the Point. "Some folks won't tell it to their young ones," he whispered. "Scairt of giving 'em nightmares for the rest of their lives. Come on, let's get out of here."

"I don't want to get out of here," Jamie objected. But Tim was a big overgrown youth and his grip on Jamie's arm was paralyzingly firm.

"I can't let ye go," he said solemnly.

Jamie stared at him in amazement, and gave his arm a sudden violent jerk, but Tim merely tightened his huge hand. No choice but to go where Tim led, back along the path past Ned's place. And all the time Tim went on in a meek, pious tone.

"Aye, I'm a lily-livered one about the old stone house down there, I can swear to that, Jamie. Brave as a lion on the high seas, mebbe, but let me get within ten yards of that stone Frenchie house on a foggy day in midsummer, and my legs like to turn soft as mush." He looked around at the foggy dusk under the trees. "I reckon it's safe to tell you about it now," he whispered. "We're a fur enough piece away."

"It don't pleasure me any to hear your chuckle-headed yarns," said Jamie.

"Seems like the Frenchie who built that house and lived in it in the old days—well, he done his wife in with a butcher knife, and then he hanged himself. It was in midsummer, and foggy, they say, and my father always used to tell me never to go prowling near the stone house when it was like this, for fear of hearing the whole thing from start to finish." He glared earnestly at Jamie from under his thick sandy brows. "Did the young ones hear her screaming?"

"No," Jamie said vigorously. The story was uncommonly vivid, and if it were anybody else but Tim Boyd telling it—well, it just might give him a cold chill or two.

"They was lucky not to hear the screams that come first. They would-n't have lived to tell the tale." He shook his head. "Of course, most folks won't admit the place is haunted. That's why you never hear the story nowadays. Even now they'll say the young ones made it up, or else some-one was aiming to scare them."

"That's what I think," said Jamie. "It was a prank. There's no such thing as ghosts."

When he'd first set out, he'd been ready to turn back at any instant because, in spite of his reasoning to Sophia, he was imaginative enough to be moved by the children's horror. But now, because Tim was barring his way with his prodigious tales of murder, he had been challenged. Maybe, he thought wryly, I only want to prove I'm braver than a Boyd. But I have to go on.

Tim grimaced in fierce determination. "I'm a-keeping you safe in spite of yourself, Jamie Bennett!" He advanced on the younger boy, crouching a little, his long arms reaching.

"This is a mighty queer place to wrestle! Why don't you get out in a field somewhere?"

It was Lark. He had come upon them before they realized and now stood grinning at their astonished faces. "I reckon," he went on impertinently, "that Cap'n Tim don't care much for wrestling out where folk could see all his foul tricks."

"Yon's a lad needs his ears lopped off," Tim snarled.

"Just you try it," Jamie warned him.

"Aye, just you try it," Lark repeated happily. He turned to Jamie. "Mother says, Please to come home, the stew and the bannock is ready and why are you obliged to be hypering around Southern Point by yourself when it's coming on night?" His grin deepened. "I said I'd be hypering with you, but she commands us to look alive and put for home at once!"

"Now you see?" Tim burst out. "She knows the story even if she's never told it to you! She knows 'tain't safe! Now will ye mind your elders?"

Jamie blushed with shame and anger. Tim had won out after all. He was sure that if his mother had ever heard such a story she didn't believe it; but she wanted him home, and that was enough for Tim.

He turned away abruptly. At least he didn't have to face Tim's leer of triumph. Lark had to hurry to keep up with him. Tim was left far behind.

"What was he babbling about, Jamie?" Lark asked eagerly. "He sounded crazier than Ned."

Jamie grunted. "He is. Him and his wild yarns."

Chapter 11

Jamie didn't get back to the stone house on Southern Point the next day, or any day after that. The fog lifted in the night, and he returned to his fishing. But as he worked he remembered the meeting with Tim, and the memory always made him grin. A body couldn't guess whether Tim really believed that tale of his, or whether he'd found something choice in the rockweed—something too big for him to carry home—and he'd been sweating for fear Jamie would find it and claim it. Jamie amused himself with wondering what the rich find might be; a locked wooden chest from a disaster out at sea, or some choice mahogany planks.

He was fishing off the east side of Brigport when a school of big pollock, driven by porpoises, traveled under and around the boat. The stream of shadowy bodies flowed past, now dark, now flashing as the sun struck through the green water. They boiled solidly around him, they struck fiercely at his lines and gave him a hard good fight. But he caught only a few before the porpoises had driven them on. He laughed aloud at the antics of the pursuers, who dove and somersaulted through the water.

The sound of his laughter in the stillness startled him, and he glanced up involuntarily at the rocky shore beyond him. He expected only to see the close-cropped turf slanting to the beach. Instead he saw, for an instant too short to be credited, his brother Lark standing at the edge of the field, silhouetted against the clouds.

He put his hands to his mouth and shouted, but even as his voice rang out across the few hundred yards of surging, glittering water, Lark disappeared. He could have dropped down behind the old stone wall or into a hollow where stunted firs grew.

Jamie stood up and began to row for home, glancing back at the beach. A seal popped up in his wake to stare at him. Far overhead a fish hawk hung in space by the powerful beating of its wings, its white head glinting in the sun.

The sudden appearance and disappearance of Lark had awakened all his doubts and uneasiness. If only he could talk to Lark, get the truth out of him by one way or another . . .

He swung forward on the oars, back, forward again; the wherry seemed to fly across the white-crested wavelets. He rounded the breaking ledge called the Cauldron. A loon's call came clear and weird on the wind, like laughter in a haunted house. But he saw and heard with only the mechanical part of his brain. Talk to Lark, he repeated to himself. Talk to Lark. Make him talk to you. Get him in a corner and clout it out of him if you have to . . . and pray it's nothing to shame us.

By the time he reached the harbor his mind was made up. There would be an understanding between him and Lark before sundown tonight.

Many of the other smaller boats were already on their moorings, or clustered around Rich Gibson's wharf, selling their day's catch. The pinky *Minerva* was back from a trip to Stonehaven.

He rowed to Uncle Nathan's wharf, to dress his fish before selling them, and found his uncle's sloop *Megan* made fast there. His uncle was not in sight, but Mark and his younger brother Will were scrubbing down the decks and making the sloop shipshape for the night.

"Ran into a school of big pollock," Jamie called to them. "I got a few before the porpoises drove 'em away. Here, take one home to your ma!" He heaved a heavy fish onto the sloop's deck.

"You clean it, Will," Mark ordered the small dark boy. "And mind you sluice the blood off my clean deck, after, or I'll have your ears." He hissed the last out between his teeth, and little Will, about to split a pollock almost half as long as he was, grinned. Mark climbed onto the wharf and crossed it, to sit on the edge and watch Jamie work below.

"Aren't you so tired of looking at dead codfish," he asked, "that you wake up in the morning and wish you never had to haul another one aboard for the rest of your life?"

Jamie shrugged. "Might be tired of looking at 'em," he admitted, "but I'm mighty partial to the jingle of coins in my pocket when Rich pays me."

Mark snorted. "That teeny handful! And did you ever hear the ring of pure gold in your pocket? Answer that one!"

"I never did," answered Jamie, "and neither did you."

Mark pounced on that as triumphantly as a fish hawk on a mackerel. "Hah! But I'm going to hear the ring of pure gold and I'm going to feel it with my fingers—come December, when the *Nereid* slides down the ways!"

The words were a jolt. Jamie looked up, and saw his cousin's dark face vivid with anticipation of adventure. "Listen, Jamie," Mark went on, "we've got our course all marked out. Hughie's grandsir gave us his chart. We'll head for St. Vincent with a cargo of hewed lumber—you figgering to load us with some of that pine from your woodlot, Jamie? In Havana we can make a fortune with it. Our beets and potatoes will find a fine market in the French islands. We'll have all the drums of dried fish we can carry, and fill up the corners with shooks from Thomas Stone's cooper's shop at Stonehaven." He gazed at Jamie with enchanted eyes. "We'll come back with a fortune, besides a load of coffee and Portoreek molasses." He held up his hand and ticked off the months on his fingers. "It's the first of September now. Three more months—three and a half— and we'll be under way." He leaned far over the edge of the wharf, staring down into Jamie's lifted face. "Are you sailing with us, Jamie? That's what we want to know."

Jamie's breath went out in a heavy sigh. For a moment, he had been hypnotized, and now, with Mark's final question, he had been cruelly awakened.

"We're counting on you," Mark's voice went on and on over his head. "My cousin Morgan Owen wants to go, somewhat, but he's fiercely afraid of the pirates down there." Mark chuckled softly. "Such tales as his father's told him, I reckon Morgan'd die of fright at the first view of another sail on the horizon once we'd reached the Bahama Cays. But he'd go if he had the chance—just to prove he's a man like the rest of us. Well, Jamie?"

Jamie was saved from having to answer. Amanda Gibson appeared on the wharf beside Mark and exclaimed, "Father's brought the mail from Stonehaven, and there's news of the voting!"

"Is it yea or nay?" asked Mark.

"Yea, of course," she said scornfully. "What did you expect? Of course we want to be a State! Everybody in the District of Maine voted yea, save for a few moldy old Federalists!" She knelt on the side of the wharf and said, "Jamie, aren't you excited?"

"Jamie's a moldy old Federalist," Mark said solemnly. "He'd have voted nay if he could. He likes everything to stay the same. As it was in the beginning, is now and ever shall be, world without end."

"That's blasphemy!" Amanda accused him, and Mark laughed. Jamie heard them only distantly. Returns, voting, districts, statehood—it was all nonsense to him.

"There's to be a meeting in Portland in October," Amanda's voice clattered disagreeably in his ears. "The delegates are going to write a constitution. William King is going to Virginia in the meantime to consult with Thomas Jefferson on how to do it. Think of it!"

"Thomas Jefferson!" Mark whistled. "Now there's a man I'd like to meet . . . Cap'n Marriot will be at the meeting in Portland, I reckon."

"Oh, most certain!" Amanda's voice took on the particular tone that always accompanied any mention of Pleasance. "And Miss Marriot is doubtless deciding how many new gowns and parasols she'll need to be presentable in Portland."

"Stand back up there!" Jamie yelled, and swung a dressed pollock high. It flew over their heads and landed with a thud on the planks beyond.

"Well, I declare!" said Amanda. "What do you think you are, Jamie Bennett?"

"If that'd smacked me in the face," Mark said, "I'd been obliged to bury your nose in it, me lad."

"That's for 'Manda to take home," Jamie said stiffly. "She'd best take it while it's still firm. Sun was hot today."

"Thank you kindly." Amanda stood up with dignity. "I don't know what ails you today, Jamie Bennett, but I sh'd think on such an important occasion as this one you'd have the civility to be a mite—"

"Civil," suggested Mark. Amanda forebore from kicking him, though one foot twitched.

"And if you're intending to leave a pollock for the Marriots," she went on calmly, "I'd be happy to send it to them by my little cousin Dickon."

"I hadn't thought about the Marriots," said Jamie, "but now that you mention it, I'll dress one for them. Pleasance has a rare gift of baking one, with milk and herbs."

"I'm sure there isn't anything Miss Prunes and Prisms don't know how to do better than anybody else." Amanda tapped one foot and stared over the harbor ledges to open sea. "I'll wait till you get the fish ready."

"No need," said Jamie. He threw out a handful of entrails and the gulls swooped down in a screaming crowd. "I'll take it around there myself."

"He hasn't had a word with Pleasance for all of a week," suggested Mark. Mark sighed soulfully. "It's what my mother calls the way of a man with a maid. He fetches her a pollock."

"He can fetch her this one, then!" cried Amanda, and the pollock flashed through the air. Jamie saw it coming, yet didn't have much time to dodge. It caught him on the side of the head with a wet and heavy thud, and knocked him off balance. He went backward over the side of the wherry.

The splash was enormous and the gulls went up with a windy rush of wings. When Jamie came up Mark was roaring with laughter and little Will was calling anxiously, "Are you drownded?"

Amanda was gone. Blowing salt water out of his mouth and shaking it out of his eyes, Jamie waded ashore. The dowsing had done him good; all he could think of now was the shock of that cold water. It might not have "drownded" him, but it had certainly "drownded" all his self-pity. For the time being, anyway . . . Gorry, Amanda was fierce! He was just as glad it hadn't happened over by her father's wharf, for the whole island to see.

He braced against a spiling while he pulled off first one boot and then the other. "Lor, what fire our 'Manda's got!" Mark wheezed. "If you don't marry her, Jamie, I reckon I'll choose her. Why, a man's made his fortune when he weds a female like that one! She'll be as much good to ye as six sons. You'd need neither sails at sea nor oxen ashore—she's got the strength to be all of 'em." He sat on a rock and clutched at his middle. "I haven't laughed so much since the time Simon Pollinger run Tim and Izzy Boyd out of his orchard with a musket, with Tim yelling, 'Don't shoot us, Cap'n, 'twould break me mother's heart!' "

He went into a new convulsion. Jamie felt his own amusement struggling to break loose, and at last he gave in to it. While little Will stood staring, Mark and Jamie laughed until they wept.

When the gale of laughter was over, Mark took his younger brother in tow and left for home. Still drenched, Jamie finished dressing his catch, then changed from his fishing clothes into the shirt and trousers he had worn to the shore in the morning and left in the fishhouse. So he was clean and dry when he rowed across to Rich Gibson's wharf to sell his fish, and no one could shout at him, "What ye do, boy? Let a big one haul ye overboard?"

Jamie was prepared to look suitably dignified when he saw Amanda; it didn't do to let a female critter think she could heave a fish at you and be let off easy. But Amanda wasn't in sight, and everyone else was so wrought up about the Separation news that no one noticed him. Caption Marriot was in the forefront of the discussion.

"It's the beginning of a new era!" he declaimed, rapping on the top of the molasses barrel with his gold-headed stick. "I wish I were twenty again! Or nineteen! Just the age of the century! It's going to be a magnificent century, mark my words, and I'd give my soul to be growing up with it!"

"Why don't you go to sea again, anyway, James?" Rich Gibson called from where he was counting out Jamie's pay from his strongbox. "You're too young to swallow the anchor and settle down ashore."

"Aye," grumbled Simon Pollinger. "You're not as hoary with age as I be. You got your Separation now—git out and make the best of it."

There was a rumble of laughter around the molasses barrel. Somebody said, "It's not clear sailing yet, Simon. Massachusetts is willing enough to cut us off from her, but it's up to Congress to make us a State."

"That shouldn't put ye too far off course," said Simon. "Send James Marriot up there to Washington under full sail with everything set, and he'll walk away with it."

Jamie went out unnoticed, rowed back to his uncle's wharf, washed down the wherry, and put her on her haul-off for the night.

At the Marriot house, Pleasance came to the back door, wearing a big apron over her gown, her hair tied on top of her head. Her cheeks were pink with the heat and steam of the kitchen.

"Why, Jamie! How nice! You haven't been here for so long!" She beckoned him into the big kitchen, which was full of a pungent aroma that prickled his nostrils unpleasantly.

"Boneset tea!" He backed toward the door.

"Don't be silly, I shan't make you drink any of it." Pleasance laughed at his horror. "Granny Boyd's down with break-bone fever, and nothing would do but a good draught of boneset tea, as Fanny Marriot used to make it." She glanced into the pot with an expert eye. "It's steeping nicely. Tim will be along for it soon."

Jamie held out the pollock. "What'll I do with this?"

"Oh, Jamie, what a grand fish!" She hurried for a pan. Jamie couldn't help wishing Amanda were here, to see how anyone should properly receive a gift.

Pleasance, making little sounds of delight, took the fish and put it away in the cool buttery. "Now!" she said, returning with a jug of milk in one hand a plate of gingerbread in the other. "Wash your hands and sit down at the table, Jamie."

Jamie would have liked nothing better than to sit for a spell in the Marriot kitchen, even if it did stink of boneset tea. But he had his promise to himself to keep; he must find Lark.

"I can't stop," he said. "I've got work to do yet."

"Oh!" She turned quite pink with disappointment and he thought suddenly how pretty she was. Her moist hair curled like a baby's around her forehead; it was queer how all these years he'd known her he'd never noticed her eyebrows, so fine and delicate and golden-brown.

"I'll come another time. I'm busy," he said, stammering over the word time.

"You weren't too busy to go blueberrying with Amanda, and doubtless you've taken her rowing over to South Island on a picnic, and she'll have you hunting for cranberries soon, and—"

It all spilled out in such a spate of sweet, angry words that he could scarce believe his ears. He could only stare at her like a great gooney. Why, for all her different way of speaking and her little wrists and delicate coloring, she sounded exactly like Amanda! He wouldn't have been surprised if she'd pitched the milk jug at him as Amanda had hurled the fish.

His heat went as swift as it had come, while he fought to keep his mouth straight and his eyes as stupid and earnest as Clover's. When she stopped for breath he drawled, "Lor', Pleasance, I dunno why you're so hawsed up. After all, a man can only be in one place at a time." He waved his hand jauntily, and left.

The path to the east side led through the Marriot woods. Once inside their shelter, Jamie allowed his grin to break free. The two of them fit to be tied, and he hadn't even worked at it. Most likely they were each vowing never to speak to him again. He kicked a spruce cone along the path before him. Girls were as unexpected, though not as big, as whales what came up under you and made you sweat while they decided whether or not to capsize you.

The breeze blew in puffs against Jamie's face, and at last the blue of the sea showed in all its early autumn brilliance beyond the shadows of the woods.

It was out beyond this spot that he had seen Lark. The boy had had time to reach the other end of the island by now, or he might have gone home.

The wind had freshened with the turn of the tide, and where there had been a lazy tumble of surf along the shores there was now an active surge. The path followed along the edge of the water. The sound of the surf was all around him. There was one chasm in the rocks called the Pirate's Den, and here the water boomed explosively, almost under his feet, it seemed . . . Strange about the surf. The longer you listened, the more you heard. Rattles and roars, groans and cries. Jamie could almost swear he heard music now. The conviction grew on him; he stopped and looked all around him, listening with his whole being.

Might be somebody tossed an old jug overboard, he thought. And it's caught between rocks where the wind can blow past its mouth . . . might be, except it's too high a sound. Too high and too sweet. Like a bird and yet not like a bird.

Then he knew it wasn't a sound his ears imagined, but a real one. Talk of will-o'-the-wisp and fairy lights, and ghosts in the stone house! This was something to tighten a man's scalp when he heard it all sole alone, out on the lonely east side of the island with the wind rising and the sun going down.

It grew faint as the wind let up for a moment. Surely it was just up there a little way . . . He climbed from the shore path toward the thicket of bay and alder and high bush blueberry; but when he had broken his way through, the music was still beyond. Here the trees cut off the wind and the sound of the surf, and now the music was very close, sweet and gay as the thistlebird's late summer song. It went up as the little black and yellow bird rose, it came down as the bird came to rest on a swaying thistletop, singing all the way.

He knew now where it was. Straight ahead, in a little clearing which he remembered well as a good spot for cranberries.

When he saw Lark perched on the broken wall, he stopped short. It was Lark who was making the music. He was playing a flute, and for all the lad knew he was sole alone in the world. His bare toes curled rapturously around a loose rock in the wall. His eyes were shut. His body moved in time to the merry tune.

Jamie's first reaction was shock; anger followed. He felt humiliated and cheated. Here he'd been stumbling along in search of something wild and wonderful that had made him forget about the things he wanted and couldn't have, and what did he find? Lark!

He strode forward and stood in front of Lark. The boy went on playing, his brown fingers moved nimbly over the holes in the flute. Jamie stood silently waiting. Lark must have felt his presence, for his eyes flew open and he stared at his brother. The music stopped, and in the stillness Jamie heard the far-off roar of surf and a ripple of wind through the drying birch leaves.

Lark lowered the flute, but he didn't take his eyes from his brother's stern face.

"Is this what you're doing when you're supposed to be milking Clover and fetching water and getting my bait and maybe helping me catch a few codfish?" Jamie asked in a deadly cool voice. "Whose flute is that?"

"Mr. Whiting's." Lark's own voice trembled a little, but his eyes were steady. "He lends it to me."

"Fine thing," Jamie said harshly, "for the parson to be teaching a boy to run off from his chores."

"He doesn't know I run off," Lark blurted. "If he did, he'd never let me lay hands on it, nor teach me a tune on it. So don't be blaming him."

"Then you've lied to him."

"I didn't exactly lie," said Lark, fingering the flute. He flushed and looked away from his brother. "He just thought that most likely I'd done my chores and that you let me off."

"Isn't that lying, to let him think it?"

"I reckon so." Lark's curly head drooped and against his will Jamie remembered how he had looked a few minutes ago as he played the flute, his eyes shut, his bare toes curling ecstatically. He sighed, and sat down on the wall beside Lark, staring at his big hands that could do nothing finer than split and gut a codfish. Well, he could mend a net, he supposed, but that wasn't making music.

He straightened up again. "How'd this happen?" He gestured toward the flute. "When did it start?"

"Last summer," Lark began eagerly. "I wanted to tell ye, Jamie. I wanted to tell you all along, but I didn't know how." His eyes were shining now, imploring his brother to believe. "Remember the time you sent me up to the parsonage with some apples and a slack-salted fish? Well, he called me in for a cup of raspberry shrub and a bannock, and then he asked me if I could still sing 'Greensleeves'. He said he hadn't heard me sing for so long, never at Meeting or anywhere else, and had my voice changed so soon, he asked me." Lark laughed at the joke, then sobered abruptly. "But I didn't tell him it was Mother who didn't want me to sing, Jamie. I just said I could still sing. So he brought out his flute and played 'Greensleeves', and I sang with him. Oh, it was grand to sing like that again, Jamie; to open my mouth and let it go, and never fear who was to hear me. And the flute went along with me, like another voice singing with me—"

He stopped and moistened his lips. "Well, we went from one song to another and he taught me a new sacred song called 'The Heavens are Telling,' by somebody with a comical name—Händel—and he said I should sing it at Meeting sometime. But I told him I couldn't, because I had promised my mother I would not sing at Meeting until my father came back . . . And that was the beginning, Jamie."

"But the flute. What about the flute?"

Lark's face was pinched and troubled. "It came about because afterwards I couldn't stop thinking about singing. Years ago when Mother said I shouldn't sing anymore, it was like asking me to stop breathing."

He'd been only seven. Yes, it must have been hard.

"But after a time I was used to it," Lark went on. "And I used to think, someday Father will come home and I can open my mouth and sing wherever I am, and not fear who'll hear me . . . It wasn't till after I sang at Mr. Whiting's that time that I began to worry. I thought, Here 'twas seven years since Father went, and what if when he did come back I had no voice left? It was what Mr. Whiting said about my voice changing that frightened me. I kept thinking, What if I wake up some morning and find out I can't make music for myself anymore? If they said you could never set foot in the wherry again, Jamie, how would you feel?"

"Sick," said Jamie, staring at the ground.

"Well, I was that sick and scared about losing my music . . . and then

I thought of the flute. If I learned to play it, and then I lost my voice and couldn't sing, I could make music in another way that was almost as good as singing. I asked Mr. Whiting, and he's been teaching me. That's all there is to it, Jamie. I hadn't ought to've run off, but Mr. Whiting didn't know I'd run off, so 'twasn't his fault." He sighed heavily and looked at his bare toes. "I reckon you'll tell him all about it, now, and it's no more than I deserve."

"I won't tell him anything, Lark, if you'll tend to your chores a little better."

Lark was pale. He'd run out of words; he held up the flute, dumbly. Jamie nodded.

"But what about Mother?" asked Lark.

"We'll have to tell her somehow," Jamie admitted. "We can't deceive her. I'll think of a way." He couldn't think of anything at the moment, but with Lark gazing at him so worshipfully, he had to say something. He felt as if he had found a brother for the first time. They each wanted something they couldn't have. Take Lark, stifling the tunes that rose in his throat for seven years; wanting music with every bone of his body the way Jamie wanted a wide deck heaving under his feet, or foreign cobble-stones ringing under his boots, and strange names on his tongue.

"You could have a flute of your own," he said. "You could earn it, if you had a mind to help me more. You'd still have time to practice."

"I'll help you, Jamie. I swear it!" Lark was almost hysterical with re-lief. "I always meant to help you more, anyway. But how can I earn a flute? We never have any money to spare."

"If you go fishing with me," said Jamie, "and pull your own weight, I'll give you a bit to save for yourself each time Rich Gibson buys our fish. It'll take a long time, likely, but you won't be feeling so deceitful." How much did a flute cost, he wondered. He'd ask Mr. Whiting. "And," he added dryly, "you'd feel less deceitful if you tended to Clover on time, too."

"I promise," said Lark solemnly, holding up his right hand. "I'll do anything you say, from this day forward."

"I believe you," said Jamie, and he did.

Chapter 12

So there he was, with a new brother on his hands, who milked Clover promptly, night and morning, kept the tie-up clean and the manger full of fresh hay; this was not to mention all the buckets of water he lugged daily for Clover from the pond behind the barn, and for the family from the spring. Lark also dug clams or gathered mussels for bait, and was waiting aboard the wherry when Jamie reached the wharf.

The first week his shoulders ached so that he groaned when he first stirred in the morning, and announced before he even opened his eyes that he was done for.

"I'm a goner," he would moan. "Sew me up in my hammock and heave me over the side, lads."

But no matter how lame he was, how sore and blistered his hands from the harsh codlines, he didn't hang to his bed. He was up and out to the milking even while his mother was saying, "But do you think he's doing too much, Jamie? He's so thin and he's growing so fast. Promise me that if you ever see a blue look around his mouth you'll bring him straight home."

"Now, Mother," Jamie comforted her. "I'm not figgering on working the lad to death. Aren't you real proud of him now that he's squared away to bear a hand?"

She smiled in spite of her anxiety. "Yes, I am. I knew he'd listen to me, finally."

Then it was Jamie's turn to be worried. Sooner or later she must know about the flute. He had never lied to his mother yet, and the longer this lie went on the bigger it grew.

* * *

Ned's barn was finished now, and Jamie was honestly proud of their accomplishment. He wished his father could see the stout beams he had hewn out with the axe. Yes, he was proud, even though he had not once driven a peg into place or swung his axe without remembering the schooner that was slowly coming to life in Rum Cove. He had never spoken to anyone about the schooner, but once Ned said to him out of a clear sky, "You signin' on for a West Indies trip this winter?"

It had taken the wind out of Jamie's sails for a moment. Then he said, trying to be casual, "What put that into your noggin?"

Ned squinted his good eye at him and laughed soundlessly. "Might be I'm readin' yer mind. Might be a trick I learned from them Ay-rabs."

"You think I want to go down among the Bahama Cays," demanded Jamie, "and have my hands and feet cut off by the pirates and my mouth stuffed with oakum and set afire?"

"There's many a Yankee ship sailed to the south'ard and never seen a pirate," said Ned. "And them two stavers—your cousin and Old Bandy-legs' grandson—they've got the look of luck about 'em. Why aren't you after 'em all a-flukin'?"

"Because they've never asked me to sign on, that's why!" Jamie flung back at him desperately.

"Aye, aye." Ned wagged his rough white head. "That's a good reason if I ever heard one. But don't use pirates for a reason next time, lad. There could be cutthroats closer to home than Campeche or Cape Antonio."

"What do you mean by that?" Jamie demanded, but Ned was off on another train of thought, talking in a disjointed fashion of events long past. There was no pinning him down to explanations. Not that it mattered. Doubtless Ned meant the scum of the New York and Boston waterfronts.

* * *

Jamie went off by himself late one raw windy afternoon to dig a mess of clams and do a little thinking. He hadn't had an hour to himself for some time now. He was not pleased, therefore, to straighten up from his digging and see Amanda crossing the wet slope of the beach.

He pretended not to see her and went back to his digging. A short way beyond him, the big gray-backed waves spent themselves in a confusion of foam. Ledges usually submerged rose dark and shaggy with rockweed from the swirling gray and white. It was a low dreen tide, perfect for clamming, and he didn't intend to let Amanda drive him home. He wouldn't talk to her. She didn't deserve it.

At last she was beside him, saying with unusual shyness, "I was just passing by on the road and I saw you. So I came down to see if you were getting many clams."

Jamie didn't look up. Just passing by! He could see her feet in her sturdy shoes, shifting a little on the wet sand. "I've been tidying up the schoolmaster's house," she contributed then.

That almost brought his head up. Schoolmaster? They'd had no schoolmaster, ever since the last one had up and left one day without warning . . . But he kept on stubbornly digging.

"Jamie," said Amanda huskily. "I'm awful sorry I threw that pollock at you."

He straightened up then and looked at her severely. "You should be. That was a scurvy uncivilized trick."

Amanda reddened. Her black eyes blazed into his. "I s'pose that was the fish you gave to the Marriots."

"It was not," said Jamie grandly. "And I'll thank you not to bring up the Marriots. Every time you speak of a certain person, you rise up like a kraken, and it's not becoming to a young lady."

"Hah!" Amanda threw her head back in scorn. "You can't be speaking of me—a certain person is the only lady on this island. Or so she thinks."

It was too much. A sudden vision of Pleasance Marriot enraged, as he had last seen her, flashed into his mind and he had to laugh. He laughed until Amanda's eyes filled with tears and she turned to run. Then he reached out a long arm and caught her, and pulled her back.

"Don't go, 'Manda," he begged her, his voice still shaky. "I wasn't laughing at you, I swear it. It was something just came to mind. Might be I can tell you of it some day. But 'twasn't you."

"I never did know you to lie to me," Amanda said, wiping her eyes with the back of her hand. She smiled from behind wet curling lashes and he felt a sudden tenderness.

"What's this about the schoolmaster's house?" he asked.

"We're to have a new teacher, so Mr. Whiting says. He's been in correspondence with him."

"And does Mr. Whiting say this one can hold his own?"

"He says all we can do is hope for the best."

Jamie shrugged and went back to digging. The last schoolteacher had simply gone aboard the *Minerva* one wintry day, when she was about to sail for Stonehaven, and had never come back. It was said by some that his natural bad health had been worsened by the pranks played on him.

"Seems like they've always plagued the teacher something fierce," said Amanda. "I wonder why."

" 'Cause nobody ever brings 'em up with a round turn." Jamie rubbed the seat of his pants reminiscently. "Once Mark and Owen and I had a hand in tormenting a schoolmaster. We climbed up on his roof and stopped up the chimney, and like to smoked him into a flitch of bacon.

When we came down off the roof that night, our fathers were waiting. To this day," he added wonderingly, "I've never guessed how they found out about it."

"What happened?"

"The thrashings we got made us decide that hectoring the schoolmaster wasn't worth the time it took to think up new torments and carry 'em out." He chuckled. "So now we're to have a new one. This is one time I'm going to be on deck when the *Minerva* comes in."

"You mean," she teased him, "that you'd stay home from fishing just for that? I didn't know anything short of a broken arm or a living gale could keep you ashore."

"Well—" He grinned. "Happen if it's thick fog or blowing great guns, I'll be there on the wharf to catch the *Minerva*'s lines. That's what I meant."

"I thought so," said Amanda, and for no apparent reason, they both burst into laughter.

It turned out to be no weather for fishing the day the schoolmaster was to arrive. It was raw and blustery, with quick, blinding squalls driving rain against a man's face like grape-shot. So Jamie could be on hand to see the arrival of the pinky *Minerva*.

Jamie and Lark and Sophia went down to the harbor in mid-morning. There was a good crowd in the store; Mrs. Rich Gibson tacked back and forth behind the counter like a stately frigate, while Amanda scudded among the talkers like a little yawlboat.

The Bennett brothers stopped inside the door and looked down the long busy room. Lark saw some of his friends at the far end and went to join them. Mark, Hugh Erskine, and Morgan Owen were in deep conversation around the cornmeal barrel; Jamie turned away instinctively lest one of them should catch his eye and hail him. At another time he would have gone to them instantly. But now the *Nereid* rode between them like a ghost ship.

He moved close to a group of men by the fireplace and showed great interest in their conversation. "Boys will be boys," Thad Boyd was saying in his usual husky drawl, "and plaguing the teacher is a fine old Yankee tradition. Gives the feller a chance to show what he's made of. We don't want none of these puling gooneys lording it over our young ones . . . 'Course," he added hastily, "I don't countenance the lads going beyond mischief, you understand."

"What do you call mischief, Thad?" Captain Marriot asked, suavely enough. "Anything short of murder?"

Thad's fleshy face grinned, but not his eyes. "You're a great one for a joke, Cap'n."

"Sail ho!" a boy sang out from the loft, and the crowd moved toward the door with a swift flowing movement like seaweed on a turning tide. The younger boys ran, eager to catch the lines and get the first glimpse of the new schoolmaster.

From the lee of the salt shed Jamie watched the pinky enter the harbor. She was wet but valiant. Slacking sails flapped loudly in the wind.

"Do you see him, Jamie?" a small eager voice asked. It was Sophia, who had followed him down the length of the wharf at the risk of her cloak filling out like a sail and blowing her overboard in a great gust of wind. She held Jamie's arm and stood on tiptoe, trying to peer over the line of boys who waited on the wharf's edge. "Jane says he's real fierce and carries a big stick, and he'd just as lief thrash the girls as the boys with it."

"Now don't you be afeard," Jamie said briskly. "Jane says plenty besides her prayers. And nobody'll thrash you if you mind your manners and study hard . . . I don't see any stranger aboard yet. Most likely he's laid out below, so seasick he can't lift a finger."

"I'm afraid of that," said Mr. Whiting's voice. The minister had also come into the lee of the salt shed. His lean face was grave. "Poor young man, he'll be doing well if he can walk ashore after three hours in the *Minerva* with the wind on her quarter. It may be a week before he can commence classes." He shook his head. "I don't know if I've been wise or not. But he wanted so much to come."

The pinky docked with easy grace, the lines snaked through the air and Lark caught the bowline, though he nearly fell overboard in the scramble. By this time the wharf was fairly crowded, and Jamie felt a twinge of pity for the victim who, exhausted with seasickness, must run the gauntlet as surely as any captive of the Indians. The cluster of boys at the head of the ladder broke apart. Mr. Whiting moved forward, his hands out in instinctive preparation for steadying a sick man.

The man who climbed nimbly onto the wharf was not sick. He looked around him, curious but not dismayed; he was not darkly tanned like the Brigporters, but neither did he have the faintly greenish pallor they had expected. A strong gust swept across the harbor and he took off his hat before the wind could; as he stood there at the edge of the wharf, among the barefoot gaping lads who would be his scholars, his hat and gold-headed stick in his hand, the wind blowing the capes of his blue greatcoat, he was a picture of complete and foreign elegance. The bleak ledges behind him, the rainsoaked wharves and huddled fish houses, the thick wall of dark spruces against lowering skies—they all belonged to some fierce dismal land in which this fine creature had stopped for a moment on his travels; and presently, it seemed, he would go on again, and it would be as if he had never been there on their wharf at all, with his sleek, dark red head and his splendid greatcoat.

The man smiled pleasantly at the staring youngsters, and said "Good morning" in a voice that was all of a piece with the rest of him.

They answered raggedly except for Lark, whom nothing could ever daunt.

"Good morning!" he answered clearly.

The young man lifted an eyebrow. "Good morning—what?"

Lark's jaw tightened. "Good morning—sir."

"That's better." The man nodded, glanced around at the others on the wharf with a preoccupied though not disdainful air, and then Mr. Whiting reached him and introduced himself. The two men shook hands, and the schoolmaster's swift and pleasant smile came again. They turned away from the edge of the wharf, and the great bustle of unloading began.

"Well, we've got a schoolmaster," Jamie said to Sophia. "For better or worse, there he stands."

Sophia didn't answer at once. Her small face in the shadow of her hood was entranced as if by some dream; her dark eyes followed the progress up the wharf of a slim erect figure in a dark blue greatcoat. He walked with a curious arrogant swing.

Sophia sighed. "I reckon," she said wistfully, "that he's even more elegant than Cap'n Marriot."

"It's not elegance he'll be needing," said Jamie. "It's powerful shoulders and fists like granite boulders, and the will to use them."

Lark caught up with them as they went up the wharf. "He's thin as a shotten shad," he said excitedly. "Why, Timmy Boyd could snap him in two with his fingers!"

Then Mark Bennett and the rangy yellow-haired Hugh Erskine fell in with them. "Did you hear the fine tongue?" demanded Hugh. "Now what would such a one want with a place like this? There's another passenger for the *Minerva*, come winter."

"Before that," said Mark cynically. "Give him a week and he'll be ready to sail, if he hasn't fell into a decline before that."

Sophia pulled her hand out of Jamie's and glared at the boys. Her cheeks were red.

"Anybody'd think you were all jealous because he's a gentleman!" she flamed at them. "Just because you haven't a greatcoat with three capes and a fine way of talking and a handsome thin nose!"

She rushed off ahead of them, her cloak flapping and her hood falling back. They looked after her in amazement and then burst into laughter, except for Jamie. "Now what possesses her?" he muttered.

"I reckon that from now on," said Lark with an air of ancient wisdom, "Sophie won't forever be wishing to be a boy."

They climbed the muddy slant to the store. From the end of the long wharf there came warning shouts and creaking of lines as the *Minerva's* freight was unloaded; up at the store the crowd had thinned.

The boys stopped at the head of the slope and looked out over the bleak wharves and the gray harbor.

"It'll be winter soon," Jamie said, and then wished he hadn't. For his cousin Mark's hand came down hard on his shoulder.

"But not for us, lad. We'll be where the sun is hot enough to cook the break-bone fever out of us, and the sea will be more blue than it ever is here, even in mid-summer."

Jamie stared stubbornly at the harbor whose desolation seemed to grow in proportion to his own; he made his face deliberately set and stupid. But Lark was openly enchanted; he gazed from one to the other, breathing fast.

"We'll be setting foot on those green isles and those warm white beaches, and smelling sweet flowers," said Mark. "When you're pounding ice off the water buckets in the morning, and staying up all night to mind the fire, we'll be warm."

"Aye, we'll be warm all winter, after all these years of freezing our gizzards," said Hugh, "and what's more—to look at the practical side—we'll be coming home rich."

"Will you take me?" demanded Lark.

"It's your brother we want," said Hugh. "You wait till you've got more flesh on your bones and more length to 'em, and then you can make a voyage with us. But now it's Jamie we want."

Jamie turned sharply and broke across the tangle of voices. "I'll give you my answer in three days. I want to go, make no mistake about it. But I have to discuss it with the—the rest of the family."

They nodded, satisfied for the moment. He left them abruptly.

* * *

"What's a serenade?" Albion asked at suppertime.

"Mercy, that's a queer question to ask," said his mother. "Where did you learn such a long word?"

"It's music," said Lark. "A kind of song."

"Then the schoolmaster's going to hear some music tonight," said Albion with pleasure. "They're going to give him a serenade. Can't we go and hear it too?"

Lark burst into laughter. "O-ho! That's a different kind of a tune altogether! Who's going to play it?"

Their mother sighed. "Oh, dear, it does seem as if these things shouldn't go on in a law-abiding community."

Jamie put down his fork and looked steadily into his little brother's round blue eyes. "Who's going to give the schoolmaster this—uh—serenade?"

"I don't know. We was to Uncle Nathan's to play with our cousin Stephen and he told us. He heard about it down at the shore."

Jamie wished Albion hadn't mentioned the serenade, which of course didn't mean music at all. Concerning the schoolmaster, it could have only one meaning. And if Albion hadn't spoken of it, he wouldn't be wondering now if he should interfere, or at least warn the man to beware.

He met his mother's glance. It was one of the times when she was completely his mother. Her dark eyes were thoughtful and sympathetic; they saw into his head. She smiled faintly at him, and when he arose from the table and took his jacket from its peg, she did not ask him to stay, though she surely knew where he was going.

Lark sprang up eagerly, but Jamie pointed a finger at him. "Stay here," he said, and Lark turned sulky but obeyed.

As Jamie shut the door behind him, his mother said quietly, "Be careful, Jamie."

* * *

The cloudy dark was warm, and smelled of wet earth and damp leaves. As Jamie walked along the island road to the schoolhouse the night felt so quiet and empty, with only a far-off murmur to remind him of the sea. He was no longer angry that the serenade had been mentioned. He was grateful for action. "Whistle for a wind," sailors said when they were becalmed. Well, someone had whistled him up a good wind tonight!

It wasn't a blow of his choosing; it wouldn't take him to the West Indies, but it would put a snap in his sails for an hour or so.

Doubtless it was the Boyds who planned the serenade. He'd seen them loitering around the wharf this morning, inspecting the new school-master with contemptuous grins. Tim and Israel had always considered the schoolmaster to be their prey alone. They'd thought Ned Converse fair game once, until he drove them off with cutlass and musket. So then they'd used the schoolmaster as a target.

Almost always they could find someone to join in with them, some of the older boys in the school who had a grudge to settle with the master for one thing or another. But if anyone had wanted to enlist his own raiding party, he'd have had to fight the Boyds first. The schoolmaster was theirs as surely as if he were a little seal they'd trapped in a cove.

The lights of the schoolmaster's house, behind the school, showed through the night at last and Jamie walked faster. He was disgusted because Providence hadn't seen fit to send Brigport a brawny young man at least as big as Israel Boyd, if not bigger, and much faster on his feet.

So his disapproval grew as he approached the house, and by the time he'd knocked on the kitchen door and had it opened to him, he wore a prodigious scowl.

The remembered voice greeted him. "Good evening. My first caller! Come in!" The man stepped back from the doorway and Jamie went into the kitchen. It was brighter than he'd ever remembered it. Most of the schoolmasters had been poor enough to worry about the price of candles and whale oil. But now a lamp burned on the chest of drawers and another on the table, and there were candles on the mantelshelf, besides a rousing fire on the hearth. The plain room was warm and gilded with light. The stranger was in the midst of unpacking. Books were stacked everywhere and the open sea-chest by the fireplace was still full of them.

Jamie looked at everything and then turned back to the schoolmaster. The man stood there waiting, smiling a little. He was as slim as a yellow-birch sapling in his flowered waistcoat and snug strapped trousers; his white cambric shirt was finely made. Jamie felt like a gorm and a scare-crow beside him. Best to get his business over with swiftly, and escape before he stifled.

"I'm Jamie Bennett," he said bluntly. "I've come to warn ye—"

The man's friendly smile turned his thin face much younger. "I'm Roger Thorne. How do you do?" His eyes were a clear gray. "Will you be one of my scholars?"

Well, he had a good grip, for all his bones were so thin and narrow! Jamie said, "I reckon I'm finished with my schooling."

"I'm sorry for that."

"You'll have my brothers and sisters," Jamie assured him, "and if ever they don't act up to snuff, you've only to let me know. They've had their orders."

"And they'll certainly obey, if you looked at them as fiercely as that." Roger Thorne laughed, and moved a pile of books off a chair. "Sit down."

"I'd like to," Jamie said, and was surprised to realize that he meant it. "But there's no time. They'll be here any minute. That's what I came to tell you about."

"More guests, do you mean? Does the island always show its schoolmasters such hospitality?"

"It's not what I'd call hospitality," said Jamie grimly. "But it's what the schoolmaster gets—sooner or later. They're aiming to do ye mischief, Mr. Thorne."

"Mischief? What sort of mischief?"

"It'll be whatever comes to their minds first. There's no telling. If only you—if only you weren't—" he blurted out and then stopped, ashamed.

"If only I weren't so slight?" Roger Thorne smiled at him. "And so citified? To tell you the truth, that's what I've been thinking this evening, since I've taken store of my—my apartments." His gaze flicked over their homely surroundings. "Not that I object to chopping my own firewood and cooking my own meals; I only wish that I'd had a bit more education along those lines." Abruptly serious, he sat astride a chair, folded his arms on the back and gazed at Jamie. "And now you're here to tell me there are even more serious disadvantages. And can you tell me also what I am to do about it?"

Jamie ranged restlessly about the room. "I was hoping for a man at least as big as one of them," he said honestly. "They're bullies, Mr. Thorne. They go by brute strength and that's what they respect . . . unless—" He remembered something he had read in one of Captain Marriot's books, and he swung around excitedly. "That stick you carried this morning—does it have a sword in it? They'd respect that."

Roger Thorne's smile was rueful. "You're a romantic boy. No, it's merely a stick and I use it to help me walk. Didn't you notice anything else this morning? I'm lame."

Jamie's flush burned from neck to hairline. "No. I thought you had an uncommon proud swing in your walk, that's all."

"That," said Roger Thorne, "is the kindest thing that has ever been said to me in all my life."

Jamie scarcely heard him. He had stopped at the old pine chest of drawers and was staring at the littered top. Flanked on one side by an uneven stack of books and on the other by a long roll that might have maps or charts, a leather case lay open; and Jamie stared at the contents of the case as a man might stare at treasure. For they were treasure, the brace of double-barreled pistols gleaming softly there against the crimson velvet lining. At that moment, Jamie thought they were the most beautiful things in the world—always excepting a ship.

The schoolmaster crossed the room behind him, his lameness making an uneven rhythm on the wide floorboards. "Oh, the pistols," he said in-differently. "Pretty things, aren't they?"

"Can you fire 'em?" Jamie asked bluntly. "Or are they just for show?"

Thorne shrugged. "I'm a fair marksman."

"Then you can drive them off!" Jamie was exultant. "They'll be as scairt as if you was Old Harry himself."

"Come now! You don't expect that I'll start my tour of duty by firing over the heads of a crowd of pranksters, do you?" He laughed and shook his head. "I'm a schoolmaster, Jamie, not a bucko mate. Let them get their games over with, toss rocks at my window, pour water down my chimney, or whatever it is they do, and then we'll all rest easy." He turned away without a backward glance at the pistols, and Jamie followed him despairingly.

"What'll you do when they come?"

He shrugged. "Why, I'll simply tell them, 'Gentlemen, you'll find less sport in hounding me than in catching a fish. So you'd best be off to your work and leave me to my housekeeping."

There was nothing to say. Not that Jamie couldn't think of plenty; but if Roger Thorne had such a conceit about the way he could handle the Boyds, why should Jamie Bennett go on making a fool of himself?

"Then I'll be leaving," he said shortly.

"Stay and talk with me. I'd like to ask some questions about the is-land. Do you often have wrecks here?"

"We had one last summer." Jamie had his hand on the latch.

"Tell me about it."

Jamie's eyes were cold. Looking for yarns, was he? He should have been on the beach when they brought the *Cynthia*'s dead captain ashore. He opened the door and went out. "It doesn't bear talking about," he said over his shoulder. "The captain was drowned."

The schoolmaster was a black figure against the light. "I've heard of that one," his voice came soft to Jamie's ears. "The captain's name was the same as mine."

"So it was. Good night," he said stiffly and tramped out past the dark loom of the schoolhouse to the road. He didn't look back, even when

Roger Thorne called out after him, "Many thanks for your company and for your warning."

The silence was unnatural; it meant, most likely, a stiff breeze before morning. When at last Jamie reached a bend in the road he stopped and looked back at the three small squares of warm light against the dark . . . Jamie gazed at the tiny bright squares, shook his head, and was about to turn home when the sound of the hard knocking on the schoolmaster's door carried to him in the stillness. He saw the door opened and the light shine out, Roger Thorne's slim neat figure blotted out by a bigger one; then a hoarse rallying shout, and the fire of torches as the raiders burst through the narrow passage between schoolhouse and dwelling. Jamie realized that they had probably been hiding on one side of the school as he passed by on the other side.

Let him see for himself it's no joke, Jamie thought defiantly. But even as he thought it, he felt the rage that the prospect of cruelty always roused in him. Cruelty to Ned, to a child, a dog . . . and in this case the schoolmaster, who might have been smug and a dandy, but who was also thin as a shotten shad, and lame into the bargain.

Jamie went back. I dunno what I figger to do, he argued with himself. He broke into a run. When he was almost to the scene, he shifted his course into the inky shadow of the woods across the road, making his way among the trunks as sure-footed as the Indian he had often pretended to be under these very trees.

The shaking red glow of the torches reflected from the schoolhouse windows. That and the din of voices made him think of the old but still horrifying tales of Indian raids. Finding two trees growing close together, he kept well behind them and watched through the slit. The Boyds had done a good job of recruiting; there must have been eight or ten in the party, but the only one he could recognize for sure was Tim Boyd.

They had brought out the substantial pine table on which Roger Thorne had been unpacking his books, and Tim stood on it, illuminated by the streaming high-held torches. He looked gigantic looming thus against the night, and his grin was turned monstrous by the flares.

"Hand up the goods," Tim yelled, "and we'll perceed with the auction. You got it there, Izzy?"

"Aye, aye!" Izzy roared smartly. This was considered to be very funny, and there were whoops of laughter as the "goods" were handed up. Jamie's teeth came together hard. Roger Thorne, hoisted from below, hauled up by Tim's big hand at the back of his neck, looked no bigger than Lark beside Tim's bulk. He stood there helpless in Tim's grip, gazing out with an expressionless face over the heads and the torches.

"Now, gents," Tim began, "we've got a very fancy piece of goods here." He punctuated his words by shaking his victim. "Of course, he ain't as fancy as he was when we got here!" The crowd roared.

Tim peered into Thorne's face, a baby delighted with the kitten it is about to squeeze to death. "Let's see if I can shake a sound out of the critter." He kicked Thorne's feet out from under him and then jerked him upright by the back of his neck. And Thorne made no sound, but Jamie saw the flash of pain across his face and knew it was the lame leg Tim had kicked.

It was enough for Jamie. He slipped across the road like a shadow among shadows.

"What am I bid for this bit of elegance?" Tim declaimed. "A schoolmaster without a tongue! You can set it in your cornfield to scare off the crows, or put it in the henyard for a roost, or bait a trawl with it . . . what am I offered? I'll sell it to the lowest bidder—"

If rage was what counted, Jamie could have scattered the crowd like a dogfish after a school of herring. But he knew that he was outnumbered. One clout on the jaw from Tim's fist and he'd be knocked senseless, to wake up and find both himself and the schoolmaster badly battered.

Jamie slipped into the back entry of the schoolhouse, always left unlocked so the bell could be reached in case of emergency. He groped for the bell-rope. For one frightening instant he couldn't find it, and began to sweat at the thought that the crowd had cut the rope. But in the next instant his frantic fingers found it, and he pulled.

At the first clang from the belfry, the tumult outside stopped. Jamie's mouth dried. I'm in for it now, he thought, and all because he wouldn't use his pistols . . . But his rhythm never faltered and the schoolbell went on ringing. The alarm flung out through the dark to the east and the west.

After the first silence there was a rush of feet outside. "Stop that blasted bell!" someone yelled.

At least there was only one way for them to reach him. And the wall behind him was stacked with firewood . . . Jamie hung to the rope with one hand and reached behind him for the hard, comforting round of a birch stick.

When the door flew open he heaved the birch. There was a grunt of pain, the invader staggered backward, and Jamie laughed silently and reached for another length of wood.

It seemed to him that he had been ringing the bell and pitching firewood at the doorway for an age, and his arms were beginning to ache and his breath run short, when all at once they stopped coming. It could have been a trap; he let go of the bell-rope, took a piece of wood in each hand, and waited. There was only silence, which told him nothing.

What he heard after that was the sound of galloping hooves. He dropped the firewood and went outside. The hooves meant that Captain Marriot was riding Hector. He'd be the first up from the harbor, but the men who came on foot wouldn't be too far behind.

Jamie walked around the school, looking for Roger Thorne. The raiders had gone, probably into the woods across the road, and from there they would get to their homes. Some would double back, to arrive panting at the schoolhouse asking, "Is there another wreck?" Time for them later; if the Boyds showed up, Jamie intended to sing out. I'll sing out anyway, he thought grimly, as he found Roger Thorne, lying unconscious where Tim had dropped him. He had struck his head against a corner of the heavy table.

A few of the men were a bit stiff-necked about being called away from their firesides by the schoolbell for anything less than a fire or a shipwreck. But they went into action after one look at the man lying senseless in the dooryard, his face streaked with blood from the gash on his temple. There was little said. One crew set to work at once to put the kitchen in order, while another group carried Roger Thorne to his bed, and looked on while Captain Marriot washed and dressed the wound. Almost everyone had turned out. The Boyd brothers were conspicuous by their absence.

"They went outside the harbor to look for herring," their father explained, no doubt believing it.

Jamie, working in the kitchen, was relieved to see that the pistols were still in their velvet-lined case. Thorne's books and his chessmen had been scattered broadside across the room.

Standing where he could look from one room into another, he wondered who among the crowd had taken part in the serenade. None of the older men, to be sure, nor the young married men. But there were others . . . They were some diligent now, weren't they? Stacking books and scraping up spilled candle grease without looking to left or right. Doubtless they were feeling queasy in the stomach, wondering if Roger Thorne were dead.

Hugh Erskine was piling Roger Thorne's clothes back into the trunk from which they'd been pulled. Catching Jamie's eye, he smiled feebly. "Reg'lar shambles, ain't it? . . . Can you see in there? They brought him 'round yet?"

"Not yet," said Jamie.

The schoolmaster soon returned to consciousness in a quiet and gentlemanly fashion, and apologized for all the trouble he had caused.

"It's we who owe you an apology, Mr. Thorne," Captain Marriot said, his face iron-hard. "Whoever was responsible for this, the decent folk of Brigport aren't condoning it."

"I'm sure of that, Captain." The schoolmaster smiled faintly. "In fact, a very decent young man warned me to prepare to repel boarders, but I didn't take him seriously, and you can see the sad result." He lifted his head and tried to look into the kitchen. "My books—"

"They're all right, Mr. Thorne," Jamie said from the doorway. "Thrown around like a hurricane was set loose in here, but that's all. The pistols are safe, too."

"Ah, the pistols." He lay back wearily. "You were right about them, I fear."

"You should have fired a few rounds into the midst of the devils!" David Owen burst out. "Then we'd know who they were by the shot in their hides!"

"A man's got no call to use firearms on prankish boys," Thad objected, but was drowned out in a wave of general agreement to David Owen's statement.

"We're supposed to be a civilized community," Captain Marriot said grimly, "in a civilized country. We New Englanders set great store by our learning, but Brigport can't keep a schoolmaster." He looked around at the others who had crowded into the small chamber. In the flickering light he scanned each face. "It's just pure luck that we haven't been called to stand around this man's deathbed as we're standing now," he said. "This was no prank tonight, but malicious mischief and it very nearly got out of hand."

"I cal'late we better see where our boys was tonight," said Thad Boyd importantly. "I know mine have been out looking for herring since dark." Then, as if he could feel the heat of Jamie's thoughts, Thad turned on him.

"As I understand it, Jamie, you was the one who warned the schoolmaster, and you was right handy by to ring the bell when things got a mite hot for him."

"That's right." Jamie glared hard at him. Thad squinted his eyes in a way that was no doubt meant to be shrewd.

"How'd you get wind of it?"

"One of the young ones told me. He'd picked it up at the shore."

"And you're sure," Thad pressed him, "that you never heard anything about no serenade till then? You never heard the word—or never even said it with your own lips—down at the harbor this morning?"

"I'm as sure," said Jamie in a remarkably quiet voice, "as I am that it was Tim Boyd who was dragging the schoolmaster around by the back of his neck tonight."

Thad choked as if someone had him by the neck. There was a murmur throughout the room, and Captain Marriot turned a stern and implacable face on Jamie. "James Bennett, have you ever lied to me?"

"No, sir."

"Then don't start now. Can you swear that Tim Boyd was mixed up in this deviltry tonight?"

"Yes, and Israel was here too. I couldn't tell about the rest."

Someone sighed behind him and he had a feeling that Hugh Erskine had slumped in relief against the wall. He wondered how many others were relieved, but he did not dare take his eyes from Captain Marriot's face.

"I know where my boys are!" Thad spluttered. "I refuse—"

Roger Thorne, who had been lying with his eyes closed, roused up and asked with an effort, "Big fellows, are they? One with a livid scar slashing into his eyebrow?"

Thad was struck speechless. It was someone else who said without surprise, "Aye, that'd be Israel."

"Thad, the rest of us expect you to call your boys on deck for this," said Captain Marriot. "And we expect it of anyone else who can't account for his son's actions tonight. If a boy of mine had got fouled up in this, I'd trice him up for the lash, but however you do it is no concern of mine, as long as you do it." He looked down at Roger Thorne. "Do you have anything to say?"

The schoolmaster turned his head carefully, his eyes narrowed as if the light hurt them. "I've got a devilish headache," he said with some difficulty, "and I swear my wits have been addled. So my words won't be well-chosen. But I'm sure of one thing. If I had the brawn, I'd attend to the Boyd brothers with my own hands." His gaze stopped on Thad, and it was as cold as his polished, elegant voice. "From the bottom of my heart I wish I could repay them for dragging me out of my house like a trussed fowl, kicking my game leg, and trying to crack my skull."

Jamie's scalp tightened. This was neither fop nor mild bookish scholar, but a man of vengeance. "For those who laid hands on me, I have no forgiveness," the man went on, "and I never shall. But as for the others—" He leaned his head back and shut his eyes wearily—"well, there were some who tried to call the others off, and I think they hadn't intended to do anything more than make a noise. Whoever they are, don't be too harsh with them. And I thank all who came when the bell rang. And now I feel so ill that if I were a complete fool I'd be convinced I was dying."

"And he looks it," hissed David Owen. "We'd best be out of here and leave him in peace." Scowling, he beckoned across the room to his oldest son. "Come, Morgan, I'd like a word with you." The crowd left, walking as softly as possible across the bare floors and shutting the kitchen door gently behind them.

Jamie was on his way out with Mark when Captain Marriot called to him and he went back into the bedchamber. "The schoolmaster wants a word with you," the captain said brusquely. "Heave to, Peter Pollinger," he called after Simon's younger son. "I'll want you to ride Hector home and bed him down, and tell Pleasance I'm staying the night here." He went out with Peter, and Jamie and Roger Thorne were alone.

The schoolmaster smiled up at him. "I apologize, Jamie Bennett. My family has often told me that I'm insufferably vain of my own intelligence and that pride goeth before a fall. They seem to be right."

"You'll be better in no time," Jamie said. "Cap'n Marriot's a good hand at doctoring."

"Will you come to see me again?"

Jamie nodded, eager to be out of the room.

"I'll hold you to that promise, then. And now, good night."

Chapter 13

One warm October afternoon when Jamie and Lark returned to the harbor after their day's fishing, there was activity at some of the wharves, but none at all at Uncle Nathan's. His sloop was at her mooring, and the wharf was deserted. This was unusual. If Uncle Nathan and several other men weren't having a political discussion in the sunny lee of the fish house, Mark might be baiting a trawl there, or mending a net.

"Where are they all flown to?" Lark wondered aloud. "Nobody much in sight anywhere. Mebbe they all had to go up and save the schoolmaster again."

"I don't think anybody'll manhandle him again so soon," said Jamie. "They should have had their fill. 'Course," he added thoughtfully, "mebbe they'll want to come down on me and take the wind out of my sails."

"Why should they? They never got larruped for what they did, and if you hadn't seen 'em there they'd have told about it anyway, because they think so proud of themselves, and they know nobody can hurt 'em."

"Somebody—somehow—will hurt 'em," Jamie said between his teeth, "and they can holler long and loud, but it won't make one particle of difference."

They finished splitting their fish and were ready to row the catch across to Rich Gibson's, when Sophia and the twins appeared unexpectedly on the path between the spruces and the beach.

"Ahoy the brig Sophia Bennett!" Lark sang out. "What's that you've got for cargo? Two barrels of Jamaica rum?"

The twins giggled appreciatively and tried to pull away from Sophia, but she held them fast. "You're not running down there and getting gurry all over your shoes," she said severely. But she was happy and excited; her smile kept tilting the corners of her mouth and sparkling in her eyes. She had grown tall in the last few months, and seeing her thus Jamie had a fleeting vision of the pretty girl she would be in a few more years.

"Do you know what's happened?" she demanded. "Do you know who came today? A tops'l schooner from Limerock brought him out. He paid them to bring him out." Her voice was awed. "Think of that!"

"Who?" asked Jamie.

"Our cousin Owen Bennett!" Albion shouted. And not to be outdone, Margery added in a triumphant shriek, "He's going to be a captain!"

Lark whistled. Jamie said, "Good. He deserves it. Let's get these fish across to Rich before he shuts up shop, Lark."

It was bad enough to have Lark and the young ones yammering about Owen like a flock of medricks screaming over a school of herring. But when Jamie went into the store to collect his money from Rich, there was Captain Marriot holding forth.

"Aye, we'll have a genuine gala this coming Saturday night! Everybody on the island must come, even the babes!" He chuckled. "We'll stow 'em away in the bedrooms, line 'em up from headboard to foot like so much cordwood! Nobody's to stay home to rock the cradle when we've got such an important citizen in our midst."

Jamie hung close to the door. Amanda waved to him from behind the counter; aware of her eyes, he tried to seem pleasantly intent on the captain's words.

"The boy's done well for himself, to be sure." Simon Pollinger shook his massive gray head in wonder. "I mind when he was a whelp, scampering all over the boats, up in the crosstrees, out on the bowsprit. Not afeard of man or the Devil, that one."

"Well, he's learned honest fear by now," declared Captain Marriot, "or Darius Pinkham would never trust him with a vessel of his. A shipmaster who doesn't know fear is a dangerous man."

"Aye . . . aye . . ." The sage rumblings of agreement went around the long room.

"I'd planned," Captain Marriot went on, "to gather everyone together for a celebration, when I returned from Portland after we draw up our constitution. But Owen has only a week, he tells me, before he takes over his ship at Thomaston. So we'll gather together to drink a toast to our new state and our new captain, all in one grand, blazing blow-up!"

Jamie slid quietly outside without waiting for his money. Lark was jibber-jabbering around the doorstep with some other boys, all of them hero-struck and sounding off about the ships they were going to have one day.

"Collect our money before you start for home," Jamie said to him curtly.

"Aye, aye, sir!" Lark responded smartly.

Jamie set off for home in the blackest depression. It was only a matter of hours before he and his cousin must meet.

Jamie tried to fight his resentment. It wasn't Owen's fault, that he could go to sea as a cabin boy when Captain Marriot offered him the chance; it wasn't Owen's fault that Jamie couldn't go. And he couldn't in all fairness begrudge Owen his success. Owen was a Bennett like himself, grandson of that British seaman who had sailed the Atlantic in His Majesty's Ship *Revenge*, and refused to return to Devon when the Revolution was over; he had the sea in his bones. It was only to be expected that a Bennett should become a sea captain at nineteen.

Jamie knew all that, and he was bitterly ashamed of his envy. That was one of the seven deadly sins. Mr. Whiting had preached a whole long sermon on Envy once, and now entire sentences came back to Jamie to torment him further. Oh, he was a sinner, right enough! If he could just get aboard his boat and row over to South Island, and build him a brush camp, and live alone in the woods on mushrooms and roasted crabs and periwinkles until Owen had gone to claim his precious ship at Thomaston!

The family supper the next night wasn't too much of a chore; what with the David Owen cousins there too, and the men wanting all the details of Owen's last China voyage, it wasn't as bad as Jamie had expected. Rounding Cape Horn took them well through the roast wild goose, and a typhoon in the China Sea carried them through the apple pudding. In spite of his depression, Jamie couldn't help being hungry after a long day's fishing, so he ate well and kept his own counsel.

Owen, nineteen now, had grown more mature in his build and his manner since his last visit home two years ago. He was a handsome young man, tall, square-shouldered, long-legged, with crow-black hair and dark eyes set in a face bronzed by Cape Horn gales and Pacific suns. With his laughter and his vivid stories, he was the prince of the evening.

In the confusion of good nights at the end, he swept a long arm around Sophia and laughed at her red cheeks. "Are you so fash to leave me, sweeting?"

"I have school tomorrow," she protested.

"Is school more to you than your big cousin who brought you a heathen doll from China?"

Sophia wriggled free, pressing her lips tight as if to keep from smiling, and Margery cried triumphantly, "Sophia loves the schoolmaster!"

"Margery!" her mother reproved her, but the damage was done.

"What, you'd choose that pretty stick-in-the-mud over me?" Owen roared in mock rage. Sophia turned blindly toward the door. It was not comic to her. Jamie pulled her to him and felt her arms go around him with a convulsive strength. He glanced at Owen with calm blue eyes.

"Our Sophie has a high regard for learning," he said mildly. "Some folks do set great store by a strong brain rather'n a strong voice."

To do Owen credit, he laughed as loudly as the rest of them. He clapped Jamie on the back and said, "When are we hypering off by ourselves to spear some lobsters?"

Somebody else interrupted so Jamie didn't have to give a definite answer, and the evening was over. But Jamie lay awake for a long time that night, watching Orion climb up past his small window . . . He tried to think of everything else in the world but Owen, and he did not succeed. He tried not to imagine Owen in Thomaston, stepping aboard his ship for the first time, meeting his mates, superbly self-assured under the eyes of his crew. But it was all he saw.

* * *

He told Ned glumly about the gala. "I could wish for an early blizzard or a screaming northeaster by Saturday," he grumbled.

"That's no way to talk," Ned reproved him. "Jem Marriot, he wants to do the handsome thing by your cousin!"

The day of the gala was as fair as only an early October day could be, with no threat of a sudden shift in the weather by sundown. By the time darkness had settled down on the island, the Marriot house was lighted from attic to cellar, and fires of hard birch or seasoned spruce burned on every hearth. Pleasance had set masses of autumn flowers everywhere; the sweet scent of late-blooming stock blended with the fragrance of the bay-berry candles she herself had dipped.

As she stood with her father in the wide red-carpeted hall, receiving the guests as if this were Beacon Street instead or Brigport, she was so pretty that Jamie was taken flat aback at the sight of her in her high-waisted gown of flowered muslin, her light brown hair caught up grace-fully at the back of her head and little curls escaping around her ears. Tiny ear-drops trembled and glittered like raindrops in the sun whenever she moved her head. Jamie had ample time to stare, for his mother must pass the time of day with the Captain. She still wore her widow's black, but her fichu and cap were delicately fashioned of lawn and edged with lace. Her dark eyes had a soft brilliance, and she seemed to breathe with delight the warm fragrances of the house.

As she moved on toward the wide doorway into the parlor, where the sound of voices rose and fell like the rote on the island's shores, the chil-dren followed her decorously. Their eyes were tremendous. They loved the richness of the Marriot house and walked reverently on the glowing Turkey carpets.

Then Pleasance chaffed Lark about being such a beau, and Lark stood there perfectly at ease, laughing and joking as if he were her age and more, while Jamie tried to keep his mind on what Captain Marriot was saying to him.

". . . proud of your cousin, eh?"

"Oh, certainly," Jamie blurted out, staring hard at the Captain. "Proud as if he was President or—or the new Governor of Maine."

That pleased the Captain, who was as proprietary about the new State as he was of Pleasance. He patted Jamie's shoulder and said, "That's the spirit, boy. And he's got reason to be proud of you, taking care of that family without a thought of sojering."

Jamie was relieved to see the Pollingers shedding wraps by the door. He moved on to Pleasance and took her hand in his.

"I thought Lark was handsome tonight," Pleasance said softly, "but that was before I'd seen you. You wear your clothes with such an air, Jamie."

"You look—" he fumbled for a word, but didn't need to find it, for she smiled at him as if she knew.

"Thank you, Jamie."

He nodded and moved away, both sorry and glad that the meeting was over, but her hand pulled gently at his sleeve. "Aren't you going to ask me to be your partner in the Portland Fancy?"

"Why—" His neckcloth was strangely tight. "Certain of it!" This time he did escape, red-faced. Oh, Lor, what ailed him to feel such a simpleton with a girl he'd known all his life, just because they were both done up in their Sunday-go-to-meeting clothes?

Entering the square parlor, he had one glimpse of Amanda perched demurely on a dainty chair with her tanned hands folded in her lap and her toes placed together just so; then she was springing up with a reckless disregard for her streaming red sash and rose-sprigged skirts.

"Jamie, come look at this wee darling thing!" She dragged him toward a miniature model of the frigate *Constitution* set on a windowsill.

"Mercy, girl," her mother called heartily after her, "you needn't come down on the boy with all sails set like that! He'll sheer off t'other side of the Western Ocean!"

Everyone laughed. "Don't pay 'em any heed, Jamie," Amanda muttered. "What do they expect of me? I'm just the same 'Manda that has to go out and turn the fish when they're curing, and row out to bring my father in from the mooring." Her cheeks were poppy-red, and her lower lip rolled out sulkily. "So how can they expect me to act like Miss Prunes and Prisms just because I'm walking on Turkey carpets and have on a new gown—" She pulled irritably at the ribbon around her waist—"and my hair done up."

"You look real staving," Jamie's whisper assured her. "You're mighty slender amidships and I'd say it was a prodigious improvement to have your hair triced up with those scarlet lashings."

"How do you mean—a prodigious improvement?"

"Just that," he said earnestly. "Far better than letting it all fly loose like a mess of old dry rockweed."

"A mess of old dry rockweed," she repeated, the words suspiciously soft. She backed off still further. "So that's how it looks most of the time! It's a wonder you could ever bring yourself to associate with me, Jamie Bennett!" she hissed, and only a silvery trill from Mr. Whiting's flute kept people from hearing her. "Any girl who runs about with hair like a mess of old rockweed—why, who could expect a Bennett to be even civil to the likes of her?"

Jamie glanced fearfully over his shoulder. The children had surrounded Mr. Whiting, and were asking for favorite tunes, while all the
mothers smiled and watched. "Listen, Amanda," Jamie whispered, "I
wasn't intending to run you down. I was just trying to tell you—" Blazes,
he was falling all over his tongue. Plague take the girl, he'd ought to turn
her over his knee. "You were all hawsed up about being dressed so fine—
I only wanted to tell ye—"

"Keep it to yourself, Jamie Bennett. Or better, entertain Miss Marriot
with it!" She whirled away and marched defiantly toward the group
around Mr. Whiting.

Jamie went moodily out into the hall. It was empty now; the last of
the guests had arrived. A murmur of male voices and laughter drifted out
from the library and he turned toward that room, then hesitated. What
had he to do with them? He was the only boy of his age without some future venture in mind; he was the only one of them all who was actually
imprisoned here on Brigport. Even the younger ones who would be listening open-mouthed to the talk could dream of exciting years ahead, of
long voyages and foreign shores, of Boston, New York, Liverpool and
Lisbon. But not Jamie Bennett. He sat down glumly on the stairs.

The schoolmaster appeared in the library doorway, saw Jamie, and
limped out into the hall. He leaned his elbow on the newel post. "I
haven't seen you since the famous night. When are you coming to talk
with me?"

"I've been drove up," said Jamie bleakly. "No time."

"Ah, well." The schoolmaster smiled. "Winter is coming. There'll be
endless time for talking then."

Albion burst from the parlor and raced across the hall to the library.
"Pleasance says are you going to spin yarns all night, because we've set
back all the chairs for the dancing!"

He was greeted with a great deal of laughter, and a group of the
younger men followed him out of the library. "We'll join you soon," Captain Marriot called after them. "We old mariners still have some tales to
tell." He shut the door behind them.

Owen saw Jamie and the schoolmaster, and headed for them. He was
splendid in a bottle-green coat and fawn-colored trousers. His ruffled
stock shone the whiter for his dark skin.

"Why the long face, Jamie?" he demanded. "Haven't you a partner
for the first dance, or can't you make up your mind?"

Jamie stared at the carpet. A tremendous pounding on the front door
was like a heavenly visitation sent to save him.

Tim Boyd reached for the knob, and the big door swung inwards. Ned Converse stood on the threshold.

The candle flames in the sconces danced wildly in a sudden breeze, and their light flickered over the strange wild figure in its tattered best; the light caught in the one good eye and made the black patch all the more sinister. For a moment no one spoke or moved. Jamie pressed back against the stairs, his arms folded hard against his chest. So far the evening had been a misery for him; now it had reached a nightmare peak.

"I've come to the party," Ned said hoarsely. He stumped in, his big white head lowered, and stared all around at them with a darting upward glance. "Where's Cap'n Marriot?"

No one answered at once. They seemed struck with a wordless astonishment. "Who," drawled Roger Thorne close to Jamie's ear, "is this imposing personage?"

"Well?" Ned's voice rose. "Struck with Spanish mildew, be ye? Not one o' ye young sculpins got a tongue on ye?"

"Well, Ned," someone began feebly. "Evening, Ned," someone else said. Owen strode forward.

"Did you fetch along your dancing shoes, Ned?" His voice pulsed with scarce-hidden laughter. "Are you ready to take a turn on the floor?"

"Young brute," the schoolmaster murmured. Jamie's hands tensed.

"Aye, I mind ye now," muttered Ned, his eye on Owen, his head lowered like an old bull's. "You'd be Nate Bennett's boy, that went to sea and riz to be a captain. But don't count your ships before they're launched, boy. There's many a master wore his title out before ever he reached the Gilberts."

Owen's laughter brought a cluster of girls and children to the parlor doorway. There was a flurry of gasps, and a child let out a frightened yelp. "It's the crazy man!" Jamie didn't have to look twice to know that Pleasance's happiness must have turned to horror at the sight of Ned.

"And were you one of those masters who wore his title out?" Owen asked.

"No, but I sailed under as many masters as you have years on you, and I learned to tell the boys from the men . . . My last cap'n, he was cap'n down into his bones, for that's all there was left of him when I saw him last, skin and bones when they dragged him off to the mines . . ." His fist came up and shook under Owen's nose. "But I'll swear he was worthy of his name till the day he died. So they can call you Cap'n Owen if they please, but I'll not set my tongue to the word till ye've proved yourself."

"D'you think that breaks my heart?" Owen folded his arms across his chest. "What crazy Ned Converse thinks of me is less than the wind going over my head. And now you'd better be off. You're turning all our stomachs. D'you still sleep with that pig? Lor, you smell of it!"

Jamie was on his feet almost before he knew it, and pushing away the crowd or so it seemed to him later. "What ails you, Jamie?" Somebody objected to his thrusting elbow. "Can't you get a good view of the old lunatic back there?"

Owen said with pleasure, "Well! One of my cousins to help me run the madman off the premises."

"No," Jamie said violently. Ned, recognizing him, was transfigured. He stumped forward and clutched at Jamie's shoulder.

"There you are, boy," he said happily. "I was a-wondering if you'd stayed fast to your own anchorage, after telling me about the party and all."

Owen's eyebrow lifted. He gazed at Jamie with incredulous distaste. "So you invited him?"

Jamie spoke in a clear, steady voice, "The party was to be for everybody on the island."

"So that's what you were doing, moping away on the stairs! Waiting for your friend to arrive."

"Friend!" roared Ned. "Aye, I'm his friend and he's mine, and neither of us'll ever find a better."

"I'm sure of that," said Owen and burst into laughter. The rest picked it up; but Jamie looked beyond them toward the women and saw his mother's pale, shocked face and the children's frightened stares. As for Pleasance, he could not bear to look at her. It was almost sacrilege, with Ned beside him holding his arm, and yes, Ned did smell! And Owen's laughter was like to burst his eardrums . . .

"Pay him no heed," Ned said to him. "Yon's an empty jug for sure. Would he ever dirty his hands to help a crazy old derelict build a barn? Would he ever sit and listen while an old man talked?"

"Why don't you take your friend home, Jamie?" Owen asked, silken-soft. "You're upsetting Pleasance. Why don't you two old comrades go down in somebody's baitshed and spin yarns?"

"If Ned isn't welcome," said Jamie, "then we will go. If he's not fit for this party, then neither am I."

Owen's cheekbones were red. His chin went up high. "You're quite the smug little hero, aren't you? Well, if this—" he jerked his thumb at Ned—"is what you prefer to the rest of us, then we take it as an insult, and you'd better go."

"This, first," said Jamie quietly, and struck him on the chin. It was so sudden that he was as amazed as anyone, but only for a moment. By the time Owen had regained his balance and started for him, Jamie was ready and this time he hit Owen's mouth. He didn't feel Owen's blows, though they must have been fierce and heavy. He was intent only on landing his own.

"Gently, lad," Ned cautioned him. "Watch out for his left hand!"

"Jamie!" his mother cried out in despair.

"Oh, stop!" That was Pleasance. "Please!"

Owen's mother was calling her son's name. "Stop, this moment!" There was a tremendous noise all around.

The library door opened on the uproar. "James Bennett!" Captain Marriot's voice was a whip.

"Owen Bennett!" That was Uncle Nathan. As swiftly as it had begun, the battle was over. The fighters separated and Jamie saw with a fierce satisfaction that Owen's nose was bleeding over his elegant ruffled stock. He himself had a cut on his chin from Owen's ring, and one ear was throbbing.

Captain Marriot strode into their midst, his mouth thinned and taut. "What is the meaning of this?" he demanded. Then the chill went out of his eyes.

"Well, Ned Converse!" He thrust out his hand. "We don't often see you at the harbor! We'll talk tacks aboard after I settle these young cockerels here." He looked austerely from one to the other. "I'm waiting for an explanation."

"That's me, Cap'n." Ned broke into gusty laughter and slapped his thigh. "I'm the reason. I come aboard of this handsome craft of yourn to watch the young folks at their games and yarn a bit with ye and mebbe try a dram, and it seems there was some who thought I wasn't fit company. And this lad—" he touched Jamie's rigid arm—"he held out for my rights."

"I'm glad he did, Ned." The Captain gave Jamie a brief smile. "But next time, lad, come to me with it. Don't settle it with blows—at least when you're under my roof." He turned to Owen, whose face was half-buried in a handkerchief. "And you remember that you're captain of just one vessel. I'm in command here. If I want anyone removed, I'll do it myself. Get to the galley, now, and clean yourself up. I'll see that you have a fresh neckcloth."

He called to the men in the library doorway. "Simon Pollinger, Reuben Boyd, and the rest of ye! Take Ned in and make him welcome with a glass of toddy. I'll join you soon. As for the others—" His frosty face warmed into a smile. "Start up the dancing! What's a little blood between cousins? And Bennetts at that!"

Mr. Whiting took the signal and began "Soldier's Joy" on his flute; Owen vanished to the kitchen, the captain to his room to fetch a clean neckcloth, and couples began to form for the first dance. Ned, beaming with happiness, had been taken into the library.

Jamie stood in the hall wiping his chin. He was a little light-headed. He grinned at all who spoke to him, and there were many who said, "Good lad!"

"Are you all right, Jamie?" his mother asked quietly. He nodded, and she went back to the parlor.

"Congratulations," the schoolmaster said. Jamie was startled; he had thought he was alone in the hall at last. "You seem to make a point," Roger Thorne went on, "of championing the lame, the halt, and the blind."

"Ned is my friend!" Jamie said sharply. "I'd just as lief admit it to anybody."

The schoolmaster nodded. If he had anything else to say, it was gone, because Lark burst in on them. "You'd've knocked him senseless if the Cap'n hadn't got wind of it! Gemini!" His awe deepened into solemn amazement. "How'd you ever get so close to Ned, with him swinging that cutlass all the time?"

Amanda ran like a boy across the hall, her hair already pulled loose from its ribbons. "I'm s'posed to be partners with Morgan Owen, I have to hurry back—but Jamie—" She stopped short, all at once conscious of the schoolmaster and Lark, and her face went scarlet. "Well, mebbe I'd ought to be more tidy with it," she said obscurely. "I guess you're right about the old rockweed." She ran back to the parlor.

"Is she daft?" inquired Lark.

"No, just a girl," said Jamie. He felt fine and flourishing all at once. The fight must have driven the vapors out of his blood.

Ned left after a good hour or so of yarning about the old days. Pleasance, who had decided that Jamie was very brave and noble, gave the old man a basketful of sweets and cakes to take home. The dancing went on until everyone was tired, and then they adjourned to the dining room where the platters of cakes and tarts had been set out, the pitchers of mulled cider and raspberry shrub, the bowls of frothy syllabub. It was surely a gala, as Captain Marriot had promised.

Simon Pollinger entertained with a sailor's hornpipe, David Owen sang Welsh songs that stirred them even though they didn't know what the strange words meant. When he had finished, someone called out,

"How about a song from Lark?"

Lark's face looked thin, somehow, and too old; he kept his head high and stared straight ahead as if he hadn't heard the query.

His mother sat composedly on a loveseat near the fireplace, her hands in her lap. For an instant, so serene did she appear, Jamie wondered if she realized what was being said. Lark stood behind her. As Pleasance held out her hand to him from the pianoforte, he shook his head.

"I don't sing now," he said with dignity. "I've outgrown it."

"Why, Larkin!" came his mother's soft protest. She turned around to look at him. "I'm sure you haven't outgrown it," she said very clearly. "Your voice hasn't even begun to change yet. And on such a night as this, when Captain Marriot and Pleasance have entertained us so wonderfully, it would be most ungrateful of you to refuse."

The boy stared down at her as if he could hardly believe his ears. Then, as she nodded encouragingly, he smiled with such happiness that Jamie's eyes smarted, and went to the pianoforte.

He sang "Greensleeves" for them, and "Bonnie George Campbell," and "Lord Randall;" when Pleasance shifted softly into "Drink to Me Only with Thine Eyes," he sang that too, and "Passing By." Then he sang the song all seamen knew, "Rolling Home." While he sang, his mother sat gazing into the fire.

After "Rolling Home," he would sing no more, in spite of all the urging. He left the pianoforte and came straight across the room to Jamie. Someone set up an outcry for Blind Man's Bluff, and so no one heard their conversation.

"I'm going to tell her now about the flute, Jamie," Lark said. "I'll ask her to walk out in the garden with me."

Jamie nodded. They were choosing the first one to be the Blind Man in the game. He had no wish to be selected, and so he walked out into the hall. He saw his mother, wrapped in her cloak, going out the garden door with Lark, and he knew he would be restless until they had come back and he had seen her face. He wandered into the library, glanced around at the books and the paintings of ships, then stood idly in the doorway, watching for his mother and Lark to enter the hall again.

Soon he saw Owen pass through the parlor archway and head toward the dining room. Jamie felt a sudden desire to speak to his cousin; it was true that Owen had begun the quarrel, but he was leaving in a day or so, and if any disaster should overtake him on his voyage, Jamie would be forever haunted by the knowledge that they had parted enemies. He walked quickly to the dining room.

But Owen wasn't alone. He stood before the fire with Peter and Luke Pollinger, and Jonathan Gibson. "What'll your cargo be?" Luke was asking. "Or is it a secret matter?"

Jamie thought to withdraw before they saw him, but Jonathan hailed him and he had no choice then. Owen turned toward him, smiling. "You owe me a damask waistcoat," he said. "I should've known better than to challenge a man who rows a wherry halfway to the Rock each day. I thought someone'd flung an anchor at me."

The others laughed. Jamie put out his hand. "I didn't figger to swing at you in the first place. It just happened. No hard feelings, I hope."

"No hard feelings. 'Twasn't the first time you've blooded me, and doubtless it won't be the last." His grin shone white in his dark face. "Our young ones will be going at each other hammer and tongs one day."

"I reckon you could use that good right arm of his," Peter suggested, "if you ever had a run-in with the Malay pirates. Why don't you take him along?"

Owen put his elbow on the mantel and considered Jamie with an amused gaze. "No use thinking of that, Peter. Jamie's got no need to see foreign parts. Why, he's rooted deeper to Brigport than that old giant of a spruce outside the Captain's front door."

"Oh, he'd go if he had the chance," said Luke.

"Not our Jamie. He'd just as lief row over the same waters day in, day out, the rest of his life, and catch codfish till he's ninety." Owen laughed. "Someday he'll even look like a codfish, from staring 'em in the face so many years. Wait and see!"

Jamie put his hand behind his back, so no one should see the suddenly clenched fist. He opened his mouth, not knowing what he was going to say, when Lark's voice called out from the doorway as clear and triumphant as a bell.

"It's not so! Jamie'll go as fast and as far as anybody here, and a prodigious lot farther than most!" Jamie swung around and Lark grinned at him. The boy was radiant, and no wonder, Jamie thought enviously; if he'd told his mother about the secret flute lessons, and she had understood, so that now they need be no longer secret, then he had not a care in the world. Across the hall, Mrs. Bennett had paused in the parlor doorway to watch the game of Blind Man's Bluff.

"That's right, lad," Owen encouraged Lark. "Be loyal to your brother."

"It's not just loyalty," Lark argued. "It's the truth! He's sailing on the *Nereid* for some Havana coffee and some Portoreek molasses!"

Jamie tried to say it was not so, but it was like trying to speak in a dream; an evil dream, in which his mother turned slowly in that distant archway and looked across the hall, past Lark, into the dining room straight at him. The triumphant ringing words had reached her over the clamor of the game. And even at this distance, he thought that he could see how pale she had become.

He had never seen her swoon before, even when the news came about his father, and the twins were to be born in only a few months. But he saw her swoon now, slipping to the floor as quietly as a sigh.

So the gala ended. Lydia Bennett was well surrounded before Jamie reached her. As the women told him to stay out of the way, he heard Lark's anguished protests.

"I only said it because Owen was smirking so! And you might go, Jamie! I'd mind the fires and the water and all!"

* * *

Sophia and the twins clung to Jamie while they watched the procession of women moving back and forth between the kitchen and Pleasance's room, where his mother had been taken.

He stood at the foot of the stairs, lonely in spite of the young ones around him. Almost everyone had gone. When Amanda joined him, he was grateful.

"She'll be all right," Amanda said. "It was just the shock, I guess."

"I know." Jamie stared glumly at the floor. "Well, it's not me so much as what happened to my father. I can't blame here for being sure I'd never come back from the West Indies."

"You should've told her about it earlier," Amanda was disapproving. "It was awful heartless, to let Lark holler it out like that. My mother says it was a crime. So does everybody."

"Everybody but Hugh and Mark." Jamie heaved a deep sigh. "They hailed me to shake hands on it, and I had to tell 'em it wasn't so."

"You mean you aren't going? You never were going?"

Jamie nodded. "Gemini!" Amanda exploded in a fashion that would have horrified her mother. "A chance like that, and you had to say no. You must've been miserable about it for a long time."

He had never appreciated Amanda so much in his life.

When they were home, and all in bed but himself, he went quietly out and walked a long distance in the October midnight. He walked until he came to open fields, and he crossed them to the sea, and looked over at the long dark shadow of the South Island on the quiet, star-streaked water.

"No matter if I don't ever get to do anything great or travel any distances," he told himself, "someday I'll have a piece of South Island, a big piece. And I'll live on my land and be the king of it, and nothing will torment me anymore."

Chapter 14

On the 11th of October, 1819, the appointed delegates met at the Courthouse in Portland to form a constitution, and to apply to Congress for admission into the Union. In the store everyone talked of the event and of Mr. Jefferson's advice. But the constitution was put briefly out of mind on that fresh sparkling day when the schooner *Nereid* slid down the beach and into Rum Cove.

To Sophia's rapture, the boys had invited her to christen the schooner. In her best gown of dark green, her red cloak blown back in the breeze, and her hood slipped off her smooth-brushed black head, she looked a picture. The boys had presented her with a bouquet of asters, goldenrod, and crimson wild-rose haws. She stood proudly on a big boulder at the *Nereid*'s bow, awaiting the moment, and while Mr. Whiting made the prayer she peeked shamelessly around to see if the schoolmaster were in the forefront of the crowd where he could see her clearly. Jamie saw, and smiled. Sophia would never forget this day, and his gladness for her dulled slightly his sharp pain of longing at the sight of the schooner.

The *Nereid* was towed around to the harbor, where she would be rigged under Dougal's direction and her new sails would presently shine under the Brigport sun and fill with the Maine wind for the first time. Jamie was soon accustomed to rowing out past her every day. Besides, he had other things to do than brood. On the days when it was too windy to fish, he sent Lark to school and he went into the woodlot and cut spruce and pine. What he had cut last year had long since been sawn into boards at Peter Pollinger's sawmill, and this prime seasoned lumber would go aboard the *Nereid*. In time, some rich planter would pay well for lumber cut on Jamie Bennett's woodlot.

After a day in the woodlot he often went to bed even before the twins, half-lulled by the sound of their voices below him as they learned their letters.

Lark's natural objection to school, which he would attend every day when the winter was upon them, had been overcome when he found that Mr. Thorne had some volumes of Scott that Mr. Whiting did not have.

So the young ones were well content these days, and Jamie supposed he could be glad of that . . . As for him, he'd be pleased to get to fishing again after a long week of windy weather.

Jamie slid toward sleep, but he was still on the edge of it when the familiar sound broke through. At first he wasn't disturbed. It seemed to be part of his half-dreaming state, a trick played by his drowsy brain . . . School bell ringing, the way it had rung another night, the sound blown and tattered by the wind . . .

All at once he rolled out from under the warm covers, groping for his clothes, his head as clear of sleep as if someone had emptied a bucket of cold seawater over him.

When he ran down the steep stairs into the kitchen, the others looked at him as if he were a ghost. "School bell," he said briefly, reaching for his coat. Lark's book slammed shut, and he went for his coat like a pollock for the bait. Their mother, Sophia, and the twins remained staring at them like painted figures in a picture.

The boys set off at an easy, ground-covering lope. "Wind's some different than what it was last July," Lark said between chattering teeth. "What do you reckon they're calling us out for? Lor, I hope it's not a fire. Nor a wreck either," he added nervously.

* * *

They didn't speak again until they reached the schoolhouse and found their young cousin Stephen Bennett ringing the bell. A boy was always left to ring the bell, so that every able-bodied man could go to the scene of the disaster.

Tonight the disaster was a ship ashore. Jamie was not surprised to hear it was the Thrasher once more. "Old Ned, he come to our house and told Pa!" Stephen shouted over the bell's clanging. "Like to scared Mother into fits when he walked in!"

Once more the grim nightmare scene on the fields and shores of Southern Point was played out, but this time it was made even more cruel by the wintry edge of the wind. Their ears and faces and hands ached with it; their eyes ran water until they could hardly see the combers rushing toward them out of the darkness. But they could hear the thud and boom all along the shore, the separate sound of seas breaking on the Thrasher, and over the distressed ship.

Jamie did whatever he could, wherever he was needed, but there was grievous little to be done. The wind, stronger than it had been on that night in July, wouldn't let them get a rope out to the vessel. A few of the crew managed to lower a boat before the ship settled too far on one side, but they'd been instantly capsized by the Thrasher's treacherous breakers. Because of an ebbing tide against a freshening wind, and a certain conjunction of currents, seas rushed at the ledge from all directions, to explode together in a terrible confusion.

Peter Pollinger and another man had brought his big yawlboat around from the harbor; by skillful handling of the craft in waters they had known all their lives, they were able to pick up most of the men who had been turned out of the ship's boat, and those who jumped from the vessel and were able to fight clear of the breakers in a brief lull. But for the three who were left clinging to the slanting deck, there was nothing to do but wait until the tide turned. If the wind shifted then, and quiet waters flooded the Thrasher, the islanders could row out from the beach and bring the captain, the cook, and the first mate ashore.

Jamie sent Lark home and waited with the others until the tide turned. Here and there the watchers built small fires in the lee of the rocks. Jamie moved from one group to another until he found Mark, Hugh, and Morgan. Huddling close to the warmth, trying to warm wet chilled feet, the boys discussed the events of the evening.

"Can't understand it," Morgan muttered. "All the while we was wading out into the surf, trying to figger a way to get a line to the vessel, those chests and barrels were a-sailing in on the tide. They was as thick as a school of herring. But where'd they all go to?"

"A hogshead like to knocked me off my feet and drowned me," said Mark. "Rum or molasses, I'd say. I should've hung on to it, but—"

"That's it," Hugh interrupted. "Nobody had any time to salvage anything then. But when we settled down to wait for the tide, and everybody turned to salvage what they could, there wasn't much to salvage. I've been walking around. Nobody's found much. Oh, a couple of chests and a barrel here and there, but that's all. And I'd have said that vessel was loaded heavy. Did it all go out again on the tide?"

"Couldn't go far." Mark squinted out toward the dark water. "Couldn't get out past the Thrasher. Tide down like this, it's like a big old tub between the beach and the ledge."

Jamie didn't contribute, but thought back to the period of confusion and shouting. Besides the ones like himself who had waded out, trying to get a line to the vessel, there had been many milling back and forth along the beach behind them like a school of herring. What if some of those, under shelter of the dark, had been salvaging the cargo and hiding it away among the rocks, while the others were trying to work out a rescue plan?

He was remembering the wreck of the brig *Cynthia*, and the Boyd brothers piling up bales of raw linen while the others worked . . . He walked along the edge of the water, away from the voices and cluster of fires like fireflies. He hated thinking of the men out there in the freezing wind, hanging to the spars on the dripping deep-slanted deck, watching the fires, wondering if they could hold out until the tide turned. And he hated equally the thought of the Boyd brothers feeding on disaster. Of course, he wasn't sure it was the Boyds. But hadn't they always been the greedy ones?

And then at last he found their fires—around a little point and doubly hidden by being built in a hollow under the bank, where flood tides had eaten away the earth. Their fire had also a windbreak which was most interesting. It was built of several large chests, like the one Mark had salvaged.

Tim and Israel lay at ease by their fire. Keeping out of the light's range, Jamie made a large circle around them, and came up behind the chests. Here were more chests, and a soldierly row of barrels and casks lined up under the bank. Oh yes, Tim and Israel had been the busiest of all in the busy crowd tonight! Only in the dark no one had guessed just what form their industry had taken. Doubtless they'd been first on the scene too, and so they'd had a head start. Jamie was quietly enraged. He walked around the windbreak of coffee chests and into the firelight.

"Look what the tide left," Tim said heartily, and Israel laughed.

Jamie jerked his head backward at the unseen Thrasher. "Tide left something else too. Another crew thought they saw Saddleback, I reckon. Lucky for you lads she had such a rich cargo."

"You calling us wreckers?" Israel rose to a threatening crouch.

Tim, sounding like his father, said blandly, "Why, no, he ain't calling us that, Izzy. He's just envious, that's all. On account of we worked a mite harder'n him, and got more. Set back and rest, Izzy."

"I ain't forgot about him ringing the schoolbell on us."

"We don't have to settle that tonight. We got all our lives. Jamie figgers to be right here on Brigport till he's a hundred 'n' ten, don't ye, Jamie?"

Jamie shrugged. "You'd ought to be grateful for me ringing the schoolbell that night. Not knowing your own strength, you could have killed Mr. Thorne, and there were some in your gang who'd have told of it." He was surprised to be enjoying himself. "One of you would have danced on air from mainland gallows long before tonight."

Neither of them answered to that, but scowled at him across the fire as if he had given them something new to think about. After a moment Israel growled, "Anyway, if there's wreckers about, I said once 'twas Crazy Ned, and I say it now."

"Aye," Tim agreed in a sanctimonious tone. "Sooner he's locked up the better it'll be for the honor of Brigport."

"Honor!" Suddenly Jamie's anger exploded into one hot cry. "Honor! I suppose it's for the honor of Brigport that you two go after a cargo like crows after carrion while the rest of us are working our hearts out to save lives!"

Israel moved with astonishing speed for one so big, and Jamie took to his heels. He had no wish to be battered into something his own mother wouldn't recognize. He fled along the hard-packed sand, around the bend toward the clustered fires, and Israel pounded behind him. He ran straight for the thick of the fires, tripped over a chest and went sprawling. In the moment of his crash he heard Simon Pollinger bellow, "What's all this? Sheer off, Israel Boyd!"

"He's been a-tossing all manner of foul words at us!" roared Israel. "All on account of we was lucky enough to salvage a mess of prizes!" Jamie rolled over and sat up, and Israel's finger lunged at him like a harpoon. "Calling us out of our names, when we was the first ones to answer the hail! Why don't he go look for him that sent that ship ashore?"

"And who might that be?" someone called out.

"Yes," Rich Gibson said. "If you think we have wreckers, name them. Don't keep blowing like a confounded whale."

"Crazy Ned Converse!"

Jamie sprang to his feet. He was glad that most of the island men were around him, but even if they hadn't been, he'd still have shouted defiance at Israel Boyd.

"That's a lie! Ned's not crazy! He knows better than to show a light where there should be no light! He heard her strike, same as he heard the *Cynthia*. I'll swear Ned wouldn't be out here showing a light any more than I would."

"Mebbe you was out here." Tim had joined his brother. "How do we know?"

"The tide's turning!" someone called, and a hush spread over the beach. A shift in the wind, a change in the sound of the water breaking over the Thrasher; though there was nothing to see, the change was as palpable as the change from darkness to daylight.

In a few hours the captain, the cook, and the mate were brought safely ashore, and though they were chilled through, none of them seemed to be developing the fearful lung fever. Of the men whom Peter Pollinger had rescued in the surf, and taken to the harbor, some were badly bruised and cut. One man had gone under the tumble of waves before those in the yawlboat could seize him.

"The Thrasher's killed again," the island people said solemnly. "Whoever named that ledge named her rightly." And then there were uneasy shifts of glances and long silences, until someone had the courage to say it. "What about this light? What about Ned?"

If Captain Marriot had been there, doubtless he would have called a meeting as he had done before. But no meeting was suggested.

"Maybe nobody wants an inquiry," Jamie said bluntly to Amanda, in the store the next day. They were in a dim corner away from the hearthside crowd, Amanda ostensibly filling Jamie's molasses jug from the hogshead.

"They talk about it enough for ten meetings," Amanda said. "That's all I hear. And I know one thing. If we don't find out for ourselves about that light, somebody'll be out here to do it for us. Cap'n Pease as much as said so last night."

Captain Pease, a big, sandy-haired, raw-boned man from Eastport, had spent the night at Rich Gibson's. Now he stood back to the fire, flanked by his mates, his mouth obstinately tight, his eyes slitted and cold as he listened to the talk around him.

"I know one thing, certain-sure." Uncle Nathan's voice cut through the uneasy murmur and rumble. "We can leave Ned in the clear. Ned's got a game leg, and this cold weather gets into it and pains like the Old Harry—and I can well believe it, having a rheumaticky shoulder of my own. So what would wrecking a ship benefit a man who couldn't salvage anything that's come ashore?"

"Besides that, Ned's no fool," Simon Pollinger stated with a sweeping glance from under his grizzled eyebrows that took in Thad Boyd. "He's a seaman. He's no wrecker."

That was a word that made them all wince, that made them look at the floor, and shift their feet. Captain Pease's face seemed carved from stone.

Jamie wished he dared speak up what lay in his head. Somebody's made some fool mistake, out prowling around with a lantern, he thought. Tim or Israel, I'll wager. So confounded greedy for every chip that comes ashore, they went scavenging by lantern light. Now they're scairt to say so, and I dunno as I blame 'em. But little good it did 'em to name poor Ned.

"My mother will be saying I've gone clear to Portoreek for the molasses." He grinned at Amanda, paid her, and left the store. Thad Boyd, standing near the door, gave him a blank, preoccupied look. Maybe Thad's putting two and two together, he thought. Maybe he'll knock those two turnip heads together till they get a little wit between them. And a good thing. They've been scaring the young ones away from Southern Point for long enough.

Outside the store the cold November air was fresh and biting in his lungs; the wind was northwest, in scudding, howling squalls that bent the birches double, blew the dead brown grasses flat, and turned the water to seething silver.

Jamie had left the settlement at the harbor, and was on the road that cut through the deep woods, when someone called to him from behind, and he looked around to see the schoolmaster following with the aid of his stick as fast as he could.

He did well; Jamie had only to slow his pace slightly. Here where the thick wall of spruces rose high on either side of the road, the wind was cut off and it was easy to talk.

"Jamie, what do you think of this story about a light?" Mr. Thorne asked him.

"I figger—" Jamie began eagerly, and then clamped his mouth shut. He was amazed that this theory about the Boyds had come straight to his lips, when he hadn't even been tempted to tell Amanda. It was a queer thing about Mr. Thorne, and it made Jamie uncomfortable, even a little resentful. He gave the schoolmaster a sidewise glance and said vaguely, "I don't reckon anybody was making mischief. If there was a light, 'twasn't intentional."

"You say if." The man was casual enough. "Don't you believe the evidence? The men and the mates of the *Cynthia* swore to it; so does the captain of the *Annabelle*, as well as the mates and the men."

"I'm not doubting their word. I'm just saying what's been said before—we aren't wreckers here."

Thorne wasn't a Brigport man; this was none of his business. Jamie stared straight ahead, and would have lengthened his stride to leave the man behind, except that it wouldn't have been mannerly.

"No opinions whatever?" the teacher asked.

"No opinions," he answered, stiff-lipped.

"You're a remarkable person, Jamie, to have no opinions. But then, everyone on Brigport is just as remarkable. Every man on Brigport is ready at the drop of a hat to argue on Statehood, free trade, the habits of lobsters. But when it comes to the *Cynthia* and the *Annabelle*, not one man on this blessed speck of rock and forest has an idea to his name—with the exception of the Boyd brothers."

"Maybe you think it's real exciting for us, having two men die in one year off the Thrasher!" Jamie said angrily. "Well, I went to the burial of one, and it wasn't anything it'd pleasure me to do again."

"I'm sure of that, Jamie," the man answered in his easy voice. "I won't mention it again to you, if you like. There's something else, though."

Jamie gave him a suspicious glance and Mr. Thorne smiled with such honest amusement sparkling in his gray eyes that Jamie was caught off guard and grinned back.

"What is it, then?"

"When did you stop going to school?"

"Oh, four or five years ago. But I already know how to read and fig-ger. And my mother made me read my father's books, and borrow books from Mr. Whiting, so I wouldn't forget how to be easy with print."

"A woman of infinite wisdom. Her price is above rubies."

"In the winter I have time to read," Jamie added. "No other time."

"It's the winter I mean," said Mr. Thorne. "You said you could figure. Do you like mathematics?"

"As far as I went in 'em . . . or it, however you say it." He supposed these questions came natural to a schoolmaster, but surely Mr. Thorne was the most inquisitive man he'd ever known, schoolmaster or not.

"How would you like to learn more about mathematics, Jamie? And then go on to navigation?"

Jamie could hardly credit his ears. He stopped in the road, regardless of the bitter sweep of wind across Jonathan Gibson's fields, and stared into the man's face. "You don't teach navigation in school, do ye? And be-sides—" he reddened angrily—"I wouldn't go and sit in with all those young ones!"

"Of course not! I want you to come to me in the evenings. I'll teach you navigation, and everything about the wide world that my books could show, and—"

"What good would all that learning be to me?" Jamie broke in roughly. "What do I need of navigation and geography? I'll be handlining for codfish in these waters all my life. Who needs navigation and geogra-phy for that?"

"Learning is never lost," the man said. "I studied to go to sea, Jamie. I was born for it, I dreamed it and I lived it. And when I was about the same age you were when you left school, I fell sick with that fever that cripples where it doesn't kill. It killed my smallest brother and baby sister; it didn't touch the next brother; and I was left—not as you see me now— but in a much worse state . . . And so—" he shrugged—"was all my learning lost? In the long days of recovery, I'd got it clearly through my head that I'd never be able to go to sea—" he smiled without self-pity— "and that was a devilish hard lesson to learn, I can assure you. But here I am, Jamie, ready to pass on to you everything I know. I passed it on to my brother once, and I've passed it on to other boys who have sailed on the high seas in my place. Forgive the long oration, Jamie. It's all to prove my original premise that learning is never lost."

" 'Twould be lost on me," said Jamie, but not with contempt. The man's story had moved him, it was so much like his own. Both of them with their heads full of plans that were more than dreams, and then— disaster. He caught himself wriggling his strong toes in his boots, flexing sinewy fingers. At least all his limbs were sound . . . It had never occurred to him before that in some ways he had been lucky indeed. They were all lucky on Brigport; the island had rarely been visited by any of the terrible fevers.

He glanced quickly at Roger Thorne. Aye, the winter evenings were overlong, and they couldn't hold sociables and singing schools and prayer meeting every night in the week. Maybe one night, or even two, out of seven, wouldn't hurt him to prod up his brain a bit in the schoolmaster's kitchen.

"Well," he said deliberately, "I might try it."

Chapter 15

The *Nereid* made her maiden voyage, to Stonehaven to collect a supply of shooks from the cooper's shop. A shook was a bundle of staves, hoops, and heads; these assembled would make a hogshead or barrel. The parts of a wooden box, tied together flat, also constituted a shook. These things alone, if the boys had wanted to fill the hold with them, would have fetched them a pretty penny in the West Indies market. But the

Nereid's cargo was to be mixed; lumber, as many drums of dried fish as they could manage, beets, potatoes, and even a dozen wooden ploughshares patiently shaped by Reuben Boyd in his hours of solitude on South Island.

Just before the season's first blizzard, Captain Marriot and Pleasance returned. The captain promptly circulated copies of the new constitution; there were to be town meetings all over Maine early in December to vote on it, and if the weather kept the Brigporters from attending the meeting at Stonehaven, they might hold their own gathering, and the votes would be included in the Stonehaven tally.

"As if," Simon Pollinger scoffed, "our puny handful o' ayes and nays counted as much as a continental!"

"But they do count," Mr. Whiting reproved him. "Each one of those ayes and nays represents the sovereign right of an American to give his opinion."

"Aye, he can give it sure enough," Simon grunted, "but much good it may do him if nobody else agrees."

Everybody laughed. When the laughter had died down, Captain Marriot said, "The constitution will take the wind out of your sails, old Shiver-the-mizzen! It's a great document to launch us into the sea of Statehood. Even if a man doesn't own property, he may still vote if he's twenty-one. There's to be money raised for the common schools; complete religious freedom; lotteries are forbidden—" He sent a whimsical glance at several of the younger men who'd recently lost a pocketful of coins at a lottery in Limerock. "And there are to be laws to regulate the practice of physic and surgery."

Amanda slid among the men till she reached Captain Marriot at the fireplace, and Jamie edged nearer, curious to know what she might say. The captain was talking with Mr. Thorne, and she took a fold of his sleeve between her fingers and pulled a little. He glanced around, frowning, and then smiled. "Well, my poppet?"

"What's religious freedom about?"

"Well, you see, lass, we have no heavy weather of it here, with all of us signed on for the same church. But in some places, what with the Baptists and the Methodists, and the Church of England-goers that were all accused of treason during the war—" He broke off short. "Can you make it clear to the lass, Mr. Thorne?"

"But you've done it very well, sir," the schoolmaster said tactfully. "I'll just take her along the channel into the harbor, so to speak . . . This is what religious freedom is about, Amanda. It's about every man in this state, and all the states, who wants to worship God in his own way, to sing his own songs and say his own prayers, and call himself a Baptist or a Methodist, or an Episcopalian; or a Roman Catholic, or a Hebrew. Religious freedom is the right of all those men and women to worship in peace."

"Can't they do it now?" Amanda's black eyes were wide.

"In some places, I'm ashamed to say, a group has been attacked only because they are different. Always it's because they are different. And the tragedy of the human race is that it fears what it doesn't understand, and its first impulse is to destroy what it fears."

The talk had died down and there was hardly a sound in the store. The schoolmaster glanced around, and colored faintly. Amanda was even more embarrassed. "Thank you for telling me, Mr. Thorne." She ducked back behind the counter.

Jamie walked to the far end of the store, to the windows overlooking the harbor. The first thin swirls of snow were eddying wildly across the water, and the wind made a high thin wail past the panes. By nightfall the blizzard would be full-fledged. But Jamie was not thinking that winter was upon them; he was not even thinking with the familiar nudge of resentment that Mark and Hugh would soon be sailing for the West Indies. For once, something else had crowded it out. Listening to the men's words, something of the truth had glimmered before him like a brilliant sunny scene glimpsed through a break in the fog. Always before, he had shrugged off the talk of Statehood as something fit only for Captain Marriot to declaim about and for Simon Pollinger to grumble about at the fire in the store.

"What is it to me?" he had asked himself each time. But not today. Maybe there was something to declaim about. Maybe one day he would find out just what it was and how it concerned him. Maybe what Mr. Whiting called the "sovereign right of an American" was more than breath and voice making senseless words. He pulled his thoughtful gaze from the harbor and looked back the length of the store. How many of them there knew what it meant, what it gave you and what it asked of you? Voting was only one side of it, he knew that. It was all tied up with the War of '75 and the recent war that had taken his father; as an American you had many sovereign rights, and sometimes you had to fight for them, it seemed.

But wasn't that the way with anything you wanted hard enough so that it never let you rest? Whether you fought with shot and shell for the independence of your country, or with endless arguments for Statehood until at last the ayes won, or whether you fought with silence to keep the course you'd charted out for yourself—there was always a battle. Nothing ever came easy.

I could fight, he thought grimly. But what have I got to fight for? . . . At once the glimmering was gone. All that's left for me, he thought, is to hold my temper, to do by the young ones as near like my father as I can, and never show envy of any man or begrudge him his good fortune.

Yes, he had enough of a battle just to keep himself in line.

* * *

The *Nereid* left for the West Indies on a cold bright day with a fair northwest wind filling her sails. Obeying the tradition, nobody watched her out of sight. It was a quiet departure, with everyone behaving as if the boys had just set off for Stonehaven.

Pleasance caught up with Jamie as he left the wharf. Her blue cloak and hood turned her eyes as deep in color as the winter sea outside the harbor. "You haven't been to see me since the party for Owen," she reproached him. "Now winter's settling in, you must come often. Please, Jamie. We'll play backgammon, and roast apples, and talk—"

"I'll come," he said cheerfully enough. "I'll fetch Lark and Amanda along too."

He hadn't known her eyes could darken so, that she could look so tall. "Indeed!" she blazed at him. "You'll fetch Lark and Amanda, will you? I was inviting you, and if I want anyone else, I shall choose the person!"

She ran away from him, calling imperiously to her father, "Wait for me, Father! I want to walk home with you!"

Jamie was a little surprised that he could afford a secret chuckle. He'd expected to be so gloomy when the *Nereid* set sail that he'd have to spend the entire day in the woodlot working the megrims out of him. But he realized that he was relieved because the schooner had gone at last. The sight of her had been a constant goad to him.

At the town meeting, a week later, all who were entitled to vote voted aye on the constitution, after a certain amount of arguing on some of the fine points; for instance, a few of the older men thought it was rather extravagant to promise to raise forty dollars a year for the education of each pupil in the common schools.

"Did Thomas Jefferson advise that?" Thad Boyd inquired in a sarcastic manner, "or did William King devise that by himself? Whichever it is, they'd ought to remember we can't all be rich squires like they be."

Simon Pollinger, surprisingly, took the other tack. "Ain't it worth it," he demanded, "to know your grandsons won't be ignoramuses? 'Course, this comes too late to do Tim and Israel much good, but we'd ought to be thinking of what lays ahead."

This carried the school issue successfully. Then there was a brief flurry about the name of the new state. At the convention several names had been proposed, Columbus and Ligonia having the most imposing ring to them.

"What about Maine?" Rich Gibson demanded. "Sure, it's the name the Frenchies gave our coast, but we've used it all our lives and it's got a familiar taste to the tongue, like our own names."

"That's how most of us saw it at the conference," said Captain Marriot. "But we promised to present the other names to the voters."

"Maine!" somebody shouted, and the others took it up in a cry that filled the schoolhouse with a triumphant roar. For a moment Jamie's heart beat hard and fast in him, for it was like a battle cry surging against his ears.

In January the application would be made to the Congress to admit Maine as a state. The General Court of Massachusetts had already passed a ruling that on March fifteenth, 1820, the District of Maine would be severed once and for all from the Commonwealth of Massachusetts.

"There'll be no difficulty about Statehood," Captain Marriot assured the Brigport men. "The Congress has been expecting this for a long time; some of us have been talking tacks aboard on the subject since back in 1815, and we've been holding the course and running free ever since."

Chapter 16

It was a soft sunny morning, and Jamie worked steadily at the chopping block. This was a Saturday, and he had let Lark off for a few hours with Mr. Whiting. In the yard Sophia had all the coverlids strung on a line, and was whacking them soundly with a brush made of yellow-birch withes.

It was a January thaw, and the sounds of crows and chickadees in the woods, and of water dripping from the eaves, were exciting even to Jamie, who knew very well that the worst of the winter was yet to come. As he rested from chopping, he could gaze at the gulls wheeling above him and think it was April.

For five minutes, anyway, he thought dryly. Likely there'd be a blizzard before the week was out . . . The gate creaked loudly and he looked toward the road to see the schoolmaster limping down toward the path.

"How do, Mr. Thorne," Jamie called. Sophia left off beating her coverlids to stand stock-still like someone in a spell.

"Good morning, Jamie . . . Good morning down there, Sophia!" He lifted his hat to her and Sophia, too happy to answer, bobbed a curtsey and turned back to her birch broom.

Mr. Thorne leaned against the woodpile and crossed his hands over the head of his cane. As always, his linen was snowy white and the fit of his coat and trousers was perfect. "Jamie, when are you going to begin your lessons in navigation? Why not start tonight?"

Jamie split another piece of birch while his mind scrambled for an answer. He'd been daft ever to agree to such foolery. What did he need with mathematics and navigation? He had all he needed to get him to the Chimney Shoal. You didn't need master's papers nor the learning for 'em if you figured to go handlining for codfish from a wherry all your life.

Sophia had bundled the quilts into the house, and now she approached them, her upper lip pulled down very long and serious as it always was when she tried not to show how happy she was.

"Well, Sophia, and where are you bound?" asked Mr. Thorne.

"For a long walk with Betsey Gibson." Her dark eyes were adoring, the smile was breaking past the stiff upper lip.

"There's some fine surf to be seen off Southern Point, I should guess, with this southwest wind."

She shook her head hard. "We never go to Southern Point. Not for a hundred dollars."

"Why?" he asked seriously.

"Jamie can tell you. We heard this awful horrible noise from the old stone Frenchie house down there once, and—" she whitened, remembering it—"and then one day afterwards Tim Boyd met Betsey and Dickon and the twins and me in the road, and told us all about how the Frenchie who lived there once murdered his wife, and—"

"So you heard that, did ye?" Jamie broke in grimly. "He made sure of it, didn't he? I'd like to push his crazy yarns down his throat. Why didn't you tell me sooner?"

"You couldn't make it not be so, Jamie. And we just never go down to Southern Point anymore, so it's all right. Nothing can hurt us if we don't go near."

"Nothing can hurt you if you do go near!" Jamie's fury doubled itself, for until now his word had counted above all others with Sophia.

"And now it's even worse," she said in a hushed voice. "Did you know Izzy Boyd was down there one day this winter and he saw the sailor who was drowned off the Thrasher?" She swallowed, and her eyes moved around warily like an animal's. "He was walking up and down the beach—the seaman was—and the fishes had been at him, and there was rockweed growing on him!"

"The Boyds," said the schoolmaster, "have the most flourishing imaginations I've ever encountered. Sophia, if you've been having bad dreams about these things, from not telling them to Jamie or your mother, you deserve bad dreams."

"But I don't have bad dreams," she answered quickly, "I just know that if I never go near Southern Point again I'll be safe, so it doesn't frighten me. All of us know it. All the grown folks say there's no such thing as ghosts, so that's why we haven't told. But they'd just ought to hear what we heard on Southern Point."

The schoolmaster smiled and gently pinched her nose. "Perhaps you like having ghosts. It makes life exciting for you. It did for me, until I grew up."

"And now you don't believe in 'em," Sophia said resentfully.

"On the contrary. I'm sure of at least one ghost. But it doesn't make life exciting, only sad."

A little frown appeared between her delicate dark brows, and as her lips parted for another question Jamie said curtly, "Get along on your walk."

After she had gone through the gate, Thorne turned to Jamie. "The Boyds are bound to have influence in one way or another, I see. Perhaps they've discovered a gold mine on Southern Point." He laughed, and Jamie grinned in spite of himself.

"A gold mine, to be sure. It's a great place for flotsam, timber from lumber vessels that have broken up outside somewhere, hogsheads—oh, there's a mort of things drifts in and the Boyds reckon to claim it all."

"Well, Sophia doesn't seem to be suffering from a superabundance of ghoulies and ghosties, and none of my other scholars are looking pale and haunted these days, so I shan't fret on their account." He dropped his hand on Jamie's shoulder, forcing Jamie to look directly at him. "I'll expect you tonight. You won't be sorry, I promise."

When Jamie told his mother, she was pleased. "It always grieved me that you had to leave school so early, Jamie," she told him.

"Yes, but—"

"You must go," she said firmly. "He wants to repay you for what you did for him, the night of the serenade. You must give him that privilege, at least."

When she put it like that, there was no argument. He left as soon as supper was over. But first he went all the way to Ned's place to see if the old man was well. He hadn't been to see him for over a week. The house was tidy and so was Ned himself, with clothing clean and patched, his white head trimmed of its shagginess. He sat at one side of his hearth smoking a churchwarden pipe, and Simon Pollinger sat at the other side, and both of them beamed on Jamie.

"Set, boy," Ned ordered him.

"I can't tarry this time. Just walked around to see how you were faring."

Simon Pollinger's laugh rumbled in his chest. "Ask how the District's faring, why don't ye?"

Jamie stopped with his hand on the latch. "What of the District, then?"

"News come today. They've gone and made old Maine fast to Missouri so we sink or swim together. Jem Marriot, he's fit to go to Washington and flatten 'em all out with a belaying pin." He shook with deep-chested laughter, while Ned stared absently at the fire. "Never saw a man take on so!"

"But what's Missouri got to do with it?" Jamie demanded in honest bewilderment. Missouri was a place, a territory, and a river. But otherwise it could have been as far away as India.

Simon forgot Captain Marriot's rage, and became abruptly severe. "Missouri's slave, you see, lad? Them Missourians, they keep slaves—like Ned here was a slave to the Barbary pirates. Oh, mebbe they ain't so savage, but slavery's slavery, wherever you put it. And Maine—why we'd be a free state. So the slave states, they'd be outnumbered in the Congress by the free states, and they don't hold with that one bit. So some gang of pirates up there, they triced us up to Missouri, and if they don't get into the Union, neither do we." He launched his great frame out of his chair. "I'm blast if it's comic, now that I think on it. I ain't been in favor of changing our situation any, but now that we're underway, and there's a prodigious lot of good men supporting it, and we been proceeding under full press of sail—well, it works the old iron up in me to see us free Maine men lashed tight to a crew of slave-owners!"

Jamie knew very little about the slave states; he knew only that he could not imagine owning another person as one owned a cow or a horse, and he could not imagine being owned. It was all very bewildering. What had a far-off place called Missouri to do with his Maine?

"I thought it was to be simple," he said slowly. "The people want Statehood, Massachusetts agrees, the Constitution's been written and accepted, the General Court cut us free of the Commonwealth—"

"Aye," roared Simon. "On March fifteenth of this year that act goes into effect, cutting us free—for what? If the District isn't a State by then, we'll be nothing more than a territory!" He ground the word out with terrible scorn. "The territory of Maine. How does that sound? Where's the proud ring of that? Why, it'll sound as if we was still dwelling in blockhouses and holding off the Injuns!"

Ned grimaced around his black patch. "It's a rare treat to see you thus. Mostly it's me that raves and the rest that laughs."

"Laugh at me, will ye? If you still had your tarry pigtail I'd hang ye by it from the rafters!"

"Nay, I'm not laughing," Ned assured him. "But you're blowing up a powerful gale over naught. It's other matters I got roiling and boiling in my brain." He squinted his good eye horribly and dropped his voice to a hoarse whisper. "Other matters o' more concern to this island."

It seemed to Jamie that Ned was staring at him with a peculiar intensity.

"What's so important?" Simon was demanding skeptically, but Ned kept staring at Jamie.

"It'll keep," he answered in that hoarse whisper. "Anything'll keep in this cold weather. When it starts to stink, then you'll find it out for yourself, Cap'n." He burst out laughing. Simon sat down with an angry grunt and kicked a burning stick back into the fire.

As Jamie left, Ned called after him, "Come aboard soon again, lad!"

"Aye," Jamie called back. Now what was bumbling about in Ned's noggin, he wondered, as he tramped back along the road. Likely it didn't amount to hand or cook, but it was important to Ned and so Jamie would go back when he had time, and listen—if the old man remembered.

In Roger Thorne's lamplit kitchen, he spoke of the Missouri business, and the schoolmaster's thin face turned somber. "I fear the Union must always be divided on slavery. The issue will grow bigger and more terrifying year by year, until—" He shrugged, and Jamie leaned toward him eagerly.

"Until what?"

"Until one faction tries to impose its will on the other. By force, if needs be. It may come in our time, Jamie. You've heard Simon tonight; well, I have heard men speak who are a hundred times more concerned with slavery than Simon Pollinger is—whose lives are dedicated to wiping it out. They burn with a constant fire. And I've known slave-owners too!"

"In Missouri?" Jamie demanded.

Roger Thorne smiled. "You needn't travel to Missouri to see slaves. I've seen them in New York. Some owners are charitable, kindly men with a genuine concern for their people. They protect them from the cradle to the grave. On the other hand—" He had been thoughtful, but now he became austere and cold. "On the other hand, I've attended an auction where slaves were being bought and sold. And that's why I know that someday the issue must be faced." With a complete change of attitude he opened the book on the table before him. " 'The New American Practical Navigator, by Nathaniel Bowditch,' " he read aloud. "Thus we commence the study of navigation."

Chapter 17

The lessons went well. At first, Jamie felt stupid as a gooney bird; it was hard to get back into the way of studying sums again. But after a week or so he had the knack of it. He studied by the fire at home and was astonished how little he heeded the young ones' racket, and how fast an hour went by. More and more he looked forward to the evenings spent in Roger Thorne's kitchen, sitting across the trestle table from the schoolmaster. There were apples in a bowl nearby, and the hiss of boiling water in the iron kettle over the fire. When the lessons were over, Mr. Thorne brewed tea and sometimes coffee, which was a rare treat. Almost always there was something good to eat; many women on the island had taken it upon themselves to keep the schoolmaster supplied with fresh loaves and buns and pastries.

During the lesson time, Mr. Thorne was all business; a teacher who made himself understood in the clearest and most simple of terms, who knew exactly how to stir Jamie's mind to reach out and question of its own eager will. Often at the end of a session Jamie felt as if he had been on a long and exciting voyage. After the lessons, when they stretched their feet to the fire and ate and drank, Mr. Thorne ceased to be a teacher and was a friend to whom Jamie talked as he talked to no one else.

He had too much instinctive reserve to chatter on and on like a giddy girl, but one night he told Mr. Thorne what he never thought to tell aloud to anyone, the story of the time when his father did not come home. In return, Mr. Thorne told him of his brother's death; a shipmaster, he had been drowned when his ship foundered on a reef.

"It wasn't a long jaunt or very important, if one compares coasting to the China trade," he said. "But it was his first ship, and he dreamed of longer voyages to South America and the Orient in the years to come." After a brief silence he added, "He was your cousin's age—nineteen."

* * *

One day when Jamie was cutting birch in the woodlot, thinking pleasantly upon the evening before him, he smiled to remember Ned's description of the teacher's ministrations, and then was overwhelmed with guilt. Why, 'twas over two weeks since he'd been down to Ned's place, and he'd promised to go back, but it had gone clean out of his head when the *New American Practical Navigator* came in.

Lor, he thought unhappily, I was glad enough to go to Ned's when I'd nowhere else.

At home he begged a fresh loaf from his mother and filled a small basket with mince-meat tarts from a fat crock in the buttery, and set off for Ned's. It was a savagely cold day, bright as crystal. The frozen ground rang under his boots, and his nostrils and throat stung with the icy air.

Half-fearing to find Ned sick or helplessly lame, he was pleased to discover him hobbling about his yard. At sight of Jamie the pigeons took wing in a great rush, wheeled overhead and returned to earth; they knew him well.

"A-ha!" Ned drove his axe into the chopping block. "So it's you!"

Jamie held out the basket silently, smiling all the while until Ned's horrible scowl should give way. Finally the man hit him lightly on the shoulder. "Oh, you're the little gentleman passenger, you are. Tripping down here so genteel-like with your basket on your arm!" His dark leathery face split into an answering grin. "Stow it in the galley, lad. We've an errand to do."

Coming out of the house, Jamie found Ned already on the path to Southern Point, and in no mood for explanations. They walked on through the winter-hushed woods. Once a white owl swooped soundlessly across the path before them and disappeared among the shadowy trunks of tall motionless spruces.

When they emerged from the woods at Southern Point, South Island lay across the water from them, its spruces a smoky blue in the afternoon sun, its dead fields golden-yellow.

"Well—" He turned questioningly to Ned, but the old man was stumping down the slope toward the walls of the roofless stone house. Jamie hurried after him. With an air of knowing exactly what he was doing, Ned pushed through an alder thicket to an opening that had been the door. With wondrous agility, considering his lameness, he scrambled down over a tumble of rocks till he reached solid ground, then stood gazing triumphantly up at Jamie.

"Deep cellar holes them Frenchies dug for themselves," he remarked. He was panting only slightly.

Jamie laughed. "What you figgering to find, Ned? The ghost of that one who did in his wife? Or her ghost, mebbe."

"Take heed of what the Book says about the laughter of fools," said Ned severely, "and git down here. Look alive, now."

Jamie obeyed. There wasn't much room in the cellar hole; rocks from the walls had fallen in all around. But there was room for him to stand by Ned and look expectantly at the old man. Ned was fiercely alert, his good eye darted and glittered.

"Now!" he said in a low intense voice. "Dig where I tell ye to dig, and be quick about it." He pointed to a rough haphazard pile of rocks below a wall which was almost intact. "Git on with it—use your hands, they ain't so precious as what you'll find."

All at once Jamie was no longer amused. His heart began to pound heavily, and the chill in his fingers and toes was forgotten before the sudden warming rush of anticipation. He began to pull at the boulders with all his strength. Some were as big as cabbages, others the size of water-buckets; and he did not have many of these to roll aside before Ned's breathing grew hoarse and there was a weird prickling along his own scalp.

Freed of the rocks piled so artfully around it, a scarred old sea chest was revealed to them. Jamie stood back, blowing on his cold fingers.

"There!" Ned said in triumph. "There!"

Instinctively Jamie hushed his voice. "Whose is it?"

For answer, Ned only grimaced. He crouched before the chest, pried at the lid. "Locked, blast 'em!" he hissed. But 'twan't locked the other day, and I can tell ye everything that's in it, if you'll take old Ned's word for it!" He sat back on his heels and peered around at Jamie, who nodded.

He was almost too excited to speak; strange fantasies of pirate gold and murdered men rattled through his head.

"Well, then." Ned laid his hard hand on the chest and drummed his fingers against the wood. "There's a jug in it, lad. A jug o' whale oil. And there's a bigger lantern than what a man uses to go out to the tie-up on a winter's night. A stout lantern to give a strong clear light out across the water."

He stopped, watching Jamie. "A strong clear light across the water," Jamie repeated slowly. "And Tim and Izzy spreading their ghost tales far and wide." Yes, it was exciting, but not in a pleasant way. He knelt by the chest and pried at the lid as Ned had done, knowing it wouldn't open but compelled to try it anyway. "Tim could have been hiding down here that day we were picking blueberries," he murmured. "He must have made the noises to scare Sophia and Betsey."

He settled back on his heels and let out his breath in a long sigh. "I laid it to them. That's the queer part of it. I laid it to them, but I never figgered it was done a-purpose. I thought they were down here stravaging for stuff to come ashore, and were scairt to say so afterwards, so they put it at your door."

"Aye, old crazy Ned, we'd ought to stow him away in irons, safe in the lazareet. I know, lad."

"When did you find out about this?" Jamie touched the chest.

"Oh, I'd had me suspicions for a long spell, but 'twasn't till after the *Annabelle* come ashore that I found the chest. When I lost the wind out of my sails in your uncle's kitchen that night, giving the alarm, your little cousins they got to fretting lest the ghosties in the stone house harm their father. Your aunt was hard put to calm 'em—they was full of murders and knives and corpse-candles, and one of 'em let Izzy Boyd's name slip. So when I knew they was out to their fishing the next fair day, I up kellick and ran for pirate waters, as ye might say. And found this. The gorms had been that hawsed up about all their molasses and coffee, they'd left it unlocked."

"The murderers!" Jamie ground it out between his teeth. "Well, there'll be an end to it now! Do they hang wreckers, I wonder?" He turned to scramble up over the rocks toward the opening in the wall, but Ned caught hold of his ankle and held him fast.

"Where ye bound?"

"Why, to get someone—Cap'n Marriot, my uncle, and all—and show 'em this."

Ned screwed up his face. "What can ye prove? There's nary a mark here to show that ever a Boyd laid a finger to this gear. It could've been old Ned—it could've been young Jamie—"

"Then how are we to stop them from doing it again?" Jamie cried. He wanted instant and furious action. "I know! I'll come down here every night and watch. I can do that easy enough. I can snug down amongst those young spruces at the edge of the woods, and there'll be no chance of 'em swinging their lantern without me to know it, and I'll—"

"Ye'll what? Come down on 'em like a man o' war and knock the lantern out o' their hands?" Ned jeered, and Jamie felt very young and idiotic and helpless. "Why, 'twould take 'em only a second to knock you side of the head and heave you over the side and let the breakers finish you off. Nay, Jamie—" he held the boy's arm in an unbreakable grip, forcing Jamie to stare into his one brilliant eye. "It's witnesses ye need, to catch the scoundrels in the act. And don't count on me, for there's only one or two would believe old crazy Ned. Now. Let's up kellick and put for home before one of the bully boys takes it into his thick head to cruise down here."

They walked back through the woods in silence. Wreckers on Brigport! Oh, Jamie had heard of them in other places, but Brigporters considered themselves a lawful people. What would this do to the name of Brigport up and down the coast of Maine? And to the name of Maine herself? Not that he cared a Continental whether Maine was state or district or territory; his own troubles and yearnings were what mattered the most to him. But still, a man had pride in his homeland whether he wanted it or not; it was a part of a man, like blood and bones and muscles, and his skill with axe or sail.

Two ships broken on the Thrasher, two men dead; one in the church-yard, the other, only the good Lord knew . . . He shuddered with cold and something else, and the rage in him gave way to a great desolation. He knew about the wreckers, and so did Ned; but how could these two, a boy and a broken old man, keep a third ship off the Thrasher?

* * *

At home he was moody, and short-tempered with the twins. Lark's whistling and singing, constant now that it was not forbidden, tormented him intolerably. He was impatient with Sophia's adoring and worried gaze. Once his mother cornered him.

"What ails you, Jamie? Is the winter over-long?"

"Aye, that's it," he said too hastily. "I'll be glad to have a boat under my feet again." And he went out of the house before she could say more.

In the store the men talked of nothing but the Maine-Missouri bill, and he listened, wanting to tell them what lay under their noses, but not knowing how; Old Ned was right, you must have proof, you must not start what you could not finish. And he gave Tim and Israel Boyd a wide berth, lest one mocking word from them should cause him to fling the wretched truth in their faces.

It was hard to put his mind on his lessons these days, and several times he was on the verge of confiding in Roger Thorne. But each time he stopped himself, and only shook his head when the schoolmaster asked him if he was tiring of his studies.

A week had gone by and he was no closer to the solution of the problem. The island still talked excitedly about Maine and Missouri. Pleasance, meeting Jamie in the road, was happily agitated.

"Papa thinks we may have to go to Washington and give Henry Clay and the rest a piece of his mind," she said. "I'm sure they'd listen to him. They'd think he was Old Stormalong." She giggled, then lifted her pretty eyebrows when Jamie didn't smile.

Still he said nothing and she put up her chin and hurried ahead of him down the wharf. It was a mild windy morning, pleasantly suggesting spring, though March was still a week away. The gulls were circling and crying over the harbor as they hadn't done all winter. The *Minerva* was due from Limerock and Stonehaven, and almost everyone was out to greet her.

As he reached the wharf Amanda caught up with him, her cloak blowing, her black hair whipping free in the wind. "Look at the surf out there!" she cried. "Look where it piles on the harbor ledges and blows high as a whole school of whales! And the water's just the color of April!" So it was, a pale billowing blue one moment, and gull-gray the next as a cloud mass blew past the sun. Spring, Jamie thought desperately. More and more vessels passing by, and the Boyds out there with their blasted lantern.

"Let's take Father's yawlboat and go rowing, Jamie," Amanda was teasing him. "I'll run away from the store for once. It'll be so wonderful wild even inside the harbor. The gulls are driving me fair crazy with their hollering!"

The *Minerva* was at the end of the wharf and already the hoist was creaking as the freight rose from hold to wharf. Mr. Whiting and Mr. Thorne stood in conversation a little distance away from the crowd. Thad

Boyd was waving his arms as he argued with Simon Pollinger. He'll wave his arms some wild, Jamie thought, when he knows what his ewe lambs have been up to.

The ewe lambs were not in sight this morning. They'd be down combing the shores of Southern Point to see what the gale had washed in.

Amanda, still running on like a flood tide, pulled his arm and said sharply, "Jamie! Aren't your wits about you? I said, Look at your uncle Nathan. He's had a letter this morning, and whatever was in it, it's made him sick." Suddenly she faltered and put her fingers against her lips. "Oh, Jamie, d'you reckon that Owen—"

His uncle's strong dark face had become strange, as if it had been suddenly frozen into stone. He stood with the letter flapping from his fingers, staring off across the harbor to the surf-smothered ledges. And a picture of Owen rushed into Jamie's mind; Owen facing him in Captain Marriot's hall, handsome and dark as a gypsy above the white stock. How he had laughed, as sure of his luck as any man had ever been since the world began!

Instinctively, Jamie took a step toward his uncle. He didn't know what he was going to do or say, but he kept on walking. When he was halfway, he knew all at once that nothing had happened to Owen; for his uncle's eyes turned toward David Owen, Morgan's father, and then, slowly, to Malcolm and Dougal Erskine, Hughie's father and grandfather.

Jamie could go no farther. He did not want to hear what he already knew. He knew, as clearly as if the words had been shouted to him above the creak of the hoist and the surf on the ledges, that the schooner *Nereid* had met with a disaster.

But there is no way of escaping these things, and within an hour everyone knew. Nothing so vast and so terrible had ever happened to the island before. Oh, Brigport men had been drowned, Brigport men had been killed in battle, Charles Bennett had been taken by a British press-gang. But to lose three lads in one fell swoop—it was almost too much to take in. To lose any one of them would have been woe enough. A pall of grief settled over the island like fog.

In the late afternoon Jamie and his mother walked to his uncle's house. They read the letter, sitting in the kitchen. It was from Owen, written in Montevideo a month ago, and sent north by a homecoming vessel. "The *Phoebe Dart* of Kennebunkport is lying alongside of us in this anchorage," he wrote. "Her captain came aboard for supper with me, and told me of seeing a small schooner, fifteen tons burden, attacked by pirates almost in sight of Morro Castle in Havana . . . The *Phoebe Dart* came down upon them and the pirates sailed off, but the three men aboard had been most savagely—" here Owen's pen had dug into the paper, crossed out words, and then begun again—"murdered. I had such a premonition I could hardly bring myself to ask the schooner's name. Indeed, I said it with him. . . . The *Nereid*. Father, Mother, if it's any comfort to you, they were buried decently at sea, and Captain MacLeod of the *Phoebe Dart* read the burial service over them. I cannot write more now. I send this to you by the *Andromeda*, her home port is Limerock."

It had happened more than a month ago.

Chapter 18

That night Jamie went to the schoolmaster's house. He was tired of walking the shores with only his thoughts for company. There was not an inch of the island that he had not covered with his friends in the years of their growing up; there was nowhere for him to walk without thinking of them.

The stars were smurry overhead and the rote from Southern Point made a long low thunder in the night, telling of a heavy swell from off-shore.

He was halfway when Lark caught up with him. "Let me go with you, Jamie," he begged. "Mr. Thorne won't mind. I'll take a book and set in the chimney corner."

"Well—"

"It's awful hard to set my mind to anything, Jamie. I keep thinking about it all, and how I asked 'em if I could go . . . And how it would've been if you had gone." His teeth were chattering, but Jamie guessed it was not from cold.

"Come along, then," he said brusquely. They walked on without speaking. At the place where the harbor road branched off, someone hailed them bravely through the dark. It was Amanda.

"What are you doing out?" Jamie asked her severely.

"What is there to harm me?" She said it pertly enough, but there was something lacking. "There's no Indians, nor bears and Lucy-vees like on the mainland, and all the Frenchie ghosts are at Southern Point shut up in their old stone house."

But while she was saying it she moved in between the two boys and took their arms tightly. "I was out walking, that's all. I couldn't bear the house." She tilted back her head, and said with longing, "It's cold but it smells a mite like spring, doesn't it? Oh, Lor, I wish 'twere April instead of February! To think of all the blizzards and the miserable cold winds between now and when the birds come again!"

Roger Thorne was not surprised to see three instead of one. He made them welcome in the warm lamplit room, and passed them apples and sweets. He had a favorite book, he said, which was too good to be read alone, in silence. Would they like to hear how it began?

The book was *Gulliver's Travels*, and a droll strange tale that took Jamie's attention in spite of himself. When the knock sounded on the door, startling them all, he felt as if he had been away for a long time, but by the striking of the clock, it had been less than an hour. Roger Thorne went to the door, while the others, stretching and blinking like dreamers awakened, waited for the interruption to be over with.

"I'd be proper grateful," said Ned Converse's hoarse voice, "if I could speak to yonder Jamie."

"Why, surely," Thorne answered courteously. "Come in, Ned."

"No, no, thankee, I could talk better to the boy outside."

Jamie awoke fully from his spell and sprang up. He climbed over Lark's and Amanda's feet, ignoring their loud whispers of astonishment. "Here I am, Ned," he called. "I'm on my way." He went out past the schoolmaster, and Ned gripped his arm.

"Come 'round the corner, lad," he whispered, "away from the door." He led Jamie into the dark passage between school and dwelling. "Them devils," he hissed. "Them devils be down on Southern Point now. And it's a sweet night for a wreck, with those seas piling onto the Thrasher!"

"They're pirates," Jamie said between his teeth. "They're no better than the pirates that killed Mark and Hughie and Morgan." His fury was enormous; he felt as if he had grown eight feet tall with it, and strong as Samson. "Well, here's the time to knock that cussed lantern galley west!"

He pulled his arm free of Ned's grip, but the old man caught at his sleeve. "You can't do nothing, boy! You git to the harbor and rouse out Cap'n Marriot and the rest! That's what you can do!"

"You go for Cap'n Marriot," Jamie said. His rage extended to everything in his way, even Ned. "If I can't do any better than butt my head into a Boyd belly like a cannon ball, I'll knock that lantern out of their hands before a ship sees it!"

With a desperate sweep of his arm, he pushed the old man away from him, heard him grunt and stumble; but he had no time for remorse. He broke into a long fast lope.

Where the road entered the woods, he stopped for a moment to catch his wind. After the beating in his ears had died down a little he heard, like an echo of himself, the sound of running feet along the frozen ground the way he had come. Not old Ned, he thought grimly. These feet were too light and swift . . . Did the Boyds have a helper, then? Someone he hadn't guessed? He stepped out into the road, setting his feet wide apart and his hands on his hips, and called, "Who goes there?"

His voice echoed from the woods behind him. There was a gasp, the footsteps slowed on the hard ground, and Lark's voice plunged breathlessly toward him. "Jamie, it's me. I slipped out behind you—Mr. Thorne said 'twasn't manners, but I was anxious-like, not knowing what Ned wanted of you—" He was close to Jamie now, taking long gulps of air. "So I heard what you said. It's wreckers, isn't it? Those ships on the Thrasher 'twasn't accident, was it?"

"It's wreckers all right," Jamie said briefly. "Tim and Israel. Now you git back and turn everybody out."

"Ned can do that. I'm with you. I'm tough as blackthorn, Jamie, and I'm fast on my feet, and if I come at old Izzy from out of the dark sudden-like I can knock the wind out of him."

There was no time to argue. If Lark had his mind made up he'd cling like a barnacle. And he might be of some use; you never could tell.

"Just one thing." He ground the words out hard. "They'd just as lief kill us as not, and nobody could prove it was a-purpose. So watch out. You understand?"

"Aye!" Lark, sprinting away from him into the woods, flung the word back. There was nothing to do but run with him.

When the woods began to thin, and the wind blew strongly through the heavy spruce boughs with a sound like rushing water, they slowed to a walk. They could hear nothing but the low roar of the rote and an occasional thunderous booming as a high sea hit the Thrasher. They walked cautiously to the edge of the woods. At first there was only the blackness before them, until a strong steady light moved into their vision, from the direction of the stone house.

"There they are," Jamie said in a low voice. Now that the moment had come, he was very calm; he felt neither rage nor fear, but a clear-headed resolution to blow that lantern out. He moved quietly forward along the narrow path. Whether both brothers were there, or one of them busy in the cellar hole or down on the shore below, he would find out when he approached the range of the lantern light.

"How will we fox 'em, Jamie?" Lark whispered.

"We've got to put that lantern out. I'd hoped to come down on them in a surprise attack, and git away in the dark before they know what struck 'em. It'd be easy enough if there's only one."

They left the path and took a direct course toward the lantern, keeping well in the shelter of bay clumps and alder growth. The lantern, unmoving now, burned yellow and bright before them. If only no vessel had yet seen it!

At last they could see it clearly. They lay on their stomachs, peering over a rim of granite ledge into the wide circle of radiance. The lantern was mounted on a stump at the edge of the bank, perhaps a hundred yards away.

"That's easy enough," Lark whispered exultantly. "Make a run for it, heave it over the side to the sea below, and—"

Jamie didn't answer. He was watching for signs of life at the far edge of the lantern's reach. Where were the Boyd brothers? Down on the sandbeach, or huddled out of the wind in the stone house, waiting for what the night would bring? One wild dash across the field to the stump, and that would be all. Better to fetch the lantern back with him, and make sure it was out, than to throw it over the bank. Spilled whale-oil, afire on water or land, would mean a light still showed after all.

"What are we waiting for?" Lark whispered. "I can be there and back before you breathe twice!"

"No," said Jamie. He still wasn't sure. The night was full of noisy movement of wind and water; the Boyd brothers could be ranging all about here. "You lie flat. If they come for me, you run. You hear me? Don't let 'em git their hands on you. You're quick and more'n a match for them playing hide-and-seek on Southern Point in the dark."

"But what if they catch you?"

"I don't reckon to let 'em," said Jamie. "Listen, we have to depend on ourselves because there's nobody to help us. Even if Ned turns 'em out in the village, they'll be long enough getting here, because Ned was about dead-beat when he reached the schoolhouse. So we're alone in this, Lark. And we have to attack fast, and run fast. And maybe we can save a vessel."

Lark didn't answer. But in the darkness behind the ledge, his hand felt for his brother's and gripped it hard. Then Jamie crawled like an Indian over the face of the ledge, and crept until the way appeared flat and open before him, though it was hard to tell perfectly with the lantern gleam so bright in his eyes. He broke into a run then, with the wind roaring past his ears, his gaze fixed desperately on the lantern.

He went plunging on until he reached it, burning his hands on the hot chimney. Down below him the big seas crashed on the Thrasher; he couldn't see the white tumble of their foam, he could see nothing but the hot glare of the lantern. He didn't dare stop to put it out; once in the shelter of the ledge where Lark waited, he'd blow it out and then he'd run for the woods, he and Lark, and lose themselves like the ghosts of the Indians.

The lantern smoked and the acrid fumes stung his eyes. But the ledge must be very near now and in another moment he'd fall over it, and Lark would catch the lantern—

He ran head first into what seemed to be a solid wall. In the same instant he realized it was one of the Boyds. He felt a horrible, outraged surprise. He swung the lantern back, ready to smash it into the enemy's face, but it was wrenched out of his hand. He was caught and held savagely secure by the back of his jacket.

"If I was a kindly man," Tim Boyd growled at him, "I'd give ye time to say your prayers. But I'm in no temper to be kindly tonight! Izzy!" he howled into the wind. "Come get this beacon and set it back where it belongs!"

The last word was somewhat strangled, for all at once he was attacked from behind by a wiry tangle of arms and legs. Lark had disobeyed Jamie and joined the fight. He had jumped for Tim's shoulders, his arms squeezed hard across Tim's windpipe, his legs wrapped around Tim's middle. Tim let go of Jamie and the lantern simultaneously, to claw away from the strangling arms.

Jamie dropped to his knees beside the lantern. In another instant it would be out.

A foot caught him savagely in the side, rolling him away; Israel's face was grotesque as a carven turnip in the light as he caught up the lantern. Tim freed himself of Lark with a vast effort, threw the boy to the ground, and held him there with a heavy foot pressing brutally on Lark's chest. In that frightening instant when they were so cruelly defeated, Jamie was proud of Lark, who made not a sound.

"We've caught two for one, Izzy," Tim said jubilantly. "A-sneaking and a-spying, they was, to say nothing of stealing our property . . . You better hyper across to the bank and put the lantern where it'll show all fair and pretty. Then we'll decide what to do with these conniving critters."

Jamie lifted himself on one elbow. "Whatever you do to us, the whole island will know it was you who did it. They've got the alarm by now. They are on the way."

"On the way to find what?" Tim laughed uproariously. "Why, we'll say we caught the Widow Bennett's two precious boys—a-wrecking—or hoping to—and when we tried to stop 'em, they fought like lions from Africky, and then run off in the wrong direction. Right—plumb—over-board!" He fetched a long sigh. " 'Twill break the widow's heart, poor woman, to know what criminals was her sons!"

"Mebbe we oughtn't to do 'em in," Izzy was doubtful. "Might be they'd take heed of this, and keep to home nights."

"And tell everyone what they think they saw down here, and keep yammering till even Paw would be all for setting a patrol around the shores, just to stop the gossip! And then where'd we be? . . . Get that lantern back to the stump, Izzy, and look alive about it."

Jamie wished he could reach Lark's hand. Was this how Hughie and Mark and Morgan felt when they knew at last they were to die? Or had-n't they any time to realize it? Maybe it had come more suddenly to them . . . He wasn't afraid, exactly; there was no room for fear when you were face to face with something so enormous. You were just so filled with wonder, trying to take it all in . . . Aloud he said, "Neither Mother nor anybody else will believe we done wrong, Lark."

"I know," said Lark. But the words were lost in the explosion that knocked the lantern to pieces in Izzy's hands with a clatter of glass and a hiss of flame and a stench of smoking whale oil.

Izzy yelped like a scared dog and Tim cursed as the dark settled about them.

"We have more pistols here." The voice came from the direction of the stone house; a calm, civilized, precise voice with an elegant accent. "They're all cocked and primed. Release the boys at once."

"It's the schoolmaster!" Tim found his voice and laughed loudly. But there was a shakiness in his laughter. "Well, well! A fancy shot! And tell me how you can see to pick us off, now that you've put out our light?"

"There'll be light enough soon. Look behind you."

Tim whirled, and Izzy lumbered about like an angry bear. Where he had flung the lamp when the chimney shattered, oil had spilled out on the dry turf and ignited from the wick; while they watched, a thin orange line of flame crept along and reached a clump of running juniper, where it blazed up in a splendid torch. Jamie thought he had never seen any-thing so beautiful. No vessel would see it and take it for a mark, because it was a moving flame and a lantern gave a steady star-like glow.

"We can pick you off with the greatest of ease, you see," the school-master went on. "We've been watching and listening for quite some time, and our tempers are in a very uncertain state. Send the boys to us at once, if you please."

As if in a daze, Tim took his foot from Lark's chest. The boys got up and walked stiffly away from the light of the blazing bushes, not looking at each other, not looking back, just staring ahead into the darkness from whence Roger Thorne's voice had come.

"Jamie!" It was Amanda, grabbing him hard around the middle, and out of sheer amazement he hugged her back.

"Steady on," the schoolmaster commanded softly. "Get behind me. They'll be suspicious in a moment." He stood with his back to the wall of the stone house. The fast-dying light from the juniper bush flickered on his face, and shone on the pistols in either hand.

"Where are the others?" Lark whispered. "In the cellar hole?"

"There's no one else." The schoolmaster laughed.

Tim bellowed across the intervening space. "If there's a crew with you, why don't they sing out? Let Cap'n Marriot give a hail!"

"He'll hold no parley with you," Thorne called back.

"What about Rich Gibson? Jonny Gibson? Peter Pollinger? Nathan Bennett?" Tim hurled the names like popple rocks.

"They don't need to talk," the schoolmaster called back. "There's no room for argument! They've seen and heard enough." He spoke softly to the others. "They're not fooled now. Jamie, you and Lark and Amanda melt off into the woods. They're desperate enough to charge blindly in this direction, and if there are four of us here, their chances of laying hands on one or two of us will be too good."

"We don't go without you," Jamie said grimly.

"Don't be an idiot," the schoolmaster chaffed him. "With this leg I'd drag on you like a sea anchor. I'll keep my back to this solid wall and the pistols cocked—I have three shots left—until the reinforcements arrive." He chuckled. "A fine lot to round up a crew of wreckers! A lame old sailor, a lame schoolmaster, two boys and a girl—and all the able-bodied men of the village no doubt snug at their firesides."

Jamie caught at the words lame old sailor. "Where's Ned?"

"He told us about the Boyds and set off for Cap'n Marriot," Amanda said. "But whether he got there or not with his wind so short—he was wheezing like a rising gale—and his rheumatics so bad—that's another story."

"Now then," Roger Thorne said decisively, "cut and run for it, the three of you. Don't head for the path. Tim's no fool, no doubt he sent Israel far out around us to guard the path the instant the juniper burned out so we couldn't see the two of them distinctly."

Jamie didn't move. "You can't see to shoot in the dark."

"I'll wait till they close in. Will you go?" The man's voice was soft but cutting.

"If Cap'n Marriot is there," Tim bawled at much closer range, "let him sing out."

The four against the stone wall froze into motionless silence. We've pully-hauled too long, Jamie thought. We'd ought to have gone when he first told us to, save that we wouldn't go without him. And now here's Tim creeping up on us bit by bit, and only the Lord knows where Izzy is . . .

"Sing out, Cap'n Marriot!" Tim yelled again, and then burst into mocking laughter.

"I'll sing out, Timothy Boyd!" The voice rolled across the fields with a magnificent note of authority that sent chills up Jamie's spine; for it was Captain Marriot's voice, sounding out from the bank where the footpath wound up steeply from the sand beach below. Suddenly there were dim lanterns bobbing like fireflies along the edge of the bank and across the field; Captain Marriot was not alone.

"Ned reached him," Amanda breathed in awe. "Spite of rheumatism and no wind, he got there."

"They must have come around from the harbor by boat," said Jamie. "Listen." And below the rising clamor of furious voices they heard the thud of Tim's feet, running away into the darkness.

Jamie stopped off at the schoolmaster's house before he went home. He had sent Lark along; Amanda had gone home with her father.

He stood before the fire, watching Roger Thorne clean his pistols and put them away in the velvet-lined case. Except for a certain pallor of fatigue, the schoolmaster wore much the same peaceful expression he wore when he opened a volume of higher mathematics or the American Practical Navigator. The pistols might have served simply as ornaments; if Jamie had not stood with him back against the stone house, he would have found it hard to believe the man had ever shot a lantern out of Izzy Boyd's hands.

"You saved my life and Lark's," Jamie blurted out, almost before he knew he was going to say it.

"You saved mine once, to all intents and purposes," Thorne answered.

"And tonight you doubtless saved a number of vessels—and men. The Boyds will do no more wrecking."

"What will happen to them?"

The schoolmaster shrugged. "I'm not sure. They'll stand trial at Limerock, and we'll be witnesses. Until then, don't trouble your mind about it, Jamie. Whatever happens to them, they will have deserved it."

"I'm not troubling my mind about them," Jamie answered. "Why should I? There's Morgan and Hugh and Mark for me to think on, and all the good things left undone because they won't be alive to do them. And when it comes to that, there's my own father. And the seaman that was drowned off the Thrasher, and Cap'n Jeremy Thorne who lies in the churchyard here."

"Captain Jeremy Thorne," Roger Thorne said softly. "Did you see him, Jamie, when they brought him ashore?"

"It was dark. No, I never saw him plain."

"If you'd seen him, you'd have seen his red hair," said Roger Thorne. He lifted a candlestick from the table, and the flame struck a coppery gleam in his own red hair.

Then Jamie knew. He couldn't think of what to say at first, he fumbled to get words out past his dry lips. "That's why—that's why you were willing to stand them off alone."

"That's why." He smiled. "No doubt the arrival of Captain Marriot saved me from murder tonight—though I wouldn't have called it murder."

"Nor would anyone else!"

"It would have been murder in Thad's eyes."

They were tired and the hour was late, but still Jamie didn't want to go. His weary mind groped for the truth. "Did you come to Brigport a-purpose?"

Thorne nodded. "The first mate of the *Cynthia*, Mr. Hathaway, brought me a strange tale. He said there was something he couldn't put his finger on. That some here laid the fault at a madman's door, but he had the feeling in his bones that it might not be an act of innocence." The man turned to gaze out the window into the dark. "I had to know the truth; for Jeremy was to have done all the things I could never hope to do, but of which I had dreamed for too many years. I couldn't let them go without a fight."

There was no need for Jamie to answer, and he didn't try. After a moment the schoolmaster went on. "Mr. Whiting and Captain Marriot had written letters to the family. I wrote to Mr. Whiting and asked if there was a berth for a schoolmaster; my mind was made up, if he should say there was a schoolmaster here, to ask for lodging and board for an indefinite period while I wrote a book." His mouth quirked and there was a somber glint of humor in his eyes. "I was determined to be here in one form or another, you see."

"Anyway," Jamie said huskily, "you found out 'twasn't Ned."

"And found out that Ned was no madman." Thorne went over to the fireplace and stood gazing into the flames. "I had suspected the Boyds for a long time, but I didn't know how I was to trap them until I found Ned wheezing and cursing in my dooryard tonight because you'd raced off on your own. He was glad enough to tell me what was up, if it meant saving your hide." He turned, and dropped a hand on Jamie's shoulder. "You're a good man, Jamie. And it's late. I'll bid you good night."

It was an abrupt dismissal, but Jamie was willing to go. He had too many things to think about.

Chapter 19

Rich Gibson, as constable, arrested Tim and Israel, and took them off to Limerock aboard the *Minerva*. Their father went along, an unusually quiet Thad who walked straight down the wharf and looked neither to right nor left. Jamie could not help feeling a twinge of pity for him.

A week of storms followed, during which Rich wasn't able to sail home. Talk in the store shifted between the Boyds and the Maine-Missouri bill. Here it was March, and the act of the General Court, cutting Maine adrift, would take effect on the fifteenth; and what of Washington and the Congress? As long as the pinky *Minerva* was tied up at the Limerock docks, there'd be no news either of the District or of the time set for the trial. Captain Marriot tied both engrossing subjects neatly into one package when he said sternly, "Of course the bill will go through—it must go through! But what a way for us to begin our history as a state, with wreckers on Brigport!"

Suddenly the wind let go, and when a fair rose-flushed dawn showed over the eastern sea one morning, they knew that the pinky would be

back; she might even have set sail before daylight. Jamie headed for the
wharf as soon as the early chores were done and his breakfast in his stomach.

"What are you all agog for?" Lark grumbled, jealous because he had
to go to school. "You'll hear about the Boyds soon enough without being
there to catch the line."

"Who wants to hear about the Boyds?" Jamie retorted. "I've heard
enough about them to last me a lifetime." He left the young ones at the
schoolhouse and went on down toward the harbor road. Why was he so
fash to reach the wharf? he wondered. Surely not to hear how fared the
battle between the free and slave states? Then he grinned. Might be that
he'd cared nothing about it before it became a tight contest; you gave no
value to a thing accomplished too easy-like. And then he'd had so many
burdens lying heavy on him. Well, he still had the burdens; might be that
he'd just grown up to them. Talk about whistling for a wind. Surely he'd
sighed enough about his troubles to blow a ship to Liverpool!

Amanda ran out of the store when he passed, crying, "She's just outside the harbor now, Jamie!" She caught at his hand and started to run
down the slope to the wharf, pulling him along; her black hair streamed
out in the mild breeze. Then she stopped so suddenly he nearly fell over
her, and there was Pleasance Marriot on the wharf, smiling at them.

"How gay you are this morning," she said sweetly. "Like two little
children, without a care in the world!"

Amanda blushed, let go of Jamie's hand and tried vainly to put her
hair in order. Then she walked by Pleasance with such an attempt to be
ladylike that she fairly minced. Jamie was angry and didn't know which
one angered him most; Pleasance for mocking them, or Amanda for paying her any heed.

He walked off and left them both without a word or a look. By the
time he reached the end of the long wharf, where most of the other men
and boys stood, the *Minerva* was in the harbor mouth.

Rich Gibson, standing in the bow, made a trumpet of his hands before
the pinky reached the wharf. "We're a state!" he shouted. "They made us
a state last week—March third!"

A great cheer rose from the wharf, echoing exultantly all around the
rocky harbor, and sending the gulls up from the ledges in a white flashing
of great wings. Up and up they soared into the fresh blue and white sky,
and their shrill crying rang on the wind.

Down on the wharf everyone shook hands with everyone else. Half a
dozen seized Jamie's hand and gripped it hard. By that time the *Minerva*

was alongside the wharf and Rich was clambering up the wharf, giving more details at the top of his voice.

" 'Twas a great battle—I've all the papers here telling about it—but Henry Clay, he hewed out a compromise and that's what saved the day for us!" He handed newspapers out all around and kept on talking. "'Missouri Compromise,' that's what they call it. Missouri, she could enter the union all right, but there's to be no slavery above the—wait a minute—" He snatched the *Portland Argus* out of someone's hands and read off the figures. "No slavery in all the states north of latitude 36°30'. 'Course, that's open to a lot of pulley-hauling, but right now all that concerns us is the State of Maine!"

The cheer went up again, and Jamie was surprised to find he was cheering too.

Most of the older men went up the wharf with Rich, while the younger ones stayed behind to help unload the *Minerva*'s freight. Jamie leaned against a hogshead and looked down at the pinky. When the Boyds' trial was held he'd be sailing for the mainland for the first time in his life. His mouth took a wry twist. This didn't fit in with all his great dreams of setting forth to make his fortune, but at least he'd be seeing some tiny bit of what lay beyond his part of the ocean. He'd see some small fraction of the new state.

For the first time he noticed a stranger standing on the pinky's deck, well out of the way. He was a lean erect man, burned to a mahogany darkness, and wrapped well in a warm cloak as if this March breeze were too chill for his blood. Now who was this? And what did he want on Brigport? There was nothing here for an adventurer. Oh, there was lodging for a traveler, for someone would give him a bed that night, but who would sail all the way out into the Gulf of Maine just to find lodging? Jamie studied the stranger intently. Wasn't there something about the back of that head and the set of the square shoulders? Hadn't he ever known someone who stood in just such a fashion, tall and straight as a spar spruce?

As if he felt the boy's intense blue gaze reaching out to him, the man turned his head and looked up. His eyes met Jamie's and held for a long moment. Then he moved to the ladder and climbed to the wharf.

Jamie watched him as if he were held fast in a dream. He felt a powerful force driving him to meet the stranger at the head of the ladder, but there were too many clustering about it. He straightened up and walked up the wharf, staring hard at the store without seeing it; the stranger's even stride on the planks behind him was faster than his own, overtaking him.

He stopped short, turned, and looked into the eyes of his father. It was a quiet meeting. None of the young men working and laughing at the edge of the wharf noticed, and the rest were safe in the store. Jamie's hands went out and gripped his father's, hard.

"I've been a year on the way," said the remembered voice. "From India."

Jamie could only say stupidly, "Did Rich know?"

His father's laughter was the same, though his face was seamed and worn and the black hair whitened at the temples. "Rich knew, though he'd scarce believe it when I came aboard last night. We made an agreement, for him to take up everybody's eye and ear so I could go quietly ashore." The laughter died. "Well, Jamie, let's go home."

By a miracle no one saw them as they passed the store, and soon they were walking side by side along the wagon tracks through the woods. It is truly happening! Jamie thought. He is here! The boy was light-headed with shock, and a happiness too great for him to realize it as such.

His father lifted his strong dark face toward the March sky, and took a deep breath. "Brigport air, Brigport spruces, the reek of Brigport rockweed in the air . . ."

Suddenly he laughed aloud and clapped Jamie on the shoulder. "Home! It's not a dream anymore, or a memory, it's real. I'm walking on the island of Brigport, by the side of a man grown who is my son."

That's me, Jamie thought, seeing himself with sudden astonishment. A man grown, Maine is a state and I'm a man. We've both grown up, and we've got the whole world before us to make our fortune in. Of course I don't want to set off now—not this instant or mebbe not this year—with my father just come home . . . His mind plunged recklessly, proudly ahead, like the *Minerva* under full press of canvas with a bone in her teeth. I've got all my life, and all the world, and what I don't get around to seeing and doing, my sons and grandsons will do and see.

Sons? He cast a shy glance at his father. 'Twas the first time he'd ever thought of sons. But that meant marriage, and he'd seldom thought of that before, either. He saw Pleasance Marriot standing in the hall of the captain's house, with bright eardrops trembling like dew and her smile soft for him; involuntarily his mind shifted to that night on Southern Point when Amanda had rushed to him in the dark and he'd hugged her hard before he realized what he was doing.

Oh, well. He shrugged. He didn't have to decide anything this early. Perhaps he hadn't even met his wife yet. He had a prodigious pile of living to do before he settled down.

How Wide The Heart

Chapter I

By the time the *Ella Vye* had pushed her stubby nose out past Owls Head Light, Ellen knew it was going to be a rough trip home. The white-caps danced endlessly toward the mail boat over a green-blue sea, and the clouds scudded in on a southeast wind that smelled cold and wet and salt. The *Ella* had twenty miles to go, with the wind straight on her nose, and her forward decks would be drenched in another hour.

Oh, well, Ellen thought philosophically, better to pitch for two hours than to roll, and there's nobody to be seasick. She stood up forward in her raincoat and kerchief, her arm around the mast, watching Vinalhaven and Northhaven fall back to port, and Whitehead and Twobush retreat to starboard. There was nothing ahead. A mist in the air obscured the hori-zon that should have shown her the long blue line of Brigport twenty miles to the southeast.

"The weather isn't giving you a very good graduation present," Philippa Bennett said behind her. Ellen smiled over her shoulder at her uncle's wife.

"It's not the first time I've gone home from school in a gale of wind. If it ever came off fine, I'd think something had gone terribly wrong with the universe, and I'd come all unglued."

Philippa laughed. "The first time I ever went out on this boat, I was the only passenger, and it was rough and wet, and I was knocked all over the cabin, and I was seasick, and oh dear!"

"And now you're as much of an islander as the rest of us." Philippa had come to Bennett's Island to teach school four years ago, and had mar-ried the last of Ellen's uncles to remain a bachelor.

"I'm so much of an islander that I'm either very bored or very helpful when other people are seasick, without feeling a qualm in my own stom-ach. Speaking of stomachs, my sister gave me a thermos of hot coffee when I left this morning. Come on back—" She assumed an expression of mock horror. "I mean aft, and have some."

They went aft past the pilothouse, where Cap'n Link gave them a nod from the window over the wheel, and went on talking with the man who stood behind him, not distinctly seen from outside.

Astern, Ellen and Philippa opened campstools. They were sheltered from the wind by the bulk of the pilothouse before them, and behind them the lifeboat hung on davits.

"Who's the man with Link?" Ellen asked.

"I don't know. He was already inside when I came aboard," said Philippa.

"Maybe he's someone for Brigport, or a salesman," Ellen said. "Sometimes, when I've come home from school, Link's been loaded. But people go back and forth in their own boats now, more than they used to, and they fly too. Nils said he'd treat me to a flight home, but I wouldn't feel right unless I went out with Link, heavy weather or not."

Philippa handed her a thermos cup of coffee. "I know. You like everything to stay the same."

"In a way," Ellen admitted. "But on the other hand, there's something marvelous about the relief of coming into the harbor after being knocked to pieces and soaked to the skin for two hours. It's almost worth the trip, that gorgeous feeling. Like when a toothache stops. It's the perfect start to a summer vacation, and since this is probably my last one, I want everything exactly right." She laughed. "Nils thinks his stepdaughter is slightly addled, but my mother knew what I was getting at. She said the trips home with Link were the high points of her school year, and the worse the trip, the better."

They ate doughnuts and sipped coffee contentedly, with the sun warm on them and the crests boiling past the rail where they braced their feet. Behind them, the mainland and the adjacent islands dissolved into a blend of misty blues and lavenders.

All at once the spring just past was like a dream to Ellen. She said to herself, But Pierce Classical Institute is still there, twenty miles inland, with this same wind making the elm shadows dance over the lawns. A week ago today we walked in our white dresses across the campus under those elms. The orioles were whistling overhead and the air was warm and fragrant, and we could hardly believe that we'd never come back anymore. We—at least I—half envied the juniors who'd be back in the fall, and suddenly I felt like crying because I'd never again scuff the elm leaves up all dry and golden around my shoes, and smell the smoke of them burning in the October dusks. . . .

Had she really felt like that? Yes, but today the only reality was the return to the island. All at once she could hardly wait; the two hours stretched out interminably, as if she were sailing all the way to Spain instead of just twenty miles away from the Maine coast.

Her mother and stepfather had come to the graduation, and they had all driven down to Limerock together afterward, but she had stayed on in the small port city a few days with one of her school friends, to have her yearly session with the dentist and buy some things for the summer ahead. To meet Philippa on the boat this morning had been a pleasant surprise.

"More coffee?" Philippa asked.

"Please." Ellen held out her cup. "What did you come ashore for, Philippa?"

"To find out whether I'm going to have a baby or not," said Philippa candidly. "I am. I called Steve last night."

"Oh, Phil!" Ellen was delighted. "Isn't that wonderful! What did Steve say?"

"You know your uncle. He's a man of few words. But I gathered that he was pleased."

She sipped coffee and looked out at the water seething past the rail. She had been a widow four years ago, teaching school to support her eight-year-old son Eric who had never seen his father, killed in the Pacific during the war. She had been through an agony of spirit that Ellen could only guess at, but now she seemed completely filled with happiness, like a clear crystal vase filled to the brim with fresh pure water. It was a queer thing, Ellen thought, what people were able to survive. They really lived a good many lives in one.

"I hope I get somebody as nice as Steve," she said.

"I don't know if there is anybody else that nice," Philippa said. "But you aren't worrying now about your man, are you? Not with art school ahead of you, and then perhaps New York with a tremendous career, traveling abroad, and—oh, everything is possible when you're seventeen, Ellen!" Her eyes were shining.

"Why couldn't I decide to be happy with a husband and family?" Ellen argued. "Maybe I'm really a domestic type after all. Look at you! Your home is your world."

"My dear girl, I'm thirty-four and I've been through the wars. I'm about twice your age, when you come to think of it. I've come home to safe harbor, and it's about time." She went on more seriously. "You aren't having doubts, are you? Cold feet? Stage fright? You know, you've been lucky in having gone away to school. There's something about island living, especially when most of the people on the island are your relations, and the island's named for your family, that can take a terrific grip on you, and never let go. This way of life is unique these days. It really puts you in a class by yourself."

"At school some of the kids, and teachers too, thought we lived in feudal splendor on a rocky crag, like some ancient clan, repelling invaders with boiling lead."

"That's not too far off." Philippa laughed. "In a figurative sense. Anybody gets in a certain frame of mind on an island. I know, and I've only been there four years, while Eric acts as if he'd been born into it. You feel utterly safe and rooted, and a little arrogant, and you're inclined to bristle up at the sight of strangers until your common sense tells you they can't touch your security."

"I know," agreed Ellen. "And bit by bit you begin to feel as if you never want to cross the moat to the mainland, and mix with non-islanders." She contemplated Philippa with thoughtful blue eyes. "But I've had lots of practice, is that what you mean? So I should be able to make the break?"

"Without too much anguish, yes. And forgive me, because it's really none of my business."

"Oh, you can say it to me all you like," Ellen said calmly. "My mother's been telling me for years. Of course we're insular, she says, but for heaven's sake it's possible to breathe without the assistance of parents, uncles, aunts, and assorted cousins. It's possible to speak to someone else besides Bennetts." She giggled. "Sounds like that rhyme about the Cabots and the Lowells, doesn't it? Nope, I'm not afraid to strike out. But I'll always love the island, and some day I'll have my own house on it. I've got the place all picked out."

"When you're a rich and famous artist," said Philippa, "and need a place to rest up in between your travels."

"Or a very unsuccessful artist who comes home and marries a fisherman after all." Ellen yawned, leaned her head back against the side of the lifeboat, and shut her eyes. She saw the island the way it would look when the *Ella Vye* came around Eastern Harbor Point, and she thought of the way it would smell when she walked up to the house: of seaweed, and the wild roses growing almost in reach of the tide. The gulls would be crying over the harbor, and pervading everything would be the smoky, silvery sunshine of this dry storm.

The engines throbbed lullingly, the water swashed by the sides, the seaworthy old *Ella* ploughed steadily forward, and Ellen was almost asleep when she heard Philippa say to someone, "No, it's not a bad trip at all. I've seen far worse."

Ellen opened her eyes to see the back of a man's head and shoulders descending the companionway into the passengers' cabin, below the pilot-house.

"Then you do know the man with Link after all," she murmured to her aunt. "Who is he?"

"Your mother must have told you about Mr. Villiers. He's our myste-rious summer complaint. Well, not really mysterious, just inaccessible."

"Oh, yes, I've heard of him. He came out on the boat one day and asked for a place to stay, and Owen rented him the empty fishhouse over in Schoolhouse Cove. Is he writing a book, hiding out from a gang, or spying for a foreign power?"

"I think he's just having a rest, though down in the store they've had him doing and being just about everything."

Ellen watched the hatchway with curiosity. A strange man living in her uncle's fishhouse was certainly deserving of her close attention.

"Oh, dear." Philippa got up, cautiously. "I've sat still for too long. And I walked on too many hard pavements yesterday after months of island grass. I'm going to move around a bit."

"I'll stay here," said Ellen. "I'm in a nice dopey mood."

Philippa moved around the lifeboat out of sight. Ellen thought, Per-haps Brigport will be showing now. But she didn't get up. It was an old game, waiting until she couldn't stand it, and then going forward to see land rising on the southeast horizon like the first landfall after a month at sea.

The rapture of homecoming never changed. It just centered on differ-ent things, at different ages. At seventeen, with graduation behind you, the rapture was made up of all the things you had known, and something different, something that came with the realization that after this summer you would forevermore return to the island as an adult, never again as a child.

She leaned her fair head back against the lifeboat and shut her eyes. Never again a child, she thought. What a strange and almost frightening thing. No wonder her heart had cried out as the solemn procession wound under the elms. . . .

Suddenly her reverie was abruptly disturbed, not by a touch or a voice, but by the sensation that she was no longer alone. She opened her eyes, expecting to see Philippa, but her aunt wasn't there. She turned her head to the right and saw the man standing halfway up the companion-way. He was lighting his pipe in the lee of the pilothouse, his dark head bent down, but she had the sharp impression that he had been watching her.

Fair's fair, she thought, and deliberately watched him. He got his pipe going, threw his match overboard, and stood looking off. He might be as old as Steve, her youngest uncle, and he might not; it was hard to tell about those strong bony features with no spare flesh on them. His brows were drawn into a frown, his eyes narrowed as if the sun glare hurt them, or as if he were thinking deeply about a difficult situation. He was deeply tanned, and wore an old tweed jacket with leather patches on the elbows.

So people do really wear those outside the movies, she thought. At that moment he turned his head and looked at her.

"Satisfied?" he asked grimly.

"With what?" asked Ellen.

"Have you got all the details down pat?" He came up out of the companionway and stood by the bow of the lifeboat, tall as her tallest uncles, but mast-thin where they were solid.

"Fair exchange is no robbery," said Ellen mildly. "Weren't you studying me when my eyes were shut? At least you knew I was watching."

His smile was a warm and startling change from austerity.

"Touché," he said. "You're Ellen Douglass. I recognized you, because I've heard all about you."

"Oh, no," said Ellen in mock dismay.

"Don't worry. All sources said simply that you were a nice girl. Nobody went into embarrassing raptures and said you looked like Rosetti's blessèd Damozel, or anything like that . . . you know."

She frowned, trying to place the reference, and he went on quite unaffectedly, making it seem perfectly natural to quote poetry aboard the *Ella Vye*. "'Her eyes were deeper than the depth of waters stilled at even.'"

She was pleased by his quotation rather than made self-conscious, because he sounded so impersonal, not like someone trying to force an acquaintance.

"I think I should tell you that I've heard about you, too," she said. "You're Robert Villiers, the Mysterious Stranger."

He seemed amused. "What do they say?"

" 'They say? What say they? Let them say.' " Ellen was pleased at having a quotation to throw back at him.

"You're an unusual girl," he observed, "or that was an unusual school, or both. . . . Whatever you were thinking when I was watching you—it wasn't exactly pleasant, was it?"

"What makes you think that?" she said warily.

"I'm an expert on dreary thoughts, frightening ones, bad dreams, and every variety of nightmare."

"This wasn't really frightening. Just something I'd never thought of before."

"Those," he said solemnly, "are the worst."

"Yes, they are," she agreed in surprise, "but I didn't know anybody else thought so."

"Hello," said Philippa, coming past the pilothouse. "Brigport's in view. How about some coffee, Mr. Villiers?"

"No, thanks." He nodded curtly at Ellen and went up forward.

"Was he actually carrying on a conversation, or just standing there?" Philippa asked in amiable curiosity.

"He was trying to find some lee where he could light his pipe, and we introduced ourselves, and that was it." But it had been such an interesting conversation, and now it would probably never be finished, she thought with a faint regret. "I guess I'll go up and get my first look at Brigport. I don't know why that has to come up first and hide Bennett's, do you?"

She went forward to where the deck was running with sea water from the bursts of spray that flew up whenever the *Ella*'s nose plunged into oncoming waves. She held onto the mast and watched Brigport change from a long low cloud to a spruce-crested land with surf breaking at its feet. In an hour now she would be home, and the old ecstasy rose in her and she stopped thinking of anything else except what lay ahead.

Chapter 2

Ellen sat on a high stool at the kitchen counter, opening boiled lobsters when she wasn't gazing at the brimming blue bowl of the harbor. "'Steep thyself in a bowl of summertime,'" she said dreamily.

"Who said that?" Her half brother Jamie, twelve, took a succulent bit of pink-and-white knuckle meat from the bowl.

"I did," said Ellen.

"I mean, who said it first? I can always tell when you're quoting. You talk different." He flung out his arm, stared glassily at nothing, and said in a breathy falsetto, "'Twinkle, twinkle, little, eeny-weeny star—'"

"Smart kid," said Ellen. "Here, Eric." She held out the bowl to Philippa's son, who was also twelve, but childishly skinny with mouse-brown hair and gray eyes where Jamie was stocky and had a Scandinavian fairness. "Don't be modest, Eric, just because Jamie's such a hog. Take a claw. It was Virgil, my boy," she said to Jamie, "and you don't know who he was, so put that in your pipe and smoke it."

At the other end of the counter their mother energetically thumped yeast dough. She was a tall dark-eyed woman, her skin the warm Bennett brown, her figure agile and slender. "It's a pretty phrase," she said. " 'A bowl of summertime. . . .' We could use some water, Jamie, as I've reminded you about ten times in the last ten minutes. If your father comes in and finds the pails empty, you'll go to the well a lot quicker than walking. You'll probably fly."

"I don't see why we don't dig our own well and have a pump in the sink," said Jamie, "or even a generator, and then we could have a bathroom and TV, and—"

His mother pointed a finger at the door. Resignedly he handed a pail to Eric, took one himself, and they left. Ellen watched them go down to the well in the field, pushing each other until Eric finally hooked Jamie's ankle with his foot, and they both went down in the tall grass with a shout and a clash of empty pails.

"I can't decide whether twelve's a darling age or a hideous one," said Ellen.

"Oh, they have their moments of charm," said her mother, "even though sometimes you wish they were still of an age to take long naps and go to bed at six."

Ellen opened lobster tails, and the kitchen was quiet except for the thumps as Mrs. Sorensen kneaded the dough. Then the teakettle began drowsily to hum, and at the same time a song sparrow sang out loud and sweet from the lilac beside the window. There was an outcry of gulls over the harbor. Ellen thought with nostalgia of the life of twelve-year-old boys on an island in summer, and of seven-year-old Linnea playing outdoors somewhere. Vacation hours were endless when you were young. You didn't worry about how to get the most out of them.

"Look," her mother said suddenly, "you don't have to open those lobsters now. I'll tend to them after I set the bread to rise. You've stayed around all morning and I know you're dying to get out. So why don't you get it over with?"

"I don't know what to do first!" Ellen laughed.

"Why don't you walk around the harbor and see your cousin? She wasn't able to get to the boat yesterday. The baby was feverish with a tooth coming through, and that kept her in all day."

"I hadn't even thought about Donna," said Ellen guiltily. "How are they, anyway? Is Gage making any money?"

"He should be, with your Uncle Charles providing the traps and the bait, and showing him where to set them. But it must all go into paying bills; they owed so many when they came here." She frowned at the dough under her vigorous brown fingers. "What they'd have done without Donna's family to fall back on, I don't know. It still seems terribly wrong to me, their getting married before she finished her training and he finished college."

"But they're going back next year and finish, aren't they? After Gage makes enough money lobstering to pay his debts? That's what they planned."

Her mother gave her a sidewise glance. "I've heard enough plans like that to pave the road from the harbor to the Eastern End. What people don't plan for is the unexpected. Like having a baby right away, and the hospital bill being so enormous. And then having to move into two rooms instead of one, which almost doubled what they were paying for rent. And the incidental expenses, even with the family contributing all the expensive gear babies have to have these days. And, worst of all, Gage's health breaking down under the strain of two jobs, his studies, and no sleep because of a colicky baby. Well, he looks a lot healthier now," she said dryly. "I suppose that's one good thing about it. He's out in the fresh air all day, and they have plenty to eat."

"But they were in love," Ellen argued. "What were they supposed to do?"

"If it's true love, I think it could have lasted through a year's engagement, with their final studies to occupy their minds. As it was, Gage didn't even finish his junior year before he broke down. He'll have to repeat that year if and when he goes back."

"You don't believe he'll go back, do you?"

"I'm afraid one thing after another will come up, and he'll never get his engineering degree, and she'll never become a registered nurse. And you can't tell me they're not afraid of it too, underneath. Gage particularly, as talented as he is. Don't you suppose there are times when he's deathly afraid he'll never do what he started out to do? He may end up as a lobsterman after all."

"There are a lot worse things than being a lobsterman on Bennett's," Ellen said lightly.

"Such as knowing that you had the gift for some special thing," her mother retorted, "and that you'd dreamed of it and studied for it all your life up to a certain point, and then threw away your chance without ever knowing what you might have accomplished with your talent."

Ellen looked solemnly at her mother. "Did you ever want to do something special?"

Joanna Sorensen laughed. "I wanted to be a lobsterman till I was twelve. And then I wanted to stay on Bennett's Island the rest of my life. I didn't expect to get married at twenty, but your father blew into the harbor in a storm, with his fiddle under his arm, and I was a gone goose."

"And when he was drowned, didn't having a baby make it up to you a little bit? So why wouldn't Gage's baby make up to him for a lost career—if he loses it?"

"The baby's a darling and they love him, but do you suppose Gage likes knowing that he started out as a married man and a father before he could provide for a family, and had to be helped by his wife's people? . . . Not that he shows it. I just have a feeling, that's all." She laughed again. "It's none of my business, just age settling on me, I guess. I forget how tough and bouncing you young ones are. Leave that lobster and run around and see Donna. She's probably wondering where you are."

"Seems funny to think of Donna tied down," Ellen said as she washed her hands. "But then, it seemed funny to think of her in training, getting such good marks, and not minding giving baths and hypos. Remember the lipstick when she was twelve, and the cigarettes when she was fifteen, and Uncle Charles so worried?"

"And secretly you admired her, didn't you?"

"I thought she was madly sophisticated," confessed Ellen. She ran up to her room and changed into Bermuda shorts and a candy-striped shirt. She put on fresh lipstick, seeing in the mirror a tall girl with blond hair curling lightly under at the nape of her neck, her features having a delicate yet aquiline strength. She had the lean build and high-bridged nose of her dead father, but her coloring was that of the blond Bennetts who now and then appeared among the dark ones. When she was little she had thought with secret pleasure that it make her look more like Nils Sorensen's own daughter.

She found a package containing a washable woolly lamb and a yellow jersey for the baby, ran downstairs, called good-bye to her mother, and went down through the field to the harbor.

It was midmorning, and most of the men had gone out to haul their lobster traps. Children fished form the big wharf, or played in their playhouses among the wooded ledges behind their homes. Jamie and Eric were out in Jamie's double-ender, hauling the traps they had set just inside Eastern Harbor Point. Gulls perched on the ledges, cats slept on doorsteps, a couple of dogs poked around the shore at the tidemark. It was an average summer morning on Bennett's Island, if any morning there could ever be called average, Ellen thought.

Suddenly the seagoing pungence of new copper paint delighted her nostrils. On a small wharf in front of one of the fishhouses, a man was painting the bottom of an overturned skiff. He sat on his heels, his back to her, whistling softly between his teeth as he drew the brush along the water line. She looked down at his broad shoulders under the faded plaid flannel shirt, the long back, the reddish drake's tail showing on the tanned neck beneath the edge of the duck-billed cap. A memory blossomed intact of a night last summer when, just for a flash, after a dance, he'd ceased to be Joey Caldwell whom she'd known since she was six, and had become an intriguing stranger whose head held all sorts of unknown things. He'd acted like a stranger too, suddenly aloof, leaving her at the door without coming in for something to eat. She had been oddly exhilarated and disturbed when she went to bed that night. She awoke eager to see him again, but for some reason he was unusually busy for the next week or so, and then it was time for her to go back to school. In the winter vacations he had been entirely natural, and she remembered now that at first she'd felt a little let down and then relieved to find him the same old Joey.

Very pre-culiar, she said to herself now, repeating little Linnea's phrase, and said aloud, "Joey Caldwell, why aren't you out to haul on a day like this?"

His head went back and he stared up at her, squinting against the sun. "Ellen," he said, his voice as soft as hers. "Hello."

She squatted down beside him, and they smiled at each other. Joey had a squarish face with a strong, deeply cleft chin, a face that could be pugnacious if its natural expression were not so mild. Freckles scattered across his nose and cheekbones were a deeper bronze than his tan, and his eyes were an even different bronze.

"I'm waiting for the tide to float my boat," Joey said. "I had her out yesterday to paint and copper her." He nodded at the white lobster boat held on even keel by strong lines between the two wharves. "Come with me?"

"I can't," she said regretfully. "I'm on my way over to Donna's."

"She just went up to her mother's about ten minutes ago, pushing the baby buggy."

"Bless you and those bright little eyes," said Ellen. "Look, the water's up around the wheel already. I'll go home and get a sweater."

On her way back to the shore she came face to face with Mr. Villiers, just going past Nils's fishhouse toward the store. "Hello!" she called to him as to an old friend.

"Good morning." His voice and his manner were remote enough to chill. She raised her eyebrows at his back as he passed, shrugged, and went down to the Caldwell wharf. The boat was afloat now on the fast-coming tide, and Joey was putting his boxes of bait aboard.

With all lines cast off, Joey held the boat *Sea Pigeon* close to the wharf with his gaff. Ellen stepped down into the cockpit and he started the engine. As the boat sped past empty moorings toward the harbor mouth, Ellen forgot the slight discomfort of the meeting with Villiers. This was what mattered, the feel of the boat under her and the feel of the ocean beneath the boat, the smells, the sights, the vast, immaculate, sun-washed blueness of her world.

They went down the west side of the island and out around Sou'west Point, where there was always a swell and a surge, always a low roar of surf against the reefs. Above the reefs the uninhabited end of the island rose high and bold against the sky. While Joey pulled rustling yellow oil-pants on over his dungarees and rubber boots, Ellen steered, trying to see how close she could come to his first black-and-yellow buoy, so he could reach over the side with his long gaff and hook it.

Then he started the warp spinning about the brass winch of the hauling gear, until the trap appeared out of the dark depths. She watched eagerly to see what he took out of the trap after he'd brushed away crabs and sea urchins, and was as pleased as he about the shiny wet tangle of six legal-sized lobsters. He pegged their fighting claws and put them in a crate, rebaited the trap from a twine bait bag stuffed with fat salted herring, speeded up the idling *Sea Pigeon* until she circled back to where the trap had been, and set it again. Then on to the next trap, and the next, in a rhythm that was as familiar to Ellen as that of her breath or her heartbeat.

She and Joey hardly spoke, but she was contented, looking all around her or watching the smooth coordination with which Joey moved in the always restless boat, the austere yet peaceful absorption in his work that made him look older than twenty-one.

She returned to that look again and again. He seemed to have grown older just since last Christmas. It was as if the glimpse of the stranger, a summer ago, had been a preview of the man to come, for she realized now that she was seeing him for the first time as a man, and not a boy whom she had always known. Was that what it was, she thought in wonder. Was that what made him as mysterious a stranger as Villiers? She had a queer, startled sensation, as if she might find out something important about him if she could only look hard enough, but she mustn't be caught at it.

They anchored in a lee cove and shared the lunch in Joey's dinner box. The water was like dark-green glass in the shadow of the spruces that grew down to the rocks.

"It looks perfect for swimming," Ellen said. "If only I didn't know how cold it really is."

"Villiers goes in every day over in Schoolhouse Cove," said Joey. "Real rugged. Dives off the rocks out there on Windward Point, where it's always deep."

"Lord, what fortitude," said Ellen. "Look, what gives with him, anyway?"

Joey shrugged. "I dunno. He doesn't bother me any. Live and let live, that's my motto." He grinned. "Pa says the women are all heifered up because they like to tend out on bachelors with pies and baked beans, but they can't get anywhere with Villiers."

"He came out on the boat yesterday when I did," said Ellen. "We talked and I enjoyed it. Today he acted as if I were a forward female trying to compromise him."

Joey laughed. He had a deep robust laugh, surprising in someone usually so calm and moderate. It had always delighted Ellen and made her laugh too, which she did now. Still, she was preoccupied. What was that thing he'd quoted yesterday? "Her eyes were deeper than the depth of waters stilled at even."

"Hey, you're getting quite a burn," Joey said in alarm. "You want to be careful. You got anything to put on it?"

Yes, a large dose of common sense, she thought. Getting all giddy because somebody quoted poetry at me for the first time in my life.

When they came back to the harbor in late afternoon, most of the other men were back. As they rounded the point and one boat after another came into view, Ellen picked out the one belonging to her stepfather, and those of three of her uncles and a cousin. The long wharf toward which *Sea Pigeon* glided belonged to another uncle, who would presently buy Joey's lobsters. She remembered what Philippa had said about belonging to a large clan in an isolated, almost self-sufficient community that bore the name of the clan. Philippa was right about what it did to one. Ellen couldn't imagine a life in which people moved restlessly from place to place without ever sleeping a night under the roof a grandfather had built.

They were almost up to the lobster car now and Uncle Mark was coming down the wharf. Jamie and Eric yelled from the double-ender in which they spent most of their waking moments. Joey looked at Ellen with somber eyes.

"There's a dance on Brigport tonight," he said. "You going with me?"

"Certainly," said Ellen cheerfully. "First I knew of it, but I'll go anywhere as long as it's on a boat."

"They better tie you up," said Joey. "First yacht that comes in this summer, you'll likely be stowing away in the sail locker."

Chapter 3

Ellen dressed for the dance after supper, with Linnea a fascinated and talkative audience. A pretty, full-skirted cotton dress and low-heeled sandals were necessary, since every other dance would be an energetic square dance.

"Why can't I go?" Linnea demanded belligerently. "Lots of kids go to the dances. Babies, even."

"The babies can sleep in their baskets. You're just at the wrong age, Funnyface." Ellen gave her already sleek hair a final brushing. "Well, how do I look?"

"All right." Linnea was sulky at first, then her admiration burst through. "You look beautiful! I hope I look just like you when I grow up. You know what? Joey'll want to marry you, I bet."

Ellen looked at her in honest astonishment, then began to laugh, and Linnea went scarlet to her yellow hair. "Don't you laugh," she said angrily. "Why can't you marry Joey and stay here like Donna?"

"Don't you want me to become a famous artist?"

"You don't have to go away for that," said Linnea with contempt. "You can stay home and paint pictures."

"Yes, but I have to learn how to do it," Ellen began, and then gave up. It was useless to argue with Linnea, whose main purpose in life seemed to be to have the last word.

She dabbed cologne on Linnea's neck and said, "There, run down and snuggle up to your father."

Linnea ran out, shouting, "Hey, everybody, smell this!" Smiling, Ellen followed her downstairs. It was just sunset, and a ball game was taking place in the field. Almost everyone was out to enjoy the leisure of this lovely hour at the end of the long day's work. Ellen's mother and stepfather sat on the front doorstep watching the boys play. Linnea perched on her father's knee, her arm around his neck.

"Isn't Ellen beautiful?" she demanded.

"I think maybe Brigport should be warned," Nils said. "Give the girls a chance to defend their property."

"Oh, I guess they're safe enough," said Ellen. "There's nobody on Brigport that I want."

"Well, if you don't sound conceited," said her mother.

"Anyway," Linnea contributed, "she's got Joey!"

"What's this?" Their mother's dark eyes were humorously curious.

"Linnie's pipe dreams," said Ellen. "Well, I guess Joey's waiting at the wharf."

"Have a good time," they said. Behind Ellen, as she walked down past the ball game, Linnea's voice was as pipingly clear as a sparrow's.

"But he does like her!"

Another voice broke in, crying her name joyously, and she saw her cousin Donna running to meet her from around the harbor. Gage came more slowly behind her. Donna seized Ellen and hugged her hard. She was a pretty girl with short, shiny black hair and curly bangs, a brief nose that Ellen used to envy, and velvety dark eyes, fringed with thick black lashes. Color glowed in her olive skin, and her lipstick was as bright and as perfect as ever. She looked radiant and festive. Ellen, prepared for a Donna whose sparkle had been extinguished by an ailing baby and too many debts, was astonished and delighted. Donna was the same as always. She might have been out on a high-school date, and Gage, casually elegant in flannel slacks and jacket, was the college man whom she'd triumphantly taken away from the class femme fatale. They were nothing at all like Ellen's mother's picture of them.

Gage gave Ellen a cousinly kiss, closed his eyes and breathed deeply. "Delicious," he said. "I'll take this one."

Donna giggled, and he said coldly, "Who are you? This woman keeps following me," he said to Ellen. "She insists I'm the father of her child."

"Where did she ever get such an idea?"

"I don't know, because he doesn't resemble me in the least. For instance, he doesn't wear glasses."

"Hey!" Joey yelled at them from the wharf. "Is that the only place you can talk?"

"I hope you don't mind, sweetie," Donna said to Ellen, "but we're going with you and Joey. We'll leave you alone, though."

"What for?" asked Ellen.

"Well, after all!"

"How obvious can you get?" said Gage. "If you haven't caught on yet, Ellen—and you should have, unless you're an imbecile—she thinks There's Something Between You."

"If there isn't, there should be," retorted Donna. "What's a summer on Bennett's Island without a love affair? And her last one, too."

"Before she goes into the convent," said Gage, taking his wife's arm and propelling her toward the wharf. "Come on, wench, and if you hold your little tongue for all of five minutes, I'll marry you tomorrow."

They were all laughing as they joined Joey aboard the *Sea Pigeon* And though Joey didn't know what the joke was, he looked happy too.

Brigport harbor lay three miles to the north across a tranquil sea. They walked up from the shore in the twilight along a winding road through woods and meadows until they came to the Knights of Pythias Hall on the height of the island. Already the fiddler was tuning up with the accordion and guitars, running through "The Devil's Dream" and "Rakes of Mallow," while the children skated happily over the corn-meal-strewn dance floor.

It was the way all dances began, whether on Bennett's Island or Brigport. Quite suddenly and sharply Ellen remembered being ten, with Joey an awkward fourteen, propelling her doggedly around the sides of the floor, practicing his newly learned waltz in hopes that by the end of the evening he'd be good enough to ask Donna for a dance. Ellen had been furiously jealous behind her meek little face, her heart thumping with rage under smocked broadcloth and flat little-girl chest. Joey was her Joey.

Joey's not my Joey anymore, Ellen thought with amusement. We're just the best friends in the world, regardless of what anyone else tries to make of it.

In the intermissions, the children raced feverishly around the building in the dark, yelping with excitement. Courting couples wandered off to the privacy of someone's orchard or the little cemetery down the road. Married women, the older ones, sat together on the benches and caught up on the news while the men stood outside and smoked.

Looking for Donna, Ellen couldn't find her. She and Gage had disappeared like a pair of lovers. If that's supposed to be tactful, Ellen thought, I'll tactful her. She joined Joey on the stone wall under the spruces across the road.

"Hi," he said laconically. After Donna's unsubtle hints, his matter-of-factness was a relief. "You like orange pop?"

Ellen didn't, but she said that she did, and was touched because he gave her his clean handkerchief to wrap around the icy, wet bottle. "I hope they don't have 'Hull's Victory' right after I drink all this," she said.

"Well, there's no law says you have to dance every dance. We could sit it out."

"I may have to. School dances are tame compared to these." Surprisingly, the orange drink wasn't bad, not too sweet. They exchanged a few words now and then. Soon they heard Donna's unmistakable rippling giggle from the road, and Ellen called her name. She and Gage came toward the spruces.

"Is that you, Ellen?" She sounded either disapproving or disappointed. "What are you doing here?"

"Nothing she hadn't ought," said Joey with dangerous mildness. "You taking care of her, Donna?"

Fortunately, a loud chord was struck up at that moment across the road.

"Come on, spouse," said Gage. "We've got to dance every dance even if it kills us. We may not get a free baby-sitter again this year. Your kid sister will want to go to all the home dances." He took her hand and led her back across the road in spite of her protests.

"I feel in my bones that it'll be 'Hull's Victory,' " said Ellen, "and I'm awash with orange pop. If I joggle, I'll probably explode."

"Let's walk it off," said Joey decisively. He took the bottle from her hand, set it beside his in the grass, and stood up.

They walked away in the dark. The noise and music and light of the hall became dimmed. Ellen stepped on a stone that rolled under her foot, and Joey took her arm and pulled it through his. The woods were silent and aromatic on one side, and on the other side, beyond a stone wall, open fields stretched down to the water which lay quiet and mysterious tonight between the two islands. Out on the horizon, the Rock light flashed at rhythmic intervals. Joey removed pasture bars at a break in the stone wall, and they walked down a grassy track to the shore. Here the blended scent of spruce, wild roses, and the whole blossoming wildflower tapestry of the fields was strong in the stillness, and the great shelves of rock were warm from the day's heat. A curve of white sand shone in the starlight, and the water crept up it with no more sound than someone murmuring to a drowsy child.

They sat listening to the water. Suddenly Ellen felt melancholy creep-

ing over her like an unexpected fog dimming a bright day, and she
wished they had not left the dance. She put back her head and tried to
concentrate on the gleaming powder of stars.

"Look, there's Andromeda," she said. Joey didn't answer, but put his
arm around her. It seemed a natural thing, and yet the strangeness came
back to her, the certainty that Joey was no longer the same person she had
taken for granted all these years. She murmured, almost in spite of herself, "What are you thinking, Joey?"

"So you're going away again," he said. "This isn't coming home. It's
just a vacation spot now."

"Of course it's home," she said. "It'll always be home."

"Not to live in. Just to visit. It'll be a summer island to you, now, all
blue skies and fair winds, a place to show off to your fancy friends, who'll
be just crazy about all the picturesque characters."

The savageness of it shocked her and she tried to get up, but his arm
tightened around her waist, and he tipped back her head and kissed her.
Instinctively she struggled, but the kiss was not so much violent as it was
self-possessed and somehow deliberate. Like something planned for a
long time, and which he intended to enjoy to the fullest. It was all astonishing, and she thought in wonder, I was right. He isn't a boy anymore.

She felt herself responding, as if she were running to meet him. And
then it was over. He had known the exact moment to end it, before she
could think better of her response. He released her. Neither spoke.

"Well, I guess we better be getting back to the dance," Joey said, after
a moment. A few minutes ago she wished they hadn't left it. Now, inex-
plicably, she didn't want to return. She wanted to ponder things. Or did
she just want to stay here with Joey between the spruces and the sea? He
was holding out his hand to her, and she took it and got up, and they
walked silently back to the road, and so to the dance.

It wasn't the same as it had been before intermission. Oh, I'm tired,
that's all, she assured herself brightly. But it didn't convince her, and she
found herself avoiding Donna's gaily curious eyes, and then thinking that
would give it away. Give what away? She tried to be bold and open, all
the time wishing she could go home and be alone.

At last it was time for "Good Night, Ladies," and they walked back
to the harbor. No one else had come over from Bennett's, so Joey's boat
was the only one to break the midnight hush. She went out of the harbor
in a soft phosphorescent rush. Ahead of them, Bennett's lay long and dark
on the star-streaked sea.

"Come on up on the bow with me, sweetie," Donna said to Gage.

"Dances always make me feel romantic." She kicked off her shoes and stepped up on the washboard in her bare feet, and led the way forward past the low hunting cabin to the bow deck. Gage followed her, and they sat down with their backs against the cabin. Ellen saw Donna settle into Gage's arms, and turned away. She watched the bubbling wake that gleamed with greenish-white fire behind the boat, but always she was conscious of Joey, and at last, with a sense of inevitability, she sat down on the washboard near him.

He stood tall and motionless by the wheel, one hand in his pocket, the other resting lightly on the wheel, watching past the two blended figures forward to where the bow pointed for the harbor of Bennett's.

It's not at all the way you think it is, she protested silently to his dark, quiet figure. It'll always be home, I'll always be an islander. I'm not really leaving it—

Her protest stopped short. What if he really meant to accuse her of leaving him? She stared at him in shock and surprise, and felt like bursting into tears.

All at once one of Joey's long arms reached out and took her hand and pulled her up beside him. He put his arm snugly around her waist in an affectionate but not lover-like gesture. In her present mood of fatigue, doubt, and self-pity, she took comfort from the contact. Standing like this, they took *Sea Pigeon* home, steady as the stars. As peace settled on her, she wished they could have gone on like this indefinitely over the night sea. When the engine stopped and the boat slipped toward the wharf with only a whisper of water, and Gage stood ready on the bow with the gaff, she felt as if she'd been awakened too soon from a dream.

Gage handed Donna onto the wharf with a stern admonition to be quiet. "You going ashore now, Ellen?"

Ellen said, not knowing when she had decided, "Thanks, Gage, but I'm going to the mooring with Joey. If I'm invited, that is."

"Doesn't seem to be anything I can do but invite you," Joey said dryly. "You've got me in a cleft stick."

"That's what I call a gallant speech," said Gage.

"Gage," Donna whispered fiercely. "Come on!" Before Ellen changes her mind, she might just as well have added. Joey backed the boat away, and they went out to the mooring slowly, with a softly purring engine. The other boats lay dimly white around them. All the houses on the shore were dark, except for a faint light in the Sorensen kitchen, and another in the little house where Gage and Donna lived.

Joey made the boat secure at her mooring and pulled the skiff alongside. Ellen got into it with a practiced lightness that scarcely rocked it, and Joey rowed ashore. She wanted to say something, and a few moments ago it had been almost clear in her mind, something harsh and definite but at the same time merciful, such as, Joey, I can't think of anybody right now. I have to go away and study. I owe it to my parents; they've been putting the money away toward it for a long time.

No, that would be cowardly, putting it on them. But if she said, I want to try to be something, it would sound as if he was right and she didn't want to be an islander anymore.

The skiff grated on the shore and still she had said nothing. When she got out, she said, "It's been a nice evening, Joey."

"I'll walk you home."

She didn't want him to—she ached with sadness and tiredness—but she waited politely while he pulled up the skiff and tied the painter. They walked up through the sleeping village. When they came to the gate under the thick black shadow of the spruces, they stopped, and for the first time Ellen became aware of the rote, the far-off roar of the swell breaking on the outermost shores of the island. It meant either the beginning or aftermath of storm. It had been there all the time, under the summer fragrance and the peace. Nothing was ever as tranquil as one thought.

"I'll say it again, Joey," she said. "It was a nice evening. Thank you."

"I guess I should thank you," he said. He took her hand in a hard grip. She thought he was going to kiss her again. "Well, good-bye," he said.

So he wasn't going to kiss her. She said with a smile, "You don't have to say good-bye yet. I'm not leaving until September."

"That's soon enough," Joey said. "The days go fast in summer."

"But you aren't going to ignore me the rest of the time, are you, because you think I'm disloyal or something?" She tried to make a joke of it. It failed.

"You're pretty hard to ignore," he said unsmilingly. "Especially when you count up how long I've been waiting for you to graduate. So I don't plan to cut off my nose to spite my face. If this summer is all there is, well, I'll make the most of it."

He let her hand go and strode rapidly away. She stood in the shadow, keeping her lips tight over the involuntary impulse to call after him. After she'd waked everybody up—and her mother might not even be asleep—what would she say to him?

Nothing. It was one of those times when there was absolutely nothing to say.

Chapter 4

The storm broke the next day, a fast southeaster that blew hard while it lasted. Ellen was glad of it, but at the same time she was too much of a lobsterman's daughter not to think guiltily of the traps that might be damaged. She dressed in her foul-weather gear and went for a long walk on the southeast side of the island, where the wind could tear at her with all its strength, and the rain could pelt her with hard, stinging drops. She climbed in and out of rocky coves between pounding surf and groaning spruces, so absorbed in the effort it required that she had no time to worry about Joey.

She was a good distance from home, and going cautiously down a steep incline slippery with wet grass, when she saw the figure of a man in yellow oilskins down among the rockweedy boulders where spray from the exploding surf flew over him in showers. He was tugging with all his might at a lobster trap that was wedged in between the rocks. Ellen went over the loose, rolling beach stones and slithered down across the rock-weed to help. But before she reached him, the man got the heavy, water-soaked trap free and dragged it by its rope bridle clear of the surf. Then he turned to coil up the long warp with a blue-and-orange buoy on the end of it, and she recognized the buoy and the boy simultaneously. Pierre was her cousin, Donna's brother.

He jumped when he saw Ellen and then grinned. "Hey! You scared me! I thought you were a ghost."

"Ghost of what? We don't have any interesting ghosts on Bennett's." They had to shout at each other over the storm.

"What do you bet? We always used to think it was haunted, didn't we? Never wanted to be caught down here with dark coming on, for fear of Indians or pirates or worse." Pierre was sixteen. Under his yellow sou'wester he looked like Donna with his dark eyes and extravagant eye-lashes, his short nose and his dimples, but he had a square and wholly masculine cast to his features. Rain had beaten red into his brown cheeks. He looked merry, healthy, and extremely attractive.

"Look at that trap," he said in disgust. "Come right ashore. If I hadn't seen the buoy in the rockweed the surf would have pounded it to pieces by night. I wonder how many more of mine are in."

He took hold of the bridle again and Ellen took hold with him. Together they dragged the trap up over the rockweed, themselves skidding and stumbling all the way, until they had it out of reach of the approaching high tide. "I had a feeling this was going on," Pierre said. "That's why I came down here. Thought I might find something."

"Well, you did," said Ellen reasonably. "Let's keep on looking. Maybe we'll find some more."

They scrambled on around the shore, sometimes following a narrow track at the edge of the roaring woods, sometimes making a precarious way over wet rocks and rockweed. Ellen spotted another blue-and-orange buoy in the gray-and-white swirl among some huge boulders, and they went down toward it, warning each other to be careful. In the midst of cautioning Pierre, Ellen stepped on a shred of rockweed and slid rapidly on her seat down a steep slant of granite as if it had been greased. A wave crashed at her feet and showered her with cold spray just as Pierre grabbed her by the back of her collar and one arm, and hauled her roughly but effectively back to the level ground. They sat there panting and laughing like idiots until they got their breath.

"Now you stay right there," Pierre said masterfully. He climbed down among the boulders, and in a lull between seas he waded out and caught the buoy. He hauled on it for a moment, but soon realized the trap was caught some distance out.

"There's eight dollars gone to the devil!" he shouted cheerfully at Ellen. "Oh well, easy come, easy go!" He cut off as much as he could salvage of the warp, and coiled it up with the buoy and toggle. "Might as well laugh as cry. Times when I'd just as soon lose all of 'em at one whack."

"I thought you were a born lobsterman."

"Well, think different for a change." He didn't say anything more, and they resumed their search. They found a good pine plank drifting in, which Pierre salvaged, and in a little while they found a third trap. After they'd hauled this one up, they decided they'd had enough wind for a few minutes, and went up into the woods to rest.

Though the tops of the tallest spruces leaned in creaking circles far above them, it was quiet down below, the dense growth cutting off the wind and the sound of surf. Ellen sat down on the forest floor, her back against a thick old yellow birch. Pierre dropped his sou'wester on the ground, took out his knife, and began looking for spruce gum.

"No kidding, don't you want to be a lobsterman?" she asked him curiously.

"Nope."

"You want to be a city slicker?" she teased him. "Is that what Lime-rock's done to you? Your father and all the others nearly died when they had to go over there to school."

"That place! Not for me! Oh, I get along over there all right—"

"I hear you have to beat the girls off with a stick."

Pierre had a devastating twinkle. "That's the best part of it," he said candidly. "But I don't want to settle down where there's sidewalks and brick buildings. Nope, I want the ocean all right, but not from a lobster boat. I want to go in the merchant marine. I always did, ever since I was a little kid."

Ellen looked at him with new respect. To her, Pierre had always been a happy-go-lucky youngster, living in the moment; but all the time he'd had his wish behind his merry dark eyes and enchanting grin.

"Well, what's to keep you from going off and finding yourself a ship when you're old enough?" she asked at last.

Pierre pried a piece of spruce gum off a trunk. "Look at that! Clear and pretty as all git-out. Here." He tossed it to her.

"Thank you kindly, sir. I never chew, but in this case I'll make an exception."

"You chewed plenty of it once. Remember all the stuff we found to eat in the woods? Fern roots, bunch-berries—" His voice trailed off and he seemed busy looking for more gum, but Ellen knew they were both thinking about the same person all at once.

"Do you think you can't go—they won't let you go—because of Charles?" she asked. Her voice was slightly unsteady on the name. Charles, oldest of Uncle Charles's children, had been drowned four years ago in a winter storm, but there were times when it seemed to have happened only yesterday. Like now, for instance, because Pierre looked so much like him, and because they were remembering the days when they'd all been children together in these woods.

Pierre nodded without looking at her. Then suddenly it burst out of him. "I've never told anybody till today what I want to do, except Charles. He knew. But now you're the only one who knows. Maybe I should start saying something to my father and mother, but I don't know how to say it. My father thinks I'll be going with him winters, the way Charles did. I have Charles's room. All the time I'm doing just the things Charles did and they're treating me just the same way. I'm even the oldest boy now—

the only difference is my name, but Marm forgets now and then, and calls me Charles."

He was not merry anymore; he looked miserable, and Ellen felt so sorry for him she could only grope for something to say.

"That's only natural, I guess," she said slowly. "It doesn't mean they don't love you as much as they did Charles. But it was such a terrible thing to happen. We've lived around here two hundred years or more, and no Bennett was ever drowned. I guess we got to thinking we'd cast a special spell on the sea so it wouldn't harm us."

He nodded gloomily. "And now it's all changed. Marm's nervous if one of us is an hour later coming in from hauling, even in good weather." He squatted down on his heels with his back against a tree, and looked earnestly at her. "I'm not jealous of old Charles. I just don't want to be him, that's all. I want to get out and see things. All those names— Panama, Rio, Valparaiso, Port Said, Marseilles—well, they do something to me. They give me an awful twisting pain just to see 'em on a map."

She knew. It was like seeing a painting or a perfect drawing that was a whole world in itself. It stabbed you inside, because you wanted so much to do something as perfect, and thought you would die if you didn't.

"Tell them that," she said.

"It's easy for you to say. You're free. Nobody ever thought different. They haven't lost a kid whose place they want you to fill. They want you to go, even if you come back in the end."

How wrong you are, Pierre, she thought ruefully. It's not that simple. Yes, they want me to go, but Joey doesn't, and when I listen to him I wonder just how clear I am in my own mind about what I want to do. And that's an awful way to be. . . . Aloud she said, "Tell them just what you told me. You're not Charles to them, really, even if Aunt Mateel does call you by his name sometimes. You're Pierre, and they want you to be happy."

"But I don't know how to tell them!" he said angrily. "I thought maybe you would. You could get around it easy. They think you're smart, smarter than Donna. And maybe you could get Nils to say something too, where he was in the merchant marine once."

"I think Nils would say plenty for you, after you broke the ice. But he won't go up and tell them something that they ought to hear first from their own son."

"And you won't either." He stared grimly at her.

"I can't, Pierre! Look, how would you like it if I asked you to tell my mother something about me because I was scared to?"

"Like what?" He grinned in spite of his woe. "Like 'Hey, Aunt Jo, Ellen's gonna marry Joey Caldwell!' "

"Oh, for heaven's sake!" snapped Ellen, so taken aback that she popped the hunk of hard spruce gum into her mouth without intending to.

"Now don't go baring your teeth at me," Pierre said with a conciliatory smile. "I just said that because I couldn't think of anything else, and Joey's the only one around here for you to marry up with. 'Course I could say it was some Brigporter, and that'd really make her holler."

"Well, don't worry," said Ellen with dignity. "I shan't ask you to break any news for me. And don't you go twitting Joey, either. We're good friends now, but we won't be for long if these absolutely puerile jokes start going around the shore."

"You mean I'm your good friend or Joey is?"

"I mean, if you help to break up my friendship with Joey by plaguing him about me, I'll really talk up to your folks then. I'll advise them to keep you in a barrel and feed you through the bung." Then she relented; it was impossible to be stern with Pierre when he tried to keep his face straight but couldn't hide his twinkle.

"Look, Pierre," she said seriously, "did you ever think of getting onto a ship through the Maritime Academy at Castine? I'll bet if you told Uncle Charles you wanted to go there, he'd help you and be proud as the dickens about it. That's a lot different from just striking out on your own."

"Well—" She could tell by his face that his mind was moving faster and faster, and she kept talking.

"You get good marks in between fighting the girls off. You like math, and you already know something about navigation. You could write to the school next boat and find out what subjects you should be taking now."

Pierre sprang up. "Come on, let's go home for a mug-up!" he shouted. "Marm was baking when I came out this morning." Ellen held back.

"Are you going to do your own talking?" she demanded.

"Darn right I am." He was transformed with eager excitement. "Gorry, why didn't I ever think of Castine before? I'm practically sure I can qualify!" He grabbed her arm and they came out of the woods into the face of the storm, singing at the top of their lungs about "the schooner Lucy Foster out of Gloucester."

But underneath the excitement of the storm and the fun of singing in the rain, as they headed toward a warm kitchen and food, Ellen was sad. If only she could help herself as easily as she'd helped Pierre. For the undeniable truth was that Joey had stirred up doubt in her. I should be so sure of myself, she thought, that nothing he said could matter to me in the least.

She went home from the Homestead by way of the road that went straight down to the harbor. As she reached the place where the ruts gave way to beach rocks, and she could see the boats lying quietly in the sheltered silver-gray harbor, she saw a ragged feather of smoke from the chimney of the little weathered workshop that Gage used. It was separate from the others, with no wharf, set between marsh and tideline so that sometimes the flood tides lapped at its doorstep. When she was small, Ellen thought it would be a nice place to live.

She hesitated. Gage was so brainy it might do her good to talk with him a few minutes, she thought hopefully. She glanced in through a tiny cobwebby window to be sure he was there—he might have just left. He was alone in the small cluttered room, leaning against the workbench, his arms folded, and apparently staring at something on the floor. But after a moment she realized he was staring at nothing.

It might have been a trick of the light which changed each time a cloud rushed overhead, but he looked like a much older, worn-out brother of last night's Gage. She felt instinctively that she shouldn't be seeing him like this, and withdrew from the window. As she walked home, she remembered what her mother had said about him. Last night it seemed an impossible exaggeration. Today Ellen wasn't sure. She wasn't sure of anything at all.

Chapter 5

The next day was full of sunshine after the storm. Ellen took her painting kit, a lunch, and a berry pail for wild strawberries, and went down to Sou'west Point. It was early enough so that the colors were still intense, the shadows deep and long, so that the faintest hollow became mysterious. The desire to get even one small portion of the scene down on canvas board was like no other desire in the world. It was a passionate eagerness that made you sad even while it made you rejoice, because you knew you were doomed to failure before you began. You knew it would never come out in paint as it really was, but you were flogged on to try by the almost religious belief that perhaps one time out of fifty you'd be able to look at your work and say, "That's it."

She selected an arm of reddish-black rock, coppery where the sun touched it, running out into a cold, sapphire sea from a turfy point where buttercups and daisies shimmered in the breeze. A single massive spruce stood over them, bent by the prevailing winds, casting its beautifully twisted shadow over the pale beach rocks below.

When, finally, she realized that one more brush stroke would be too much, she knew also that she was exhausted. Leaving her paintbox open, her brushes and palette uncleaned, she lay down on her stomach on a warm rock and put her face into her folded arms. The climbing sun soaked hotly into her aching muscles, and she was lulled by the swash of the water and the distant hum of engines. All sounds became one, so at first she thought the voice was part of her half dreaming.

"It's good," the voice said. "Very good. I'm astonished. . . . Are you asleep?"

She rolled over and sat up, shading her eyes against the sun, and the man became Mr. Villiers instead of an anonymous black figure.

"Do you really like it?" she asked politely. "Or are you just being kind to the child?"

"If you weren't such an obviously well-brought-up child, I'd suspect you of malice." He sat down on the old timbers. "I think your work is very good. You've taken a hackneyed subject and given it a morning freshness."

"Thank you. But it was all by accident." She looked at her picture critically, and was secretly pleased by it. When she'd finished it she'd been discouraged and frustrated. But it did convey something, after all. She tried to hide her pleasure, but couldn't, and glanced shyly at Villiers. He nodded at her.

"You may not do as well when you learn how to do things not by accident," he said. "Maybe you should stay here, and paint as naturally as a bird sings."

"I don't see how anybody can be hurt by learning their business from the ground up," she said. "I don't know anything. At school we barely scratched the surface."

He nodded absentmindedly, tapping his pipe against the timber. "So you're not afraid to put your talent to the test. That's all to the good. Where are you going to study?"

She named the school in Boston.

"I almost envy you." He began to fill his pipe. "Are you as calm about this as you look?"

"It's the calm of exhaustion," said Ellen. "And besides, September's a long way off. It's not real yet."

"You know," he said, "sometime when you're two or three times the age you are now, you'll look at the children around you and think how blasé they are, how much they take for granted, when they should be quivering with anticipation and shooting off sparks of joie de vivre when you touch them."

"I'm not blasé," objected Ellen. "And I don't take things for granted. At least, not anymore," she added scrupulously, remembering the last few days. "Lots of times people are afraid to show emotion. Either they're too locked up in themselves, or else the feeling's too deep for them to express."

"Yes, that's so." Something in his tone recalled the curtness with which he'd spoken to her on the path. She looked away from him, and he said in the other, pleasanter tone, "So you're really excited, are you? You know what you want to do, and ache to do it?"

She looked at him in wonder. "How did you know about that part?"

"Oh, you have a sort of dedicated look at times, the look of someone who's found her vocation." His smile made him look amazingly younger and companionable. "You'll like being a student in Boston. Feeding the ducks in the Public Garden, looking in the importers' shops on Tremont Street, running for rush seats at the concerts, wandering through the art museum—"

"Oh, stop!" Ellen hugged her knees. "I'm trying hard not to think of it all summer for fear of being too worn out by September to care." They laughed, and then he became abruptly serious.

"It's this summer that could be dangerous."

"How? And why?" She looked at Villiers quizzically.

"Because you're an artist who hasn't yet developed a hide like a suit of armor in regard to everything but your work. Because you've the vulnerability of youth added to that of the artist, and because summer on this magnificent place could be a shatteringly beautiful emotional experience, and make you believe all sorts of things that aren't true."

"Like what, for instance?" she challenged him, because she was uneasy.

"Well, for instance—" he had an impersonal coolness. "—It would seem a pity, a great waste, not to be in love in summer on an island, wouldn't it?"

She laughed. "So Donna thinks. Yes, it would be a great waste if that's all anybody had to do—be in love and think about it. That's two-thirds of it, you know. The thinking. Finding poems that fit, and hearing special songs on the radio, and sighing at the moon like Yum-Yum in *The Mikado*."

"And what's that thing about crossing out letters and coming up with friendship, love, and marriage?"

"And counting with apple seeds," she chimed in. " 'One I love, two I love, three I love, I say. Four I love with all my heart, and five I cast away.' " They both began to laugh. "Will you share my lunch," she asked finally, "and tell me more about Boston? I guess I want to anticipate after all."

"Hadn't you better clean your brushes first?"

"That mess doesn't look as if I'm very serious-minded, does it?" Feeling hungry and extraordinarily happy, she cleared up her things.

After lunch they separated, he to resume his walk around the island, she to pick strawberries for the family's supper. She thought of him most of the time as she picked. He had been an easy companion, sometimes an unexpectedly witty one. He had told her many things to do and to look for in Boston, which made her feel that she already knew some of the most unusual and exciting aspects of the city. She only wished she'd asked him why he was so curt when he met her in the village; then she was glad she hadn't asked him. It might have spoiled something which in its own way had been perfect.

She took an old wood road home. Here was something else to strive for, the effect of straight spruce trunks like shadowy pillars moving off to infinity. . . . Well, she'd have time to try it. The whole summer. She'd work and work.

She had the painting to show the family, strawberries for their supper, three perfect, bleached sea-urchin shells for Linnea's playhouse, and a buoy slung over her shoulder for Jamie. It had an unknown name on it, which meant it had drifted from far off, and Jamie could keep it for one of his traps. She felt perfectly at peace with her world. She knew what she wanted, and the summer had at last begun to be what it was supposed to be.

Chapter 6

Joey came up to the house that evening, admired her painting with an honest, open respect, and asked her to go for a walk. The day had been so perfect that she half dreaded going with him, for fear he'd make her uneasy again and shake her newly recovered strength of purpose. But oddly enough he was the same cheerful matter-of-fact Joey he'd always been. His behavior at the dance might have been pure imagination on her part, though she knew it wasn't. Still, she was glad to put that out of her mind, and the walk turned out to be fun. They ended up at the Eastern End, where Ellen helped Philippa piece a crib quilt for the new baby while Joey and Steve played cribbage.

They wandered back through the woods arm in arm, stubbing their toes on rocks and roots as they picked out constellations overhead, and parted at the gate with a hard brief squeeze from Joey and a "See you."

Suddenly everything seemed to fall marvelously into place. She didn't know why, unless Joey had at last decided she could paint and was determined to, so he was giving up with good grace. Anyway, she was grateful.

For the next week they were good companions, playing pool at the clubhouse, visiting at one house or another, walking all over the island. She went hauling with him again, spent an afternoon painting buoys for him while he patched traps, and on one splendid day she, Joey, and Pierre went deep-sea fishing. They came back sunburned, exhausted, and smelling gloriously of the big codfish which they distributed to everyone on the island.

It was a week to remember because it was so exactly as she had wanted her summer to be. Every day she put in a few hours' work; she scowled and struggled with the difficult boat shapes, gulls in flight or at rest, men at work, children in fast motion, the cat stretching. There were the skeletons of trees, and the problems that went with making rocks look like granite crags or long-petrified lava. To reward herself for keeping at the hard things, she worked in oils and pastels, splashing color with an increasing boldness, happily remembering Villiers's praise. He sounded as if he knew; surely he had no reason to be merely kind to a strange young girl. Though she saw him only at a distance these days, the hour spent with him was still vivid in her mind.

The gallery grew, the family admired, and so did Joey, and she was positive now that he saw how it was with her. Some wanted to stay because their world was here, some wanted to go, like herself and Pierre, but not necessarily forever. This was home, no matter what Joey said. You never stopped being an islander.

After the end of the memorable week, Joey couldn't come up every night, and his afternoons were spent either in tending his gear or in catching up on his sleep. The herring were moving in, and Joey was in Steve's seining crew. It meant that the men were out every night in Steve's forty-foot *Philippa*, looking for herring. The shiny, silver fish were used for lobster bait, they were sold to mainland sardine-packing factories, and almost everyone along the coast liked them to eat, fresh or salted.

When the herring came, everyone shared the excitement, and the whole island was delighted when Steve's crew stopped off Nate's Cove one night and captured what they estimated to be about five thousand bushels. Last year a mainland crew had put dories in the cove early in June and held it for the whole summer, taking out sizable loads of herring at annoyingly close intervals.

The men made a pocket in the net to hold their catch until the sardine carrier could come out from Port George on the mainland, and took a night off to catch up on sleep. So Ellen wasn't expecting Joey when she sat on a boulder by the gate one evening, making a quick sketch in pastels of the harbor at sunset.

"There's Joey!" Linnea sang out from her swing under the old cherry tree. Joey was coming up by the well, his boots thumping hollowly on the path. He was staring straight ahead, his eyes narrow, his mouth severe. He must be tired, Ellen thought with sympathy. He should have stayed home and gone to bed.

Linnea ran out through the gate to greet him, gazing at him with as much rapture as if he'd been Young Lochinvar come out of the west.

" 'Through all the wide Border his steed was the best,' " Ellen chanted.

"What's that for?" Joey said unsmilingly.

"Don't you remember?" she teased him. His eyes disconcerted her. "You must have had it in the sixth grade. I did. It was one of Miss Allison's favorites."

"Oh." It was a terse sound. "Ayuh, I guess I remember. I came up to ask you if you want to go around and see the herring in the pocket."

"I do!" cried Linnea, hugging herself and jumping.

"Another time, Linnie." He kept his eyes on Ellen. "Tonight I'm just taking Ellen."

Linnea blushed with humiliation and disappointment. Her lower lip rolled out. "I never go anywhere or get anything!" she burst out. "I wish

Ellen would get married and have a baby! Ricky's awful cute, and Susan Bennett's so stuck up about being an aunt, she's just plain horrid."

Ellen looked at her in dismay and then felt her sense of humor cracking through. Joey ceased suddenly to be austere and broke into laughter. Linnea, blushing, uncertain, and yet defiant, cried, "Why can't I be an aunt before I'm ten, when it's fun? There's babies in every Bennett family almost, except ours!"

"You're our baby, Linnie," Ellen teased her, "and this is a Sorensen family." She got up. "I'd love to go, Joey. I'll put something warm on. Come in, or go out to the barn if you want to see the rest of the family." She grinned. "On second thought, maybe you'd better not go out there. Jamie's learning to milk, under protest."

"I guess I better not, too. Sight of me might cause that cow to r'ar up and throw the milk pail in Jamie's face, or him to throw the pail at me." Joey leaned against the gatepost, and Linnea, delighted at having a captive audience, at once began to talk. Ellen went into the house.

The cove with the herring was at the eastern end of the island, and so *Sea Pigeon* headed away from the sunset.

They passed by Eastern End Cove, where Steve's house seemed to be set in a field of green plush. The land rose beyond it toward the massive phenomenon of nature called The Head. The boat passed around under The Head, and started down the other side of the island. At last they came to where the herring were, in a deep narrow cove walled steeply with rock on three sides, and with spruce forest growing down to the very tops of the walls so that the cove was densely shadowed. The square of net corks that marked the pocket glimmered in the last trace of light from the eastern sky. When the engine was shut off the only sound at first was the wash of the wake against rock. Then, as that died away, the evening calls of the thrushes and whitethroat sparrows fluted back and forth through the dark woods with an eerie sweetness.

Ellen and Joey sat side by side on the engine box, silent, as if both felt the same about this hour that was slipping so subtly from day into night. Finally Joey stirred, got up, and brought the skiff alongside the boat. "We'll go over and take a look," he said. "They'll be starting to fire now, any minute."

At the pocket, they held to the edge of the net and looked down. The herring were a dull silver mass, swimming round and round. Stragglers were darting streaks of light. "We figure we've got about five thousand dollars' worth of fish there," Joey said reverently. "If that's so, my share will be around a thousand."

"That's quite a nest egg to gather in one night," Ellen said. She knew better than to exclaim too loudly. Fishermen always took these things with a cautious satisfaction, knowing that it might not happen again this year or even next. She dipped her hand in the water and lifted it, watching the bright drops run off her fingers. "Did you ever swim at night when the water was firing?" she asked.

"I never plan to swim any time, unless I fall overboard and have to," said Joey.

"Oh, you're like all the rest of them around here," she mocked lightly. "Anyone would think you all had hydrophobia. But there's one thing I'm promising myself now, this instant: to go swimming some night when the water's firing."

"You'll freeze into a long blond icicle."

"I'm not saying how long I'll stay in." She looked back at the herring and felt what she'd been trying to stave off with her talk of swimming: the pity for all trapped things that she thought she'd left behind with her childhood. It made a little shudder go over her.

"Cold?" Joey said instantly.

"No, idiotic," she said. "I suppose anybody can carry a thing too far. Can we row around a while and watch the oars stir up fire?"

"Sure." The oar blades whispered in the water and left silver whirlpools. Liquid fire ran off the lifted tips. The birds had quieted, and the stars were out. From far off through the dark came the cries of gulls. The hour was lovely, mysterious, and sad. Joey rowed as if time didn't matter and it didn't . . . until September broke into Ellen's mind like an enemy attack, and Boston burst in behind it, full of crowds and buildings, of hurried hours all running into one another, of niggardly patches of sky and garden, of dirt and suffocating scents. And the school! She'd be like a foreigner coming into a strange country, knowing neither the language nor the customs, and then what good would it do to belong to the Bennetts of Bennett's Island?

The dory glided slowly over the water, but her thoughts rushed on like the panic-maddened herring in the pocket when an oar disturbed them. What if her talent wasn't really much? Perhaps everyone, in love and pride or simply wishing to encourage her, had actually misled her. Not intentionally, of course, but what did any of them actually know about painting? The art teacher at school had been enthusiastic, but you could lead the art classes in school and still not have a deathless gift. At the big school in Boston she'd meet people whose best might be so much better than hers that it could break her heart. Villiers had complimented her on clear thinking. How smug I was, she thought bitterly. Like Linnea saying, "I never forget to say please and thank you." And Villiers might not have been sincere.

Suddenly *Sea Pigeon* loomed above them, and the skiff gently nudged the curving side, like a calf greeting its mother. Joey held the skiff steady while Ellen climbed aboard, then he followed her and went astern to tie the skiff's painter. Ellen stood by the engine box, her hands in her slacks pockets, her shoulders hunched together so hard that they ached.

Joey came back. He took her in his arms almost before she knew it, and he felt blessedly solid and real. She put her hands on his shoulders, but didn't push away. "Oh, Joey," she murmured confusedly, on the point of blurting out all her fears to him. In her sadness and anxiety, combined with the old but never threadbare spell of the island night, she didn't move. Joey kissed her. Once he had protected her in the schoolyard, and now he stood between her and the specter of defeat in Boston. She kissed him back, in loving gratitude, and he whispered her name unsteadily.

"I've been waiting for this," he muttered. "I thought you'd never grow up. Last year there was one time, but I wouldn't say anything. I was waiting till you were through school." He kissed her again, his embrace tightening until she felt overwhelmed, not only by his strength but by something in herself.

"Let's sit down," she said shakily. "Joey, I—"

He drew her down beside him on the washboard and kept his arms around her. "I want to marry you," he said simply. "I made up my mind when you were fifteen that I'd ask you as soon as you were old enough, and now you are. You're through school, and you've come home. And I've got a thousand-dollar nest egg in that pocket to start our house with."

"Joey, I'm not home for good," she heard herself saying. "I have to go away—"

"No." He took her chin in his fingers and turned her face up to his. "You don't have to go," he whispered. "Stay with me. Don't go. Please don't go, Ellen. This is where you belong."

His pleading caused a queer, weakening tenderness unlike anything she had ever felt before, but his last words gave her the strength to break away from him. He didn't try to hold her, but sat quietly watching her as she stood up and stepped back out of his reach.

"Don't say anything more tonight, Joey," she said. "This has struck me all of a heap. Marriage!" She laughed softly and incredulously. "I've never even thought of it except as something, oh, far off and hardly real."

"This is real," he said with a curiously chilling self-assurance. "And you'd better start thinking of it that way. I told you I've been thinking about it for a long time. Working for it, planning things out. I've got more than my share of these herring, you know. And that's earmarked for the new house. But what I've got in the bank is going to build me a thirty-eight-foot boat next winter, with the biggest, best marine engine I can buy."

His grimness faded before an endearingly shy and pleased grin. "I wasn't going to tell ye till she was all built and ready to launch. But you might's well know she's going to be called Ellen. Ellen C., I'm hoping."

"Joey," Ellen broke in, not knowing what she was going to say, wanting only to stop him before she burst into tears. But he was unstoppable. He put his arm around her waist and held her snugly. "Means I can go a lot farther for my winter fishing, and I can go out when it's rougher, too. We really haul in the money then. Price goes up to a dollar a pound sometimes, and if you come in with three or four hundred pounds, that's a pretty fair day's work, isn't it?" He laughed, and hugged her harder. "You can have everything you want in the house. We'll get a generator, and you can have an electric kitchen if you want, though Marm swears by gas. 'Course we may no more'n get the house built than we'll be moving across the harbor."

He stopped, and she knew he was waiting for her reaction. "What for?" she asked.

"This is my real long-range plan," he said in a quietly tense voice. "I've been talking to your Uncle Mark about the business."

"What?" She braced back against his arm and stared into his face. He tried not to show how pleased he was by her astonishment.

"Ayuh," he said sternly. "When he gets ready to up anchor and retire from buying lobsters and keeping store, I've got first refusal of the whole works, from stem to stern."

"Joey, this is—well, I don't know what to say!"

"Don't say anything! Just listen. It's not going to be long. He's always growling and growsing about having to be up all night when it storms, watching that lobster car, and never getting to go anywhere. Gemini, he and Helmi could go round the world in real fancy fashion with what money he's got socked away, and then live the rest of their lives without a worry." He rushed jubilantly on. "A lobster buyer on one of these islands, where we've got practically the whole ocean to fish without running on anybody else's territory—well, we make money and he makes plenty off us."

He whistled. "Every time I see the mail boat unloading freight at

Mark's wharf, the boats in around the car and him down there buying
two or three thousand pounds of lobsters a day and making a nickel
apiece on 'em when the smack comes, I think, 'That's for my darlin' and
me and our six kids!' They'll have college if they've got the brains, but at
least one will have to learn the business, so we can go places—"

He stopped for lack of breath, laughing. Ellen didn't know whether
to laugh or cry, she felt so shaky. His excitement and ambition were as
much responsible for the way she felt as his proposal. Everything was
bound up together. She was in all his plans and it hurt her and honored
her, made her happy and sad all at the same time.

"It sounds absolutely wonderful," she said. "And I know you'll do it.
But don't count—"

His arm tightened instantly. "Don't count on what?" he asked
fiercely.

She felt something like panic. It would be so easy to say Yes, we'll do
it together. To put all the uncertain, unknown things away from her and
face an exciting future with this new, intense, and really dynamic Joey.

"Don't count on what?" Joey demanded again, and turned her fact toward his. She couldn't tell him the truth, that she mustn't answer until
she'd searched her heart and soul.

"Don't count on Mark giving up too soon," she said at last. "He
growls a lot, but he's too young to retire. He wouldn't know what to do
with himself."

She felt Joey relax. He laughed happily. "He says he wouldn't mind
being a plain old rich lobsterman and letting some young squirt do the
growling and the worrying." He kissed her lightly and, she noticed with
respect, quite expertly. "Got anything to say? I haven't given you much
chance to get a word in edgewise."

The moment of near-panic was gone. "Let's go home," she said. "I'm
hornswoggled, Joey. I'm fair scunnered. I want to go home and think."

He was still under the spell of his own plans. "I s'pose we've got to go
through just so much backing and filling to make it official," he said.
"Okay. You think like all git-out for a couple of days, and then we'll see
about a ring."

He hopped up and started the engine. As they circled the island in the
soft summer dark, she tried to analyze her feelings, and couldn't. She only
knew that something had kept her from being swept along with him, but
that for a few moments she'd almost lost her footing and it had been a
sweet and exciting thing. But something had held her back, and what it
was she didn't know.

Chapter 7

Ellen expected her thoughts to keep her awake, but when she awoke she realized she hadn't lain awake at all. Pure fatigue had overcome the disturbance in her mind. So now in the cool island dawn, listening to the thin crying of the gulls, she tried to give Joey and herself the most sober consideration.

It was difficult. Yet people spoke of proposals as if they were the simplest thing in the world. All you had to do was say "Yes," and you'd live happily ever after. Nobody ever mentioned the curling sensations in the stomach, and the awful sensation of coming face to face with a dilemma that had just too many horns. She thought in awe, If just being asked to get married can make me feel like this, what about actually getting married?

She burrowed down under Grandmother Bennett's log cabin quilt and wished she could wake up again and find out it was still yesterday morning. Then, because she had never been a coward, she sat up straight in the chilly room. "It's happened," she said, scolding herself severely in a stage whisper. "All you have to do now is make up your mind. That's all." She smiled rather grimly.

She could hear Nils's muffled movements as he moved about in the kitchen below, making coffee. Presently her mother would go down, and they would have breakfast together, sitting at the table in the sun porch. Ellen tried to count up all the breakfasts they must have eaten like this before the children were up. And she tried to imagine Joey and herself in their forties, but it was not possible. It was just a blank, which for some reason was so disturbing that she got quickly out of bed.

As she brushed her hair before the mirror, she was faintly surprised to see that she looked as she always did in the morning. "Well, what did you expect?" she demanded of her reflection. "A halo? A luminous fog? Heart-shaped pupils in your eyes with Joey's picture on them?"

She heard Jamie go downstairs; even when he tried to be quiet he was noisy. Then Linnea began moving around in her small room under the eaves, sounding like a kitten trying to make a bed in a sewing basket. Ellen dressed quickly and went down to the kitchen.

"There goes your intimate breakfast hour," she said to her parents. "You should never have had children if you wanted to preserve your romantic illusions."

Her mother laughed. Nils gave her his slow, warm smile. "Oh, we make out all right. This is the best time of life, didn't you know?" He kissed Joanna and went out. Ellen watched him walk down to the harbor and thought of herself, watching Joey go out to haul. I wonder where we'd build the house, she thought, and pulled herself up short.

She spent the morning weeding the vegetable garden, a good occupation when you had serious thinking to do, but the trouble was that she couldn't seem to think any better than when she was in bed.

Her mother, having got the day's baking out of the way, came out to weed too, and Ellen wondered what her reaction would be if she suddenly announced, "Joey asked me to marry him." It was tempting, but she decided against it, knowing full well that her mother's first question would be, "Do you want to marry him?"

And she couldn't answer. That was the whole trouble; that was what had turned her into a mental lightweight today. Suddenly, after years of knowing exactly what she wanted, she didn't know at all. It was as frightening as finding out that the solid sands of Schoolhouse Cove had turned to quicksand as she walked on them.

In the afternoon she went around the harbor to Donna's small house. Joey had gone to haul early that morning, and now the long-awaited herring carrier was on her way out, which meant that when Joey finished hauling he'd be helping to load the carrier over in Nate's Cove. Ellen was glad there was no chance of meeting him while she felt so unsure of herself and everything else.

Even before she reached the house she heard the baby's screams, and she began to run. Something dreadful must have happened to make small Ricky shriek in such desperation. She hurried into the house by the back door, crying, "What is it, what's wrong?"

"Nothing!" Donna shouted back at her. "Nothing but the whole darned world!"

She sat in a low rocking chair with a red-faced squalling baby across her lap—not in it, because he was much too active for that. She was trying to pull a minute pair of knitted pants on over his thrashing legs. When he wasn't thrashing he kept stiffening into a small arc of fury.

"Has he got a pain?" Ellen cried anxiously above the uproar.

"Oh, he's just being cussed!" Donna's face was as scarlet as Ricky's, her lipstick half off as she kept biting her lip. Ellen realized uncomfortably that her cousin was trying not to cry. Ricky gave a particularly violent lurch and almost threw himself off Donna's lap. She sat him down hard.

"Now you just stop that!" she said between her teeth.

Without thinking Ellen took a long step forward and picked up the child, who was briefly astonished into silence. "Let me have him," she said quickly in the lull, feeling Ricky already beginning to brace rigidly away from her. "You go clean up and fix up, or lie down, or whatever you want to do, and I'll see what I can do with him."

It was a brave gesture, because if his mother couldn't handle this eight-months-old fury, how was a stranger to do it? But it was too late to regret her gesture now, because the tears burst suddenly from Donna's eyes and she fled for the stairs saying unsteadily, "Thanks—you don't know what just fifteen minutes will do." More words floated brokenly down the stairs. "He's only cranky because I am, poor little monkey!" And then her door banged, and Ellen knew she was crying.

Ellen was worried but there was no time to give in to her worries. Ricky had his second wind. He let out a loud wail and pushed back from Ellen with all his strength. It took all hers to keep him from bouncing backward out of her arms. Holding him tightly, not speaking to him, she hurried out of doors to give Donna a complete respite. She felt as if somebody had just handed her a giant salute with a lighted fuse and there was nowhere to throw it.

Well, at least there were no close neighbors to come running to windows as she walked around the house with him, although everyone around the harbor was probably hearing him. Ellen's forehead and neck were wet. Poor little frantic thing, she thought in compassion, shaken by his angry woe and the rigid defiance of his slim, small body.

"See the gulls flying," she said as a gull swooped close to them, dropping a mussel on the rocks to break. Ricky screamed louder. "See the boats coming in," Ellen said with desperate enthusiasm. "Oh, Ricky, see the pretty boats!"

His face close to hers, Ricky's eyes were drowned in a fresh torrent of glistening tears. He bawled his outrage to the sky. If only a dog would come along, or a cat. Or Gage. But his boat wasn't anywhere in sight yet.

She went back around the house. Beyond the lines of Donna's washing an open meadow began, stretching across to Long Cove. Without any plan of action Ellen walked out into the meadow until she was a good distance from the house. Her arms and shoulders ached from trying to hold on to the struggling child, and she set him down on the warm ground among the tall grasses. She sat down a little distance from him and looked off at the sea.

Quite suddenly Ricky was silent, except for shaking, sobbing breaths. She didn't look around. Then there were small rustlings and a grunt. This time she did look around, cautiously, and saw Ricky studying a spray of daisies that waved enticingly on a level with his eyes. A small frown which Ellen found delicious appeared between his delicate light-brown eyebrows. He studied the daisies for what seemed a long time, his hands resting on his bare knees. Now that he was no longer convulsed with rage, she saw how much he looked like Gage, how thoughtful his gray eyes were when they were no longer flooded with tears.

Finally he decided to pick the daisies, rolled off his small rump onto his knees, and began to creep. Ellen watched without speaking or moving. He reached the daisies and put out a hand for the certain one he wanted. He grasped the blossom and pulled it off, then frowned at his doubled fist. Ellen reached over and broke off another daisy, with a stem. She held it out to him silently. He dropped the crushed head and gripped firmly the stem of Ellen's gift. At the same time his eyes met hers and he smiled a shy, faint, but curiously adult smile.

Ellen felt a wave of wrenching, almost frightening, tenderness. She wanted to reach for him, to put her cheek against his moist and fragrant skin and feel his silky brown hair, but at the same time she didn't want to spoil this perfect little interlude in the meadow, just Ricky and herself and the daisy.

So they sat quietly for a few minutes while Ricky contemplated the flower. But Donna would be wondering where they were. Regretfully she held out her arms to him. "Let's go see Mama," she said.

Still holding the daisy, Ricky was content to go with her. Now he leaned trustingly against her shoulder, one arm around her neck, and the painful tenderness was very strong in her.

As they reached the house Donna called from an upstairs window. "Give me a few minutes more, will you, honey? I want to really do my face. I haven't had a decent chance for days, with that darned tooth of Ricky's kicking up. Gage must think he's married to the original sea hag."

"All right," Ellen answered. "I'll keep him as long as you say. Maybe I won't give him back at all."

Donna's answering laugh sounded natural once more. "This morning I'd have sold him to you for three cents. But I guess I'll keep him for another day."

Ellen walked on around the shore. Now Ricky was interested in the gulls and the boats. A cat obligingly stalked a crow on the beach. Ricky laughed and made observations in his own language.

He was such a perfect little being, Ellen thought in wonder. And he belonged to Donna; she had made him. How could she ever bear to be angry with him, or even casual? Why wasn't she overcome with astonishment and pride whenever she looked at him? Ellen felt something very like awe. Because of Ricky, Donna was invested with a dignity and strangeness of her own, and all at once, Ellen felt as young and inexperienced as Linnea.

"What you got there?" Pierre bobbed out from under the stern of a boat he was painting. "That your lunch? Hi, Rick, ol' boy!" Ricky frowned his tiny delightful frown and shrank back against Ellen, tightening his arm around her neck. She was no longer a stranger to him; he loved her, he was dependent on her, he clung as if she were his mother! She could hardly speak.

Pierre was laughing. "I don't blame you, Cap'n. You got a good berth there and you want to hold onto it. Just don't let Joey see you." He winked impudently at Ellen and ducked back around the boat, then came back and said more seriously, "I told them, Ellen. You know. And it's going to be all right. How'd you know?" He looked genuinely puzzled.

"I know how most parents are, that's all," she said. "I'm glad you've talked to them, anyway. I'm terribly glad. Have you written to Castine?"

"Last boat."

"Hi!" Donna's voice carried across the water from the doorstep. Pierre answered with a piercing whistle, which pleased Ricky, and went back to his painting. Ellen walked very slowly back to the house. A new and tremendous idea had taken hold of her and was shaking her heart, or so it felt. If I married Joey now, she thought, by next summer I could have my own baby.

It was something she had never thought about before. Oh, as a little girl she had thought about growing up and having babies, but it hadn't been quite real. Now, in the space of twenty-four hours, it had come close enough to touch; she was touching it, in the form of Ricky.

"How's Mama's sweetie?" Donna asked tenderly, and Ricky leaned away from Ellen toward his mother and was taken into her arms. So that was that. She had lost him, and she felt something very like jealousy, but not for long. My baby will come to me like that, she thought proudly. He'll always be ready to leave anybody else for me.

"Come on," Donna was saying, "let's get away from here and go over on Schoolhouse Cove beach. I'm tired enough of this house to burn it down."

"It's a darling house," Ellen objected, "and you keep it spotless. You're a far better housekeeper than I'll ever be."

"Compulsive." Donna turned down the corners of her bright, newly done mouth. "I scrub till I'm exhausted, and then, when Gage comes in so tired, I'm no comfort to him. And don't ask me why I work so hard!" she burst out furiously. "You and those calm innocent blue eyes of yours!"

"Well, why do you work so hard?" Ellen persisted.

"You'll never know. You're one of the charmed ones. You don't have my lovely precious horrid gift for biting off more than I can chew." She handed Ellen a blanket and the pink plastic utility bag. "Oh, come on."

Walking behind Donna on the narrow path around the shore, watching Ricky's bright, contented expression, Ellen cherished her new discovery. What would her baby look like? She remembered belatedly that Joey would be its father, felt suddenly abashed and shy, and went back to thinking simply but intensely about a baby of her own.

The long curve of Schoolhouse Cove was deserted. No one moved down on Windward Point where Owen's fishhouse and Villiers's camp were. The girls spread out the blanket and lay down in the sun on either side of the baby.

"Donna," Ellen asked abruptly, "what was wrong today? Are you sorry you married before you finished school? Do you hate being tied down?"

"How could I be sorry when I have this precious lump?" Donna's face was muffled against Ricky's stomach, and he was playing with her hair. "And besides, somebody else might have got Gage, if we'd waited. I couldn't have stood that! But—" Her voice died out.

"But what?" Ellen urged after a moment.

Donna rolled over and looked at her with a curious, appealing earnestness, as Pierre had looked at her in the woods that day. "I envy you, Ellen, because of what I said a little while ago. You're too smart to bite off more than you can chew."

"How do you know what awful idiocy I might commit?" Ellen asked humorously. "Donna, is all this just on account of Ricky's teething troubles?"

"That's just on the surface. There's a lot more to it than that. Nights when I was walking the floor with him—Gage was so exhausted I wouldn't let him get up—I did more thinking than I ever did in my life before." She smiled wryly. "So I'm not going to pester you and Joey anymore. Gage says it's beginning to sound as if I resent your freedom." She seized Ricky's big toe and cried gaily, "Crab got Ricky's foot!"

Ellen knew that the moment of confession was past, and she hadn't really found out anything about Donna's marriage. Donna, laughing with her baby, now seemed as completely serene as a cat lying in the sun with her kitten. And for Ellen nothing at all had changed since the moment when she realized that a baby of her own was within her reach, the moment when she knew that marriage meant something more than staying home on the island instead of going away to school.

And now she could hardly wait until she saw Joey again.

Chapter 8

Now she could hardly wait for evening to come. Joey would be up after supper, and they could go for a walk, out through the woods behind the barn and across the Bennett meadow to Goose Cove. No, that was too much under the eye of the Homestead. They could go up through the old Bennett orchard, surrounded by sheltering walls of tall old spruces, or down on the west side to watch the sunset. That was as far as her actual planning went. What they would say to each other would come naturally, one thing leading to another.

As she and the younger children did the supper dishes, she was with them but not of them, her minding wandering in some pleasant golden landscape of her own. Then she became aware that Jamie was patiently saying her name, and she smiled at him. "What is it?"

He was carefully wiping a dinner plate. "How about coming up to the clubhouse with Eric and me tonight, and we'll play some records and you help us practice waltzing?"

"Oh, Jamie, I'm sorry, but I can't. Why don't you and Eric waltz together, the way they do at West Point? Or with Linnea?"

"With her?" Jamie looked at his younger sister as if the suggestion appalled him.

Linnea flushed scarlet and said with dignity, "I wouldn't anyhow. They'd squash my feet right out flat."

"And I'm not going to shove old Eric around the floor either," said Jamie with equal dignity. "I can't help what they do at West Point. I want to learn to dance with girls."

"Why don't we go up some time tomorrow then?"

"And have every little twerp on the island watching us?"

Linnea laughed loudly. "I wouldn't strain my eyes!"

"Besides," he went on, "if you're waiting for Joey to come up tonight, he won't. They're going out seining again. Right now," he added, pointing. Through the window Ellen saw Steve's forty-foot *Philippa* going out of the harbor, three big orange dories in tow.

"So they are," she said brightly. "Well, it looks as if we go dancing after all."

Allowing Eric and Jamie to take turns propelling her around the floor at the clubhouse was somewhat of an anticlimax after the tremendous exhilaration of the afternoon. But she assured herself that Joey would come to her the first moment he was free. She knew that the seining had to come first, and the lobster traps couldn't be neglected, either.

The clubhouse was a low building set back from the harbor among the spruces. The islanders had built it for their dances and parties. There was a small kitchen at one side, and a room at the other side where the men could play pool. In between was the large man room with its polished dance floor, the old upright piano donated by an old-time summer resident, the big pot-bellied stove. A wide porch almost encircled the building.

For dances, music was provided by three boys who played the accordion, guitar, and violin. But the ancient phonograph, given also by the long-ago summer visitor, still ground out its equally ancient waltzes for generation after generation of youngsters. They might practice square dances in the schoolyard in recess, but they learned the refinements of One, two, three, One, two, three on the clubhouse floor. Now Ellen guided and counted through the summer evening until it was too dark to see, as her young uncles had guided and counted when it was her time to learn.

When they cut back across the meadow toward the house, she decided to say good night to the family right away and go to bed, to think quietly of all that had happened to her today. She'd think of Joey.

I must be in love with him after all, she thought, her heartbeat quickening. Perhaps this is the way it begins, not like a thunderclap, but slowly and secretly, with someone you have always known.

But there was no way to be quiet tonight, not at once anyway, with Uncle Owen's laugh bursting out of the house at them.

"Hey!" Jamie yelped happily, and he and Eric sprinted toward the door. Ellen stood by the old cherry tree, feeling a reluctance like pain at leaving the soft, silent night. Owen filled any house he entered with the vigor of his personality; everyone was either sparked instantly with excitement, or exhausted. Tonight he was a discord, and Ellen felt guilty about that, remembering how massive Owen's shoulder had been to a very small girl perched on it, how his wiry black hair had felt to her fingers when she clutched it to steady herself, and how he'd been as gentle as Nils if she feel asleep against his chest.

So she walked quickly toward the house after all. Her mother and Aunt Laurie were making coffee and cutting cake in the kitchen, her uncle and stepfather were in the sitting room, Nils knitting trap heads while Owen smoked his pipe and talked. Linnea was in bed, but the boys sat side by side on the studio couch giving their uncle an unblinking and fascinated attention. Ellen set the cups and saucers out on the dining room table. When the coffee was ready and the men came in, Owen hugged her to him.

"You counting the days till you get off this rock pile and into the big city, sweetheart?"

"Live one hour at a time, that's my motto," said Ellen. "Or, as my mother's so fond of saying, 'Don't be wishing your life away.' "

"How'd we ever get such a cautious one in this clan?" demanded Owen. "Paying attention to what her mother tells her! Must be your influence, Nils. You've put a hex on the kid." He stood her off to look at her, and she smiled into the weather-browned face with the lively dark Bennett eyes that would always be young. He gave her a little shake. "Now what are you thinking? That you know all about it, and your life's as clear as a chart? Well, you'll be heaving that idea over the sides before the year's out, missy."

I've already heaved it, she answered him silently, but still smiling, and he gave her hair a tug and let her go.

"As soon as each of mine gets to be twelve," he said, "I'm giving 'em a dollar and a compass and sending 'em out to make their own way in the world."

His wife said with affectionate exasperation, "They'll be lucky if you let them go off to high school. And by the time Holly's eighteen you'll be meeting boys at the door with a rifle and demanding a complete clearance from the FBI before they can even walk her across the island to the clubhouse."

"Darn right," said Owen enthusiastically. "I know the ropes. I was a boy once myself. Ellen, don't you go throwing yourself away on one of these island hellions."

"Well, there's only one old enough," Nils remarked in a mild voice, "and he doesn't seem to be much of a hellion."

"Joey's too steady. What's the matter with 'em these days? All want to settle down young. Look at Gage. Cares of the world on his shoulders."

"Oh, I don't know," Ellen said. "I don't think he's sorry. Anyway, he and Donna never have to worry about dates." She laughed, and Owen scowled at her.

"They should both be out playing the field, instead of trying to figger how to pay for the next baby." There was a sharp pause around the table, and then Owen grinned. "Just guessing."

"I'm never going to get married," said Jamie. "I'm going to sea to get away from women."

"I'm going to be a test pilot," said Eric. "Then I'll have a good excuse not to get married. It wouldn't be fair to a woman to marry her."

"Another country heard from," said Nils pleasantly. "And it's close to nine. Good night, boys."

Eric and Jamie carried their glasses and plates into the kitchen. "I'm walking as far as the beach with Eric!" Jamie called, and the screen door slammed behind him before anyone could answer. Ellen got up.

"I'm going out for a little walk before I go to bed," she said. "I'll break up any long discussion by the beach."

But she met Jamie coming up past the well with the cat draped around his shoulders like a fur piece. She said good night to them both and walked on through the village and across the marsh to Schoolhouse Cove. Away from the lamplit windows she felt delightfully alone and free, yet safe.

The tide was high, and under the stars the cove glimmered like a huge sheet of black glass, except where the tiny wavelets broke along the beach in fine phosphorescent lace. She took off her sneakers and walked along the edge, lifting her feet high to see the bright drops run off her toes. Soon the water felt warm around her ankles. She began to be happy in a way that had nothing to do with Joey, with school, with anything else but being alone at night on the island and walking barefoot in the firing water.

She walked out further and then plunged in and began to swim just as she was, in shorts and blouse. She meant to circle back to shore and go home, but after the first shock the water was so exhilarating and she felt so full of life that she kept on. She did remember to swim parallel with the shore and not outward when she wasn't swimming in circles, diving under, popping up again, and in general cavorting like a seal.

She felt like a seal when at last she climbed onto a familiar huge boulder at the edge of the water. You could swim to it at one end and jump down to dry land from the other. She sat above the water, watching the luminous drops run down her arms. A little distance away there was a stir of light in the water and she recognized a round dark shape. A real seal had come to see what was going on. They were curious creatures. She whistled as if to a dog, and the motion stopped. She whistled again, and the "seal" whistled back.

Her heart jumped, and then she laughed aloud. "You must have been with a circus," she called. Villiers's voice answered her, as matter-of-fact as if they'd met on the road.

"Are you decent?"

"Soaked to the skin, but dressed to the teeth," said Ellen. She found herself resenting his presence here, just as she'd resented Owen a little while ago. But it was too much to expect that this experience should be perfect. He swam over to the rock and held onto it. His uplifted face was pale in the starlight, sharply marked with the dark eyebrows.

"I see you found the Rock of Exile," he said.

"Why do you call it that?" she asked.

"I saw a photograph of Victor Hugo sitting on a huge boulder like this overlooking the sea. He was exiled from France, you know, and this photograph was called 'Rock of Exile.' " He spoke less seriously now. "What are you when you sit on it? A mermaid? The Lorelei?"

"Well, when I was small this was sometimes a castle, sometimes a ship, sometimes the Inchcape Rock. My cousin Charles was always Sir Ralph the Rover. I did try being the Lorelei once, after we learned the song in school, but the boys all threw jellyfish at me instead of being lured." She moved over on the rock. "Coming aboard?"

"Thanks." He pulled himself up beside her. "What an astonishing place for a conversation."

"Isn't it?" Ellen agreed.

"It wasn't very wise of you to go swimming alone."

"I kept my eye on the shore."

"Oh yes, I must remember that you always do." She suspected he was making fun of her, but she couldn't see his expression.

"I'd like to offer you a hot drink," he went on, "and show you a book of photographs that came in my mail today. Is that permissible?"

His tone was dry, almost flat. Suddenly she was surprised by the strength of her wish to make the right answer. She must sound old enough, poised enough, not coy or silly or forward, nor affronted as if she

suspected him of wrong motives. Because she didn't suspect him; and besides, she sensed that it was important to him to have his offer received
for what it was, a gesture of friendship, of sharing something which gave
him pleasure and might also please her.

"I'd like to see them," she answered. "What are they?"

"Paintings by American artists. Oh, Sample, Etnier, Burchfield,
Wyeth—ever hear of any of them?"

"Of course!" Now she was really excited.

"Will you swim it or walk it?"

"Walk. I've had my swim, and the air's warm."

Her clothes were already starting to dry on her, and besides, she'd
never felt the cold.

The camp seemed to grow out of the slope, and the path went on up
to the top of Windward Point. Ellen had played here often as a child, but
tonight it seemed foreign, almost exotic, as if Villiers's presence among familiar things turned them all unfamiliar. Yet she was not uneasy with
him.

He reached inside the door for a flashlight and lighted her way in.
"Not being used to female visitors, I don't have a complete wardrobe by
Dior to offer you, like someone in the movies," he said, "but I can give
you a robe to bundle up in."

"All right," she said agreeably. He went up the ladderlike stairs to the
loft and came back down again with a dark wool robe, which she pulled
on over her drying clothes. He lit a lamp and went back upstairs again.
"Shall I build the fire?" she said.

"Yes, go ahead. There's dry kindling." So there was, and a wood box
neatly stacked with spruce. As the flames crackled through the kindling,
she looked around at the room where she had once played dolls. The
rough plank floor was darkened and smoothed by years of wear, the
board walls mellowed by age, so that even the marks left by generations
of fishermen who cleaned their paintbrushes on the handiest place were
blended into a pleasing whole. The stove was well blacked, the old teakettle reflected lamplight from its clean sides. The bare table by the small
windows looked as if it received a daily scrubbing. The black iron sink
was also dry and clean. Oh, he was a housekeeper, this one, she thought in
pleasure and amusement.

She felt a pang of homesickness, not for the playhouse days but for
the little camp itself, so small and perfect a place, fitting one as a snail's
shell fitted the snail.

The dry spruce caught on and the kettle began to hum. Villiers came down from the loft dressed in flannels and a turtleneck pullover. He looked surprisingly young in the lamplight. "What a host! I might at least have given you a towel for your hair."

He opened the old sea chest against one wall and tossed her a towel. "And a new comb. You see, I'm prepared for ladies after all."

She smiled as she began to dry her hair. With younger men you had to keep talking or they thought you were bored. She felt astonishingly at ease with Villiers whether she talked or not. But perhaps it was the place.

"How about hot chocolate?" he said, taking a saucepan from the row hanging behind the stove.

"That sounds a lot nicer than coffee."

"It is. And your aunt sent me a loaf of new bread this morning. We'll have that, too." He set another lamp on the table. "Sit down and look at these while you're waiting." He laid the book of photographs before her. She wrapped the towel like a turban around her head to keep her hair from dripping, and became at once lost in another world.

When he set a tray on the table she sighed like someone waking, regretfully, from a dream. She closed the book and put it carefully out of the way, got up from the table, and began to comb her hair.

There was a mirror over the sink and she stood before it, but she saw in the warm lamplight only the bemused face of a stranger, a lost girl who was not sure that she wanted to be found.

She combed her hair slowly and then went back to the table. He had set two places with mugs of foamy hot chocolate. The brown loaf waited on the old breadboard, the butter on a blue plate beside it. She was glad he didn't ask her at once what she thought of the pictures, but pulled out her chair for her in silence.

But she had to say something before she could eat. "How did you happen to have those prints just now—today?"

"A friend sent them to me. They happened to arrive today. That's all." His gray eyes changed somehow, grew more penetrating. "Why do you ask?"

"Because—oh—" She shrugged. "I don't know, unless it's because I'm suddenly overcome with guilt. I haven't had a brush in my hand today." Or even thought of painting, she added silently.

"I suppose a certain amount of guilt is good for the soul, if it's not enough to swamp one completely, which sometimes happens. Then the salt loses its savor, and wherewith shall it be salted?" he asked lightly. "Are you sorry you saw the pictures?"

"No—"

"But you have reservations. I wonder why. Don't worry, I shan't ask."

"That means I can't ask you any questions either," she said.

He began to slice the bread, looking thoroughly absorbed in what he was doing, but she noticed a taut look around his mouth that she had seen once before. "If you wonder who I really am and where I hail from, I'm really Robert Villiers, and I'm neither an international spy nor an escaped convict."

"My favorite criminal is a jewel thief," said Ellen. "Are you sure that sea chest isn't full of emeralds?" She felt a personal triumph when he laughed and the taut look went away. "But you know so much about painting, and the way anyone feels—I just thought that perhaps you're an artist. They used to come here a great deal. So it wouldn't be strange."

"Your chocolate's cooling off," he said.

Obediently she lifted the mug to her lips. "Don't let my patter deceive you. Anyone can learn it."

She knew this was the end of her questioning. Any more, and he would lock himself away from her.

The chocolate and the bread and butter were good, but there were her own thoughts circling round and round, crying without end like the gulls over the harbor. It seemed as if they'd been doing it almost since she came home from school, prepared for what was to be a perfect summer. To escape for a little while, she began to tell him how this had once been her playhouse, and before she knew it she was re-creating the whole fabric of an island childhood, patterned not only with her adventures but those of her more colorful and reckless cousins.

He seemed to enjoy listening, slumped back in the old scarred chair, smoking his pipe. Sometimes he asked a question, and she realized he wanted to keep her talking. It dawned on her in the middle of a sentence that perhaps he too wanted to keep certain thoughts at bay, and for an instant she almost lost track of her story. Then she threw all her resources of color and rhythm into it to make it especially good.

It was. He put back his head and laughed and laughed. "Thank you!" he said at last. "Thank you very much, for the pleasantest evening I've had in years."

It was time to go, while he was still laughing and she was still feeling the glow of a rather special performance. She stood up and took off the robe. "It's a little damp, but I'm practically dry. Thank you for a nice evening, too."

He got up. "Can't I lend you a jacket? And I'll walk you home."

"I'll run all the way home. And it's warm, there's still no wind. I think today's been a weather breeder." With her hand on the latch, she took a last look around at the bare and exquisitely clean little room. "The hot chocolate and bread and butter were better than anything else I've eaten all day."

"Seasoned by guilt, no doubt."

"No doubt." She smiled at him and said good night. He stood in the doorway while she went down the path to the tumbled beach rocks and thence to the firm damp sand. They said good night again in soft voices. Light from the windows streamed out over her head.

Halfway around the village she looked back and saw the long yellow splashes of reflected light on the faintly heaving black water. She had said she would run all the way, but she went slowly back to where she'd left her sneakers, sat down on a driftwood log to put them on, and then went home. There were no lights at the harbor now. It must be midnight. There'd been no clock at the camp, and Villiers wore no watch. But it wouldn't matter about the time. Her parents, not knowing about the swim, wouldn't have worried. They knew she was as cautious and sure-footed at night as a cat.

She went noiselessly up to her room. Once the lamp was lit, and she was undressed and in bed, she took her sketching pad and tried to draw Villiers. It was unsatisfactory. She could remember in every minute detail how he looked stirring the chocolate, cutting the bread, and then sitting back and smoking while she talked. She could remember every shade of expression, every line in his lean cheeks, the way his lids drooped or his eyes lit up in pleasure or amusement, but she could not get it down. She gave up at last, crumpling the papers and determining to burn them herself.

It had been a long day, a difficult day in many ways. But she was physically tired and her body betrayed her almost at once, straight into sleep. Then on the verge of sleep she came wide awake, hearing Villiers's voice coming up from the sea in the dark. "I see you found the Rock of Exile. . . . What are you when you sit on it?"

Was he an exile? From what, from whom? And then he spoke of the salt's losing its savor. He could have meant himself, his work. She was tantalized by a dozen questions, all the time knowing she must never ask them.

It was not until morning came, and she was on her way across the island in a windy dawn, to capture a stormy sunrise from Fern Cliff, that she remembered Joey. It's those pictures, she thought accusingly. They made me forget everything else except that it was a terrible thing to let one day go by without painting something. . . . Even now I can't spare Joey a thought till I see what I can do with this sunrise.

Chapter 9

The flaming sunrise over a gunmetal sea that coldly reflected the sky's fire was soon wiped out by rushing storm clouds from the east, and by the time Ellen started home, carefully carrying her wet sketch, there was a rising roar of surf along the eastward shores and the gusts of wind pushed violently at her back. There was no sign of Villiers when she passed Windward Point, no smoke from the chimney.

Most of the men, having wakened like her to the signs of storm, were having a leisurely breakfast for once. It would be no day to go to haul. So the harbor was quiet except for the usual gulls. But as Ellen went by the long beach a fisherman untying a skiff's painter straightened up, and it was Joey.

"Hi!" His grin was radiant. "I thought you were still under the kelp, along with everybody else. What you got there?"

She put down her paintbox and held up the sketch. "Don't come too close," she warned, "or it won't look like anything. It's just an impression, everything was changing so fast."

Joey pushed back his duckbill, cocked his head, and squinted at the sketch. "By gory, that's a real john-rogers sunrise you got there," he said admiringly. "Seen 'em just like that myself. If that's the way it looked we're in for more than a smart breeze, I'd say. Something real dirty."

She felt pleased. She always was a little self-conscious about showing her work to friends and family, feeling that they would say it was good anyway. But Joey was too candid to put on an act. She felt a surge of affection toward him just for the picture alone.

"It's dirty already," she said. "Look, starting to rain. I've got to get this under cover."

"And I've got a string of fifteen traps out around The Head," said Joey. "Brand-new four-headers, nylon heads, new warps, everything. I don't figger on letting any easterly chowder 'em up—at least not till I've had 'em overboard a while longer. I'm going out and bring 'em in. You come too."

There was no stopping to think. The freshening gusts of wind and the rising sound of breaking surf on the east side were to her like bagpipes. "I'll put this in Gage's fishhouse. It's nearest." She ran back past the huge anchor half sunk in the sand between marsh and beach, and put her things in Gage's shop, standing the wet sketch carefully up on the bench against a can of paint. She had dressed in warm slacks this morning and a heavy Norwegian-style sweater she used for skiing, so she was ready for the boat.

The harbor was sheltered from easterlies, but the boat began dipping her bow jauntily into waves as soon as she rounded the point. As they passed the Eastern End Cove, Uncle Steve waved to them from his wharf where he and his dog stood looking at the weather, then grinned and shook his head.

"Thinks I'm crazy as a coot," Joey said to Ellen. "Going out to bring traps in. He'd never bother, unless they got word of a hurricane coming. But I've got my way to make and a house to build."

He looked soberly at her when he said that, and she gave him a quick smile and frowned intently at a buoy they were passing, as if she were trying to read the name on it. A house. Marriage. The decision was still there to be made, and yesterday she was so sure she was ready to make it. But something had happened since yesterday. What, she wasn't sure.

There was no more time for talk. As they came around The Head, *Sea Pigeon* wallowed and pitched, and took a shower of spray over her bow. The eastern sea was a gray-and-white expanse of rushing crests, and the Rock was indistinct on the horizon. The wind blew more spatters of rain into Ellen's face. She squinted against it for sight of the first black-and-yellow buoy appearing and disappearing among the crests. Joey was watching too, while all the time the great swells crashed at the base of The Head and slid back with deceptive slowness to begin a new assault.

Joey gaffed in the first buoy and hauled the trap aboard, the boat circling slowly as he did so; with this trap dripping on the washboard and sea urchins falling off the laths, he swung toward the next buoy. It was a slow process against the wind and the deepening seas. The buoys were hard to find; the boat must always be kept heading out away from the steep mass of rock, while the water tried to carry her toward it. The rain came harder, pelting into their faces. Wanting desperately to be a help, Ellen looked for buoys until her eyes burned. All that mattered was now, the instant; finding the traps, getting them aboard, getting them home.

Her hair was already drenched. That'll rinse the salt out of it, she thought wryly, astonished to find out how far last night had retreated before the pounding reality of the moment.

"How good is your engine?" she shouted at Joey.

"Brand-new Chrysler!" he shouted back. "Shouldn't stop on us now, not after what I paid for her!" He grinned from under his sou'wester, and shoved another big trap along the washboard to make room for the next.

"If it does stop, I hope Uncle Steve is watching from up on The Head!" she called back.

"Lot of good that'd do us," Joey said cheerfully.

They both laughed, excited and exhilarated by the challenge of the storm around them. Eventually they were past The Head and running almost broadside to the onrushing seas that broke along the uneven shore in a long line of white explosions. Ellen felt as if she had been soaking wet for her whole life and had never known a calm sea, a steady boat. But at last the fifteenth trap was aboard, and they could go home.

Joey looked back over his shoulder at the way they had come. "Feather-white," he said amiably. "Don't look so good, down in the water as we are with this load on. Guess we'll keep on going into Schoolhouse Cove."

Running slowly, cautiously, they went along. As usual there was a heavy run off Windward Point, but the boat rode the breaking swells like her namesake and then they were inside, with the high point a sheltering wall at their backs. The rain pattered with a strange gentleness on almost calm water. Ellen's head was ringing. She and Joey grinned at each other. "After you unload these, are we going back to the harbor?" she asked.

"Ayuh. On foot. I guess Owen will let me tie up here till this blow is over."

The boat eased up to Owen's wharf, built in an L shape to shelter a boat from the southerly storms that crashed into this cove. Watching it come closer to them, Ellen saw the subtle blending of colors in the spilings and rockwork, the green marine growth on the lower rungs of the ladder and the tawny brightness of the rockweed lying like thick manes on the big boulders of the shore. Then she lifted her eyes in anticipation of the pleasure of seeing Owen's fishhouse and Villiers's camp snuggled in their warm mossy grays and weathered silver against the green bank where wildflowers danced and dazzled in the rain.

Villiers was there. He stood by the door of his camp, his hands in his pockets, watching them come in. Happily she waved to him, but he didn't wave back. As far as she could see, he gave no sign of recognition, but turned and went up the path to the top of the point. He walked along the ridge toward the road, an erect dark figure silhouetted against a sky of storm. When the boat reached the wharf, she could see him no longer.

The snub hurt her. She was glad that Joey, busy with the gaff, hadn't seen either Villiers or her unanswered salute. Well, all right, she thought angrily. How would you like it if I'd snubbed you last night? When Joey stopped the engine she jumped onto the washboard, and then to the ladder and climbed up on the wharf.

"Come on, chum," she said, rubbing her hands together. "Let's get them there traps stowed away."

"Look, I don't hold with women working like pack mules," said Joey. "Go on up to Owen's and get dried out, and I'll come up when I get through here."

"Save your breath," she advised him. "I like being soaked. Feels natural. Look, you get them up on the wharf and I'll coil up the warps." Getting the traps aboard in such a hurry, he hadn't bothered to put the rope and buoy safely inside each one.

He grinned and shook his head as if she were a nine-days' wonder, then got up on the wharf and began hauling the traps up over the edge. At last they had a neat double row of traps on the wharf. Outside Windward Point the surf crashed so hard that sometimes they saw a jet of spray fly up over the ridge, but here in the lee the air felt so warm and the rain churned up the good smells of fresh rockweed and of wild roses growing in brambly thickets almost in reach of the tide.

"Well, that's done," said Joey, as he lifted the last heavy trap to its place. "Good morning's work. Let's see, these fellas cost about eight dollars apiece to build, and with lobster prices up, they'll pay for themselves in a couple of hauls and after that they'll start working for the house. Let's say they'll pay for the kitchen, huh?" He took off his sou'wester and ran his hand through his hair.

"Let's go up and see what Laurie's baked for Owen's dinner box," Ellen suggested hastily.

"No, wait. Come on in the shop, huh?" He led the way up past Villiers's windows, where she had sat last night lost in the book of pictures, and into Owen's fishhouse. The remains of a fire still snapped faintly in the oil-drum stove, showing that Owen hadn't been gone for long. Ellen stood nervously inside the door while Joey looked around the shop with a fixed interest in details that showed he too was nervous. Her stomach knotted as she studied the back of his head. Suddenly he turned and faced her, his amber eyes fixed on her face.

"What's the answer?" he said. "Have you had time enough?"

"No." She heard her small but firm voice with surprise.

"Look, you shouldn't have to think!" he said angrily, color rising under his freckles. "If you like anybody well enough to marry 'em, that's it. You know it. You don't have to think."

"Yes, you do," said Ellen. "After all, it's not like making up your mind whether you want to go to a dance or not. It's deciding about your whole life, not one evening. You've been thinking, haven't you?" she argued reasonably. "For a long time. You told me so. Well, I haven't. Marriage was something that would happen someday, but not right now. I guess I've been thinking about everything else but."

"Oh, I know." Joey kicked savagely at a shaving with his rubber boot, then dived under his crackling oilskins for a cigarette. "Your education. No wonder you can't put your mind on marrying a common lobsterman."

She would have laughed if she hadn't been so angry.

"Don't be silly," she said, knowing she shouldn't say it. "My father's a lobsterman, and so are all my uncles, though I don't know why I should have to tell you. I'd probably be one too, if I were a man."

"I said 'common,' " said Joey loudly, glaring at his cigarette. "The Bennetts aren't common lobstermen. They're educated."

"If you mean that most of them went to high school, so did you," she retorted. "Oh, I know we've got a doctor and a couple of teachers in the family somewhere, but they don't belong to the island branch.—Oh, look here, Joey, nobody else, here or there, has anything to do with the way I feel about you. That's just between you and me."

"What's between you and me?" He stared at her. "I'm beginning to figure there isn't anything. At least on your side."

Color rushed up into her face. "That's not so, Joey! Just because I didn't rush into your arms the minute you asked me, as if that was all I'd been waiting for—as if I only planned to go away to school because you hadn't proposed to me yet—"

"What I said before still goes," said Joey with ominous patience. "If you want to marry me, you'll know it without thinking." His tone changed suddenly and so did his face, from stubbornness to a warm, pleading eagerness. "We belong together, Ellen! You can see that if you let yourself. You're born an island woman. You know all the ups and downs of it, the good parts and the bad. You know when to be scared and when it's time to worry without coming all apart at the seams like some old vessel on the rocks. And we'll get a chance to see the world before you're old, if that's what you want, but we'll always have the island to come home to, because we're islanders and can't dig in anywhere else." He grinned at her. "I figure to have traps out when I'm ninety and the kids are running the business."

She leaned back against the wall and shut her eyes. Pictures made by his words wheeled dizzily through her head, but she couldn't get a firm hold on any of them with Joey standing so close to her, fierce and intent. She opened her eyes and said wearily, "Everything you say is true, Joey. I know it. That's all the more reason for me to think, can't you see?" She looked into his eyes, trying to will back their sturdy, uncomplicated friendship, and attempted a little joke. "Maybe it's my New England conscience, but whenever anything looks so darned easy and perfect I haul back. I can't help it. It's automatic."

The joke failed. His lips were a straight hard line and his freckles stood out against his pallor. "There's only one thing you have to know," he said. "Whether you love anybody or not. . . . All this lollygagging, making excuses, wanting time to think about it! Why don't you come right out and say you don't want me? It'd be a darn sight more honest."

They stared at each other bleakly. In the silence she could hear the long roar of surf on the end of Windward Point.

"I've never been accused before of dishonesty, Joey," she said. She turned and went outside and climbed up to the path. The wind swooped at her with a roar, flapping her wet hair, deafening her ears so that if Joey shouted to her she didn't hear. And she didn't look back to see if he were shouting. What with Villiers's snub and Joey's accusations, she felt as if she wanted to see neither of them ever again.

She hurried home, the wind at her back helping her, not looking toward Owen's house in case somebody should see her and beckon her to come in. Joey didn't catch up with her, and when she did look back no one was in sight. When she reached the schoolhouse she had to slow down from sheer lack of breath, and the weight of her now-sodden clothes. Suddenly her legs felt trembly and weak. It's reaction, she told herself. Balancing in that bouncing boat for so long, I can't walk straight on solid ground. . . . But she wasn't sure.

She sat down on the schoolhouse steps, her elbows on her knees and her chin in her hands, staring bleakly up across the Bennett meadow to the Homestead and the rain-blackened rise of forest beyond that. She tried to blame Joey for the way she felt, but she couldn't. Oh, that remark about being a common lobsterman was silly even if she shouldn't have told him so; no man wants to be told he's being silly when he's just got

himself worked up into a fine rage. But what he said about not needing to
think, about her not being honest—wasn't he half right? Shouldn't she
know something deep inside herself, instead of blowing first one way and
then the other, like the weathercock on the barn when the winds were
variable?

But I do know something, she argued. I know that I'd love a baby.
And I know that when I was out there getting the traps aboard, I felt absolutely safe and natural. It was as perfect out there in its own way as it
was with Villiers last night. Joey and I have almost everything in common
. . . almost. . . . She got down off the doorstep and started home.

Soon she came in sight of the harbor where the boats rode at their
moorings with their bows pointed to the east, and the gulls sat on the
ledges with their white breasts also to the wind. And for the first time in
her life, the place that she loved became a torment to her. She wished all
at once to be away from there, so that she could think without beauty's
breaking in.

Chapter 10

At least once a summer the island women put on a supper in the clubhouse for some good cause, and this year it was for a lobsterman's family
who had been burned out of their home on one of the tiny islands in the
bay. Ellen, her ideas of a leisurely summer shattered once and for all by
Joey's behavior, volunteered at once for the job.

"I'll clean the clubhouse before and after, and decorate the tables too,"
she said. "The kids will be my committee. Just these three." She fixed
Jamie and Eric with a cool eye; Linnea was willing anyway. "Any more
will turn it into a circus."

Jamie yelped in pain. Eric was too polite, but she could tell by his
withdrawn expression that he was thinking up a way out.

"All I want from you is two days' work," she said. "Can't you give
that much for a poor family that's lost every stick of furniture and all their
clothes? And lobster prices way down because it's shedder season?"

"Well," said Eric.

"When do we start?" said Jamie rudely.

"Not until the day before the supper," said Ellen. "If we do it too far ahead, somebody'll be up there dropping gum papers and getting the lamp chimneys smoked up after I've washed them."

"I can hardly wait!" cried Linnea. She went around telling her contemporaries that she was on the committee for the supper, thereby provoking remarks like, "I s'pose you think you're some special, Miss Lady!"

For some reason "Miss Lady" was the worst thing one could possibly be called, and long before the actual day of work began Linnea had been in two braid-pulling affrays, and had kicked one of her boy cousins in the shins when she was wearing shoes and he was barefoot and therefore unable to protect himself except by pursuing her with a handful of rip bait.

"He called me Miss Lady," Linnea wept as Ellen scrubbed off the bait smell in a tub of rain water and suds.

"And that's a deadly insult," Ellen soothed her, "because a lady you'll never be."

"That's right!" Linnea agreed tearfully, and then gave her a suspicious look. Ellen laughed. Secretly she half envied her little sister her freedom of expression. There were times, when she saw Joey duck into someone's fishhouse rather than meet her, or stand to one side of the store with his face stiff and blank if she came in, when she'd like to kick him in the shins. And Mr. Robert Villiers too, she always added, to be completely fair. She hadn't seen him except at a distance since the day of the easterly.

I was perfectly happy without knowing him and without being proposed to by Joey, she thought. And now I intend to be perfectly happy again. . . . But it wasn't the same, and she was angry at being cheated of the dreaming and painting hours she'd anticipated. This was an out-of-joint summer, and she was hating it.

What she resented most, she decided as she worked in the clubhouse kitchen, was the fact that she no longer was sure of what she wanted. She polished lamp chimneys until they looked like soap bubbles, while across the lane the field was a pool of midsummer sunshine. Everywhere she looked there was loveliness. Each season had its own beauties, and she thought with longing, All the things that Villiers told me about, in Boston—what do they matter if you don't hear gulls crying and see the water leaping against the shores, or a boat coming home in a winter sunset with a bone in her teeth?

She saw herself on the wharf, the cold wind beating at her clothes, watching a white boat fly harborward across a silver-flecked sea, with Joey at the wheel. She saw him coming ashore, his teeth flashing in his salt-streaked face, his oilskins stiff from the spray that had dried on them.

They'd walk around the harbor and into a little house like Donna's, so bright and warm against the winter winds, so particularly their own. After he'd pulled off his boots and washed up, they'd sit down to their supper—two married people, not two children playing house.

Mrs. Caldwell of Bennett's Island. Going to sleep on the island, waking up on it, raising children on it, growing old on it. . . . Ellen Douglass, a student in Boston, knowing no one who knew her island. She'd be a curiosity to the others, who might even dismiss her home casually as some queer little place way down east. . . .

All at once her self-pity disgusted her, and as she set the lamps in place on their wall brackets she sang aloud in a sickly sweet whine:

"'I'd rather be somebody's darling
Than a poor girl whom nobody knows!'"

There was a clatter as of stampeding cattle on the porch, and the children rushed in. She'd given them time off to go down to the wharf and watch the mail boat come in.

"A girl came on the boat for the Campions!" Linnea shouted, with the frenzied triumph of the one who got to tell it first. "She was some seasick!"

Jamie snickered. "And there wasn't anybody else on the boat but that rope salesman. You know the one. He wouldn't lift a hand if you fell overboard."

"Couldn't, most likely," observed Eric. "He was pretty green around the gills too." They were supremely patronizing, having the equilibrium and stomachs of young gulls. They felt they hadn't got their money's worth from a trip on the *Ella Vye* unless it was rough enough to keep the decks under a continuous deluge of salt water.

"She started to cry when she saw Mrs. Suze Campion," said Linnea. "Everybody was looking at her. She said she'd go right back home again, but she couldn't face the trip."

"Women," snorted Jamie.

"Some day, my boy," said Ellen, "I hope you have a good galloping case of mal de mer so you'll know just what it's like. And who was it came home from the polio clinic on Brigport looking limper than a shirt on a hand-spike?"

"Hey, that's right!" exclaimed Eric, looking at Jamie with pleased recollection, while Linnea burst into victorious laughter.

"All right, men," said Ellen briskly. "Let's set up the tables."

She heard more of the girl at dinnertime. "I felt so sorry for the poor little thing," her mother said. "She probably wished she'd die on the way and be buried at sea. But a rest and some hot food in her stomach will set her right."

"Who is she?" Ellen asked.

"A grandniece to Suze Campion, from Pennsylvania. She probably thinks this is the last frontier out here."

"Poor Joey, living right next door," said Jamie. "They'll most likely ask him to take her walking around the island, picking flowers." His eyes were sky-blue innocence. "Take her on moonlight sails, and stuff like that." He clasped his hands to his chest and said in falsetto, wearing an expression of idiotic vivacity, "Oh, Joey, isn't it just marvelous! Oh, what lovely daisies. Oh, what lovely bait. Oh, what a lovely sunset. Oh, what lovely muscles you have!" He dropped his voice to bass. "The better to hug you with, my dear."

"Joey can't hug that girl," Linnea said furiously. "He's Ellen's boyfriend. Mama, Joey can't take that girl out in his boat and hug her, can he?"

"Not without her permission, anyway," Ellen interposed. "So don't worry, sweetie."

"Anyway, she's real plain," said Linnea with satisfaction. "Got old red hair."

The day of the supper Ellen and Linnea gathered armfuls of wildflowers and spruce boughs. Ellen laid the evergreens down the center of each long table like a garland, with nosegays of varied flowers at close intervals. All over the island, women were baking beans, steaming brown bread, setting rolls to rise, concocting a fabulous array of salads, pies, and cakes. Favorite relishes and pickles were fetched up from the cellar shelves. In the afternoon two women arranged a table of handiwork at the head of the room.

"Your pictures ought to go real fast, Ellen, you just didn't put a high enough price on 'em, real oil paintings and framed and all," Mrs. Foss Campion, one of the women, said.

Ellen flushed with pleasure. One scene showed Steve and Nils mending seine aboard the *Philippa*, tied up at Nils's wharf with the harbor behind them. The other showed Joey's boat rolling in the chilly gray sea under The Head on that stormy day; a figure in yellow oilskins was just hauling a trap aboard, and a gull rode the wind overhead. Nils had framed them.

She thought herself they were rather good, aside from the pang she felt remembering how she'd parted from Joey that day. I wonder what Villiers will think of them, she thought. Oh well, he probably won't show up at this rustic little affair, so he'll never see them. She shrugged and said animatedly, "That quilt is the most gorgeous thing I ever saw!"

"I always say there's nobody can piece a quilt like your Aunt Mateel." They fussed with draping the quilt over the old upright piano so that its full prismatic beauty would draw the eyes of everyone who entered. Chances would be sold on it, and the lucky number drawn.

By suppertime Ellen would have been happy to have a sandwich and milk by herself in the deserted house, but everyone thought she had no problems and was as peaceful as she looked, so she washed and dressed and went off to the supper with the rest.

"Where's your cole slaw?" somebody whispered as the contributors set the food on the tables. "I want to be real handy to that. . . . Jo, did you bake your graham rolls? . . . Helmi made some of that Finnish bread you like, Foss. . . . Pea beans are good, but I like yellow-eye best. Where'd you ever find Jacob's cattle beans, Vi?"

Men's laughter. "No, I don't want to set there. I come up here on purpose to git away from the wife's cooking. Every time I eat Nora Fennell's pie I wonder if I didn't marry the wrong woman." Nudges in the ribs and more laughter.

Maternal tones. "Don't you start sliding on this floor! Mind your manners, or you'll be kiting for home before the shindig starts. . . . Don't you ask for coffee, just because you think you're out of my reach!"

In one of the Brigport boatloads there was a visiting minister, and as soon as he asked the blessing everyone fell to with huge enthusiasm. Ellen discovered she was hungry in spite of everything.

They were just starting to eat when the last contingent of Campions arrived, Suze and Asenath with their guest. Their weathered middle-aged faces were alight with smiles as they came in, and Ellen didn't blame them, for the girl who had been variously described as seasick, tearful, and a poor little thing was as pretty and as perfectly turned out as the teenage models in the glossiest magazines. Red hair, yes, in a short and apparently casual aureole around a pointed face with wide eyes. She wore something mint-green that emphasized a tiny waist, and her sandals were hardly more than child-size. No wonder the Campions were as delighted as children with a new toy. No, a new kitten, Persian and adorable.

The girl's eyes were roving shyly about the long room, and Ellen caught them and smiled, receiving a tentative smile in return. The rest of the Campions made room at their table, and Ellen went on eating, not before she saw Jamie and Eric nudge each other and stare entranced across the room.

Joey wasn't at the supper, but his father and mother were. "Joey's been so tired lately, what with seining every night, almost, and taking care of his traps," Vinnie explained to Ellen's mother. "He can't seem to get enough sleep, so he thought he'd pass things up tonight. 'Course, he's not much for dances anyway." She smiled at Ellen. "Unless Ellen gets him out. He'd r'ar up for her."

So nobody noticed anything wrong, but of course nobody knew that he was really serious about her. She smiled back and said, "I wouldn't disturb him. I know he's been working hard and there comes a time when nothing matters except sleep."

"Well, I guess there's plenty of partners for you tonight, anyway. Three boatloads from Brigport, and even a crowd from Stonehaven. My, won't they have a lovely sail home in the moonlight!"

After the scanty ruins of the pies and cakes were cleared away, it was time to draw for the quilt. The smallest child present, except for Ricky, was a two-year-old from Brigport. He drew a card from a mixing bowl, and was presented a stuffed percale horse from the fancy-work table. Owen Bennett, having the loudest voice in the community, read the winning number.

"Sixty-three. Who's got sixty-three? Isn't one of our crew, is it, Laurie?" he called to his wife, and everybody laughed. "Laurie smiled and shook her head, and Owen said, "Well, that's life. Never won anything yet. Who's sixty-three? Somebody strangle those noisy young ones on the porch, mine included. See if one of those bashful fellas out there has sixty-three."

"Here it is!" someone yelled from outside the door, where some of the men had gone to smoke. Pierre came in grinning, and everyone applauded him wildly.

" 'Tain't me," he said. "I'm just carrying his ticket. He's one of those bashful fellas. He says he gives up, and you draw again and see if somebody off the island gits it."

"Nope," said his uncle vehemently. "He won fair and square, and besides, he's got us all worked up wanting to know who he is."

"Gorry, you never advertised a mystery man on your posters," said someone from Brigport. "Fetch him in here."

"Well, it's Mr. Villiers," said Pierre.

"Well, I never!" a woman exclaimed. A pleased stir went through Bennett's people. Because they've caught him out, thought Ellen. This time they think he can't get away. He took some chances on the quilt just to help out, and now he's caught, and they're all glad he's going to be embarrassed. . . . Then and there she was on his side against everyone else.

Chapter I I

He came into a hush that wasn't broken as he walked the length of the hall to where Owen stood by the stove. He was as erect as a guardsman but seemed at ease, even smiling a little as he came up to Owen.

"You're sure you don't want to draw again?" he said.

"Nope, we're all set on you having that coverlid to brighten up your bachelor existence," said Owen, thoroughly enjoying himself as a master of ceremonies. "As a matter of fact, you'll likely get a lot of offers now that you're so well set up in household furnishings." He took Villiers's arm and swung him around to face the room. "You ladies from Brigport and Stonehaven, I want to make you acquainted with one of our most illegible bachelors, as the fella says. That means he can't read, but that's no serious handicap."

He must be hating this, Ellen thought, her hands clenched under the table. Each ripple of laughter made her hotter. Yet if Villiers was embarrassed he didn't show it.

"I think most of the ladies would rather have a chance at the quilt than at me," he said.

But Owen had infected the rest and Donna called out gaily, "It's yours! Put it in your hope chest!"

"Ayuh, he's keeping it all right, but we have to make a presentation." Owen scowled around the room. His gaze stopped at the Campions' entrancing little redhead, then hurried on to Ellen. His grin dazzled. "Come up here, miss, and do it all shipshape and Bristol-fashion."

Ellen didn't move, though everyone turned toward her and Linnea was bouncing with delight. Owen strode around the table and took her arm. "Come on, darlin' mine." She had to give in, and there she was facing Villiers, her cheeks hot, trying to tell him with her eyes that she was loathing it too, and seeing his face go politely blank.

Owen took the quilt from the piano. Somewhere Ellen found words. "I hope this quilt lasts you for a long, long time," she said, "and that every time you look at it you'll remember when you lived on Bennett's Island. Of course, we all hope you won't leave us just yet." She smiled, held out the folded quilt, and felt him take it. He nodded and said thank you, and it was over. She turned to go back to her seat, but Owen held her arm.

"As dance committee for tonight, I'm starting the dance right now— as soon as the squeezebox and fiddle get set—and these two are leading off in the first waltz." Everyone applauded wildly, boys whistled, and the musicians scuttled for their places.

She had never felt so helpless in her life, but it was Villiers who took the situation in hand. As "Over the Waves" began—it was always the boys' first tune, easy to limber up with—he put his arm around her and swung her out onto the floor. Soon everyone else was out and they were just one couple among many. Gradually the tautness relaxed in Ellen. He was a smooth and authoritative dancer, and she enjoyed that. But she couldn't think of anything to say. She felt woefully young.

He didn't seem to feel like talking either. He's probably just dying for this dance to end so he can make a decent retreat, she thought. Well, I'm dying for it to end too. What if he did think Owen was being a—a kind of country clown? I know how wonderful Owen really is! If he's looking down on us for our simple fun, no wonder he didn't want the quilt. She knew she was being unreasonable, swinging from one extreme to the other, but she couldn't help it. And then she heard herself saying softly to his jaw, "Why didn't you want the quilt?"

"For a very uncomplicated reason. It seems wasted on me. I think a woman should have it. Or at least a family man."

"I know it's just a homemade—"

The arm around her tightened abruptly, like a warning. "Don't depreciate anyone's handiwork. The quilt is a work of art and you know it. I know at least ten women, who consider themselves highly sophisticated, who'd give your aunt anything she asked for a quilt like that." His crisp tone softened. "And don't look for ulterior motives."

"Did you see Joey and me the day of the storm?" she asked abruptly. "Yes."

"Oh." She felt flat. "I thought perhaps you didn't recognize me. Or didn't see me wave."

"Oh, I saw you. I didn't feel conversational, that's all."

Why hadn't she thought of that? Again that wretchedly young and awkward feeling came over her. Wouldn't this dance ever end? Yet, when she thought it was about to end, she wished it wouldn't. They circled the hall again and she looked cautiously up at Villiers's face. He was gazing past her head, apparently serene, even pleased with himself and the evening. Now and then he nodded to someone he knew. And it occurred to her that he might be enjoying this dance because it was with her.

He swung her around Jamie and a little Brigport girl, who had stopped to argue about who stepped on whom, and she saw Joey standing in the doorway watching her. "Hello," she called softly as they passed him.

He jerked his chin in a sort of salute and didn't answer. Then she lost sight of him, and when she looked again he was gone. She felt a little hurt and lost; she and Joey had always had a good time at the clubhouse things. It didn't seem right to have him angry with her.

The dance was over, and Villiers led her to the bench against the wall to which Joanna and Nils were just returning. "Thank you," he said to Ellen in a low tone. There was some general conversation with her parents, and then he went through the nearby door into the room where some of the nondancers were playing pool.

The next dance was a square dance, "Lady of the Lake." Steve came to ask his sister out, and Nils took Linnea. Ellen looked about for Joey. Pride be darned, she and Joey had been friends too long; she'd ask him to dance this time. . . . She saw him. He was leading the Campions' redhead onto the floor. She came up to his shoulder and he was bending his head interestedly toward her as she said in a sweet, worried voice, "But I never did this before! You'll be sorry you asked me!"

"Oh, no, I won't," said Joey with unexpected gallantry. "You'll learn it real quick, Amy."

Well, tit for tat, thought Ellen wryly and sat back on the bench. Someone said, "May I have this dance?" She looked around quickly. A big youth with a brown crew cut stood over her. He grinned ruefully. "I'd ask for the pleasure of this dance, except that 'Lady of the Lake' isn't a pleasure for me yet. But maybe it will be, with you," he added politely.

Ellen stood up. "It's fun after you really know it by heart."

"I know. That's why I'm grimly driving myself through it. . . . I'm Fritz Galbraith. I came in the Stonehaven boat."

"I saw you," said Ellen, smiling.

"Did you?" He was ingenuously pleased. "I saw you right away too. And I asked your name. Ellen Douglass. Sounds like a Walter Scott heroine. . . . I bought one of your pictures, the stormy one. Well, I suppose we have to get lined up," he said reluctantly. "You're sure you wouldn't rather go outside and talk?"

"I'm sure I'd rather dance," said Ellen, smiling, and he grinned back.

"Onward and upward. Remember Thermopylae!"

It turned out to be great fun. Fritz pranced through his part like a clever bear, so happy with himself and everyone else that it was catching. Whenever he joined Ellen he said joyously, "How'm I doing?" and she assured him he was doing marvelously. Sometimes she caught a glimpse of the Campions' redhead being tenderly steered from one figure to another, or nestling against Joey's chest and imploring him to swing her very slowly because she got so dizzy. In fact, before the dance was over she got so dizzy that when she and Joey promenaded down the hall they kept on going straight through the front door, and somebody whistled after them.

Joey just isn't the type to start necking right off, Ellen thought. Or is he? Just because he never kissed me until last year doesn't prove anything.

The rest of the evening was busy, with Fritz trying for every dance but sometimes losing out. Joey did not come near. When somebody else was dancing with the new girl, he stayed outside on the porch.

"I declare," his mother said to Joanna, "I never saw Joey so active at a dance before." She gave Ellen a worried glance. "I'm sure the Campions have pushed him into this, and he doesn't know how to get out of it. I hope he's got gumption enough not to walk home with her."

"Oh, Joey's got gumption for the things that count," said Ellen, not quite sure what she meant but apparently satisfying Joey's mother, who looked relieved.

Fritz, getting her once in a Liberty Waltz, said, "May I have the last waltz and walk you home? I know where you live."

"I'm sorry, Fritz. I—I'm walking home with somebody else." It was true. With her mother, she thought grimly.

"Oh." He was disappointed, but a cheerful loser. "Sure, you would be all dated up, anyway. Who is he?" He looked interestedly around the floor. "That older guy who danced with you first? Where's he gone, anyway?"

"Probably home," said Ellen. "No, he's not the one."

"Well, look, can I come over from Stonehaven some day, and—"

"All join hands!" Owen called, and she was glad there was no more chance to talk.

In the brief intermission that gave everyone a chance to rest up from the long square dance before the last waltz, she went out into the kitchen to get a drink. She considered slipping out the back door into the spruces and escaping. Whoever asked for the last waltz would expect to walk home with her, and she wanted to walk home with no one. Except, she added in bleak honesty, Joey. And he seemed to be well taken care of.

She glanced back into the hall. Nobody was looking in her direction. She could be out of sight in an instant.

Her hand was on the doorknob when someone spoke her name. It was Joey, tall and awkward in the kitchen doorway, staring at her with angry anxiety. "Can I have the last waltz?"

She felt silly with relief. "I don't know!" She laughed. "Are you free?"

"What do you mean by that?" he demanded angrily.

"Nothing, except that—"

The accordion struck up "Let Me Call You Sweetheart." She moved toward Joey and into his arms and out onto the floor. Fritz, of all people, was dancing with Amy. He beamed at Ellen.

"So he's the one!" he called.

"What's he mean by that?" said Joey suspiciously as the two couples whirled apart.

"He wanted this dance, but I was saving it for you."

He was pleased, she could tell, and that pleased her. "What if I hadn't asked ye?" he said gruffly close to her ear.

"Then I'd have snuck out and gone home alone."

"No need to ever do that when I'm around," said Joey masterfully, and they finished the dance in contented silence.

They took the long way home in the moonlight, up into the woods where they found a black-and-silver orchard bewitched and motionless in the night. They sat on an old fragment of stone wall.

I'm so glad to make up with Joey, I must be in love with him, Ellen thought. I'll know when he kisses me.

But he didn't move to kiss her right away. "Some dance," he said.

"Yes, it was a nice one. Amy's darling," she added generously.

"Oh, she's all right, I suppose. Wants to go haul with me tomorrow, but Gemini, I don't want her! A hundred traps makes a long day, I don't want any women along. I don't know why Asa can't take her."

"It'd be a lot more interesting with you. You're young, for one thing," she added seriously.

"Will you come?"

"I'm sorry," she said honestly, "but I'm on clean-up committee for tomorrow. You know what somebody's sure to say if I run off with you, much as I'd love to."

"Old biddies," he muttered. "Well, maybe it'll rain. Or blow. Or come in foggy. Come to think of it, we haven't had much fog yet for August."

"Well, don't go praying for it, or everybody will bless you—I don't think."

"If I get stuck with her I'll only haul about fifty. That'll be enough to get her good and sick."

"Don't you sound mean!" she said softly. "And she's such a pretty little thing."

"How come Villiers was at the dance tonight?" he said unexpectedly.

"I don't know. Everybody was surprised, I guess."

"What did Owen have to drag you into it for? Getting you up there for that foolishness about the quilt?"

"Are you mad?" she asked him in hushed astonishment. "Good heavens, Joey, you know Owen!"

"And pushing you into the first dance with him—"

"So you were there all the time," she said. "Skulking around outside. If you'd been in there, we could have had the first dance together. I'd have said it was promised."

"Good thing I wasn't there," he muttered. "Might've spoiled your fun."

"Joey Caldwell," she said bluntly, "are you trying to pick a fight?"

"No! But everybody could see what a good time you were having with Villiers, and you acted as if you knew him a darn sight better than anyone else does, too! And what I want to know is, has he got anything to do with the way you're dragging your feet?"

She stood up. "No, he has not." She kept her voice quiet. "I think of him as a very nice and interesting person. But that hardly constitutes a raging passion, does it?"

In the moonlight his face was pale and stern, unfamiliar to her with its dark-shadowed eyes and the mouth cut like a stone statue's. In spite of her hurt and anger she was intrigued by the planes and angles thus revealed, and her anger began to slip away from her, even when Joey said, "I know how you looked and how he looked."

"And how did I look with Fritz Galbraith?" she asked gently. "And how did he look?"

"It was different," he said stubbornly.

"Oh, Joey." Her voice was mournful. "I don't want to fight. I'm so happy to be with you tonight. We've been friends for almost all our lives." She put her hand on his shoulder, waiting, hardly breathing, and after a long moment he put his hand over it.

"I don't want to fight either," he said, "but it seems as if everything rubs me the wrong way these days. Sometimes it's as if I never knew you at all—or else you're somebody different every time I see you." He stood up and drew her toward him, his hands on her waist. "But I know one thing. I won't ask you again to marry me. It's got to come from you. So I'll be waiting." He kissed her gently, then slid his arm around her and started back to the path that would lead them out of the enchanted black-and-silver orchard and back to the village.

Chapter 12

So there was peace between them. Or was there? Ellen wasn't sure. But then, she was sure of so very little these days. The island remained the same, and so did the family, lovable or maddening, sometimes surprisingly sensitive or appallingly obtuse.

And of course one other thing stayed the same, the thing which until now had been almost more important than anything else: what happened to her when she took a pencil or brush in her hand.

On the afternoon following the dance, she sat cross-legged on the old wharf, working furiously to get a dory as it lay on the incoming tide. A dory was one of the hardest things in the world to draw, for ideally it should look as sleek and slender and light as a mussel shell, but one wrong line could turn it into a heavy, sullen block of wood on the sketch pad. She worked fast as the dory twitched airily this way and that, and all the time she was conscious of the sun on her head and shoulders, of an ant crawling over her legs, of children, a dog, a young gull peeping like a penny whistle, men's voices from down beside the wharf where they were fitting a new propeller to a boat.

I should get Asa and Foss working, down there under the curve of the bilge, she thought. Good in oils. The side of the boat catching the sunlight, the men in the shade, the mossy old wet wharf spilings and barnacled rocks behind them, and then the new brass propeller in their hands all agleam in the shadows. . . . She saw it, but how could she leave when she almost had the dory?

"May I look?" someone said softly, and she started nervously and looked around. Red curls caught the sun. Amy Harper, in brief pink shorts and sleeveless blouse, stood beside her. She smiled trustingly down at Ellen. "I never saw an artist at work before. Ooh, it's a boat!"

"I'm not an artist," said Ellen. "I'm just trying."

"It looks like fun." Amy sat down and hugged her knees. "All those cute little drawings. I've never tried it."

Go ahead, said Ellen silently. Get a perfect dory at the first whack. No use trying to work now, with someone sitting there watching expectantly for her to perform. Her mood was gone. But of course Amy couldn't know that. She smiled at the girl.

"How do you like the island?"

"Oh, I adore it!" Amy cried. "I never dreamed it could be so beautiful! Wasn't last night simply fabulous?" She looked out at the harbor, smiling to herself and humming "Let Me Call You Sweetheart."

"Did Joey take you to haul this morning?" Ellen tried a gull, neck outstretched, shrieking a warning at another gull not to land near him.

"Oh, yes. Isn't he simply fabulous?" She put her hand to her mouth and her eyes grew round. "Maybe I shouldn't say that, but of course you know it already, and I always say what's the good of having a boyfriend that nobody else goes for?"

Ellen gave her a sidewise look, but Amy's little face was as innocent as a kitten's turned toward a butterfly. "Anyway," she went on, "it's just wonderful of you not to get mad because he wanted to show me what it was like."

"But why should I get mad?" Ellen asked calmly.

"Well, after all!" Amy giggled. "I know how I'd feel if a new girl appeared in town and my man wanted to show her the sights—"

"What's your man like?" Ellen interrupted brightly.

"Oh, he's all right," Amy conceded. "He's going to be a lawyer. He's working for the Park Department for the summer, cutting hedges and mowing grass and things. But you know, just since yesterday he seems so young. The boys around here are so—so mature!"

Ellen said, "Well," which seemed a good, safe, noncommittal statement.

"Your cousin Pierre's a real doll, with those eyelashes," said Amy. "He's going to take me around—is it Sou'west Point? Where the Raven's Nest is?"

"Yes," said Ellen. "Pierre's fun."

"But still, I like men to be a lot taller than me, don't you? Joey makes me feel so—oh, I don't know!" She hugged herself rapturously and wrinkled up her nose, then again looked elaborately embarrassed. "There I go!

I don't know what you must think."

"About what?" asked Ellen, wishing Joey could overhear this. He would be positively scarlet to the tips of his ears.

"About me! Running on so about your man!"

Ellen felt suddenly like shouting, "Oh, for heaven's sake, he's not mine!" Instead she got up. "I'm glad you're having such a good time. It's nice for the Campions too, having you here."

"Dear old Aunt Suze and Uncle Asa," said Amy, then cried out delightedly, "Here comes Joey now! Guess what! He's going to take me fishing out in the harbor!"

Joey came by Gage's fishhouse and advanced to where the dory was tied. Without looking around to where one man was loading a skiff with traps, another was splitting a codfish, and several others lounged in the door of a bait shed, he put fishlines and a couple of herring for bait into the dory, untied the painter, and pushed off, swinging himself over the side.

"Hey, Joey!" someone called. "Which one you taking?"

"How do you manage to git all the girls, Joey?" somebody else teased. Joey's jaw was long and tight, and he didn't look around. He rowed out into deep water and then headed for the outer end of the wharf.

"You'd better not keep him waiting, Amy," said Ellen.

"I guess not!" Amy dimpled. "I don't want him mad at me!" She ran lightly over the planks, turning to call back, "Thanks awfully, Ellen. You're just fabulous not to mind!"

It must be sincere. Nobody could be that corny on purpose. Joey's head appeared over the wharf as he stood up in the dory, holding it to the ladder, and Ellen smiled and waved at him. "Catch a lot of pollock!" she called. He didn't answer, just stared at her bleakly.

"Oh, my!" gasped Amy. "These ladders, Joey!"

Ellen left the wharf. Mindful of the others who'd been watching the byplay, she didn't intend to give anyone a chance to say she'd gone home in a huff, even though she did feel definitely huffy. She went around the beach and did a sketch of Gage's fishhouse.

Gage came along the shore from his house. He never looked quite like a fisherman in spite of work pants, rubber boots, and duck-billed cap.

"Do me one sometime as a souvenir of my days as a lobsterman, Ellen," he said. "I'll frame it and hang it where I can always see it. It'll keep me humble, if I ever get into a spot where I'm in danger of getting too big for my boots."

"You seem pretty cheerful."

"I am." His smile was happy. "There were times this summer when I thought we weren't going to make it, but I've done so well this month that if I were superstitious I'd be scared stiff. We haven't told this to any-body else, Ellen—" He dropped his voice. "—And I suppose that's super-stition in a way—but we expect to be going back to school before long."

"Oh, Gage," she said softly. "I'm so glad."

"I wake up in the morning with an idiotic grin on my face. I love everything and everybody. I'm glad I've had this year down here, don't get me wrong. I'm glad there was such a place where we could come and get our feet back under us." He blew out a long breath. "But a civil engi-neer is what I was meant to be. I'll be building highways and bridges yet."

"I'm ashamed to say I haven't seen Donna for a week. But I'll be she's happy."

"Well, with reservations. She doesn't say much, but I guess she thinks if she's too overjoyed something might happen. . . . In another year, if we can find a good day nursery, she could finish her training." He couldn't keep from smiling. "Look, Ellen, if I get to M.I.T. eventually, which is what I want, we'll all be around Boston at the same time."

"That sounds wonderful." She kept her eyes on her work. If I'm not here with babies of my own, she thought.

"You'd better drop around and assure Donna that Little Amy's no menace," he said dryly. "She's all fussed up. I told her you had your mind on your work and not on Joey, but she won't believe it. She thinks early marriage is good for everybody."

She didn't one day, Ellen thought. "Do you?" she asked.

"That depends," he said after a moment, his voice very quiet. "I'd be a heel if I denied that there have been high spots in our marriage that I wouldn't swap for a million dollars, or that Donna and Ricky mean my life to me. But I'd be a hypocrite if I denied that sometimes I've felt like one of those lobsters I haul up in a trap. Pegged so I couldn't fight, thrown into a crate, next stop the kettle. I used to wish I was a happy moron with no talents whatever. But knowing you've got something and can't use it—" He pushed back his cap and wiped his forehead. "Just thinking about it makes me sweat. I'm glad you're going to study, Ellen. Don't let anybody talk you into giving it up until you've found out just how good you are."

Mother was right, Ellen thought in awe. She said almost exactly what Gage is saying now. But it wouldn't be the same for me, a woman. How could it be? Aren't women meant, first and foremost, to have babies and a home?

As if he were answering her thoughts, Gage said, "There's your whole life for marriage, and a world of men to choose from. And that's enough from the old philosopher for today. . . . I've got to bait up. I guess I'll bottle some essence of corned herring to go along with the sketch of the fishhouse."

"And I've got to go home," lied Ellen. She didn't have to go anywhere. But she thought angrily as she walked through the village, I should tell Joey tonight it's yes and put an end to it once and for all. Then everybody will leave me alone. And Amy will stop gurgling at me.

Joey didn't come up that night. Eric, coming from the Eastern End after supper, announced that he'd met Joey and Amy coming through the Eastern End gate. They were going out to Fern Cliff to watch the moon rise.

"She told me," he said. "Gorry, she runs on, doesn't she? Bet Joey won't have any ears left by the time she leaves. He looked kind of funny when he saw me. Poor guy."

"Poor guy nothing!" said Jamie. "I bet if she was homely he'd find a way to get out of it."

Ellen went to bed early and shut out the moonlight. She wasn't upset because Joey was out with Amy, she told herself angrily. It was just that the moonlight was too beautiful not to be shared. She'd like to go back to the orchard again, but not alone. An almost frightening sadness seized her at the thought and she felt like someone standing completely isolated at the center of a swirling, laughing crowd.

A message got through to her from the outer world the next day in the form of a note from Fritz Galbraith. "I've got your painting in my room," he wrote, "but would rather have a picture of the artist. This is by way of asking where I can reach you in Boston this fall. I thought I'd get back to your island to see you, but have to push off sooner than expected, to greet an ancient uncle from California who refuses to come to Maine because he thinks the snow lasts all summer. . . . So will you please, please write me at the address below and tell me if I can show Boston to you and you to Boston?"

She smiled in spite of herself, remembering the happy bear. The letter was nice to have, even if she didn't know whether she would answer it.

At sunset that night, everyone around the harbor saw Joey's boat head out toward the west. Amy stood by Joey at the wheel. The setting was familiar; it was to be a sail around the island, coming home by moonlight. Ellen was out rowing Linnea around the harbor in Jamie's double-ender when they went, and as the rowboat danced in the wake Linnea cried indignantly, "I hate that Amy!"

"No, you don't," Ellen said. "What did she ever do to you?"

"And I hate Joey too! Why didn't he take you?"

Why, indeed? Ellen had felt a real twinge at sight of them, and wondered if it was simply because she'd like to sail around the island with Joey as they used to do, or whether it was acute jealousy. She smiled at the angry child and said, "Aren't we having fun? If I was with Joey, you and I wouldn't be out here."

To her dismay Linnea's eyes filled with tears. "I thought if you m-m-married Joey," she stammered, "you w-wouldn't go away, but you don't even c-c-care!"

"I do care, Linnie," Ellen said.

"No you don't. You'll go away, and then next year Jamie and Eric will go away to high school, and—and—" She wiped her eyes on her sweater sleeve and wept again.

Why she is like me, Ellen thought in astonishment. And I never knew it. She worries the way I used to. She wants everything and everyone to go unchanged, world without end.

"Linnie darling," she said softly, "you'll be so busy and so happy, you won't have time to miss anybody."

Linnea bowed her head onto her knees and gave herself up to weeping. She'd had a long day, full of the usual rapturous ups and devastating downs. Ellen remembered herself as a child, lying in bed crying softly because she was so tired that the sheer beauty of the gulls flying homeward in dark silhouette past the evening star was too much to be borne.

She turned the double-ender toward the shore. Linnea stopped crying, and except for a sniff and a hiccup she was calm and cheerful by the time they reached the house. After all, her father and mother were there, looking as usual, and Philip the cat. All the important parts of her small personal world were as yet unchanged. Uncle Steve and Aunt Philippa had walked up from the Eastern End, and that added to her sense of security, hearing the laughter and voices downstairs as she fell asleep.

In the morning, Ellen thought, she won't care whether I go or stay. As for herself, tonight she would not shut out the moonlight. The island was hers, the moon was hers, and she needed no one else with whom to share it. Last night she'd been emotionally about as old as Linnea.

She left quietly by the back door, cut through the velvet, dark woods and into the lake of light that was the Bennett meadow. Little scarves of mist looked luminous and artificial in the hollows. She came out above Schoolhouse Cove. Sitting on a rock still warm from the day's heat, she gazed across the pale shine of water at Windward Point and the spark of light in Villiers's windows.

The hour she had spent with him there was still with her, even though for days she did not consciously think of it. I wish I could go back, she thought now. I wish I knew him well enough to tap at the door and walk in and sit down at the scrubbed table and talk a while. . . . She heard the faint throb of an engine in the silent night: Joey's boat, somewhere along the outer shores. Then it stopped.

She couldn't sit still anymore after that, and walked the length of the beach. Were Joey and Amy sitting on the engine box? Was Amy whispering, "Ooh, I'm scared," or "My, I'm cold." And Joey—

I might call on Villiers at that, she thought, walking faster. Tell him I've come to see how he and the quilt are getting along.

But there was no light by the time she'd climbed the bank to his door. Her tap seemed thunderous in the hush, and afterward she could hear her heart beating.

It was like Walter de la Mare's poem, "The Listeners." Everyone in her English class liked it, without really knowing why. " 'Tell them I came, and no one answered,' " she said aloud, and turned away from the door, and climbed up onto the point.

There was something about an empty house . . . if it was empty. But what if he had seen her on the beach, recognized her in the moonlight, and had blown out the lamp and gone upstairs?

The picture hurt her pride and instantly she wanted to hurt him. If I marry Joey, she thought fiercely, I'll turn out to be just what he thought I wasn't. He could say I let him down, as if I owed him anything, a stranger and a darn strange one at that!

How right was Joey when he accused Villiers of being responsible for her indecision? That day in early summer when Villiers had come upon her while she was painting—had he flattered her so much that she'd been trying to live up to his picture of her, rather than be what she truly was? Who was right about her, Joey, Villiers, she herself, or even Fritz Galbraith, who simply saw her as a nice girl he'd like to date in Boston this winter? Or Gage?

When she came to the harbor she turned off around the shore. Maybe Donna's and Gage's happy atmosphere would infect her. She tapped at the back door and let herself into the kitchen. The Aladdin lamp was bright in the sitting room.

"It's me," she said softly, going toward the light. Only Donna was there, lying on the couch.

"Oh, hello," she said thickly. Her nose was red, her face was blotched, and she had a handkerchief in her hand.

"What have you got, hay fever, for heaven's sake?" said Ellen.

"I wish that was it." Donna's voice broke and she turned her face away from the light. Quickly Ellen drew the shades.

"No use sitting in a goldfish bowl," she said briskly. "What's the trouble? Can you use a cup of tea?"

"You and my mother. Think a cup of tea cures everything." She sat up drearily. "Did you see Gage anywhere?"

"I haven't seen anybody."

"He's probably committed suicide by now." Donna blew her nose.

"Not the way he was this afternoon!" But dismay knotted her stomach. Now what? "Apparently half the island's out wandering lonely as a cloud tonight," she went on.

"Why didn't you go with Joey and protect your property?" But the old spirit was gone from Donna's voice.

"Look, if Joey can't take care of himself, that's his lookout. I know you were afraid of somebody getting Gage before you did, but—"

"I wish somebody had got him!" Donna burst out. "And I wish somebody had carted me off to a padded cell and kept me there till I got over thinking I wanted to get married!"

Appalled, Ellen went out into the kitchen and put the kettle on. When she came back, Donna poured out the story.

"We may be having another baby. I've been worried sick about how to tell Gage, he's been so happy, and writing letters to the university and everything, and all week I kept hoping I wouldn't have to tell him anything. But tonight he kept at me, wanted to know if I was unhappy at leaving the island and the family, or what, so finally I had to tell him." She stared bleakly at the playpen in the corner. "He didn't say a word. He just looked—well, stunned. Then he got up and went out. That's all."

Thank goodness for the kettle. It was beginning to boil and Ellen went back to the kitchen. Donna came out, looking plain and defeated. "But he's been working so hard—we've saved every possible cent—to take care of school, and now—" She broke off.

Ellen couldn't think of anything to say. She poured boiling water on the tea bags.

"What I'm afraid of," Donna said drearily, "is that someday he'll resent us. The children and me. Me most of all, for making him lose so much."

"I think Gage is too honest ever to blame you. After all, it takes two to make a marriage."

"I didn't have to say yes, did I?" She began to cry again. "You think you can't live without somebody, you have to have them right this minute or you'll die, and then one day you wake up, but it's too late. And I love Gage so. That's what makes it worse."

"And he loves you. He told me that you and Ricky were his whole life."

"Not quite," said Donna, with a sad little smile. "Not quite his whole life."

She began to sip her tea. They sat silently at the table, until there was a step outside and Gage came in. He looked drawn and ill.

"Hello, Ellen."

"Hello, Gage. I'm just leaving."

"Don't hurry." But it was perfunctory. He kept watching Donna, who looked up at him with drenched eyes.

"Good night," Ellen said, but neither answered. As she shut the door behind her she heard Gage say, "Come on, honey bunch, we've got to think of the little feller. This isn't his fault." A great sob burst from Donna and then Gage was murmuring things too private to be overheard.

They'll be all right, Ellen told herself. But she wasn't sure of it. She hurried home, eager suddenly for the companionship of the older people who had fought their early battles, lived through their young griefs, and shown that it could be done.

Chapter 13

She lay in bed the next morning, wondering what energetic and absorbing thing she could do with her day when she didn't really feel energetic. A good thick book down on Sou'west Point, away from everybody, seemed the most inviting suggestion.

She heard Nils going out, the sound of rubber boots on the grassy path, the faint squeak of the gate and the murmur of his voice as he said good-bye to Philip, the cat. The children weren't stirring. Except for a small noise now and then from down in the kitchen, as her mother moved around, the house was quiet in the sunrise. An engine started up in the harbor, and then another. A gull called repeatedly as it passed overhead. Then she heard the squeak of the gate again, and this time the rub-

ber boots came toward the house, and they didn't sound like her stepfather's. They were faster.

"Why, hello, Joey!" her mother's voice said, almost under the open
window. "I was just about to get some beets from the garden."

"Is Ellen up yet?" Joey sounded tense. Ellen's apathy departed. She
jumped out of bed, pulled on a robe, brushed her hair quickly, and went
downstairs and out into the dewy grass.

"I'm up," she announced.

"So you are," said her mother with humorous surprise. "Well, I'll go
pull my beets."

Joey and Ellen remained by the rain barrel, Joey scowling and Ellen
smiling faintly at him. "What's the matter?" she said.

"Look!" he burst out. "She wants to go on a picnic over to the sand
beach on Brigport tonight. She's been talking about it ever since she got
here. Our beaches aren't good enough. Guess she thinks it's Hawaii or
something over there, all that white sand."

"So?"

"So you've got to come too."

Ellen tightened the belt of her robe and wriggled her toes enjoyably
in the wet grass. "Why?"

"Because I want you to, that's why. Gorry, I can't say no to her, living
right next door! Asa and Suze keep beaming at me all the time, they're so
tickled. But at least I can ask who I want in my own boat!" He was quite
red.

"Well, won't Amy mind? If she thinks it's just going to be you two,
coming back in the moonlight—"

"I don't care what she thinks!" said Joey violently. "It's still my boat.
Look, you get hold of Pierre, huh? He and your uncle are staying ashore
today to work on their wharf, or I'd nail him when we're out. We've both
got traps on Old Hoss Shoal. Ask him to come too."

"She did say she thought he was a doll," Ellen said, relenting. "All
right, I'll talk to him."

Joey sagged against the rain barrel. "Whew! I woke up about ha'past
three with that trapped feeling." His smile was quick and brilliant. "See
you, then. I'll bring in a mess of lobsters for us. She's going to make a
cake. Claims she can cook."

"Probably she can," said Ellen. Joey made an ambiguous grunt and
strode off. Ellen watched him go, suddenly depressed. The word
"trapped" reminded her of Gage and Donna.

Later in the morning Ellen went down to the shore, where Uncle

Charles and Pierre were repairing their wharf. "Can I talk to your hired man for a minute, Uncle Charles?" she asked.

"Sure, as long as he keeps on working." Then his dark face softened in a grin. "Guess he's earned five minutes off. I'm going over to the store for some cold pop."

"Make mine root beer," Pierre called after him. He finished prying up a rotten plank, leaned the pinch bar against the pile of new planks, and mopped his forehead under the black curls.

"You do have nice eyelashes," Ellen said thoughtfully.

"Huh?"

"Amy says they're divine."

"Oh, her."

"Well, aren't you impressed?"

Pierre gave her a look from under the divine lashes. It was a little difficult to interpret. She went on quickly. "We're going on a picnic to the sand beach tonight, and we want you to go too."

"Who's we?" asked Pierre suspiciously.

"Joey and I. And Amy, of course. It was her idea."

"She doesn't want me along. All she wants is Joey. Boy, what a dope she is. I don't mean because she wants Joey," he added hastily. Ellen smiled.

"Didn't you have a nice walk the other day?"

"Oh, lovely. Joey was still out hauling and she nearly broke her neck and both ankles trying to keep his boat in sight. All I heard about was Joey. He's so manly. He's so masculine. He's so tall." Pierre's slight build was a great trial to him. "Tell you one thing: If I had me a steady girl on the island, Amy would think I was wonderful too."

"Meaning?" Ellen asked lightly.

"Meaning I wouldn't go on her lousy picnic tonight, but you'd better go. You're the reason she thinks he's so wonderful. Like the guys who make their living hauling other guys' traps. Too many nights in the moonlight with her snuggling up under his arm, and Joey won't know whether he's afoot or horseback."

"Thanks," said Ellen.

"You think I'm kidding, don't you?"

"What makes you think Joey and I are steadies? We don't act that way, do we?"

Pierre contented himself with a sound that was at once a sneer, a snort, and a villainous laugh, and picked up the pinch bar again.

"I wish you'd come, Pierre," Ellen said as winningly as she could, and this time he gave her the charming Bennett smile.

"Darlin' mine, I don't believe in wasting my sweetness on the desert air, as it says in that poem we had to learn in school."

"Maybe if you recited some poetry to Amy, she'd think you were so intellectual," said Ellen, but she had no hope of persuading Pierre to come.

Before she went home she went around the harbor to Donna's. But no one was home. Gage, of course, had gone to haul, and Donna must have taken the baby and left as soon as he did, probably seeking some comfort from her mother. Ellen washed the dishes and put the oatmeal pan to soak. She felt a wave of guilty relief that she was not in Donna's position; not because of the babies, but because of Donna's state of mind at the present.

At home she made brownies for the picnic. Eric and Jamie, coming in from hauling their traps, had a warm sample apiece. They offered to go to the picnic in Pierre's place when she told them Pierre couldn't go, though not why. Linnea wanted to go simply because it was a picnic, and involved going somewhere in a boat.

"Look," said Ellen, "we can have a family picnic over there, and it'll be a lot more fun than this one."

"That's what people always say when they don't want kids along," Jamie remarked. "That it's not going to be fun. Then why are they going?"

"That's a good question," said Eric.

"To which I can't think of a good answer," said Ellen. They all laughed but Linnea, who looked puzzled.

"Just the same," said Jamie, "Pierre's crazy as a coot not to go on a picnic with that lollypop."

"Yeah man," agreed Eric. "Let's go down to the harbor. Maybe we can take her for a row."

They went out rapidly. "They're foolish," said Linnea. "Why do girls even look at boys? I'm never going to!" She left.

Joey was disgusted when Ellen told him Pierre wouldn't come. "What's biting him?" he growled.

"There was something else he had to do," she said vaguely. "I didn't get it all. Maybe he owes Uncle Charles more work, or something."

"Well, we'll survive, I suppose," Joey muttered.

If Amy was disconcerted at sight of Ellen on the Caldwell wharf, she didn't show it. "Oh, hello!" she trilled. "Don't you look darling in those skinny slacks! I wish I was nice and tall."

This had the effect of making Ellen feel like a bean pole. "Sometimes I think being small has its advantages," she said.

Amy giggled and wrinkled her nose.

Joey handed her into the boat as if she were fine bone china. Ellen got aboard without help. She always had, and didn't intend to become suddenly helpless now.

The slight wind had gone easterly, no surprise after several days of heartbreakingly lovely, calm weather. Brigport looked near enough to touch, as bright and sharp as an island cut from paper and pasted on a luminous sky.

"Fog before morning," Joey said to Ellen. "It's lying offshore now. Maybe move in by dark."

"Then give the word to start for home when you feel like it."

"Can't we come home by moonlight?" cried Amy.

"Not if it's foggy," said Joey.

"Oh, I've never been out in the fog!" Amy looked entranced.

Though it was three miles to Brigport harbor, it was only a mile across to the long white sand beach. They anchored offshore and rowed in. By the time the lobsters were cooked, in a kettle of sea water over a driftwood fire built among the rocks at one end of the beach, sunset was edging each little aquamarine wavelet with gilt lace. Joey and Ellen did the work, while Amy wandered up and down the beach, ecstatic over mussel shells, periwinkles, and sandpipers. Her cake was good. Ellen could congratulate her wholeheartedly on that.

"Thanks, darling," said Amy. "You're sweet. My mother raised me to be a good cook. She says that's the most important thing for a woman to be." She looked solemnly at Joey. "No career, she says, is more important for a woman than being a good wife."

"I guess I'll have another of those brownies, Ellen," Joey said.

When they were through eating and had cleaned up, and Amy had collected a sizable heap of driftwood and shells, Joey was content to sit still, and Ellen was never tired of watching the sea and the forever-changing sunset colors. But Amy was restless.

"Let's explore the island!" she suggested.

Joey all but groaned, then rallied manfully. "I've got a better idea. Let's sail around the harbor and get ice cream, and then go home."

Anything delighted Amy. So they helped transfer her collection from the beach to the skiff, thence from the skiff into *Sea Pigeon*, while she chattered happily the whole time. Whoever gets her is going to be talked to death, Ellen thought. Joey was so obviously silent that she made a special effort to be responsive to Amy and keep the conversation going, but she felt tired and edgy behind her good-natured manner.

At the harbor the usual group of young people were around the store, eating ice cream cones and drinking pop. The older men sat inside, smoking and talking. On the fringes were the youngsters like Jamie and Eric, torn between the fascinating yarns they might hear from the men if they listened long enough, and the exuberant good spirits outside the store. They were old enough to look at girls with curiosity, young enough to mock at them and prefer a man's world.

The middle group gave Joey and the girls a large welcome. "Hey! Where'd you get two of 'em? That's no fair! . . . How's that critter manage it? He's the shyest thing feet ever hung on and was called a man."

"That's what does it," Ellen said. "Still waters run deep."

"She means," said one girl, "why don't you men ever shut your mouth five minutes and be interesting instead of loud?"

Ellen had gone to school with most of them in the years when Bennett's had no school and she boarded with a Brigport family. She knew that every one of the boys, who ranged from sixteen or so up into the early twenties like Joey, was a self-supporting lobsterman. Listening to them now, watching one try to throw another while the girls laughed or applauded, she understood what Amy meant about their being grown up. Right now they were acting no older than Jamie or Eric, but at work they were as wise about the sea as gulls or seals. They had to be self-reliant, able to think far ahead and to make intensely serious decisions on the spot. And deep in them, for all their gay foolishness, they had a fierce love for the wild, beautiful world around them. Otherwise they would have fled from it for the cities, as a few others had done.

Amy expanded like a blossom in the sun. She was an enormous success and let the boys know that they were, too. Lashes fluttering, dimples deepening, nose wrinkling, laughter bubbling, she gave them the full barrage. Ellen, keeping a straight face, mapped the girls' reactions, as their natural friendliness and good manners struggled with incredulity.

"Did you knit your sweater yourself, Ellen?" Phillida Robey asked, coming over to look at the stitches. Under her breath she said, "Oh, brother. Is it real or did somebody make it up?"

"It's real—I think. She's just a harmless little thing having a ball."

"Is Joey bored stiff, or just grim with jealousy?"

Joey sat on his heels, his back against the wall of the store, looking out at the harbor through narrowed eyes. Ellen felt a little twist of something not pleasant. Was Joey grim because the others were getting the full treatment which hitherto had been directed at him alone?

"He wants to get home before the fog sets in," she said.

"Well, he'll have to drag her off by the hair of her head. Are you sure she's harmless?" Both girls laughed, but Ellen was uneasy. She saw Amy as a featherweight whose flirtatious ways were those of a pretty kitten but that didn't mean a male would see her in the same light. Joey might possibly find her female and fascinating.

Suddenly Joey got up and went into the store. Ellen followed after a few minutes and found him leaning against the counter, apparently listening while two elderly men compared their experiences on the Grand Banks. She said in a low voice, "I can smell fog out there, Joey."

"Ayuh. We better get going. She ready?"

"She'll be ready if you tell her why you want to go. After all, she doesn't know anything about the fog," Ellen said reasonably.

"I guess not," he muttered. "Picnic." It sounded like a bad word. They went outside, but Amy was not in sight. Neither was half the crowd.

Phillida Robey said, "They've gone up to Sam's to play some records he brought home from the mainland. Amy just loves Elvis. He's so virile."

Ellen glanced quickly at Joey's austere face, and then out at the water. The afterglow was fading, and the fog was clearly visible outside the harbor. It came in rapidly as the air cooled after sunset. The horizon was already hidden.

"We'd better go after her," she said.

Joey's mouth was hard. "Not me."

"Well, I'd like to get home," said Ellen, trying not to sound sharp. "We should have told her about the fog. I'll go."

She went up the road away from the harbor, which was soon hidden by the spruce woods. She felt tired and cross, and wasn't sure with whom she was cross.

Joey should have started home as soon as they'd eaten, instead of grumping around. But, on the other hand, Amy shouldn't have run off like that. And then there was always that nagging little question: just what was Joey grumping about? This morning he'd behaved as if it was a difficult chore to squire Amy, but tonight if he wasn't actually jealous he was giving a good imitation of it.

Well, all right! she thought, lifting her chin and walking faster.

They weren't at Sam's, which was a good ten minutes' walk from the harbor. His mother said, "Land o' love, Ellen, they lit in here like a bunch of seals after a school of herring, grabbed Sam's records, and flew off again. Said something about Clem's new record player."

It was quite dark by the time she got to Clem's, which was high up on the island near the Knights of Pythias Hall. The first warning streamers of fog were winding among the trees. She heard Elvis long before she sighted the house. Clem's people had their own electricity plant, and the house blazed with lights and noise, incongruous in the island night.

Everybody greeted her happily and wanted to know where Joey was.

"Waiting to go home. It's coming in thick of fog."

"By gorry, it is!" They piled out of the house. "Better stay over tonight, Ellen," said Clem. "Call up from the store and tell 'em you're fogbound. There's plenty of stray bunks around, huh, Ma?"

His mother nodded and smiled. "You know you're welcome to stay, Ellen."

"Thank you, Mrs. Allard, but it's up to Joey."

"Then let's go ask him!" Amy piped.

"Hey, Pa, can we take the truck?" Clem called to his father, who was knitting trap heads in the kitchen.

"Ayuh, but look out for that rock sticking up in the road by the Robeys' pasture."

"Don't you go fast now, son," his mother cautioned him.

"Not with Amy beside me. We'll go real slow, won't we, sweetie?" Amy giggled. Everyone piled into the old pickup, which rattled alarmingly and seemed to have no springs left. No danger of speeding; if he'd gone over twenty miles an hour it would have flown apart. It sounded even now as if one good bump would do it.

The general air of festivity grated on Ellen, and she would have walked back to the village in peace and quiet if she hadn't been afraid of losing Amy again.

The harbor was full of fog. "Just like in the movies," Amy rhapsodized. "You know the kind they blow out of pipes, and people walk around in it in their dreams?" The boys found this deliciously nonsensical.

Joey, standing in the yellow light from the store windows, was silent as Amy leaped lightly down from the truck and ran to him, seizing his hands.

"Clem's mother says we can stay! Won't that be fun? All we have to do is call up."

"I just tried," said Joey. "The cable's out somewhere in the bay, so I couldn't rouse anybody. So we go home. Not that I figgered on staying, anyway," he added with bleak honesty. "You girls can stay if you want to."

"If you're going home, so am I," said Ellen, thinking with longing of her own room, whose supreme charm was the fact that Amy wouldn't be in it. She was surfeited with Amy, as if she'd had too many chocolate malteds with whipped cream.

"If you won't stay, Ellen, then I can't." Amy sounded hurt. "Aunt Suze would think it was queer. I don't see why you won't stay just to please me. Joey can tell everybody we're here."

Ellen was saved from having to answer when Joey turned and strode down the slope toward the wharf. Somebody chortled. "There's a gink who knows his own mind," a boy said. "Better grab him before you lose him, Amy!"

"Oh, Joey, are you mad with me?" Amy flew after him.

"Look out you don't trip on the wharf and fall overboard!" one of the girls called, adding softly, "I hope." More laughter. Nobody seemed grieved, not even Clem. Only Joey and Ellen were out of sorts, for reasons quite unfathomable to Ellen.

The fog was dense when *Sea Pigeon* moved slowly down the long harbor. As they approached the mouth, the boat rose and fell on long deep seas moving in from open water. Ellen had been out in the fog at night when it lay in a thick band over the water, but left a starry sky visible overhead. Sometimes the moon had turned the mist luminous. But often it had been like this, with the fog band high and dense enough to hide the stars and dim the moon. She was not afraid, but she was not comfortable either, and she wouldn't be, until they were in the home harbor. Everything was queer in the fog; the engine sounded different, you saw shapes that weren't there, and sometimes missed things that were there.

Joey's compass swung in its little box by the wheel, but you had to have common sense along with the compass. Well, Joey had common sense. She sat quietly on the washboard while Amy, bundled into Joey's jacket, talked excitedly.

"Wait till I write home about this! Mom and Dad will have a fit!" Nobody answered, but she didn't seem discouraged.

On their left a high wall of rock rose through the fog, throwing back the clattering echo of the engine. The surf at its base flickered like something alive. It was one of the ledges that guarded the harbor mouth, now magnified by fog and low tide. Somewhere ahead of them lay the biggest obstacle of all, a rocky scrap of islet to be circumnavigated before they could set a straight course for home. In daylight Tenpound was a charming little place where a Brigport man kept sheep and where bluebells grew. In the fog it meant innumerable reefs and ledges that would be out of water entirely or half submerged. The islet grew tremendous in Ellen's mind, as she knew it did in Joey's. This was where a compass couldn't do everything.

Amy stood close to Joey's elbow. "Can you really read that thing? My goodness, when I was in scouts we had to box the compass and I never did get it straight!" Joey didn't answer, but she wasn't squelched. Finally he spoke sharply across her light prattle.

"Ellen!"

She went up to the wheel.

"How about getting up there and watching for breakers?" he said.

"All right." She stepped up on the washboard.

"Be careful you don't slip. The deck's wet."

"I'll go on my hands and knees." She crept up past the roof of the low hunting cabin and stretched out on her stomach on the forward deck, one arm hooked around the pawl post. Now let's try and see the breakers, she thought gloomily. Staring into the fog gave you all sorts of illusions. A flashlight was no good; it just reflected glaringly back at you from the opaque white wall that scared you half to death. The dark was preferable to that.

It seemed as though *Sea Pigeon* had been creeping along for hours across the deep dark swells before Ellen caught a flash of motion to her right. If she looked straight at it she missed it, but always it was there at the corner of her eye.

"Breakers!" she shouted, pointing, and felt the boat swerve outward.

There were other areas where the seas broke in churning white on half-hidden ledges, other eternities of creeping onward. There was a special kind of eternity when the engine stopped, and she thought it had failed until she realized that Joey had stopped to listen for the foghorn from the Rock. But they could hear nothing but the low roar and swash of water all around them. It was music when you lay in bed or on a safe rock with the water breaking below you, but menacing when you were out in the dark and the fog.

Ellen's hair was drenched with the wet wind, her sweater was laden with moisture, her slacks were wet where she lay on the deck. Her eyes burned with trying to see through the fog, as her head rang with trying to hear above the engine.

For a long time there were no breakers. We've gotten by Tenpound, she thought in relief. In a little while we'll see Uncle Steve's light at the Eastern End, if the fog isn't too thick. At least there should be a bright place in the fog. She relaxed forcibly, because if you looked for something too hard you defeated yourself. Her neck and shoulders ached, and she folded her arms and laid her head down on them. From under her lids she watched the sameness of the gray. You hardly knew you were moving.

Almost as if on the edge of sleep she had a vision of Villiers's room. She didn't know why, but she didn't question it. She saw the lamp on the table, smelled the fire, felt the dry, solid floor under her feet. In a minute now she'd see him—

Suddenly the boat dipped violently in a trough bigger than the rest, and all her senses leaped cruelly awake. Whiteness boiled not ten feet off the starboard bow, it seemed.

"Breakers, breakers!" she cried, flinging out her arm as if to push forcibly against the shore. The engine sound changed, clattered and roared; they backed in a rush, and Amy kept crying, "What is it? What's the matter?"

Ellen scrambled down into the cockpit. The boat was moving forward again, and everything looked the same. But Ellen knew they had turned around. Now the seas were following. "Where are we?" she asked.

"We were going out by The Head," Joey said. That meant they'd almost missed the island and started for open ocean. And it was breezing up all the time; she didn't let her thoughts go any further than that. She realized then that Amy was crying like a terrified child, like Linnea.

"It's all right," Ellen comforted her. "We know where we are. We're on our way home. Look, that big yellow glow in the fog is the Aladdin lamp in my uncle's sitting room." The words as she spoke them were like poetry to her. Unseen in the night, marked only by the diffused glow, the island was there.

She went back up on the bow. It wasn't necessary now, but she wanted to be there. Queer how the vision of Villiers's room had come to her. Seen from the long lonely time of vigil, the hour spent in the bare scrubbed little place almost represented paradise.

And yet she didn't resent the hour of fog and dark and fear, but looked back on it as something hard and challenging and, now that it was over, oddly satisfying. She hadn't been comfortable, straining eyes and ears for breakers, all the time conscious of the responsibility for Amy; but she and Joey had been working as a team in an element they knew perfectly. You had to know all the dangers around you as well as the good and safe things before you felt at home in any element. And she had felt at home up there on the deck, feeling the steady throb of the engine through her body, perfectly confident in Joey at the wheel. . . .

Now she pounded her fist softly on the deck. "I'm two persons!" she whispered into the foggy wind. "I've never felt like this before, and I don't think I can stand it much longer!" For the first time she felt a glimmer of understanding for the poor souls who couldn't stop being two people, and were so frightened and confused that they tried to run away from the world.

Suddenly the lights of the village set a half-wreath of luminous beads around the harbor. The boat seemed to fly without effort across the smooth sheltered waters. They were home. She went down into the cockpit, and saw with a peculiar lack of surprise that Amy stood snuggled close to Joey and that he had his arm around her.

"I was just terrified, Ellen!" Amy burst out.

Joey said earnestly, "She was all shook up."

"And no wonder!" Ellen exclaimed in what seemed a revoltingly hearty tone. "We could be chugging straight for Spain right now."

Amy was in no hurry to leave Joey's arm, even though it was necessary for him to gaff up the mooring buoy, make the boat fast, and bring the skiff alongside. She required a good bit of reassurance and steadying as she stepped down into the skiff. Joey had stopped being grim and was almost tenderly considerate. Ellen thought of offering to row so he could keep his arm around Amy, but decided he would consider the offer sarcastic, which it would be. So she sat quietly in the bow seat, jumped ashore when they beached, and held the painter while Joey got out. He gave the skiff a mighty heave so that Amy could step out with no effort at all on dry land. With the help of his hand, of course. Both hands.

"Well, I guess I'll go home." Ellen made up a yawn. "Thanks for taking us, Joey. And thanks for the lobsters and the ice cream, too."

"Wait," Joey began, and then Asenath Camption's drawl interrupted them as he came down the beach.

"Well, here ye be, safe and sound. I told Suze Joey was part gull, but she's been as jumpy as a three-legged cat with fleas."

"You didn't have to wait out here for me, Uncle Asa!" Amy didn't seem pleased.

"Hi, Asa," Joey said robustly. "Guess I'll let you take Amy in tow while I walk Ellen home. She's been my bow lookout tonight. More good to me than my compass."

Asa cackled. "I always said that about a pretty girl, myself. Come on, Amy. Your aunt's got hot cocoa ready for you and I dunno what-all."

"Good night, Amy," Ellen called after her.

" 'Night, Amy!" Joey shouted with almost indecent cheerfulness. "Mighty good cake!" Amy didn't bother to answer.

"What's she sulking about?" Joey murmured as the others disappeared into the fog.

"It's no sense explaining," said Ellen sharply, "because if you're not a girl you'll never in a million years understand what it's like to be one." She started up the beach and Joey came with her. "You should have gone with Amy," she protested. "It was her picnic. I can find my way home."

"What's ailing you?"

"That's a romantic speech if I ever heard one," said Ellen. They were passing the bait sheds, and she drew a long breath. "About as romantic as the smell of old herring on a hot day."

"Oh, Gemini," Joey breathed in exasperation, and hooked his arm tightly around her waist "Come on, now." He marched her between two fishhouses and around to the front of one. They were securely buttressed by a wall behind them, stacks of traps on two sides, and only the unseen harbor before them.

"Look," he said. "Are you mad because I was cuddling her up on the way home?"

"Why should I be? After all, she was scared."

"Well, what could I do? She kept hanging on to me like a little kid."

"I know, what could you do?" Ellen agreed. "Look, Joey, I'm not mad with you about anything, but I'm tired enough to drop in my tracks. So let's say good night."

"I'll walk you to the door," he said sternly.

"All right, but no discussions." They walked through the village, where the lamps made great balls of light in a fog so thick that the waterfront disappeared as soon as they left it. There was a sound of rising wind in the trees.

Joey sniffed, his head lifted. "Wind'll shift again before morning and blow clear," he said.

"Mm," Ellen said. What was she mad at? Not at Amy, certainly not. At Joey, for cuddling her? But he'd chosen to walk her home, and she was still cross!

When they reached the gate, the cat chirped at their feet, and Ellen picked him up. Something must be done about herself and Joey, and soon, she thought as they walked the last few yards to the house, the cat purring and nudging her chin with his broad damp head. Somebody's got to decide something. We're neither fish nor fowl nor good red herring.

Chapter 14

The sun parlor door opened and her mother's voice came warmly to meet them. "Hello! I was just going out to listen for an engine, and there you are, like the ghosts os two drowned sailors." She laughed. "Where are the boys? Don't tell me you haven't seen them." Joanna was too calm. Ellen's heart jumped sickeningly in her breast. She and Joey went into the house, Ellen holding the cat tightly. Nils stood in front of the stove.

"Didn't they catch up with you over at Brigport and come home with you?" he said.

"No," said Ellen. Her mouth felt queer, as if she'd better hold it stiff or it would shake. This was disaster, the kind you thought always hit other people. Except that there'd been Charles, lost somewhere between here and the mainland four years ago in a blizzard. The cat squirmed politely, and she put him down and smoothed his rumpled coat.

"To begin with, they went without permission," her mother was saying. "Around sunset they took the double-ender and rowed across to the sand beach. They were supposed to be hauling up their flounder net, here in the harbor."

Joey said hollowly, "We left the sand beach around sunset and went to the harbor."

"Don't blame yourself," said Nils. "They still had a good hour to get home in before the fog started coming in. But they told Mark when they left that they were going to track you down and come home with you."

"We never saw them," said Ellen. She sat down, trying to think but not knowing what to think about.

"You're soaked," said her mother. "You'd better change right away."

"I was up on the bow watching for breakers. The fog's awful—" Her voice trailed off, and she scrubbed at her burning eyes. How long ago that was, and all the time the boys were out somewhere, two little boys in a double-ender—

"Steve and Philippa don't know yet that they're gone," said Nils. "I guess somebody'd better let them know."

"Do you suppose they're staying over there?" Ellen asked eagerly.

"The trouble is, the cable's out so we can't call, and besides, they think they know so much, they could have started back alone just as well as not." Only the color in Joanna's cheeks showed how nervous she was.

"Somebody's got to tell Steve," Nils said. "I'll go along down there now and pick him up and we'll go over to Brigport and knock on everybody's door." He took the big five-cell flashlight from the shelf. "If they're not over there, then it's get out and take a fine-tooth comb to the bay before they row themselves halfway to Boston—or Spain."

Something fell into place for Ellen at the word "Spain." "We almost went out by The Head. Joey!"

Joey's face, gaunt with worry, lighted up. "I'm on my way."

"I'm going with you." She jumped up, then turned back toward her mother. "Unless—"

"No, go along. You'll feel you're doing something."

"All right." Ellen kissed her mother's cheek and ran out behind the men, grabbing another jacket on the way. Nils and Joey were walking fast, ahead of her.

"If you do find the kids," Joey was saying earnestly, "well, I'll be in after a while and I'll find out. If you don't, and you have to roust everybody out, well, I'll have a head start, and that extra hour might be the one that counts."

"For heaven's sake, don't get lost yourself," Nils said.

"He can't with me along," said Ellen. "I'm better than a compass, he says." She tried to laugh. Nils touched her shoulder.

"Good luck to us all," he said.

"I'll pick you up at Mark's wharf," Joey said to her, and she ran around to her uncle's place. With Mark and Helmi on their way up to stay with her mother, she went down on the wharf to wait for Joey. They left the harbor in company with Nils, the two boats running side by side until they reached Eastern End Cove, where Nils turned off toward Steve's wharf. The yellow light still shone through the fog. Philippa and Steve would be thinking that Eric was even now on his way home from the harbor through the Eastern End woods, after an evening at his Uncle Charles's house or his Aunt Joanna's. He was supposed to be home by nine-thirty. Ellen wondered if it could be only that now; it seemed as if they had been creeping through the fog all night.

This time, knowing they were going out around The Head, it was not so frightening. Ellen stood by Joey at the wheel, too proud to put her arm through his, though the contact would have been comforting as she tried not to imagine the boys somewhere in the oblivion before them. A double-ender was such a light shell of wood, a jagged ledge in surf could drive a hole through it and sink it. She resolutely shut her mind against the picture, and fought off the sickness in her stomach and the dreadful bone-melting fear in her legs.

They went out around The Head and then Joey stopped the engine. They listened and heard the swash of water along the sides, the dull thunder on the shores, the faint moo of the Rock foghorn, but no human voices. Joey cupped his hands around his mouth and shouted, "Jamie!" But the sound was made small by the immensity of fog and night around them.

It's no good to try, Ellen thought. No good at all. Worse than a needle in a haystack, because no haystack is three thousand miles wide.

Joey lit a cigarette. "What I figure is," he said almost conversationally, "that if they did miss their way and get out by The Head, and they got a glimpse of the breakers, they'd follow them around. Keep 'em always in sight, knowing that was land."

"What if they didn't see any breakers?"

"Holy mackerel, woman, they ought to know which way they're going by the wind and the sound of the foghorn! They aren't a pair of numbheads!"

"All right, all right." She was meek because she was so frightened.

They crept along the outer shore of the island, this time knowing where they were as long as the uneven line of shaking white showed to their right. They passed the mouth of the cove where Joey had taken her to see the herring in the net, and had asked her to marry him; that was the time that had set the whole summer out of joint. If he was thinking of it now she couldn't tell, but she remembered the tranquil dusk, and the whitethroats and thrushes singing, like something from another life.

Joey stopped the engine and she was violently startled. Ahead of them, low in the fog so that it was only slightly higher than the level of the boat, a light swung in wide circles and crosses. It looked weird and supernatural, like a small sun gone crazy.

"I don't suppose they had a flashlight," she said quite calmly.

"If they had, they wouldn't be signaling from there. They'd be high-tailing it for home. That's on the eastern side of Windward Point, and somebody's right down to the water's edge."

He started the engine and they moved slowly forward toward the light, which contented itself with blinking at intervals to keep them on course. When they saw the first glimmer of surf at the base of the rocks, Joey went in as close as he dared and stopped the engine again.

"Hello!" he shouted.

"Hello!" the answer came faintly back. Joey took his flashlight and turned it on the shore. In the beam the fog writhed and steamed like

Amy's artificial movie fog, but it didn't seem as thick as it had been a while back, for presently they made out a figure standing on the rockweedy boulders just out of reach of the water. It was impossible to recognize it or the voice, but the words came carefully spaced and distinctly uttered.

"Someone calling from Green Ledge! Out on Green Ledge!"

Ellen's heart leaped. She felt giddy with relief. "Thanks!" Joey shouted back. He reversed the engine and headed out past the end of Windward Point. The fog was thinning, for when she looked back the point rose behind them, and the glow from Villiers's lamplight shone up into the murk over it. Then she saw the tiny light bobbing along the crest, and it came to her all at once that it must have been Villiers who had called to them, not Owen or anybody else. Villiers, walking around alone in the fog, thinking whatever thoughts kept him awake night after night, hearing the voices blown on the wind, and then the approaching engine, knowing something had to be very wrong.

Green Ledge rose ahead, a round rocky islet where the gulls nested. They were flying and crying anxiously in the fog, because someone was there. The instant Joey stopped the engine in the comparatively smooth lee, the boys' voices came, and the excited clamor of the gulls nearly drowned them out. "All right, all right!" Joey shouted. "Hold your horses and save your breath!"

"Are you telling the kids or the gulls?" Ellen wanted to laugh foolishly.

"Telling the gulls, There'll be plenty of people telling the kids something when they get home," said Joey.

In a few minutes the double-ender came out around a big jumble of boulders that looked as if a giant had pushed them off the top of Green Ledge. Eric was rowing. Grinning weakly, strangely silent, the boys came aboard. Joey tied the double-ender astern. Nobody had much to say. The boys were blessedly safe, solidly alive, and now you could be angry with them for what they'd done to their fathers and mothers, and because everybody else would have turned out of bed for a search party, if someone hadn't happened to hear them yelling from Green Ledge.

"We'll head straight into Schoolhouse Cove and put them ashore," Joey said to Ellen.

The boys said nothing, just kept together in the stern. It was only a few minutes into Schoolhouse Cove, and visibility was improving all the time as the wind kept shifting toward the west.

As Joey's boat edged in to the foot of the ladder, Villiers spoke from the wharf. "I've got hot drinks on the stove for you."

"So it was you down there," Joey said stiffly.

"Yes. I was walking around, heard the voices, and was just going up to tell Owen, when I heard your engine. I thought there might be some connection. Who was lost?" He turned his light down onto the boys' squinting upturned faces. "Oh." He switched the light off. Someone else might have made a facetious remark to make the boys squirm, Ellen thought, but Villiers seemed unconcerned, now that they were safe.

Joey was making the peapod fast to a spiling. "All right, you kids get up that ladder. You too, Ellen. I'll go see if I can catch up with Nils."

"I'll go too," she protested, but he took her elbows and propelled her toward the ladder with such a steely grip that it startled her.

"You've been out long enough. You're soaked now."

With her hands on the ladder, she still hung back. If she could only tell him—if the others weren't there—that it was important for her to stay aboard the boat with him. That's when I think I feel all the things you want me to feel with you! she shouted at him silently. That's when I know how close we are!

"Go on," he said sharply. She went up the ladder as fast as she could, and when she reached the top she knew without putting it into words that she had made up her mind. He backed away from the wharf and headed out of the cove.

"Come in, all of you, and have some hot chocolate," Villiers said.

"The boys had better go straight home. Their mothers are waiting."

There was no protest. Jamie and Eric melted away like shadows, and she was left alone with Villiers.

"But you'll come up," he said. The vision of the little room was warm and sweet before her, but she shook her head. She had started to become one person again, and she had to hold tight to that person. She could not stand being divided any longer.

His fingers lightly touched her hair. "Wet," he said. "You're always drenched when I see you. I shall have to call you Undine. . . . You're sure you won't come in?"

Her throat was tight. "I have to talk to Joey."

"Joey's gone." How kind he sounded, but how tentative, as if he were asking a question which she couldn't answer, but which must be answered just the same.

"He'll be back," she said. "I'll wait at the harbor."

She went up the path to the point. He came behind her. She had been on the boat for so long, balancing against rolling seas, that now she felt unsteady, but she was thankful that he didn't reach out to steady her.

"Good night," she said, "and thank you for hearing them. You don't know what we've all been through tonight."

He didn't answer and she realized he was no longer behind her. She was alone on top of Windward Point.

Now she could cry if she wanted to, and she did, all the way across the island in the softly blowing fog. At the harbor she sat down on the beach with her back against Gage's shop. Now she felt calm and rested. It was a good thing to have made up her mind. An impressive thing, too. She felt a little shaky with the importance of it. It meant no looking back, no giving up to regrets.

As the wind swung steadily around to the west, more stars appeared and outlines were clearer all around her. She wondered briefly how Gage and Donna were getting on, but her own affairs were too urgent. She couldn't escape them for a moment, and it was time she stopped trying to escape them.

In a little while she heard engines through the beat of the surf, fading, growing stronger, fading again. Then they became really strong and she knew the boats would soon come through the harbor mouth. She listened to the familiar sounds that followed when the engines stopped, the rattle of mooring chains, Joey calling across to Nils, and then finally the rhythm of oars as the men rowed ashore. Nils went to the Sorensen wharf, but Joey came to the beach.

As he came up by Gage's workshop she spoke to him. "Hello, Joey."

"Oh." He stood stiffly still. "Hi. Thought you'd be snug under the kelp by now."

"No, I was waiting for you." She felt embarrassed. Why couldn't anybody help, instead of just standing there like the granite rocks of The Head? She said swiftly, "Come on into Gage's shop. It's time to talk."

"About what?" He followed her into the dark little place smelling of fresh wood and pot warp.

"About you and me." There were times when you had to plunge. "There's no easy way to say it, Joey. I'm not going to marry you."

He was silent for a moment there in the dark, and then said quietly, "I guess I knew that. It's Villiers, isn't it?"

"No!" she cried in sharp astonishment. "For heaven's sake, Joey, what put that in your head?"

"I saw how you looked dancing with him—"

"Because I like dancing with anybody who's a good dancer?"

"It was different," he said stubbornly. "I said so before, and I say it now. . . . Tonight there was something funny. I could feel it. He didn't speak to you or you to him."

She felt worn out all at once and leaned back against the bench. "Oh, Joey," she sighed. "I was all worked up about the boys and getting them home. Villiers just didn't exist right then—oh, what's the good of trying to explain?"

"But you like him," Joey said relentlessly.

"Of course I like him. I like being with him for one reason, just as I liked being with—well, Fritz Galbraith the other night. I like being with a lot of people, because each of them thinks or talks in some way special to them. And it does something for me. Can't you understand?" she appealed to him. "Don't you like different people for different things?"

He couldn't or wouldn't see. "I s'pose I'm the kind you're easy with, like an old shoe," he grumbled. "No excitement."

"That's not so, Joey," she argued. "You can give off a lot of excitement. You almost swept me off my feet this summer. I had to fight darned hard, believe me."

"But you did fight." He pounced on that. "Because you don't love me. That's it, isn't it?" He swung toward the door. "Let's get out of here."

"No!" She caught his arm with both hands and dragged him back, felt him resist rigidly and then suddenly give in and reach for her in the dark. She let him put his arms around her.

"Listen, Joey," she said eagerly, letting the words come as they wanted to. "I do love you! But not with the marrying kind of love. Not now, anyway. I know we could make a good life together, Joey, but both of us have to be ready to begin that life, and I'm not ready yet. . . . And Joey, we've got something else in common that we haven't even talked about."

"What's that?" he said gruffly.

"Friendship. We've been friends all our life, and we should have a right to be honest with each other, and that's what I'm trying to be. When you told me I was dishonest that time, I was trying so hard to be honest that it hurt." She moved away from him. "And along with that, I was trying to be everybody's idea of me, so I nearly split up in about a dozen little pieces. I just had to make up my mind finally to be what I think I am." She laughed sadly. "It was quite a job digging down through all the layers."

"So you love me, but like a sister," said Joey cynically. "So we'll always be friends, and God bless you." He lit a cigarette and in the match flare she saw his face, curiously young and vulnerable. She felt much older than he at the moment.

"Joey, I'm not saying we'll never be anything more than friends! I'm not shutting and locking any doors! I'm just—Joey, are you afraid of anything that's new and strange, anything that you haven't known all your life?"

"What do you mean?"

"Take Amy, for instance," she said cautiously. "She's new and unknown. And it has been kind of fun, hasn't it? Not half so grim as it could have been. Come on, own up, Joey." She prodded him mischievously in the ribs. "It didn't exactly pain you to cuddle her up and soothe her fears tonight, did it?"

He backed off from her. "Hey! Cut it out! What are you trying to do, salve your own conscience?" But she gave him another poke, remembering from their childhood days how ticklish he was in the ribs. He grabbed her wrists and they tussled like two boys in the dark, until they broke into foolish laughter and fell weakly against the bench.

"Do you give up?" she demanded.

"Give up what?"

"Don't you admit that after Amy showed up you were glad you weren't engaged right out in the open? Because Asa wouldn't have asked you to take her around. It hasn't been half bad, except that you felt kind of guilty about me."

"Listen," he said furiously, "no matter about now, I'm going to marry you some day."

"Tell me Amy's fun," she said remorselessly. "Come on, tell ol' pal Ellen."

"All right, all right! But just for now she's fun, see? Not forever! Some day—"

"Joey, if we do get married—some day—we won't have any regrets. I won't ever be able to say you kept me from finding out what I could do, and you won't ever be able to say I kept you from being a— a—" She groped for words, and Joey supplied them.

"A bachelor seal?"

They broke into laughter again, this time complete and helpless, and infinitely relaxing. In it, their whole long understanding and companionship was restored, made even stronger than it was before.

Chapter 15

Coming out on the *Ella Vye* on a morning in June was far different from going in on a September afternoon. The old boat cruised over a sun-lit blue sea toward the mainland hills that were the smoky purple-blue of grapes. The islands of the bay offered the enchantment of strange woods and unknown beaches; here and there a white sail held another sort of enchantment.

Ellen stood by the forward mast, not needing to hold on or to be bundled up against icy spray. The sun shone on her bare head and arms. Bemused by the lulling motion of the boat and by what she saw around her, she wondered what she truly felt about leaving the island.

She was glad nobody else was on the boat; she didn't have to make conversation. It was a little early for Pierre or the other students from Brigport to be going back, but she had clothes to get and wanted to be settled in her room in Boston, and familiar with it, before she started school.

She sat down finally on the warm deck and put her back against the mast. What were they doing at home now? She saw the harbor on a summer afternoon, the activity around the shore, and suddenly and overwhelmingly she was homesick. Was anything worth this? If she'd said yes to Joey she'd be back there now, out in a boat or going blackberrying—whatever it was she'd be free, she'd be home—

She smelled a whiff of tobacco smoke and looked around. A man had come up to the mast. It was Villiers. Smoking his pipe, he looked off over her head toward the mainland.

After a moment she said, "I didn't know you were aboard."

"You were too busy saying good-bye. And everybody was too busy saying it back. Nobody noticed." He sat down on the forward hatch and kept watching the mainland, his face calm and absorbed. "How do you feel? Like an amputated limb?"

"I don't know how an amputated limb is supposed to feel." She was lifted, however reluctantly, out of her passionate surge of homesickness. "But I can imagine how somebody feels to wake up without a leg or an arm. It was always there, and now it isn't. So—." She shrugged. "But then, in a way I always felt like this when I went back to school. It's not new, really."

"Except that this year you had a choice."

She glanced at him sharply, but he still looked past her, drawing meditatively on his pipe. "What do you mean?"

"You could have stayed. I was surprised to know that you were leaving. At the first of the summer you were very sure of yourself, and then you grew less sure by the day, didn't you?"

She wouldn't answer that at first, and then, because she'd started out with him by being completely honest, she had to go on with it. "Yes. . . . I guess I was always too sure of myself. I'll never be that again. Right now—" She tried to make a joke of it. "—I'm as uncertain as a jellyfish."

He nodded. "There'll be plenty of times like that in your life. And you'll be all right as long as you're not afraid to admit they exist. Setting yourself up as the master of your fate and captain of your soul gives you a hard part to play."

"I should think it would be good for anyone to have terribly high standards."

He gave her a slight ironic smile. "My dear girl, we're not talking about the same thing. You can cling to your high standards without thinking you're infallible. If you convince yourself that you are always in perfect command and never make a mistake, you can let yourself in for making some absolute bloopers, one of which might be fatal some day."

"Did you ever?"

"Why do you suppose I speak with such fervor?" He laughed. "You're looking at a man who had to be practically broken on the rack before he'd admit that he wasn't what he'd pictured himself to be. The trouble was, he'd clung to the picture for so long that he couldn't believe there was anything else in the world for him but that, and he'd go spinning out into oblivion without it to hang on to."

She looked at him in respect and awe, wanting to know more but too sensitive to ask. She searched for a way to keep him talking. "Do you think Gage is wrong to hang on to his picture of himself as a civil engineer?"

"No," he said thoughtfully. "At least he should have a chance to find out if he's a good one."

"He's going back to school this fall," Ellen said. "They were scared at first, when they found out about the new baby, but they've decided they can do it. At least they're starting out again debt-free and in good health, so that puts them far ahead."

"Good for them," he said. They were quiet for a little while. The mainland was closer now; they could make out the city of Limerock at the foot of the hills, bowered in green elms. A two-masted sailing yacht cruised abreast of them, taking the waves with an effortless, gliding rhythm.

"When I was little," Ellen said, "I thought the people on yachts lived a sort of magic life, like one long holiday."

He glanced across at the schooner. "Next week they'll be back at their desks dreaming of this."

"I know it now. But I wish I didn't. It makes them too ordinary."

"Like me," said Villiers. "You know, I rather enjoyed being the Mysterious Stranger. It felt like being a character in a novel, not quite real. But now I'm no longer that."

"Oh, yes, you are," she protested. "I still don't know anything about you, except that you've been disappointed in what you set out to do. But I don't know what that is, so you're still the Mysterious Stranger."

She couldn't read the expression on his face, but she felt that it was important to her, if only she could understand it. Tinged with the irony he showed so often, it was as if he were questioning himself and laughing at himself, both at the same time. After a moment he said, "It seems foolish and wrong to keep it from you, after all my sermonizing. The picture is of myself as a painter; not just any artist, but one of the rare ones. A genius, in fact. A revolutionary genius. This is where the high standards and the self-deception combined and almost succeeded in destroying me." His dry tone gave the words more impact.

"But they didn't completely destroy you," she said hopefully.

He shook his head. "I thought they had, when I went out to the island last spring, without knowing where I was going, or caring. I simply wanted a place to hide away and let the destruction complete itself. You see, last winter I was forced to see the truth, to admit at last that I wasn't a Renoir or a Picasso, a Bellows or a Wyeth. I'd been running from that truth for so many years that when I did face it, I was sunk. So I ran again."

"What helped you? You have been helped, haven't you? You look different from the way you looked two months ago," she said timidly.

"You helped me. Talking to you that day on the boat, and then later on the shore, when you were painting, I realized what I wanted to say to you; that no one should run from the truth, but toward it, bravely and with open arms."

"Toward it," she repeated softly, "bravely and with open arms."

"Because it's life, don't you see? It's all life, and it's your life, whatever you find out about it. You know, the heart is only supposed to be as big as a clenched fist, but in reality it's as wide as the world. There's room for almost everything in it."

She nodded, bemused as the ideas took hold. But she hadn't forgotten something he'd said earlier. "You said you thought there was nothing else for you but your picture of yourself. Was there something?"

"Of course," he said calmly. "I was trained for museum work. But I couldn't see it. Not until I found myself talking to you and seeing my words set off sparks in you as they're doing now. Then I knew there must be others to listen, and somewhere among them might be one of the rare ones. Oh, I fought it. Bitterly, sometimes." His mouth twitched. "You noticed that, didn't you? Anyway, the job is waiting."

"I'm glad," Ellen said. "Not just because the job is there, but because you want it. Where is it?"

"A little old lady with a vision left to a small town in western Massachusetts a million dollars for an art museum. A lot of people thought it was a crackpot idea. They'd rather have a civic center, a stadium, something of that sort. But the museum's been built, and I have a conviction that someday soon it will be tremendously important not only to that town, but to half the state."

"Do you suppose I could come out and see it?" Ellen asked shyly.

"I'm hoping that you will."

Now across the dancing sunlit crests they could see the wharves and the busy harbor life. The schooner had headed up toward Vinalhaven, but a diesel trawler laden with fish and riding low in the water was rolling in past the breakwater. It would not be long now before the noises and the scents of the city would surround Ellen like a suffocating and confining cloak. . . . But it's life, she reminded herself quickly. It's all life, and it's my life, and everything that goes on around me, everything that touches me, away from home and at home. . . . Joey in the fog, Fritz at the dance, what I'm going to do tonight, and tomorrow, and every day hereafter, and whatever happens to me. The human heart is wide enough for everything and everyone it wants to hold. . . . She'd never thought of that before, and it was a subtly exciting discovery.

"I heard you that moonlit night," Villiers said quietly. "When you knocked at the door and said, 'Tell them I came, and no one answered.' I was inside."

"Then why didn't you answer?" she asked as quietly.

"For the same reason you didn't come in on that night of the fog."

She gazed at him steadily. "I had to talk to Joey."

"That's what you said," he agreed, with the faintest emphasis on said. She felt the color in her cheeks, but she continued to look at him steadily, though it was an effort. After a moment he said in the gentlest voice she had ever heard him use, "It's all right, Ellen. We have a long time to get to know each other. I'll see you this winter now and then, if I may. And I'd like to show you my museum."

"And I want to see it," she exclaimed, not knowing whether she was relieved or disappointed by the way he'd diverted the conversation, but certain that she was completely, excitingly alive.

He got up then and walked aft. But she knew by now that his abrupt departures were part of him. She sat alone, watching the great harbor of Limerock enclose the *Ella Vye*. Her friend would meet her at the boat and Villiers would go off in another direction. He would probably leave for Boston on the late afternoon plane. She would not see him again until— she shut her eyes, and saw herself coming out of school in an October rain, and Villiers crossing the wet pavement to meet her; or perhaps it would be as late as the first snowfall. But the time would come.

In her jacket pocket she had a postcard for Fritz Galbraith with her Boston address, and tomorrow she'd mail a card out to Joey, promising a letter as soon as she was settled. He'll appreciate it by then, she thought humorously. Amy will be gone. . . . No sense wondering if Joey missed her this afternoon; he was letting Amy help him paint buoys, and she'd probably get a smudge of paint on her nose the very first thing, the way girls did in stories and the movies. And he'd wipe it off with such gruff tenderness. . . .

Oh, but it would be nice to see him at Thanksgiving, Ellen thought cheerfully, and smiled at the fast-approaching mainland as if at an old friend.

Other Books by Elisabeth Ogilvie

*Available from Down East Books

Bennett's Island Novels:
>High Tide at Noon*
>Storm Tide*
>The Ebbing Tide*
>The Dawning of the Day*
>The Seasons Hereafter*
>Strawberries in the Sea*
>An Answer in the Tide*
>The Summer of the Osprey*
>The Day Before Winter*

The Jennie Trilogy:
>Jennie About to Be
>The World of Jennie G.
>Jennie Glenroy

Other Titles:

My World is an Island	A Dancer in Yellow
The Dreaming Swimmer	The Devil in Tartan
Where the Lost Aprils Are	The Silent Ones
Image of a Lover	The Road to Nowhere
Weep and Know Why	When the Music Stopped
A Theme for Reason	The Pigeon Pair
The Face of Innocence	Masquerade at Sea House
Bellwood	Ceiling of Amber
Waters on a Starry Night	Turn Around Twice
There May Be Heaven	Becky's Island
Call Home the Heart	Blueberry Summer
The Witch Door	The Fabulous Year
Rowan Head	The Young Islanders
No Evil Angel	Come Aboard and Bring Your Dory

About the Author

Like no other writer, Elisabeth Ogilvie brings to life the people and atmosphere of the island fishing communities along the Maine coast. Though she grew up in Massachusetts, Miss Ogilvie has lived in Maine since 1944. Thanks to her perennially successful writing career she was able to live and work on Gay's Island, Maine for much of that time and many of her novels are set on the Maine coast. She has written more than forty books and now lives in Cushing, Maine.